1-99

Georgina Evans is the author of this, her second novel. She loves to travel but her home is undoubtedly where she lives on the Shropshire-Wales border, where she loves to walk. She believes in ghosts and the hauntings of past experiences.

DEDICATION

For my daughters Leigh and Chrissie. Boo!

Georgina Evans

THE CROSS OF SOOT

AUSTIN MACAULEY PUBLISHERS™

LONDON · CAMBRIDGE · NEW YORK · SHARJAH

A CIP catalogue record for this title is available from the British Library.

ISBN 9781787105492 (Paperback)
ISBN 9781787105508 (E-Book)

www.austinmacauley.com

First Published (2017)
Austin Macauley Publishers Ltd.
25 Canada Square
Canary Wharf
London
E14 5LQ

ACKNOWLEDGEMENTS

My thanks go to Christine Wright for her patience and fabulous editing. Also, to Justine Picken for her read through and invaluable suggestions.

PART ONE

The first part is another story.

It tells of the wizened and brooding chant of the piped voices that led me there.

CHAPTER 1

Wayne was two years ahead of me. He was going to be a policeman and he was unique at my secondary school because he actually showed some ambition and knew what he wanted to do with his life. Wayne was arrogant. He was very good-looking. Tall and dark and when I knew him, his hair was feathered like Rod Stewart's and he broke the school rules by wearing a red tartan scarf. I wondered what the police force would think of his rebellious behaviour. As a sixth-former he had privileges, one of which was being allowed to drive his car and park in one of the bays in the staff car park. Wayne was very fortunate to be in a position to do this but in essence he was a working-class spoiled brat. His parents doted on him. He was their only son and in their eyes, I am convinced, he could do no wrong.

None of Wayne's family had been to university and I am sure that in the Smith household such a possibility had never been discussed. A career in the police force was mapped out for him.

At the end of summer term I had just finished my O-levels and Wayne his A-levels. As a student in the early 1970s, probably not unlike now, I had to make decisions some months before I left school about my future, although mine had already been made for me by my father. There was never any conversation at home about me moving into higher education or working in a profession. I had wanted to be a nurse; I think I would have been good at it. I have a caring nature so I felt I would have been a perfect candidate and if I passed my O-levels I could have become a State Registered Nurse but no, father had other plans for me.

He already had a job lined up for me in the car factory where he worked. We lived in the West Midlands and in those days that industry was thriving. We owned our own house and dad had a car. Mum worked too, part time as a dinner lady, in the primary school where I had once attended. I was to become a secretary and I had no say in the matter whatsoever. There would be no long summer for me languishing in the park with my friend, or, shopping in the Birmingham Bullring.

I was going to be a working girl and earn my keep and I was to give my parents £2 a week for the pleasure. This would leave me with £2 for clothes, girlie trivia and to save.

I suppose you could describe me as an ordinary teenager. I had an eclectic choice in music as I would listen for hours to Pink Floyd and Diana Ross. Rock glamour was just coming on the scene and I had a huge liking for David Bowie and then Marc Bolan. That glittering world was beyond me. I had platform shoes, which my father called ridiculous and a tank top that I wore over my checked shirt and wide bottom trousers. I wasn't allowed to wear make-up, however, each Saturday me and my friend Linda would go to Woolworth's toilets and, using toothbrushes, we would put food colouring in our hair; red and blue in streaks and then we would return at the end of the day to wash it all out drying our lank curls under the heated hand drier. When I wasn't with Linda, mum would take me on the bus to British Home Stores and buy me flannelette vests and knickers and long white socks for school. We would go to the restaurant and she would buy me tea and an iced bun and she always said,

"Don't tell your dad," which I never did. I am especially good at keeping secrets.

I had a selection of ribbons for my mousy hair. Blue for school and chequered green and yellow ones for weekends and holidays. I wore thick-rimmed spectacles for reading which made me look ugly but I was blessed with straight white teeth like my mother.

Wayne's popularity attracted prettier girls than me. His girlfriend was called Samantha and if you knew her well enough you could call her Sam. She was Wayne's top prize, his trophy. Without a doubt she was the most beautiful girl in the school.

Samantha headed up the girls' trampoline club and she was already competing at international level. She wore her blonde hair in a neat twist. Her blue eyes had a permanent spiteful gaze as she rejoiced triumphantly in her own self-satisfied beauty. She was tall for a girl, about 5' 10" and she towered over her managed coterie of small admiring girls who smothered her with false compliments.

Sam and Wayne made a perfect couple. She could wear heels next to him and he still looked taller. He was 6' 4" and captain of the basketball team. Together they paraded themselves at school

At assemblies they were picked out by teachers to be respected as good examples and role models. "Sam and Wayne should be excellent role models to you all," they would say. "Work hard and be dedicated like them and the world is your oyster." I had never seen an oyster but I thought them rather small and slimy so I thought this was an odd metaphor.

They were often gossiped about and as the academic year wound down the topic was about the end of year disco. We didn't have 'Proms' in those days. Our dances comprised of Mr Granger, head of P.E., bringing in his record player and collection of vinyl which he played at full volume in the school hall. In those days the boys stood watching as we female teens jigged around our handbags. The boys would sometimes leap into the dance area with their hands on their hips leaning in and out to a Status Quo record that Mr Granger would oblige us with. This was as wild as it got. When the dreaded 'slowies' played at the end of the evening, which was normally around 9 p.m. or sooner, if Mr Granger wanted to leave early because he couldn't stand the sight of us any more, Linda and I would dash for the bus avoiding the groping hormonal boys whom we mostly deplored. In many ways I was dreading the end of term disco. It meant having to go back after we had officially left which seemed silly but Linda was so looking forward to it I could not really refuse to go along.

The week before the disco, school was filled with boring games and quizzes as the teachers tried to fill our vacant lesson time. Lessons had ended as we had all sat our exams. We viewed our teachers more like jailers keeping us all cooped up like little sheep, concerned that we might riot and take over the place at any moment. As I mentioned, Wayne wore a tartan scarf so who knows what our army of spotty comrades may have got up to next.

For the vulnerable new September intake, as part of their induction, it was traditional for leaving pupils to put on activities for them. This included dance and drama, tours of the classrooms and sixth-form block and participating in team sports. As I was not particularly good at anything I was never asked to show pupils around or to participate in any activities. On the last Tuesday, before I left school forever, Linda and I agreed to amble over to the sports hall to watch Sam and her crew on the trampoline. Linda and I were like sisters with our hair plaited neatly laying across our slim shoulders in our smart navy uniform, sensible shoes and our ties askew but fashionably displayed in large 1970s knots.

Samantha enjoyed being the centre of attention and Wayne was strutting with his mates around the row of four trampolines. He seemed to be pretending that he was interested in the occasion but I detected a note of jealousy in his eyes as everyone else was focussed on his girlfriend. He was watching her as her pert breasts wobbled slightly as she jumped up and down to warm up on the top trampoline. About twenty new wide-eyed pupils were gathered and Linda and I shoved our way through to the front to watch Samantha gracefully leap and swizzle and tumble. Her agility drew gasps from the crowd and her fan group clapped in amazement. She was wearing a white Airtex shirt with her initials stitched in blue cotton. S.S. Samantha Stanley. She was barefooted and her neat toenails were painted in black. That wasn't allowed but she seemed to have got away with it.

My eyes drifted away to Wayne. He didn't realise that I was watching him. Linda, as was everyone else in the hall, was fixated on Samantha. In that moment I sensed that something was going to happen between us but I didn't know what. It felt dangerous and as I watched his beady black eyes his shoulders were haughty and his bravado, to overcome his jealousy, was evident to me. My mind was trying to picture him and Samantha having sex together. I knew nothing about sex. My father, who controlled what we watched at home on the television, would get up and turn it to another channel even if a wildlife programme showed animals or birds copulating. I had hints of course. Linda and I would spend hours reading through our favourite teenage magazine to pick up facts and details but in the main they were only filled with stories of girls with broken hearts and tips on how to get the attention of a boy you fancied. Everything about sex, boys and penises was a mystery and one that I wasn't yet ready to explore for myself. It was rather weird that I found myself wondering what it was like for the role models of our school to be having sex together at that moment.

Wayne must have sensed me staring at him as he turned to look at me as I stood transfixed next to Linda. His gaze seemed to draw me in and I blushed. I watched as his eyes looked me up and down caressing the contours of my body as if he was virtually undressing me. This was the first time that anyone from the opposite sex had looked at me in this way and I grew even redder. Then he seemed to smirk at me and by some kind of telepathy or body language, I got the message that he was not enamoured by what he saw.

Suddenly, I felt Linda tense next to me and a unanimous intake of breath as the hall was stunned into silence. There was a scream and then a rushing of staff pushing through the crowd to Samantha who lay bleeding from her mouth on the trampoline.

"Did you see that?" said Linda.

"Yes," I lied.

"Oh my God," Linda said in her thick Birmingham accent, "she didn't half come down with a crack."

Apparently, Samantha had good flight into the air when she attempted her triple somersault but she landed awkwardly with her two front teeth embedded in her knee. There was a lot of blood and she was not happy.

"Get me off this fucking trampoline!" she screamed at Miss Barker, the P.E. teacher, spitting out blood from her swollen mouth.

"Come on Sam," she replied. "No need for that language, think of your audience."

"Fuck them!" Samantha said.

Then Mr Granger began to hustle us all away and soon we heard the bells of an ambulance. The new intake were satisfied with their entertainment for the day and some had even giggled when Samantha swore at them.

Linda and I retreated to the common room and on the way we picked up our magazines from our old leather satchels hanging in the wee-smelling cloakroom. Actually, we were in no mood for reading as all we wanted to discuss was what had just happened to Samantha.

"Well, she ain't gonna be going to the disco with them tayth is shay," Linda said. She continued enjoying the gossip.

"Hey, I wond-urr who Wayne will take to the disco now? Ee can take me if he likes!"

I laughed and then I thought that this would be the question on all the girls' minds. On reflection I doubt whether anyone ever considered asking how Samantha was doing.

"Let's bunk off early on Friday and go to the Bullring and we can try out that lovely sky blue eye shadow for the disco. If we put it on in the shop we can wear it all night!"

Laughing, I agreed, although part of me was worried what my dad would say about me wearing make-up. As it turned out it he wasn't at home when I left on that Friday. I wish he had been. He would have stopped me from going out. My life after that night would have been very different.

In truth, I didn't want to go to the disco and something about the way Wayne had looked at me had made me feel very uncomfortable.

News of Samantha's accident spread around the school and was much exaggerated. We gleaned that she had lost her two front teeth and she definitely wasn't coming to the disco.

I chose not to mention the moment I'd felt I had with Wayne in the sports hall to Linda. The way in which Wayne had looked at me disturbed me and I wanted to sweep it from my mind.

Friday arrived and teachers began to smile. Mr Granger even came and ruffled my hair and said,

17

"Goodbye Rachel."

"Rose," I said under my breath.

The last day of school had a nice relaxed atmosphere and no one was bothered when Linda and I sneaked out to venture into town. We caught the bus using our school passes for the last time. The bus conductor even wished us well and we felt sad to leave old friends but nervously excited to start our new lives in the workplace. Linda was going to be a receptionist at a veterinary practice in a posh part of the city. She was mad about animals and she kept lizards and hamsters and all kinds of small rodents and reptiles in her bedroom. This was unfortunate for her younger sister, Sharon, who hated them and shared a bedroom with Linda. Sharon and Linda and her animals, their five brothers and parents were all crammed into their three-bedroomed council house but they seemed to manage very well. As an only child I sometimes envied the banter and kinship of Linda's family. Linda and Sharon were the only girls and there was a big age gap between them and their older brothers. One of Linda's brothers was leaving home to get married, one was joining the army, one was going to work on the rigs in Scotland and the others were at work in the same factory as my dad. They always teased me and Linda but it was fun and they gave us nicknames like Thorny for me (Rose – thorn – hence 'Thorny') and Linda was always 'Lindy Lou.' I think having such a big family gave her more confidence than me. No one really noticed what Linda got up to but I was always under the spotlight. She was brave and adventurous but I was timid. I was frightened of going to work. What would I say if people spoke to me? I wasn't prepared for being a grown up.

The only person I spoke to at length was Linda and sometimes my mum. I don't recall ever having a conversation with my dad about anything. He just used to laugh at me when I watched 'Top of the Pops' and much to my shame he called

David Bowie and Marc Bolan 'poofs' for wearing make-up and high heeled shoes.

Mum and dad had friends called Trevor and Pat. Trevor worked with my dad at the factory but his wife didn't go to work. She had dyed vivid red hair and long fingernails painted pink. She wore the sky blue eye powder that I liked and she smoked like a trooper. They had all known each other for years and would go for drinks at our local pub. Recently mum and Pat had got into the trend of dinner parties. Mum would make prawn cocktails, cook steak with different sauces and she bought a variety of frozen gateaux for dessert. On the dining room table were leftover Liebfraumilch and Portuguese rosé wine bottles. She would put candles in them. I wasn't allowed into these parties but sometimes I would listen and peep through the crack in the door to hear the adult conversation that I had been excluded from. On many occasions I would hear Pat talking to mum about me.

"Ann, she's a funny little quiet thing, your Rose."

Mum would shrug her shoulders.

"And, she's got a funny little accent," Pat would say.

Mum would defend me and say that I was a bit of her and a bit of Alex. Mum was Welsh and dad was from Scotland. He was a fierce Catholic and we went to church every Sunday come rain, come shine. Mum sometimes invited the priest, Father O' Dowd, to Sunday lunch. He would drink mum's German wine, eat our food and barely say a word to any of us until he left and then he would bless us all. Dad would say that he was a nice man and a good priest despite him being Irish but that was the way of the *Catholic Church* he would mutter. Dad was such an ignorant man and, I felt, a racist. He controlled my mum and he controlled me and I was going to be working in the car factory on Monday morning whether I liked it or not.

As Linda and I sat on the bus I thought about what Pat had said about me. I was quiet and I didn't have a thick Brummy accent like Linda and her family. I liked the way she talked. Her accent sounded like she sang each word and she always made me feel calm. She laughed and giggled at everything and sometimes I found myself laughing out loud with her not really knowing why. She was rabbiting on about the eye-shadow and whether she would get away with nicking some tights from Marks and Spencer again, when an inexplicable shudder ran down my spine and I went pale.

"You all right? You've gone pale. You ain't got your monthlies 'ave yer? We always 'ave them together and we've got another week to go yet... "

"No, Linda. Not my monthlies, just a strange feeling came over me. It's nothing. Come on, here's our stop."

We jumped off the bus and ran into a big department store. We both thought it very grand. The ladies behind the beauty counters were perfectly made up and they seemed to sniff at us, me and Linda in our school uniforms, half children, half women as we dipped our fingers into the cosmetics and splattered and patted makeup on each other until the ladies had enough and shooed us away.

Next we went into Marks and Spencer and Linda nicked some black tights shoving them up her school blazer as cool and as calmly as still water.

Linda came back to our house, her disco clothes stuffed in her school bag and we went to my room to get ready. Mum and dad were at the pub with Trevor and Pat, it being Friday when work finished early. Mum left a note to say that I should make me and Linda beans on toast and there was pop in the fridge. She had also left me some money for my bus fare and for a drink at the disco. I cooked the beans on toast and afterwards Linda helped me wash up.

"It's so quiet in your house," she said.

In my bedroom Linda fiddled about with my clothes and finally we sorted something out for me to wear: a short beige A-line skirt, black tights, white platform shoes and a green blouse. She brushed my hair out of their plaits in turn and when she finished she announced,

"There you go Rose E. Howard, Miss Secretary extraordinaire."

"Oh, God, don't remind me," I said as I took a look at myself in the mirror.

I did look different dressed and made up like that. Older somehow but I didn't feel at all like the person staring back at me.

We were among the first to arrive at the disco. Mr Granger nodded at us.

"Hello Rachel," he said.

I nodded back not bothering to correct him this time.

"Any requests for the night?" he asked.

Linda butted in before me.

"The Jean Genie. It's our favourite. Oh yeah and Metal Guru."

When the assembly hall was bursting, I heard Mr Granger shout out, "And this one is for Rachel and her friend."

We threw our handbags to the floor and a big group of girls all swung about as we moved to the rhythms of David Bowie. That's when I noticed him there, sitting on the stage: Wayne, swinging his legs and drinking from a can. A beer can. He was watching the scene with his usual gang. I was surprised to see him, thinking he must have far better things to do than come to our poxy disco. I was just about to nudge Linda and then I noticed him staring at me again. I thought he looked puzzled and was probably trying to work out who I was. I flattered myself that I was a different person this evening in my black tights and short skirt. Not a pair of long white socks in sight. Then he and his mates shifted and I guessed they'd gone outside for a fag.

When the record had finished, me and Linda picked up our bags and went to the drinks table to buy some pop and crisps.

"You'll never guess who's here?" I said.
"Who?" replied Linda.
"Only Wayne Smith."
"Nay, yam fucking kidding."

Linda and I danced a few more dances but Mr Granger didn't have the same taste as us in music and we sloped around the hall feeling bored. He played a, heavy rock single and we became spectators watching the boys as they jiggled on the dance floor sweating out of their pimples growing pinker and more pustular by the minute. Some of the other girls came to talk to us and we chit-chatted about what we would be up to the following Monday. Stephanie Parks was going to college to train as a chef and we were all aghast wondering how she had managed to work all that out for herself. We thought her very brave. In the main most girls were off to work in some industry or another. The girls staying on for sixth-form weren't even at the party.

"Nay, they'll have their noses in a book, yer know, revising like," someone said.

"More like they'll have their noses in someone's trousers," retorted Linda which made us all laugh as silly and infantile as it sounded.

I needed the loo so whispered to Linda that I wouldn't be a minute. The loos were situated at the back of the hall down a small corridor with boys on the left and girls to the right. The toilet cubicles were full of graffiti. Written in red ink were exclamations of what Kevin Collins had done to Caroline Dickens which probably weren't true. There were girls' signatures, "Tina woz 'ere," "Sandra loves Rod Stewart." Foolish and innocent and stupid. I had a wee and washed my hands. I looked in the mirror and straightened a piece of straying hair and freshly made up my lips in red knowing that I'd have to come back here again soon to wash it off before I went home. I checked my watch. It was 8.30pm. Give it another fifteen minutes and then we'll head off, I thought.

I left the toilets only to find Wayne Smith and two of his cronies waiting for me outside.

"Rose Howard, you're a surprise. You look like a right tart," Wayne said.

I went to walk past but Wayne and his mates blocked my way. They had all been drinking but Wayne was drunk. Very drunk. He grabbed my arm.

"Come on luv, yer knaw yer want to. I've seen yer looking at me."

"I don't know what you mean," I said trying again to push past. A guilty thought rushed through my mind as I recalled staring at him in the sports hall.

His mates were leering at me as Wayne put his hand up my skirt. I was so shocked that I screamed which seemed to cause the chain of events that followed. One of Wayne's mates put his hand over my mouth and they dragged me into a cubicle in the boys' toilets.

Wayne's two friends stood guard as Wayne molested me, pulling at my tights as he savagely attacked my breasts with his rough hands. I tried to scream but he covered my mouth with his hand. I was pushed up against the toilet and it dug hard in my back as he tugged until my pants and tights were around my ankles. Then he entered me, shockingly, disturbingly, hurting me. All the time his mates watched outside the cubicle and then they began to shout words of encouragement to Wayne.

"Come on Wayne, take her, take the stupid fucking bitch."

He pushed into me harder the pain surging through my body. I shook and felt the sick coming into my throat. As he delivered his goods into me and his body shivered, I was sick

23

all over his sleeked black hair. It dripped down his neck in blobs splashing onto his tartan scarf. At first he seemed unaware of me. I was curled in pain, limp and frightened, until he felt the sick slither down his neck. He jumped up.

"Fucking hell!" he shouted at me. "You dirty fucking little cow."

His mates were guffawing. They grabbed him out of the cubicle and I could hear the sink filling and the splash of his hands with water to rub away my sick. Then they went and left me there, sore, scared and hopelessly crying.

After a while I got up and began to pull up my pants and tights. I could feel sticky stuff between my thighs so I grabbed some toilet roll and rubbed as much off as I could. I dared not look too hard as the gooey mix was pink with my blood. My body was trembling and I was in shock although I didn't know it. I went to the sink and washed the make-up from my face. I dampened a paper towel and washed myself again between my legs. I could smell him and I couldn't wash the smell away as hard as I tried. I was sore and I felt like someone had shoved a balloon and inflated it inside my vagina. Standing tall, I smoothed my hair and pulled my clothes together.

Ian, a particularly acne-ridden boy from my year, entered the toilets. He took one look at me and taking in my horrified appearance he hurriedly left. I went back to the hall.

"Did yer 'ave a poo?" Linda said laughing. "You were ages. I was just gonna check you hadn't fell down the pan!"

Some of the other girls were still there and they joined in with Linda chortling.

"Let's go home, Linda."

"You all right Rose, you've gone pale again. Sure it ain't time of the month?"

I shook my head keeping it low making for the exit holding Linda's hand tightly until I was running fast away to the bus stop. I didn't speak on the bus on the way home. I felt giddy and my stomach ached. Linda was chatting enough for both of us and when she got off at her stop, I was glad. I was so ashamed of what had happened to me I didn't want to tell anyone, not even Linda.

When I arrived home, mum and dad were watching the television. Mum shouted to me from the lounge as I stood in the hallway shivering,

"Did you have a good time?"

I didn't answer and made my way to the bathroom and ran a hot bath. My bones and muscles were tight and I was sick again until there was nothing left in my stomach. I soaked in the bath and cried.

There was a bruise on my back like the map of the world. I slid on my nightie and went to bed and cried all night into my pillow.

CHAPTER 2

Monday came and I started my job at dad's workplace. The pink blobs continued to dribble into my pants for a few days and my due period never arrived.

My colleagues were pleasant enough but I heard them remark that I was the quiet sort.

"Quiet ones are the worse ones," I heard Gail say to Tonia as they smirked at my expense.

I found work uneventful. Each day I typed, copying the scrawling writing from a lined pile of papers left by the manager. Unknown to him, I would include words that made up the contents of his letters. Once there was a Mr Ennis and I typed a 'P' in front of the 'Ennis' smiling to myself as I placed the letter in the 'out' tray. Despite how miserable I was, I was glad to still have a sense of humour.

I knew the manager's name, Mr McGregor, but I never met him. There were a lot of Scots and Irish working at the factory and I realised why dad liked it here so much. All the men had the same background and most of them talked to the women in the same way. Some of the fruitier men slapped the secretaries on their bottoms. When they did this, I would stare hard at them in disgust and I quickly gained a reputation for being a prude.

I was there for six months until I could not hide my bump any longer. Gail commented on my waistline and when I didn't give an answer she made the right assumption. Somehow the news got to my father, probably Gail spreading it around the factory. One cold January night my father was waiting for me in the hallway. His dark presence hung like a tenacious snake slithering silently, waiting for its prey.

"You've got something to tell me Rose and I want to know who the father is!"

His voice was rugged and angry, his raw Glasgow accent at its peak. My mother sat afraid, not looking at me. I looked over at her for some sympathy. I wanted to tell her what had happened to me but she had her head down, biting her lip, avoiding my eyes.

"You cheap harlot! Do you know how embarrassing this is for me at the factory?" he declared.

"But dad, I was raped. Please, dad."

I saw tears roll down mum's face as dad lashed out and hit me hard across my face. I fell back submitting to his wrath until he had forced Wayne's name out of me. His only interest was in who the father was; he never asked about me or how I felt. He made me feel dirty as if I had done something wrong. "But it wasn't my fault dad, *please,* dad."

Eventually, his wrath subsided and I ran upstairs crying bitterly. My top lip was swelling from where he'd hit me. I lay in the dark feeling ashamed, humiliated and afraid of what was going to happen to me.

Since the night that dad had confronted me, I felt that mum had tried to catch me on my own wanting to speak with me but dad would make sure that she couldn't. Every time we started a conversation up he would pop. It seemed that his only aim in life was to prevent me and mum having a moment together. He seemed obsessed and I couldn't understand why. Eventually, mum and I managed to have a snatch of time. Dad was snoozing in front of the television watching Celtic play football. Mum looked up from her magazine and inclined her head towards the kitchen. We both crept out and I watched her, as I had done hundreds of times before, fill the kettle and make us tea. Her shoulders were hunched in stress as she stirred sugar into our cups. Firstly, looking over my shoulder with a worried look, she threw her arms about me. We both began to cry. She held me so tight I thought I was going to faint.

"Ignore your father," she said anxiously.

She was agonising over what she wanted to say to me. Her face was etched with concern.

"It'll be all right, darling. No matter what happens I'll always be here for you. Ring me at school, he won't know. He's just worried about things from the past coming out. He's such a proud man."

Naturally, I wanted to ask her what things from the past but before I could dad came in. He looked suspiciously at mum and then at me.

"Having a nice wee chat eh, girls? I hope you were not talking about that thing growing in your fat little belly. You brought this on yourself and personally, I can't wait for you to be out of this house. I've made all the arrangements. Look at you standing there with all the cheek in the world drinking my tea that I worked hard to pay for. You don't deserve it."

At that he knocked the hot mug from my hand so that the tea ran all down my front. I ran upstairs to my room and I could hear him shouting at mum. After a while I heard the slam of the sitting room door as he went back to watch the second half of the match. I lay on my bed crying trying to recall the softness of my mother's arms around me. It would be better for both me and mum if we never talked about my situation. Although I found it hard to bear his violence and his insults, I didn't want mum to bear the brunt of them too. Sadly, I made up my mind never to talk with her on our own again. Soon after that, I learnt of dad's arrangements.

Events moved quickly, the banns were read and suddenly I was walking down an aisle in a damp church with only my father, Linda, Pat and Trevor present on my side. The pews on the right side were taken up by Wayne's parents and his two sisters. They all scowled at me as if this predicament was all my fault.

Father O' Dowd married us, his eyes averted from the pregnant lump that stuck out before him. My mother could not bear to be there. I went through the motions of the wedding service feeling sick and faint. I barely remember any of it.

At work, Gail and Tonia sniggered and made comments about my increasing belly. Soon afterwards I left. I just walked out, not saying goodbye to anyone. My baby was due in a month. I had to give up my job on account of my condition and there was no possibility of me returning once the baby was born.

I'd moved in with Wayne to a high tower council flat. He had been living there since he left school and started his course at Police College which was coming to an end. His family and friends had given him sparse furniture which included a double bed, a scruffy uncomfortable brown sofa, a table and a couple of hard backed wooden chairs. There was nothing cosy about that place and Wayne hardly ever seemed to be there.

I was numb. I moved about like a robot. I felt sick every day. Some days I vomited and sometimes it was just the feeling of nausea that overcame me. I was pregnant but I had lost weight. I didn't think about the baby growing inside me. It repulsed me as it only reminded me of how violently it had come to be there. Wayne repulsed me even more and the only conversation that we had was when I told him he would have to sleep on the couch. He accused me of being a cold, frigid bitch and that as his wife he had conjugal rights, to which, I informed him that he had no rights over me and as far as I was concerned he was a drunk and a rapist.

Thankfully his course meant that he often stayed over at the police college or over at Samantha's with her new front teeth. When he graduated, a week before the baby came, I pitied the people of Birmingham. How could it be possible that such a person could be responsible for the safety of others? I knew where he was, of course, but I didn't care. I felt I had been forced to be his wife purely to redeem my father's embarrassment and there was nothing, nothing in this world that induced even a crumb of care for Wayne in my heart.

Linda sought me out. It was refreshing to see her. The first time she visited she looked around the austere flat and said,

"Crikey Rose, it's like a bloody morgue in 'ere!"

I knew what she meant. I wanted this baby out of me and thinking beyond that I had no clue. I had no clue what I was going to do. I had no clue about making a home for myself and a baby.

On her weekend visits, she would bring me a bowl of her mother's Irish stew and make me tea. Linda was enjoying her new job and she would chatter on about the vet's clients. She also spoke enthusiastically about one of the partners and she confessed to having a big crush on him.

"Ee won't wanna be seen with a girl like me, I suppose Rose, but 'ee ain't half smashin'."

If she touched the subject of my pregnancy, I would grow tetchy and she would change the topic rapidly. Linda always had something to talk about. Around the time of my seventeenth birthday, which fell shortly before the festive season, she brought me a big box of chocolates and I saved them for Christmas Day to eat for my lunch. I thought of Linda at her house with her friendly and happy family around her in a glow of warmth and twinkling Christmas decorations festooning their small home and I wept feeling sad and alone. The door knocked and it was her, my friend grinning and holding out a plate covered in foil. Underneath, her mother had given me a

30

Christmas lunch with all the trimmings and a bowl of Christmas pudding. I was amazed at her generosity knowing the number of people she already had to feed from her small income. Linda stayed for a while and whilst I tucked in to my lukewarm meal Linda frankly told me that I should pull myself together and that I should stop feeling sorry for myself.

In a few months at work, Linda had blossomed. She wore her hair up and her puppy fat was replaced with womanly contours. I thought she had grown too. Her happiness shone through and I hoped that the vet would take some common sense and ask Linda out on a date. There was no one lovelier. Linda hadn't given up on me and I was forever grateful for her friendship. Her words made sense and I understood the gravity of them but I had no concept of how to, 'pull myself together'.

On 12th April labour began. Labour pains cannot be described. My body was young and the worst pain I had ever had in my whole life was the pain I'd felt when Wayne raped me. Cramps wrapped themselves around my back niggling as my tender loins jerked and pulsated. My waters broke and flooded the bathroom floor. I was alone. Wayne was with Sam probably shagging the pants off her. I flushed out images from my mind of the two of them having sex together, a vulgar and distasteful thought now, quite different from my vision that I had in the school hall when I was still a child. The thoughts gave me nightmares. The pains overtook me. I dragged myself to the phone box on the corner and telephoned for an ambulance.

I screamed as the baby pulled at my womb and I thought I was going to die. The midwife was impatient with me and lacked any understanding of the agony I was going through. She came at me with a syringe with a long needle and thrust it into my thigh. Then she turned on the gas and air and I sucked every last ounce out of the canister.

Patrick was born after twenty hours of labour. He was perfectly formed as he lay in my arms. I no longer cared who his father was or how he got here. I loved him. I bent my head to kiss his cold head, my poor dead baby. Still born.

The midwife attempted to take him off me. He was wrapped in a blue blanket, his lips matching its colour, but I held on. I didn't want him to be taken away. I was traumatised but the act of giving birth changed my feelings. Despite hating the baby in my womb my mind was now willing for him to live, to cry and breathe and look up at me as I held onto him not believing that there was no breath in him. I loved him and could not bear to let him go. Eventually the midwife wrestled Patrick from my arms and I never saw him again. I don't even have a photograph but I will always remember his face, his tiny pink body and the smell of my first-born son.

At first, Father O' Dowd would not allow Patrick to be buried in consecrated ground because he hadn't been christened. My father, at least put pressure on the priest and my baby was baptised in death at the undertaker's Chapel of Rest. My poor child's white coffin was lowered into a dark hole under the low spring sun. Linda came with me and out of the corner of my eye I saw my mother. She was under threat from my father and too afraid to come and talk to me. He was probably at work and would not know mum had come. I understood her anxious look. I didn't approach her fearing we would be seen and that father would later find out. I hated my father and the chauvinistic power he had over us. Linda held her arm around me. Mum nodded and smiled over at me. No one else came. Not even Wayne.

I moped around the dingy flat, my breasts longing to suckle my son. My body was wretched and imploding on itself whilst the streaky white lines on my belly decreased and faded as time passed. I mourned and I wept and I kicked the sofa and screamed at the top of my voice. The bleak light charged my mood as each day I flopped defeated into my bed. Occasionally, I dragged myself out to pee or make tea in a cup that was lined with green mould. I would scrape it out and then fill it with tea and when the tea ran out I would fill it with water. Through that summer I only ventured out to sign on for my dole money. I had visited the Labour Exchange when Wayne had first moved out, grateful for the little money I received and the independence that it gave to me. I would collect my money from the post office, cashing in my giro in the long queue of the unemployed but I never spoke to anyone. I hardly spent any of the money. Perhaps some bread and canned tomato soup. I would change a pound note for coins to feed the electric meter so that I could warm the soup that tasted like plastic. As summer changed to autumn my depression deepened.

Linda's visits grew rarer. The vet had asked her out on a date and she was in love. Her weekends were spent with him. I didn't blame her, I was not good company. Finding it hard to sleep, when I did manage to drop off I would dream. Dreams that seemed real. One dream reoccurred. I would be standing in a field of corn shimmering in a golden hue. My arms were outstretched at each side and I was staring at a beautiful view far into the distance. I wore a cloak of black velvet that billowed lightly as a lady walked toward me, a mirror image of my stance. She would call to me as she glided through the light.

"Rose, Rose, come home."

"Who are you?" I would cry.

"Rose, you know who I am. I am Eliza. Come Rose. Come to make things well."

Eliza would embrace me, her touch was soft and warm like a gentle breeze until I awoke feeling surprised that I was back in the flat.

I was skeletal and my eyes were filled with sleep debris so that the day the letter came I could hardly read it. Rubbing my eyes I read an eviction notice. The rent hadn't been paid for months, not since Wayne had gone. Now I was going to be homeless; to be abandoned on the streets. I was fearful but I was resolute. There was no chance of me returning home. My father hated me. He was ashamed of me and he blamed me for what had happened to me.

That day I ran a deep bath and cut my hair, which was thick with dirt and gunk, into a haphazard short style. I pulled on some jeans, my Parker coat and sneakers and slammed the door behind me. There was no way I was ever going back there and there was no way that I was going to continue my life in this sorry and pitiful state. I dreamed of Eliza and the fields of gold.

PART TWO

The bed of blood

CHAPTER 3

I'm not sure where my determination came from but my dreams, I'm sure, had a hand in it. Or, perhaps it was the change in my mood. The dank, sullen black clouds were lifting and as they drew away part of my soul lifted with them.

Autumn grey skies had softened and the golden leaves reflected showers of light as the sun tried hard to smile through as I made my way to the high street and my local bank.

Over the years I had been depositing my pocket money and then the few months of wages I'd earned and it was the usual clerk who recognised me. I withdrew the whole amount and he looked at me surprised.

"I'm going away," I said and as I did I realised that this was the first person, apart from Linda's rare visits, that I had spoken to for months.

I headed towards the main Birmingham bus station looking for a destination of no particular choice. I inspected the board trying to work out the multiple timetables. There were two elderly women sat waiting with net scarves tied under their chins and handbags held firmly on their knees. I overheard their conversation. They were chattering about a previous weekend trip and I listened to them describe the hills and the sheep and the valley where a stream ran through it. A place where they would take a picnic and sit and watch the birds. It was called Churchbury and from their description, Churchbury seemed to call to me. I checked the timetable and there was a bus due in an hour so I went to the milk bar for a malted drink and waited. I stared down at the froth on top of the cup and felt dizzy. I wasn't sure what I was doing. It was an adventure like no other and I knew that whatever happened this was going to be a fresh start for me.

I thought of Wayne, my father and Father O' Dowd and decided that I would never think of any of them again. Linda crossed my mind. Maybe I should have let her know I was leaving. It was an impulsive action on my part. She would've chatted to me and made me rethink. I decided to contact her when I reached Churchbury.

Hopping on the bus, I bought my ticket and sat by a window and enjoyed my journey out to the countryside where I had never been. Hazy motorways fizzled into oblivion and green fields scattered the hillsides. There were tractors cutting the corn followed by flocks of crows and strangely, sea gulls. There was no sea for miles. Tower blocks were replaced with towering trees in lush verdant forests and I closed my eyes picturing myself treading on fallen pine cones cracking beneath my feet and dozed off. I didn't realise I had arrived until the bus driver called out to me.

"Last stop, Churchbury, Miss, Miss?"

Half asleep, I jumped off the bus and as the driver pulled away I looked around me. I was in a street with buildings in all manner of architecture and filled with a variety of shops. A butcher, baker, grocer, chemist and a black and white pub called, The Callow Arms. There was a hustle and bustle of people moving around in the shadowy sunlight. An inviting little tearoom with a big window and tables covered in blue and white chequered cloth, stood on the opposite side of the road. I went in and ordered tea and an iced bun. Each was delicious and

I realised that I hadn't eaten properly for ages and I greedily gobbled the bun and ordered another one. The pretty young waitress brought a second one and I enquired whether she could recommend a bed and breakfast in the town.

'Dawn House' was a large double fronted terrace house just off the main thoroughfare. There was a sign in the window saying, 'Vacancies'. Net curtains hung at the windows. A little path led to a red door and on each side were green-leaved bushes bursting with berries waiting for winter. Wrought iron window boxes were filled with trailing fuchsias. The cream painted bricks were fresh. Mrs Davis answered my ring and surveyed me. She was wearing rubber shoes, neat navy slacks and a fresh blouse with a half size pinny tied around her waist.

"Just a single room? For yourself, is it? How long for, dear?"

Located on the top floor, she led me to my room and I muttered that I didn't know how long I would be staying for but probably a week. She looked at my rucksack.

"Are you a walker? We are just ending the summer season. Albeit, the autumn is going to be very busy as we already have an overspill from the hostel school party and then there's some of our regulars who do their best to avoid the busy times. Of course, we then have half-term and then Christmas and New Year so you are lucky having called on the spot for us to have a vacancy. I'm afraid I'll have to ask you for a week in advance. That OK with you?"

"Yes, that's fine." I handed her the money and despite her tone I thought that she seemed to be a very kind lady and there was curiosity and sympathy in her eyes. I probably looked a mess, my hair unkempt, my clothes unwashed but she seemed not to judge me.

"Breakfast is at eight thirty prompt, put your bag down dear and follow me, I'll show you the dining room." Obediently, I followed. The dining room was at the front of the house and looked out into the street. The net curtains meant that you could look out but that no one could see in. It had a wooden floor and six tables of various sizes set for breakfast. Nice art work and ornaments decorated the room and with its pale yellow walls it had a relaxing aura.

"I suggest you sit here in the morning," she said pointing at a table for two at the window.

I nodded and gave her a rare smile.

My room was also pleasant. It appeared to have been converted from the loft space and rather cleverly had a window that filled the length of one wall. I peered out and watched the clouds scuttle over tall peacock shaded azure-green hills spotted with sheep not far in the distance. Below was the street, quieter than the main thoroughfare but lined with a few shops and another inviting tearoom. I yawned and lay down on the top of the plump bed and fell asleep.

When I awoke, the room was dark and I fumbled for the bedside light. Checking my watch, it was seven o'clock and I was hungry. The landlady had given me my own key so I decided to head for the pub I'd seen hoping that they would also serve food.

When I walked in, all heads in the lounge bar turned to look at me. I suddenly felt self-conscious but with an inner grit I headed to the bar and ordered myself a lemonade and then found a seat by a hissing fire to read the menu and I ordered the broth. A few men stood at the bar, obviously locals, and the walls were covered in black beams and old horse brasses. The barman brought a steaming hot bowl with a plate filled high with crusty bread. I was desperate to tuck in but the barman wished to engage in polite conversation.

"You a walker?" he said. Lying, I said, "Yes."

Not satisfied with my short response he sat beside me.

"Broth's hot, don't burn your mouth. Where you off to for your walks then? Up to the Callow Stones?"

"Hmm, remind me, I left my guide on the bus and I can't remember how to get there from here. You see, I've not been here before."

My inquisitor began to impart extensive information on the surrounding area with marvellous local knowledge and he found a pen and paper and drew me routes for circular walks. I hadn't even considered walking but as he spoke my mind turned to the idea and I made a plan to take a long walk the next day. He was friendly and I learnt that his name was Brian. His hair was on the greasy side and I noticed a boil on his neck. His trendy tee-shirt was black with the name of a heavy metal band across a skull and he was skinny in black jeans and high top baseball boots. He also told me that my landlady and her husband were very nice people. Customers returned to their bed and breakfast year after year. I nodded my head in agreement.

By the end of our conversation and feeling a bit like Goldilocks eating the bears' porridge, my broth was at the right temperature and I wolfed it down. I dallied for a while, ordering a hot drink and then returned along the street to my bed feeling slightly rejuvenated from my meal but also with the excitement of a new beginning stirring in my heart.

When I went down to breakfast, I was surprised to see that the dining room was full, mainly with grey-haired men and women, some in groups and some as couples. I was the only person on my own and I sat at the table by the window which Mrs Davis had reserved for me. Breakfast was delicious and I filled up fuelled for my walking day. The other guests had nodded at me when I entered and some had cheerily greeted me.

I found a shop that sold walking clothes so I purchased a pair of boots and a woolly jumper. I wore them out of the shop asking the assistant to throw my dirty pumps in the bin and then went and bought some chocolate and a canned drink. I had Brian's drawing and made my way to the end of the high street where to my surprise the countryside suddenly opened out in front of me.

The morning had started with misty rain but as I ascended the hill the weather cleared. Not being very fit, I stopped at short intervals and took in the view. It was simply majestic. Hills and vales were speckled with cottages where chimneys looped smoke into the clear air. As I climbed higher the vista grew wider and deeper and an overwhelming sense of being alive overcame me. My sense of loss didn't leave me but all of a sudden I was overjoyed to be alive. I wanted to live. My wonder was heightened and I breathed in the pure air. I didn't know what I was doing coming to this strange and wild place but the features of the landscape calmed me. Inside I knew that somehow I belonged here and all that had occurred to me in the past was going to be laid to rest. I was young, so incredibly young, but I was not aware of it as my head seem aged by trauma and restlessness.

At the top of the hill I sat for a while and nibbled my chocolate. I was feeling hungry and was glad that I'd had such a magnificent breakfast. I pulled Brian's drawing from my pocket and studied the route. I figured that I needed to bear to my left heading down a steep valley which would bring me back to my starting point. My feet felt hot in my new boots so I unlaced them and took them off. I rubbed my toes and feet which ached from the unaccustomed exercise. My walk had made me warm and the sun was reaching out in rays across the hill tops. I made my rucksack into a pillow and before I knew it I had fallen asleep. I was weak from anaemia. The hospital doctor had prescribed me iron pills after the birth of Patrick but I never took them. I was too busy wallowing in my own miserable grief to think of such things.

It was a cold hand that woke me. An awakening caress of dusk. I looked around trying to make out the path in the haze of sunset. Inside I panicked a little but I knew, according to Brian's route, that it wasn't too far back, so I pulled on my coat and boots and began to walk in the direction that I thought was back to Churchbury.

My new jumper and boots kept me insulated but there was a chill in the air and nightfall was creeping in. Soon I couldn't see the path before me and I realised that I was hopelessly lost. I was afraid to tackle the tumbling steeps, not knowing how deep or precarious they were, so I kept walking along the top of the hill. I could see the lights of Churchbury below and so I decided to complete a semi-circle hoping that there would be a link path or road that would take me back down. I found myself thinking about the broth at the Callow Arms and Mrs Davis' wholesome breakfast. I steeled myself to carry onwards. Meandering along, thoughts from my past whisked their way into my head. I couldn't stop them; they were intoxicating. I wanted them to go away, to disappear, but they just kept on spinning around making me angry and sad. I yearned for happy memories but none came. An hour's walk and I was no closer to finding a path. The Churchbury lights had faded until I could no longer see them. Feeling frightened, I thought I may die of the cold but I had a speck of hope that I would find a way. Otherwise I resolved that I would sink down into the heather and lay there until dawn. As the darkness fell into a swarming curtain the night grew colder. The wind whistled through my jumper and my jeans held the cold in them so that my legs felt like ice. My joints felt weak and my muscles were stiff and sore. I trundled on with a blind faith that all would be well. Frequently, I stopped to rest and to focus my eyes into the black ink. I would startle a sheep or two who would look up at me in surprise. At last I saw a musky light in the distance, far away but gleaming in a smoggy mist, nestled in the hand of the sloping and domineering landscape. I trundled on keeping the light in my view. Thankfully soon the earth beneath me became hard as I stepped out onto a road. I looked both ways and concluded that the light was upward. I carried on up the lane until I came to two large gated pillars with hideous mythological animals sat upon them. In hushed growls, they seemed to be warning me not to enter. As I turned through the entrance, the moon stopped hiding and lit my way along the deep rutted track which I tenaciously followed winding here and there. Night animals skulked in the bushes and looming trees offered up eerie noises making me jump out of my skin.

Unexpectedly, the track stopped in front of a long wall that seemed to have a house built in it at one side. It was very dark but through the arch I could see the light that had first attracted me. Two huge iron gates stood open into a courtyard and an ancient house. The light was mustard and hung like an unwanted friend. I went to make my way into the courtyard and just as I did so I caught my foot on weed covered metal that once had clasped the two gates in marriage. My ankle bent and I winced in pain as I fell head first onto the hard cobbled ground.

As I got up I felt muddled and my ankle hurt like hell. Blood from my head trickled into my eyes. I zoomed in on the old house that creaked as the chill wind blew seeping into its worn wood and plaster. From an upstairs window I could see a woman and I waved. She moved quickly away and I thought that she was probably going to let me in through the arched wooden door. I limped towards it and I stood patiently expecting her to come. I graciously waited for a while and then as she did not appear I tugged on the iron rod. The sound of the bell was hollow and seemed to peel and echo from inside as if in an amphitheatre. I could feel my ankle swelling and bent down to untie my lace. A creak came from a door within a door and instead of the woman, the door was opened by a bearded man. There were two large vicious looking dogs at his side, not dissimilar to the mystical beasts I had seen gracing the gateway to the track. They had their mouths drawn back bearing their tomb-shaped teeth and they were snarling at me. The man held

44

them by their collars as if in attempt to stop them from lurching at me.

"What do you want?" he said gruffly. He looked past me to check if anyone else was with me.

"I'm sorry but I'm lost and I've hurt my ankle. Can you help me please?" God, I had sounded so pathetic.

He seemed to make a gurgling sound in his throat as he gestured for me to come in.

"Sit there!" he said. He pointed to a tall-backed carved wooden chair with a floral moth-eaten cushion.

My ankle seemed to scrape across the tiles and as I sat down the stink of the hall filled my nostrils.

A grand crystal chandelier lit the vast space but only two or three light bulbs were working and cobwebs straddled around it. The room was panelled with grand pictures and a sweeping staircase. There was dog poo everywhere and I rifled for a tissue from my rucksack to cover my nose. The man had disappeared through a door with his dogs and I thought that he had gone to telephone for help. He returned, this time without his dogs, and in a husky granular voice ordered me to follow him outside. In the corner of the courtyard was a truck with an open back and he pointed at the passenger side for me to get in. He never spoke one word to me as he drove me back to Churchbury. He smelled of body odour and his clothes reeked of an unknown smell, like chlorine. In him, I recognised an aroma of sadness, reminding me of myself when I had suffered alone, but his stench was much worse. It was as if he had gathered the scent of despair and loss making his own doleful perfume and storing it to make a unique and unpleasant fragrance.

When we arrived at Churchbury High Street, he asked me where I was staying and as he opened his mouth his breath smelled of onions as he spat out at me. I subconsciously tried to speak through my teeth not wanting to inhale his breath.

45

"Dawn House please," my voice mimicking a ventriloquist.

He pulled up the truck with the engine still running and waited for me to get out. Not once did he offer to help me and as I struggled, trying not to put the weight on my ankle, he impatiently revved the engine. I shut the door and turned to say thank you but he instantly drove off leaving me standing alone on the roadside.

In and beyond the thresholds of my mind, I cannot explain why this man evoked my curiosity. He drew out some empathy from deep within me. There was some deep magnetism that tugged at me. He bore an expression on his face that made me think of Jesus on the cross. He was sad and his eyes were imploring, as if he was asking why he had been forsaken. I watched him drive away with an odd sense of intuition that our paths would cross again.

Mrs Davis was beside herself to see me and insisted on running me a bath. She was very kind and warm and I enjoyed the free tenderness that she showed towards me.

"I'll just nip and call Derek, our policeman," she said. "Just to let him know that you are back. We were a bit worried when there was no sign of you. Another hour and Derek would have arranged a search party."

I suddenly felt very silly causing all this trouble. Mrs Davis handed me a towelling dressing gown.

"Slip this on, dear and when you come out just knock on my door, the one that says private, and I'll attend to that ankle of yours. You poor thing."

My ankle had stopped hurting as much and I could wiggle my toes so I guessed it was not broken and that I had probably torn a muscle or ligament. After a hot bath, I went to find Mrs Davis' private rooms and tapped the door.

"Come in dear, come in. Don't mind Arthur he's just off to bed, aren't you dear?"

Arthur nodded and smiled. His head was bald and the light from the ceiling made his head shine like a polished apple.

"Am I?" he replied. "Here's some tea and a bit of Mrs Davis' fruit cake." As he handed the delicate china to me he pulled up a footstool.

"Doris used to be a nurse you know. She'll take care of that foot for you. Quite a worry you gave us. Can I ask you to let us know where you are going and what time to expect you back Miss Howard in future? Our regulars always follow this policy."

"Of course," I said once again feeling mortified at my immature actions.

Mr Davis had generously blue twinkling eyes. I noticed that one of his cardigan buttons was in the wrong hole and he had a faint whiff of pipe smoke about him.

Mrs Davis gently took my ankle and moved it around watching my face to note how much pain she was causing me as she twisted it about.

It was easy to imagine her being a nurse. Her hair was neat and swept into a bun and her hands were gentle. She looked at me with her kind brown eyes and said, "I think it's worth you seeing Dr Comickery tomorrow. I don't think it is broken but he can give you some pain killers and check to see whether you need an x-ray or not. I'll bring breakfast to your room in the morning, to save you coming down the stairs and I'll ring the doctor for a home visit. I don't know what you were thinking staying out until this time?"

I apologised profusely and she gave me a reassuring grin.

"You're not the first to get lost up on those hills, my dear and you won't be the last but heed Arthur's words and let us know what your plans are in future."

"I will," and "sorry," I said. "The man who brought me back. Who is he?"

"That can wait until tomorrow, dear. Let's get you into bed."

47

Mrs Davis held my arm as I hobbled back to my room. She tucked me in as if I was a small child and folded the edges of the sheets neatly under me. I found that gesture comforting and when she reached for the light and said, "Goodnight", I felt some happiness because she gave me a sense of restorative faith in other people.

"Goodnight," I said warmly.

The doctor called the next morning. He removed the bandage and examined my ankle. Then he took some fresh bandages from his case and deftly wound them around my foot until it felt tight and secure. He was casually dressed in jeans, a cream shirt and wool green tie and a jumper and a tweed jacket. Aged around forty, he had thinning foppish blond hair. He saw me watching him.

"Ah, yes, I'm very good at bandaging due to the amount of injured walkers we get here," he said reading my thoughts.

"I'm going to give you an injection for the pain and a prescription for some painkillers which Mrs Davis will pick up from the pharmacy for you. I'm afraid they'll be no walking on that foot for a few days so give it plenty of rest and you should be all right to take some gentle exercise in about a week. How is that for you? Are you staying here for long?"

He looked around the room noticing that I had few belongings.

"I'm looking for a job in the area."

"Well, as I say, give it some rest and good luck with the job-hunting. It's very seasonal but you should ask at the Callow Arms they may have the need for a barmaid."

I studied his face and recalled that he had been one of the men in the bar the other night.

"Thank you and thank you for coming out to see me. I'm sorry for all the fuss I've caused."

He patted my leg.

"You are very pale. Can I just take a look in your eyes? Hmm, as I thought, you are a bit anaemic. I'll add some iron pills to your prescription," he said as he got up to leave.

Hesitating at the door, he asked,

"Was it Felix who brought you back last night?"

"If Felix is the rough man with no manners and lives in a spooky house in the middle of nowhere then yes it was," I replied with a hint of haughtiness.

Dr Comickery had a concerned look.

"I must visit him sometime," he said not really talking to me. "Good morning Miss Howard, take care. Rest that ankle."

I heard noises from downstairs. It was Arthur and Doris clanking around serving breakfast to their guests. As promised, Doris brought mine to my room laying the tray on my knees filled with toast and tea and jam and two boiled eggs. I questioned her about the man who had brought me home whom I now knew to be called Felix.

Doris did not seem to want to give much away but she told me that Felix was a recluse and he spent all his days farming his land over the hills and down in the valleys. He rarely came into Churchbury and no-one saw him.

"Well, I think he still hunts and shoots. He used to be a regular at the Callow Arms," she added.

Basically, he could die in that old house and no-one would ever know. A bit like when..."

Doris cut off short.

"Oh, that's all too gloomy. Let's concentrate on getting that ankle better shall we?" She took a deep breath.

"Dear, I don't want to be nosey but you do seem quite alone. Have you any family?"

"No," I lied. *More lies, I thought.*

Doris stroked my hair.

"So, what are your plans? Exciting ones I hope, a young attractive girl like you. How old are you dear?"

"I'm seventeen, nearly eighteen, and yes, I do have plans. May I stay here until I've sorted things out? I'll pay my board of course."

Hearing my age, Doris took an intake of breath. She sighed.

"As I told you Rose we are coming up to a very busy time and we are thoroughly booked but you can stay until the end of the month. How's that? I'll make you lunch and dinner. No charge for that, dear. On the house as they say."

I beamed up at her my smile saying it all.

I was grateful and whilst my ankle mended over the next few days, I whiled away the time with a choice of books that Doris brought for me to read. My mind wouldn't concentrate on the books as I could not get my experience with Felix out of my head. I wanted to learn more about him. He intrigued me and I wanted to know more of the reasons behind why Doris had cut her story so short.

I wondered what had happened to him. I had no idea where he lived but I promised myself that I would find him and his old house again. There was mystery surrounding Felix and I was inexplicably drawn to him. There was something in his deep brown eyes that was luring me in.

I had forgotten to mention to anyone about the woman in the window I'd seen that night or to add about the disgusting state of the house. I realised the doctor probably knew about the conditions that Felix was living in, hence his comment to me, and I wondered if he would get around to visiting him. I thought that he would need to concoct and take Felix a cure for loneliness.

As I languished in my bed recovering, I thought about Felix and the old house and a plot weaved itself in my mind. Perhaps Felix needed a housekeeper? I needed a job and that man certainly needed some domestic help. I also needed some time to myself but my pot of money would run out at the end of the month and then what was I to do? For the first time, in a long time, I wasn't dwelling on the past, I was thinking about my future.

Once my ankle had recovered sufficiently I returned to the Callow Arms. Brian would be the one to tell me about Felix and although I would not reveal the true nature of my enquiries, I would encourage him to inform me of everything he knew.

Brian greeted me with a warm smile. He had changed his tee-shirt and this was a navy blue one with a half-naked woman provocatively pointing a gun towards his fly. I saw the doctor at the bar who winked at me whilst pointing at my foot with his thumbs up and I meekly smiled back. It was still a shock to my system to be surrounded by people who were kind and thoughtful and who had a genuine interest in my well-being.

After some customary chat, I began to ask Brian about the man who had brought me home the night I got lost and hurt my ankle. At first he didn't seem to want to impart what he knew but then after a little cajoling, he told me what he did know which really wasn't a lot.

Felix's family had been in this part of the country for centuries and generally owned the land as far as your eye could see. His forefathers had donated the money to build the town hall. The majority of his ancestors held formal positions throughout the history of the town. That was even his family crest on the pub's sign, he remarked.

When Felix came to inherit the manor house, he married his childhood sweetheart. Something bad had happened to her but Brian was vague about what that was and either did not know or wasn't about to tell a girl from outside the area its local secrets. Skirting around this subject made me curious and as Brian wove his tale I became more intrigued. I asked Brian how I would find the Manor again.

Brian looked at me strangely, his mind probably trying to work out this young woman in front of him. I was beginning to work things out for myself and a rising of maturity seeped through my veins like an intruder in a distant land waiting to settle and be nourished by the act of waiting there.

"Don't be going up there, Rose. Honestly, it's not worth it. Felix will run you off his estate as soon as he looks at you. Keep to the footpaths if you head off that way. In fact, you are very lucky that he brought you back. No-one ever sees him in the village, he's practically a recluse."

"I just wanted to say thank you, that's all."

"Trust me Rose, don't bother."

But I was bothered. I have asked myself the question a million times. Why in the world I would go back to that neglected place, back to that churlish man but there was no denying those instincts inside me, just like the ones that had dragged me out of the flat to the bus to Churchbury. I had to listen to them. I had to tune into those innermost thoughts and feelings that would bring me to my destiny even if I didn't know what that was at the time. At my young age of fancy, logical thoughts were not part of my plan. I did manage to draw out of Brian the location of the house and its name, "Callow Crest Manor." He told me this was on account of the Callow Hill nearby. He also told me, that unlike the accidental trek that I had taken to find it over the hills in error, the school bus would drop me off at the Manor gates. I wheeled out of him the time and place of pick up from Churchbury and promised myself to take the trip as soon as my ankle was properly healed.

My month with Doris and Arthur was up and I gave a fond farewell to the middle-aged couple whom I had grown to like very much.

"But where are you going, dear?" Doris asked. A worried furrow creased her brow.

"Not far, not far at all," I reassured her. "I'll be in touch soon."

There was an arrogance about me. A self-assurance of my youth that I would not be returning to the boarding house as I waved goodbye. I took the short walk to the bus stop. The bus was crowded with schoolchildren of all ages eager to return home. Children create their own particular smell and their odour took me back to my schooldays which seemed like more than a hundred years ago. Some of the children gave me side-way glances as they wondered who I was. I wasn't much older than some of them. I studied the girls with some envy wishing that I was a schoolgirl again with loving parents who would have a meal ready for when I got home, who would buy me clothes and give me my own bedroom.

I asked the driver if he could drop me at Callow Crest Manor. He looked at me curiously but replied simply, "Yes."

The bus grew less noisy as children jumped off at different points along the winding lanes. I gazed out of the window. The days were shortening and the autumn temperature had dropped kissing the meadows and wild flowers a fond farewell.

"'Ere you go luv," the driver shouted calmly as he stopped the bus. "Callow Crest Manor, but I ain't got no idea whys you should wanna be going up there, luv. It don't go anywhere but the old house and no-one from these parts has ever been given a welcome up there in many a year."

I smiled at him but gave no answer as I stepped off the bus. The day was clear as I greeted the mythological beasts that I had seen on my first night. In the daylight I could see that they were actually a breed of dog, which type I didn't know, but they stood there smartly and sternly guarding the Manor House that lay hidden about a quarter of a mile behind them.

I took a deep breath and walked along one of the furrows in the ground. Even the track screamed out that it was unloved. It needed repairing and the only vehicle that you could drive along it would be a tractor, or, I thought, a truck like Felix's. I watched the ground as I walked picking my way carefully not

53

wanting to twist my ankle again. I turned a corner and the Manor House leapt out in front of me with no warning. It was standing stately in front of me. The building in the arched wall that I had seen was a gate or lodge house built with a roof of mock turrets and a big bay window facing out into the glorious countryside. The gates of the arch were heaved back and I saw the lynch hasp that I had tripped over covered in weeds but sticking up like a sore thumb. I stood looking up at the Manor, its lofty rooftops reaching towards an endless blue sky that shimmered as buzzards marauded through the air soaring on invisible thermals. Ancient rugged stones marked out the landscape, sculpted like giant's chairs waiting for an ogre to sit on them, away across the golden-lit hills behind me.

The Manor sat in a carved natural bowl and the bricks shone in honey-coloured hues glowing amid the mossy courtyard. Dried-up weeds scattered the cobbles and the heavy wooden door was like a mouth and the windows were eyes. Squabbling crows in the chimney stacks were lulled and seemed distant in the stillness of the day.

Above the door was a crest worked into the stone with faint remnants of paint colours: Three leopards, a harp and a black hand on diamond blocks of faded lapis lazuli, gold and bishopric purple. The Manor had once been a very grand house but had tired with age, bleached by its history.

Another deep breath and I pulled the doorbell hearing its familiar sound echoing and sheering the void inside.

Felix didn't answer. I knew someone was at home because his truck was parked in the courtyard and I could hear the yapping of his dogs. I rang the bell again and this time he appeared from a door in the wall at the side of the house looking dishevelled and suspicious.

"What do you want?" he said.

"I'm Rose. You helped me a while ago and took me back to Churchbury and I just wanted to come and say, *'thank you'*." I gave him my most charming smile.

"Well, you've said it," his voice terse and rough.

And at that he turned to go back through the door.

"No! Wait, please," I implored. "I have something to ask you."

He stopped, his shoulders hunched. The dogs were barking louder.

"Whatever it is you think you wanna ask me I can tell you right now the answer is no, so dunna bother asking." Again he turned to walk away.

"Please, please. Please help me. Look, listen, I need a job." I was speaking frantically as if time was running out. "I can't go home, I'm not a runaway or a criminal or anything like that but I just can't go back. Let me work for you. I couldn't help notice that your house is in a mess, actually a dirty disgusting mess (he did not grimace at my honest, unkind words) and I can do something about that. If you let me come and work for you and give me bed and board you won't have to pay me, I just need somewhere to stay. I mean your house is full of dog shit and you can't live like that!" I stuttered. "I mean, I mean, it's so beautiful and deserves to be looked after."

He stood facing me waiting for me to finish.

"Go away, Miss and don't bother me no more."

He left me standing there as he went back through the door and I could hear him shout at his dogs to shut up.

Speechless, I stood still for a moment and looked towards where he had gone. I went to the door and opened it. It led to a garden of some description, overgrown and messy. There was a small courtyard and a door leading into the Manor so I went towards it. Those dogs knew I was there and began to growl and bark loudly. Boldly, I ventured on and entered through a lobby into a kitchen. He was sat by an unlit hearth with a dog at each

55

side holding them by the scruff of their necks to prevent them from rushing and probably killing me.

"That house by the gate, I could live there, I'll be no trouble."

He sniffed and let go of one dog to wipe his nose and milky snot smeared the back of his hand. The dog went to move towards me but he commanded it to sit and the dog obeyed.

He turned to look at me.

"Piss off!"

I didn't know what to reply to that so I left. Once again my mind was hurtling and spinning and I wished for it to stop. What was I to do now?

I decided to take a long walk and headed off towards the giant's seats on the far off hill reckoning that if I kept my eyes on the sky line the way there would be easy to find. I walked for an hour at last reaching my destination. Shades of green were splattered by the giant's rocks, dropped from his bag, scattered here and there in piles. I climbed to the top of the largest crest and looked out towards spectacular vast undulating valleys that curved extending to the horizon. There was no one in sight and I sat for ages taking in the view. From here I could work out my trail back to the Manor. On the way I marked out identifiable spots to follow on my return such was my determination to persuade Felix about my plan: A boulder shaped like a lion's back, a tree bent and hooked like a witch's face.

How was I going to persuade Felix? My thoughts made sense to me but I realised that he would not be able to make as much sense of my need for a job and a place to live as I did. He had made it very clear that I was unwelcome. I hoped that I could convince him of the mutual benefits. I would focus on the evident need for his living conditions to be changed for the better. Lying down I stared towards the sky and I recalled last night's dream; for I had dreamt of Eliza.

Eliza's voice sang a song of mournful lament whilst her open arms beckoned, wishing to gather and smother me in her sorrowful embrace. "Come Rose..."

As I looked down the valley to where a tractor was chugging bringing in the corn, I thought, *I belong here.*

The walk back was gentler and mostly downhill so it took me less time and it was easier on my ankle which was feeling sore. Chunky raindrops began to splatter and splash and the sky grew grey and torrid. In a moment the deceptive lull had turned into a raging storm and thunder crashed and lightning tinged the ground. It seemed so close that I was scared and I began to run as the water soaked my clothes and skin. I was wise enough to know not to shelter under a tree so I kept my pace tracing my route back to the Manor. When I arrived, I was drenched and cold as I made my way to the grand door to ring the doorbell.

Something made me look up. I saw a light in an offset window and there was the woman staring down at me whom I had seen before. She began to gesture to me frenziedly pointing towards the gatehouse. She flicked her arms in its direction and I worked out that there was where she wished for me to go. I dashed across finding the door open and turned to wave back at her but she and the light were gone. I creaked open the kitchen door and noticed a black metal sign beside it. In cream writing it said, 'The Lodge'.

CHAPTER 4

It was late in the morning when I woke in a room that was filled with light shining through a dun-coloured window. It was a grim room, lime washed and the walls were streaked in a nicotine ochre. There was a fireplace whose hearth was covered in soot and twigs from the remains of a bird's nest. My bedding smelt fusty and yet, despite my desolate surroundings, I leapt out somehow full of vigour and anticipation.

Pulling on my jeans and a tee-shirt I padded out into the hallway. The bedroom where I had slept was the only one and along the corridor was an old-fashioned bathroom furnished with a rolled top cast-iron bath, a toilet that was dirty and stained brown and a sink that was filled with dead flies, spiders and clinging webs.

I had a pee and pulled the rusty chain. The cistern kicked in creaking and blustering as it refilled. The sink taps leaked dribbles of fermented water in shades of russet.

Above the stairs was a classical window and to the disgrace of the carpet it exposed its shabbiness as light flooded in. My feet stuck to it as I stepped down the stairs. I wished I'd put some socks on but I'd left them in the kitchen to dry when I'd entered last evening.

At the end of the staircase, to my left was the front entrance facing out towards the Manor. It had a solid oak door with iron fittings and a porthole window letting in tender sun beams. To my right was a closed door and through here was the sitting room. It was a good size with a mullioned bay window looking out across the moors. Etched over the fireplace was the same crest as above the Manor door. By the hearth was a shabby chair covered in a canvas cloth and the floor was bare wood full of splinters.

Under the stairs was a cupboard filled with buckets, brooms and mops. Then I entered the kitchen where I had left my soggy socks and boots to dry. A rustic table and four pine chairs stood in its centre. A rocking chair sat by a beige-coloured range cooker and the kitchen was fitted with a Belfast sink, high and low cupboards and a wooden counter streaming along the curvature of the thick walls. The linoleum on the floor was a mismatch of vibrant colours and was enough to give me a migraine if I stared at it for too long.

I gazed across the kitchen feeling just like the squatter I was. Squatter. This was my focal point, this was going to be my ammunition to make him change his mind. To make Felix, a man I barely knew, change his mind. Oh, for the innocence of youth!

Would he realise that if he didn't agree to let me stay he would make me homeless? Had I imagined that look in his eye when I had searched for some sympathy from this man?

I yearned for the luxury of a cup of tea. There was a kettle on the range but I didn't know how to work it so I decided to walk across to the Manor hoping for an electric version. As I took the stroll across the courtyard I made a mental list in my head of items I'd need for cleaning, such as bleach and disinfectant. Also, new bedding and I guessed a new mattress judging from the bites itching on my arms and legs. From now on I would sleep on the top of the bed and light the fire in the room to keep me warm. That would be OK for now but I knew that in the long term there would be many more things I would

59

need to ask of him. I wondered how I would broach this with Felix. I swiftly put any thoughts out of my head that he might say no.

Just as he was going to leave in his truck, his two dogs yapping in the trailer behind, he turned and saw me. I think he knew I had stayed overnight as he got out to confront me.

"I thought I told you to piss off," he said.

"Well, I did for a while and then I got caught in that storm and as I had nowhere else to go I returned here."

Then I added,

"The lady in the window said that it was all right for me to stay and she directed me to the Lodge which by the way is nearly as bad as this place. You really could do with my help around here."

Felix looked up at the window with a puzzled expression. I thought he looked pale and for an instant a flicker in his face seemed to soften him a little.

"You saw her and she said you could stay? Did you hear her speak?"

"Well, not exactly but she pointed towards the Lodge," I nodded confidentially.

"Quite adamant actually, she gestured for me to stay in the Lodge, perhaps she realises that you need my help and that I have nowhere else to go. I could help the two of you, yes, both of you."

Shrugging his shoulders, he said, "Three-month trial then. Let me know what you need."

I was amazed that he had agreed to let me stay. I didn't want him to change his mind so I remained quiet and stood in disbelief as I watched him drive away with his hounds grimacing at me as they rested their heads on the side panels. They never took their eyes off of me until the truck turned and I was out of their view.

Before I entered the Manor, I looked back through the arch. Clouds of dust rose above the hedges as his truck rattled away and I could see the moors stretching towards the horizon, the heather creating a fading purple. In front of me, a row of leaded windows faced out like pools of eyes watching and waiting. I looked up to the window where I had seen the woman staring at me, half-expecting her to be there, but all I could see were the reflections of tiny clouds weltering in the expanse of the October sky. It was unexpectedly warm and the ground was drying. The baa, baa, of the sheep traversed and hovered in the air and I turned to enter the Manor through the door within a door where Felix had led me through on that dark and dismal night. As I stepped into the grand hall I recalled Felix's sour and cool behaviour towards me.

The unpleasant pong pricked at my nostrils and caught at the back of my throat. Looking into the gloom, I decided this would be the first room I would tackle. I wanted to make this hall a warm and welcoming entrance. Entering the kitchen, I sensed the long-lost touches of a woman. A jug that perhaps had once held flowers sat as a centrepiece on the pine table and the frayed curtains were flowery. There were dainty teacups and plates on the oak dresser which encased one wall and the shelves were lined with dusty lace-edged runners.

The range-cooker was splattered with grease. Cooking pots were welded with burnt fatty grime and stood lonely on its top. Under the sink was a moth-eaten curtain in red and white gingham hanging on a plastic wire where the metal ends had rusted and stained the fabric.

On the counter top I spied an electric kettle and I sighed with relief and filled it. Amongst the dirty, disorganised higgledy-piggledy furniture and utilities I thought of my mother's kitchen. In her kitchen there was a place for everything and everything in its place. Unlike this kitchen she had modern things. Her brand new food mixer took pride of

61

place amid her matching electrical items, like her beige toaster and kettle decorated with brown flowers. In the hub of this creaking house and despite the mess, I could see the potential and I yearned to bring it back to the place of forgotten love, folds of gathering and some order to resemble my mother's home.

Behind the sink curtain I found a duster, a tin of dried up lavender polish, some disinfectant and a tin of liquid that I didn't recognise as the label had come off. It smelled like carbolic antiseptic so I decided to use it. In the drawers of the dresser I found some musty tea-towels and off the kitchen in the boot room a smelly mop and bucket. Thus armed and revived after my refreshing tea, I set to work in the grand hall.

The first thing I did was to clean up the dog decay. Some of the foul excrement was covered in a furry mould. My stomach heaved and lurched but I had a great determination within me and I set about removing every inch and puff of the disgusting stuff.

I used the unknown liquid to clean the floor and I tied two tea-towels to my feet to dry it off as I then took to the task of polishing the furniture.

The medieval tiles breathed as I opened the small door to let in the air. If felt like the first time in a long time that the outside freshness had graced the inner sanctum of Callow Crest Manor. Quickly, in the daylight shining through, I realised that the floor would need scrubbing, mopping it alone would not be enough to remove the stains, so I decided to leave that chore until the end of the day.

As I worked my way around the hall, I forgot the time and it wasn't until I had cleaned out the fire grate and had gone outside to dispose of the foul mess and ashes that I realised the morning had passed. The sun was low over the watching hills as I walked around to a small arch at the side of the house.

I found the neglected kitchen garden. It was totally overgrown but there were some flowers in dusky pink amongst the weeds. I found the bin and chucked the debris in.

The garden looked as if it had once been delightful. There was a portion that I guessed Felix still used as it was freshly dug. I was no gardener then but I surmised he was growing potatoes and root vegetables and runner beans which grew up a bamboo scaffold. I picked some of the pink flowers and took them into the house seeking out the pretty jug on the table.

In the centre of the hall was a heavy, round, oak table. I had polished it, wetting the lavender polish onto the duster and it was already gleaming. I washed the jug and put in the flowers placing it in the centre. The hall look transformed. I had only skimmed the surfaces but it glowed in a new light.

The portraits of ancestors, whom I assumed once lived here, seemed to gaze at me in gratitude. Those grand men in their gold and crimson suits and strange hats bedecked with jewels, struck poses astride antiquated maps in a weird dimension of their own styling and looked down on me with uncanny familiarity.

I was now quite tired so I headed for the kitchen and found some bread and cheese which I ate greedily. I wrote two notes for Felix. The first I left on the kitchen table was a list asking for cleaning products. At the bottom I scribbled that I wished to speak with him about the condition of the Lodge and that I required a certain amount of new things.

Next, I bravely wrote on the second page,

"*Please do not allow the dogs to use this entrance. No dirty boots to be worn in here either.*"
Thanks, Rose.

I went back to the hall and got on my knees and scrubbed at the tiles working my way so that I ended at the grand door. I was pleased with my methodical way of working and as I pinned my note to the door I exited through the small door. Closing it behind me, I felt great contentment for my day's work and a renewed hope for my future. That night I slept like a log.

The next day, I awoke early feeling refreshed but with slightly painful muscles, a reaction to my rigorous cleaning regime. When I went to the Manor, I was pleased to see that Felix had observed my requests as there was no dog mess in the hall and no muddy footprints on the tiles.

In the kitchen I saw that he'd replied to my message.

'Cleaning stuff here by noon today. What do you want in the Lodge?'

And then he had written, '*I expect an evening meal – why wasn't there one last night?'*

The cheeky bugger, I thought. How dare he? I had worked so hard yesterday. As I recalled we had no agreement about me cooking anything, he had just said that he would give me a trial. How was I to know this included making his dinner?

Soon I calmed and when I thought about it, it seemed like a good idea. I had barely any money for food myself and I could not survive on bread and cheese alone. If I cooked his evening meal then this would give me some time to talk to him and I soon cheered up at the idea of some company. I left him a reply saying that because I had so much to do in the kitchen, I would not be in a position to cook for a few days and I offered Sunday lunch.

When I had cleaned the fire grate in the hall, the ash dust had settled on my polished furniture and pictures, so today I was going to plan things more effectively.

In the kitchen, it took me half a day to clear out the fireplace and polish the surround and beautiful wooden mantelpiece until it shined. Then, I gently washed the delicate ornaments replacing them, as much as my memory would allow me, to where I had found them. Above the mantel was a picture of the Manor and I lightly dusted it and cleaned the carved wooden frame. It fell from its hanging and luckily I caught it by grabbing one corner before it crashed to the floor. It was heavy and I leant it against the wall whilst I got a chair to stand on. As I rehung the picture something fell from its back. Yellow and creased it was a piece of brittle paper and I squinted to read its contents:

'Callow Crest Manor in the year of our Lord 1578.' By his Grace, Francis Robert Langley, Lord of Callow.

I wondered whether he was one of the gentlemen from the pictures in the hall. I stood back to study the image and I noticed that very little had changed since Sir Francis had painted the scene. Something about the windows was different but I could not fathom what it was. I was then disturbed by Felix who arrived carrying a large brown box which he placed on the table, his two dogs beside him. He was dishevelled as ever and he bid his dogs outside as I stood my ground disconcerted.

"Cleaning stuff," he grunted.

His voice was Neanderthal as if he could not make complete sentences.

I began softening my voice not wanting to raise his temper.

"Felix, I am grateful for this job, really I am..." I wanted to say more but he cut me off.

"What do you want?"

"If I am to keep on top of things then I would prefer the dogs didn't come into the kitchen. It's simply not hygienic and you can't have them pooing everywhere. I'll make the boot room cosy for them and move their baskets into there."

I was feeling brave because I could see how much Felix loved his dogs.

In another Neanderthal reply he said, "Dogs belong in here."

"Let them come in after supper and sit by the fire but I am making their beds in the boot room and that is that if you want me to do my job properly."

To my surprise he nodded and said, "Leave a note of everything you need for the Lodge."

Then he left and I heard him calling the dogs to his heels.

I cleaned out their baskets and hauled them into the boot room which was large with neat rows of coat hooks and upright stands for boots and wellingtons. There was a boiler which heated the water so the dogs would be kept warm and there was one long empty wall for their baskets. Opposite the kitchen door was another door leading out to the garden; the lobby I had come through to speak to Felix to persuade him to let me live here. Inset in the end kitchen wall was a modern glass door which opened out onto a lawned area. From here the view swept for miles and I noticed a lake at the end of a sloping wave of a hill and a path hewn out of the sod that meandered down to it. Screwing my eyes, I could see a little boat house, its red roof glinting in the noonday sun. The ripples from the lake swished grey and ducks bobbed up and down coursing for refreshment. There was a building which seemed to be a church as I could just make out a tower. Why, when Felix had all this, was he so bitter and sad?

Outside the glass door were some seats and a table turned end up. The metal had been carved like wood and they reminded me of the style seen in Victorian paintings. They were heavy but I managed to drag them to an upright position after they had probably been discarded there for a century or more. No one seemed to care.

I made some tea and sat for a while watching the birds and butterflies flitting about and the shimmer from the lake dissolving into the sinking evening sun.

I worked tirelessly for those few days and I felt exhausted but the kitchen began to gleam. By some miracle I had worked out how to use the range and it had taken me another half a day to clean it. Felix must have noticed the changes and thankfully he observed my demands by keeping the dogs in the boot room. The days were growing colder and shorter and once the range-cooker was lit it heated the kitchen and the hearth looked inviting as I had gathered pine cones to fill its vacant heart.

Sunday greeted the day with the last of autumn's ebbs and flows and summoned winter to adorn the waiting sky. I rose early and went to the Manor. I commenced by laying the table with pieces of crockery from the dresser. In one of the drawers was a white linen cloth and I flapped it into the air like a sail cloth before spreading it over the table. I ignored the brownish crease marks where it had been left folded by someone. *Who?* I thought. For the first time I recalled the lady in the window.

Had she left it here? Where was she now? I had been so busy that I had forgotten about her. I wondered whether I should mention her to Felix. Perhaps she could join us for dinner? Although I hadn't ventured upstairs I had never heard a sound from up there. I doubted myself that I had seen her. Perhaps she was a vision of my own making caught in the strange shadows that swept across the Manor's face. Whether she existed or not, Felix had seemed to change his mind about me staying once I had mentioned her to him. I thought and wondered why the mention of her had made him change his mind? Perhaps he was humouring me thinking me quite mad. I decided to leave the topic for another day and to concentrate on preparing the dinner.

On the table, Felix had left a bloody joint of beef with vegetables, a carton of cream and some cooking apples that looked bruised and battered and I surmised that he was hankering for an apple pie so I did my best to make one.

Filling the serving dishes from the dresser I put out carrots, roast potatoes, cabbage and peas. Remembering my mother's

67

Yorkshire pudding recipe and heating the fat in the tin before I added the batter, they rose light and fluffy. I was so proud of myself. I was nearly eighteen and I had never cooked a Sunday lunch before but I realised how much my job depended on it. My apple pie looked sturdy as I placed it in the oven timing it to serve after lunch.

Naively, I thought that Felix would be grateful for my cuisine but he never spoke. He didn't wash his grimy hands before he sat at the table. He eyed the dishes and I watched as he made a pile on his plate. He hungrily scooped food into his mouth, the black under his nails showing through. He had purple scars and red fleck cuts in his skin. He devoured my offerings and gulped and used the back of his filthy hands to wipe the grease from his chin.

I politely nibbled the food on my plate aware that he was watching me waiting for me to finish. He was staring hard at the range oven and then back at me until I got the hint and left the table to serve my apple pie. It was just about cooked and steaming in the middle as I cut a large slice and gave it to him. He grabbed at the cream and poured it lavishly on the pudding, again, not uttering a word. I carried on eating my meal until he had finished.

"Cut up the beef and give the bone to the dogs!" he said.

He scraped the chair on the floor tiles and got up and left. Tarbo and Buster must have smelled the meat on him as they whooped loudly and whined as he herded them off to the truck.

I stared at the table and looked round the kitchen bewildered that the only evidence that he had been here were his dirty plates. I cut myself some pie and poured on the remains of the cream. It tasted fine but not as nice as my mother's. Then I cleared the table and washed the dishes. Slicing the leftover meat, as Felix had instructed, I placed it in the fridge and left the bone in the boot room for the dogs to fight over later.

My routine was very basic and it was a chore keeping on top of the kitchen and the grand hall and cooking for Felix. The winter bore down and I found a radio and I would listen to music as I continued in my tasks, a light relief from the twilight domesticity that Felix and I dwelt in. The only station that I could tune into played classical music, something I had never taken an interest in, and far from the silver booted bands of my choice. Nevertheless, I would find myself humming away to Mozart. My three-month trial was left unspoken like so many things between us. I grew confident that the time would pass and that Felix would let me stay.

On a few occasions, when I went back to the Lodge, I fancied I had seen the woman in the window. Sometimes, I would wake from a dream and peer across the courtyard at the musky light that had first drawn me there. I would see her standing in the dark, her contours lit by a candle that flickered in her shallow breath, as she seemed to call to me. I was curious to know who she was and I wanted to ask Felix about her but somehow the chance never came.

I often dreamt of Eliza, her mellow form swathing me.

"Make well Rose, be still, be still child," she would whisper. "The time will cometh."

Eliza bore no resemblance to the woman in the window who seemed to be desperate and clawing.

I would leave Felix notes asking for money and I would traipse down the track to the bus stop for my welcome visits to Churchbury. Felix never questioned what the money was for and the exact amount would be left on the table. In Churchbury, I would call on Mr and Mrs Davis who were busy with their walkers and sometimes, if not too busy, they would make me tea. I think they were befuddled by me, this young girl working up at the Manor, yet they were always pleased to see me.

Occasionally I would stop at the tea room and order tea and an iced bun. I always thought of my mother and would replace

69

her words with, *'Don't tell Felix'*, rather than '*Don't tell dad.*' I wrote to mum, I had given her a PO Box number and I would check every week at the Post Office to see if she had responded but she never did. I would bump into Brian who would beg me to come and work at the pub as they were desperate at this time of year, busy with holidaymakers, but I would refuse and promise to call for a drink with the intention of never doing so. My birthday was drawing near and I longed to be eighteen. I would feel more like an adult. I yearned for mum to send me a card.

A large Christmas tree was placed in the market square and twinkled merrily. Mistletoe hung over shop doorways and shop windows were filled with Christmas goodies. I wondered whether I should buy Felix a present. I imagined a big Christmas tree in the hall sprinkled with baubles and a holly wreath over the fire. I ordered a turkey from the butcher and a vegetable box from the grocer. I had quickly learnt that Felix's name was respected amongst the shopkeepers and that I could add things to his account as I wished. My short trips to Churchbury were always a welcome break.

Callow Crest Manor was spacious. Felix was starting to arrive home earlier on the winter's nights so after I had finished for the day I would explore the rest of the house before he came home. Firstly, I wandered into the rooms leading off the grand hall. After this experience, it dawned on me that the task of cleaning the house was too mammoth for me alone. In its heyday, a variety of servants must have worked here. Brian had told me about the massive acreage of land that Felix owned and the tenant farmers who paid him rent plus the cottages that he rented out too, so I figured this was where he received his wealth. Felix owned three horses, hunters, that he kept in the paddock and now and again I saw him galloping across the moors. His long hair flowed out beneath his cap which he wore all the time, even at meal times. The cap was grimy and I could just make out the tweed pattern the colours diminished. His beard had grown long and flimsy and there were flecks of grey and ginger amongst the brown straggly hairs. I noticed that when he went hunting he looked less dishevelled. He smelt of lavender soap and dressed smartly.

I felt lonely as I wove my way through the never-ending house. Discovering the dining room, which was Georgian in style, it had deep, soft bobble trimmed damask curtains hung at the window in duck-egg blue. The faded wallpaper was a similar colour and when I pulled out a sparsely filled bookcase I could see the original tints behind it. Bright exotic birds stood out from the blue and were nibbling at burgundy berries. The wallpaper was once dazzling and the furniture was symmetrical in a mellow tone; unlike the heavy carved oak that adorned the rest of the house. On the floorboards lay a large rug, almost touching the sides of the room and it was spotted in creams, pink, rose and brown patterns in good taste and not at all like the lino in the Lodge. A grand piano sat in the long mullioned window with its lid down.

Silver gilt frames covered the surface and I would gaze at the photographs of Felix's ancestors who stared back at me as if wondering who I was. There were scenes of hunt gatherings in the courtyard where sniffy-looking women sipped from horn cups, their tiny frames hugging monster-sized horses. All around, hounds, banded as brothers, and shooting their tails haughtily in the air smirking eagerly at the Huntmaster. I sensed their excited anticipation ready for the thrill of the hunt.

In one photograph, a fine lady in Edwardian dress sat regally. In another a more youthful woman, with her head slightly turned to one side to show off her long neck dripping with a pearl necklace, had a faraway look. She was beautiful and I wondered if she was the older woman's daughter. Perhaps the swan-like maiden was Felix's mother? Next to her was a handsome man, seemingly older who may have been her

71

husband, Felix's father. Perhaps they were still alive but if they were why were they letting their son live like this? I was never very good at mathematics but I was trying to work out the age gaps between them all. Family scenes were all remembered here atop the piano and I was glad to shake the dust away and chat to them as I cleaned the room.

The long table, with twelve seats, was set for dinner. Fine china and silver and cotton napkins made up the places where no-one sat and crystal glasses gleamed in the weakening glare of sunlight shining through the south facing window. The chandelier was still filled with semi-burnt out candles and the faceted drops shimmered when I opened the window to let the air flush through the stifled room.

A pair of chairs, in keeping with the rest of the room, sat in front of the marble fireplace and on each side of the fender stood finely sewn-silk screens to stop the ladies of the day becoming too flushed as they reclined next to the fire. This room had a calmer feel than the others and even though it was dusty and faded it had a glow of a feminine nimbus. It was a long room, adequately divided into an eating and entertaining space as it was not encumbered by the sweeping staircase whose architecture seemed to wrap around the other rooms. I'd let myself sink into one of the chairs and taking the photograph of the pretty woman, I would sit and pretend that I was the lady of the Manor. I would idly engage in conversation to the lady named Vivian. Her name was scrolled at the bottom of her beautifully-poised black and white photograph. *"Why is Felix such a filthy arsehole, Vivian?"* I would ask.

Vivian would stare out, not speaking of course, but I imagined her responding by lifting her shapely swan neck to listen to my jabberings. She looked so glamorous, her style of dress like someone between the wars. I envisaged her reclining against the piano entertaining brilliant and fascinating people. Vivian looked like the kind of woman who would smoke cigarettes from a long holder and blow the smoke in little cloudy puffs. This room conjured images from the past and from her stature and clothes, I could tell that she was a distinguished and graceful woman.

There was an old wind-up gramophone and I put on a record. I danced around, feigning a Charleston dance to a jazzy sound and the startling squeaks of a clarinet cheeped until I could almost smell gardenia corsages spilling out their perfume, envisaging Vivian and her friends moving to the music and stopping to gossip about exotic things. I imagined, that naturally, all the men longed to have a moment in time with beautiful Vivian as her long red nails caressed the piano.

Next I discovered a library. The walls of this room were stuffed and lined with bookshelves sagging under the weight of master books and first edition volumes. Leather bound oblong books were laid open on round and rectangle tables showing maps of the world. None of these showed Australia or the Americas so they must have been very old whereas others showed some parts of the continents. The readers had discarded them, no longer of curiosity and the pages were left open where they had last been read. A meticulously-carved wooden surround filled the space between the mantelpiece and the ceiling and at either side female figures swathed in Grecian costume, similar to those on the helms of sailing ships, held up globes to support the deep coving. Fine porcelain and silver rested on shelves gathering dust. In the flickering light of the oriel window was a terrestrial globe on a tilted axis. The wood panelled room was dark and to begin with I was afraid to touch as I didn't want to disturb anything. It was as if someone had just got up and left the room as if expecting to return but never doing so.

There was a tall, slim table, which reminded me of the podium in my parents' church and chained to it was the Langley family bible. I promised myself to read it one day as it would be my gateway into Felix's family. It was thick and bound in black leather with gold letters. On a cursory glance I saw the pages coloured and scribed by hand. I wondered what family secrets it held.

There was another room, a small snug. This room was warm and quite cosy. It was furnished with the usual Manor dust, just as neglected, as all the other rooms seemed to be. In years gone by someone had removed the wooden panelling and replaced it with panels of vibrant wallpaper. I felt comfortable in this room and I would have gladly sat here in the evenings as it had an oversized fireplace and the décor was to my liking. Yet, Felix would not budge from his place by the hearth in the kitchen.

There was no telephone at the Manor and Brian had told me that this was because Felix had strongly objected to having the telegraph poles erected across his land. I thought it odd that he showed concern about the features in the landscape and yet cared little for his grand ancient home and its contents.

As I inspected each room I looked for signs of the woman in the window. There were traces of ash in the fireplaces but they had burnt out long ago. My logic told me that if there was someone else in this house then they weren't keeping warm by any of the fires which I had come across and cleaned. It puzzled me to think that there could be anyone else. I did all the cooking and I knew exactly what was eaten. If there was someone in the window they would have starved to death in the time that I was here. I hadn't noticed Felix taking food to any other room. But when I mentioned I'd seen a woman in the window, Felix had agreed for me to stay. Perhaps it was a ghost? Perhaps it was his mother? I wanted to find out.

I regularly stopped my work at around 5 p.m. so that I had dinner on the table for 6 p.m. ready for Felix's return. The times he arrived back were erratic and if he arrived too late I would cover his dinner with a plate and leave it in the oven ready for him to serve himself. I would find the remains the next morning. He always left crumbs across the table and his dirty dishes in the sink. This made me feel more like a slave than a housekeeper but I never complained. I was so relieved to leave the despair and sadness that had befallen me in Birmingham.

I began to work on the Lodge. Communicating by notes, Felix gave me money for a new bed, to have the chimneys swept and to replace the flooring on the stairs, sitting room and in the kitchen. The linoleum no longer gave me a headache as I had chosen a plain beige flooring, following this theme for carpet throughout the Lodge. Felix never visited. No one ever visited.

Buster and Tarbo unsettled me and I think they resented me for banishing them from the kitchen. One evening, when I was feeling overly tired and preparing dinner, Buster tiptoed in. I glared at him feeling wary. Buster was trained and knew the routine by now. He knew he wasn't allowed in there until after dinner. He padded over to the hearth and cheekily curled up on the rug but not before giving me a challenging look as if to ask me what I was going to do about it. Angry, I went to the rug and began to tug at it hoping to dislodge him. "Buster!" I bravely shouted, "OUT!" Feeling the rug move beneath him Buster fumbled about and then, steadying himself, he turned and growled at me. As he bore his jagged teeth it was like he was making a curse. He bowed his head and bent his front legs ready to pounce. I stood my ground, not from bravado but from fear.

I sensed Felix first before hearing his voice commanding Buster into the boot room as he entered.

Buster's fierce face looked disgruntled and then Felix spoke again ordering Buster out. Buster succumbed, his maddening eyes meeting mine as he left and went to lay next to Tarbo.

I turned to look at Felix who was standing in the garden doorway. He nodded at me and I noticed that he was carrying a basket full of vegetables and he set it down on the table.

75

"For casserole?" he said.

"For casserole," I repeated.

After that the relationship between Felix and I felt different to me. Perhaps it was my desperation in seeking kindness in another human being. But I felt certain that Felix had saved me from Buster who may have attacked me; the dog was at least threatening to bite me. Perhaps Felix recognised my vulnerability.

As the winter drew in, dinner times relaxed and Felix and I started to have conversations, a few sentences at first but he spoke to me with some semblance of respect which I appreciated as I had endured some loneliness over the autumn months.

In my bones, I sensed that Felix held emotions of loss. For some people loss is worn in their heart, like my own. Felix's sense of loss was exposed and raw and it seemed to have destroyed his soul; his reason for living. He had become vague and uncertain of the world in which he was surviving and he had become isolated and disconnected to his surroundings and other people. The only thing was that I had no idea of what had occurred to bring him to this point.

We talked mostly about our day. He told me what he had done on the farm and I was genuinely interested to learn how he worked his ghastly dogs and how he rotated the crops, managed livestock and went to market. He spoke enthusiastically about his work and I would listen attentively. He seemed to be busy all year round and now it was winter, I thought there would be less for him to do. I was wrong. He told me about the barns full of cattle, sheds full of equipment in need of repair and winter grains to sow and sheep to tend. He explained how the neighbouring farmers pulled together at this time of year, sharing labour and machines and places to store feed.

I'd rightly perceived that there were subjects that we would not discuss: Our personal lives and things from the past and definitely nothing about the woman in the window. My birthday was nearing. I decided to mention this to Felix one evening, when he was in a mood of engagement and to my surprise and delight he suggested that I went to the cellar to choose some wine.

"Pick some port too." He was being kind.

I seized my opportunity. "Felix, who is the woman in the window? Shall I invite her to my birthday meal? Does she live here?"

His face grew dark and his brow furrowed as his jawline grew tense.

"Now you listen to me woman," he said viciously.

"This is my fucking house and don't you forget it and go prowling around. There is no other woman in this house but you and you're only here 'cos I'm foolish enough to let you stay."

He muttered words under his breath that I could not make out. It was clear that the mention of the woman made him angry so I didn't speak again and cleared the table. *She must be in my imagination, I thought. Was I going mad?* I had a lot of time on my own to think about things, perhaps it was just a trick of the light that made me think someone was standing in the window. I tried to brush her from my mind but she would never completely disappear.

CHAPTER 5

I had never gone down to the cellar. I had also never properly explored upstairs. I was curious to take a peek at Felix's room and I imagined it to be unkempt. He rarely left clothes out to be washed. He did expect his hunting and shooting gear to be clean and ready but most days he wore a checked shirt and jeans beneath his overalls.

Part of me did not want to find any more rooms to clean as I was finding it exhausting enough keeping on top of the ones on the ground level. I wasn't prowling – I was trying to do my job and I would repeat this to Felix if he accused me of poking my nose in again.

A couple of days before my birthday, I opened the door from the kitchen that led to the cellar. Immediately a rush of loitering and festering aroma of damp came towards me. I switched on the light and a single bulb lit my way into the blankness. There was another switch at the bottom of the steps and I made my way down to it. Cobwebs stroked my hair and I had a feeling of trepidation as I feebly placed each foot on the cold stone. I flicked the switch of the second light and I was instantly overwhelmed by the size of the cellar. It was vast. There were rooms leading off the main area and the ceilings were strongly vaulted and multiple racks of stored wine lined the walls. Spider webs levitated and everywhere was coated in a sandy dust.

Where was I to begin? I knew nothing about wine and the cellar stretched out under the length and breadth of the Manor crammed with bottles lying on their sides. In no particular order, I picked out bottles from the rows and noticed they were labelled with the name of the wine and a date. A lot of the wording was in French and I wished I had paid more attention at French lessons, as I tried to decipher the meaning. Some of the dates were as old as the Manor, dating from the sixteenth century and I tried to picture which person from the portraits in the hall had begun to build this collection. I thought the vintage bottles would probably taste vile. After a while, I worked out that that there was some process in the labelling as the dates for the younger wines were in the racks nearest to the door. I chose a bottle of 'Chateauneuf Calcernier' dated 1844. When I held it to the light, it looked like sludge so I replaced it and found a younger bottle of red wine dated 1958.

I suddenly remembered that Felix had asked for some port and wondered where I would find it. I stood in the middle of the larger room, down from the cellar steps and I stared out hard at the rows, my eyes squinting and scanning the racks. On the opposite side, where I had chosen the wine, were more racks but the bottle tops were different. I read the labels. Champagne, not what I was looking for but adjacent I found more racks filled with an assortment of shaped and coloured bottles. The labels read, cognac, sherry and at last I found squat bottles filled with dark liquid labelled, 'port'. I checked the labels but I had no idea which to choose. Selecting a method from my childhood and closing my eyes, I turned around three times with my arm held out and my middle finger pointing. I opened my eyes, slightly overbalanced and not in the place where I had started. My eyes had adjusted to the shady light and in front of me I saw a door. Intrigued I crept towards it. I was still clutching the 1958 wine. A thick woven curtain was drawn back and there were two steps leading up to it and the key was in the lock. I stared at the door. It was nearing time for Felix to return so I turned to grab the first bottle of port I laid my hand on and returned to the warmth of the kitchen. I would go back to the cellar when I had more time to discover what was behind the hidden door.

On the morning of my birthday, I laid the fire at the Lodge ready for my evening return. On my last visit to Churchbury, I had treated myself to a glossy magazine and I was looking forward to relaxing in the bath and then sitting in the glow of my sitting room to read it. I had bought some curtains and a wing back chair which I kept by the fire. Scouring the second-hand shop in Churchbury, I had purchased some ornaments and pictures to adorn the room. This was my sanctuary and I loved it. I had also treated myself to an artificial Christmas tree and I had one present wrapped beneath it: A bottle of aftershave for Felix. Heavenly light filled this space and I would sit by the fire enjoying its heat at the end of my day's work when I would rerun the conversations I'd held with Felix, trying hard to find the person beneath his hardened exterior.

On the way over to the Manor I noticed the truck in the courtyard. Felix was at home. It was strange for him to be about at this time of the morning. When I entered the kitchen, I realised why. Felix was stroking Buster who was lying on the rug, his gruff form motionless and quiet. Buster feebly lifted his head noticing me come in and Felix turned and saw me.

"He's been like this all night," he said.

I watched him gently stroke his dog, his rough hands pulling through his hair tenderly and I was transfixed for a moment.

"Can I do anything?" I asked.

Felix answered in a mild manner.

"Could you check on Tarbo? She's locked in the boot room. She'll need feeding."

I didn't answer. I nodded and went to check on Tarbo. She was sitting anxiously on her bed and her eyes were mellow as I bent down to pat her.

"Don't worry Tarbo, Buster will be all right."

I filled her bowl with a can of dog food and gave her some fresh water suspecting that she wouldn't touch either.

Back in the kitchen, Felix was cradling Buster in his arms until the dog took his last breath and Felix began to cry. Tears ran down his cheeks as he held Buster close to him. As much as I hated that dog, seeing Felix in grief moved me to tears. I moved towards him and placed my hand on his shoulder. He reached up and placed a hand on top of mine. He said,

"Rose, I'll bury him in the garden."

I set about my usual routine and later I heard him come back for Tarbo and the rev of the engine as he sped off in his truck for the day. I had left the wine and port on the dresser in anticipation of my birthday celebration but I thought this was unlikely to happen now so I carried on as normal. I was fed up and I was feeling sorry for myself so I headed to the cellar deciding to take a look through the mysterious door. The perfume of long ago permeated the stale air. I stiffened. It was creepy and my eyes took time to become used to the diffused atmosphere. I took the two steps up to the door and pushed hard. It didn't move. I stepped back to the floor and rotated the key and pulled hard at the metal knob and the door opened with ease. The smell of the iron lingered on my hand and I stepped up to see where the door led. In the muted light I could make out the turn of a spiral staircase etched out of the rock. There was no switch so I went back up the cellar stairs to root out a torch and returning, shone it into the dark crevices. Amazingly the walls were free of webs and spiders and as I wound up I touched them feeling their blank coldness. My head was full of thoughts of those men in the portraits and the likelihood of them scouting this way forward centuries before me. The woman in

81

the window sprang to my mind and I had a strange pull upwards fully expecting her to be waiting for me at the top. Abruptly, the stairs ended and a tiny landing offered two ways to turn. One, to my right, was up two further steps and was draped in matching cloth to the curtain below. I pulled it back and there was a door with a lock but no key. I tried the key from the other door but it didn't fit. I tried pulling and pushing but it would not budge. I could not fathom where this would lead, perhaps to the attic rooms?

I tried the door facing me and this opened outwards but it snagged on something bulky. I squeezed through and found myself standing behind a tapestry. I gathered one end together in my arms and soon realised that I was in the first floor gallery near to Felix's bedroom. This made some sense as it was probably a short cut for servants to take up drinks and food in times gone by. I was curious about the other door and I wondered where the key could be?

Directly in front of me was a small door. I had discovered that Felix's bedroom was down this corridor. I had sneaked in one afternoon, the hairs on the back of my neck rising but after quickly opening the door I left in a hurry not wanting to be caught there. I had glimpsed a four-poster bed and flowery mint green wallpaper.

I crossed to the small door opposite to where I had come out and loitered for a while outside. I grasped the handle and turned it. The whole gallery and the doors leading off were lined in wood panelling. As I opened the door it creaked. The grandfather clock along the gallery struck ten clattering out its resonant chimes as my heart vibrated, reverberating in time. Inside, the room was plain and sparsely furnished. My stomach churned. An odd smell overpowered me. I put my hand over my mouth and examined the room. A large wardrobe flanked one wall and clothes were in a heap on the floor. The white plaster and paint was peeling and one of the window panes was broken so the breeze caught the thin curtains and they flapped making a noise like a butterfly's wing. Trying to hold my breath from the stench I walked to the window. A marvellous view beheld me as a rampant ripe green carpet rolled down to the lake. From here I could see bushes, once clipped in topiary and I could make out prim shapes, a crown, a peacock and what looked like a teapot skirting the path to the water.

A double bed with iron ends and two bedside tables, one piled high with shooting magazines, see-sawed against the wall. Two lamps peeped out with lopsided shades tarnished where the bulbs had burned them. A cool wind came through the broken pane. Goose feathers coiled above the bed. The bed was unmade so I plumped and tidied the pillows. Then I pulled back the faded yellow satin bedspread.

My heart was silenced.

I blindly ran from the room down the gallery to the sweeping staircase and sprinted back to the Lodge and flopped into my chair. I could hardly believe what I had seen and I felt sick. My lungs were gulping for air as I breathed faster and waited for my physicality to calm. My fingers tingled and I was trembling. I went to the kitchen. I made tea and sipped it, adding scoops of sugar trying to steady myself. When I had pulled back the bedding, to my horror, the bed was filled with blood. Stained dried blood, the colour of rust, spread out like ink on blotting paper. The mattress seemed to have been eaten away. There were insect eggs and holes where vermin had munched. What shocked me more was that it seemed to have been in that condition for years. Questions rang in my head. Whose blood was it? The woman in the window? Had Felix killed her? Was I safe here?

Recalling Felix's curt words to me about prowling I didn't want him to guess I had been to this room, so I steeled myself to return so I could try to leave the room as I had found it.

I went up the main staircase and turned right along the gallery. I passed Felix's bedroom and the door to his bathroom. I noticed the tapestry, concealing its secret door behind. It was endowed with delicate stitching. Hunters were arranged around a clearing in a wood and carried bows and arrows. Their costumes were delicately sewn and women observed the scene posed with one arm across their chests, their flaxen hair in long plaits. Unlike the men, they were floating in spectral clouds. In the middle was a unicorn stitched in pure white. An aureate sun beamed rays to light the view. The unicorn had a mortal wound causing blood to seep along its trunk, the arrow striking hard and strong. One finely dressed youth carried a golden bow and he was evidently the champion of the animal's undoing. It was a cruel scene and yet by some strange paradox it was serene. I thought of the door behind it and the steps upwards and I wondered again if the blood in the bed belonged to the woman in the window.

In my rush I had left the door wide open so I was glad that I had returned to close it. I scrunched the pillows and soft satin quilt, not pulling it back to reveal the revolting mess beneath and shook them to their original untidy places. I looked back and shuddered. My soul was full of dread never wanting to broach Felix about what I had found but knowing that one day I would have to. My eighteenth birthday was one I shall never forget.

I went back to the Manor and busied myself trying hard to shut the bitter thoughts from my mind. Felix returned early looking dreadful and just for that evening I allowed Tarbo to lay on the hearth rug whilst I prepared dinner. Felix sat at the table, forlorn and not speaking. His presence there was disturbing. I felt sickened by the thought of him keeping the blooded bed and it disgusted me. He'd been angry when I raised the subject of the woman in the window and I was afraid of rattling him again, thinking and afraid that he may be a murderer.

Our dinner was eaten with no exchange of words. Afterwards, Felix sat by the fire with Tarbo at his side staring into the flames. I finished the dishes and went back to the Lodge grateful to be there.

That night, as I bathed, I heard Tarbo howling. She howled the night long mourning for her companion. From my bedroom I saw the gallery light and guessed that it was Felix going down to comfort her.

There was also a light in another window offset to the others. It was a good two or three feet higher. She was there. The lady was watching me and she seemed to beckon me. She was wearing a sheer nightgown and the gloomy light lit up the outline of her slim and slender body. Long Titian hair flowed from her nightcap and her bony hands tapped at the window begging for my attention. The black night was still and I heard her whisper like the hoot of an owl.

"My boys, where are my boys?"

I pulled my curtains hard across. This was all too much for one day and I buried myself under the blankets with a hot water bottle. The embers of the fire were dying and I tried to sleep.

After a fitful night, there were bags under my eyes. My hair needed washing but I had not got the energy so I tucked it into a ponytail. It had grown quite a lot since I had taken out chunks with blunt scissors and was growing back thick and lush. I opened the curtains and saw that Felix was gone as was his truck. I looked over to the window where I had seen the woman. There was no light and the glass was dark.

I hadn't been out for a walk for ages and today I thought the fresh air would do me good. I packed a lunch and left through the boot room. The bed where Buster had slept lay empty and I recalled his snarling mouth and in truth I was glad that he was gone. Outside, the sky was pitched in aluminium streaks and rain threatened. Undaunted, I walked across the cottage garden towards the burnt out milking parlour based at the end. It was a derelict building made of red brick and lime mortar. When I reached it an ivy-clad door stood ajar and I pushed through. Here was a walled garden. I was astounded that I had never noticed it. It must have been an acre in size and the walls protected gnarled fruit trees from the driving moor winds. A battered greenhouse leaned against one wall. Most of the windows shattered and I could make out the remains of weeds poking up inside.

At the other end was a door in a wall so I crunched my way over the frosty grass and opened it. The cold December hoar panted as I went through to a vista of rolling moorland. Flecked here and there were sheep grazing on the hardened cud resilient to the stern weather. There was a gate and stile leading up to a hill and I climbed over ready for an adventure of my own. The path up was an easy walk but I stopped halfway to take in the view. Nestling at the top of the hill was a circle of trees resolute in the landscape bent to one side from the prevailing west wind. They were spruce or some other winter green species; my botanical knowledge was limited. I hadn't seen any trees like this in Birmingham. I made my way up towards them. By the time I reached the top, sprinkles of rain had begun to fall and obscured my view so I scurried into the middle of the trees to shelter. A group of standing stones circled the centre and one had fallen supported by the uneven ground so that it looked like a sacrificial table. I sat on it and opened my rucksack ready for my lunch. As I ate I saw erect stones, dappled in the rain, standing weary in solitude. The ferns and long grass grew in shrouds and moss clung to them. They seemed to cast pagan spells under the canopy amid the bracken and I felt this was a magical place.

The path to the stone, where I sat, was well trodden as if someone regularly visited here. I listened intently to the birds and the rustle of scurrying rodents in the vegetation. Peaceful and calm and alone. My body yearned to be still but my head kept jamming, whirling around with thoughts of the woman in the window and the blooded bed. I speculated that Felix had hurt her in some way and locked her in an attic. Apart from seeing her at the window, I had never heard anyone moving about the Manor. Yes, it creaked and yawned and the old oak beams succumbed to a stretch now and again but I had never heard the presence of any other human. That made me think. Perhaps she wasn't human. A ghost? It *was* an irrational thought but it had been distinct in my brain for a while. I wondered, had Felix killed her, in their bed?

My mind thought about Brian and the tale he had told me about Felix being aloof and that something tragic had happened to his wife but he would never finish the story. What had happened to her?

The rain cleared and I left, my mind in turmoil. As the rain dispersed I could see the Manor, the winding path trailing back to the stile.

Sitting in a dip, it was surrounded by heathland and rippling hills, giving it some protection from the wild elements. The roof zig-zagged and I could see the walled garden and the lake beyond. The Lodge was also visible. I looked across to the row of windows in the gallery.

There was a tower. I could never have noticed it from the ground because it was set back from the roof. I quickly gleaned that this was the window where the woman had beckoned to me.

Before I left for the track back down, I trod across the dampened grass through to the other side of the ring of trees. I could see for miles and far out to the west where valleys slumbered and transgressed into Wales. The views from up here were breath-taking and as the sky brightened I saw the outline of another grand house in the distance. Its shape was geometrically square with lawns and neat borders wrought formally around it. There were cottages spotted in abundant pastures clipped after the autumn harvest now covered with a winter's frost. Smoke twirled from chimneys and blackened bonfires choked the air.

Country lanes were mapped out like veins threading through the landscape. Along a lane I saw Felix's truck chuffing towards a track leading up to where I was standing. Fumes were spewing from the exhaust where Tarbo sat in the open back, her tongue lopped to one side, as she scanned the horizon seeking out unwary sheep.

He was the last person I wanted to encounter so I dashed back through the circle and tracked back towards the Manor. I jogged along, tentatively jumping over scattered rocks. I still feared hurting my ankle, and strained to hear the engine of the truck approaching the trinket of trees. I was almost there. The sound of him stopping his truck carried lifeless down the hillside and I heard the slamming of the door as I reached the stile. I went to the kitchen, lit the fire, stoked the range and made some tea.

CHAPTER 6

Clocks in the Manor had disregard for accuracy as they all chimed at different moments. It was around noon and my trek to the top of the hill and back had taken me less than two hours. I heard the abrasion of wheels in the courtyard and I was surprised. This could not be Felix. He had no time to return so soon.

I went to the door and parked on the cobbles was a 4×4 car; blue and shiny. A petite, blonde-haired woman was getting out and as I stood at the door within a door she smiled and waved at me. She wore a bright white blouse, dark navy slacks and her shoes were navy too with cream leather heels. Her smart blue blazer looked neat and expensive. Even in the chill of December she wore sunglasses to pull back her locks. They sat on her head reminding me of Mickey Mouse ears.

"Hello," she said taking my hand to shake it. "I'm Bunnie, Felix's sister-in-law."

I gawped never expecting that Felix had any living relatives. I quickly brushed myself down hoping that she would not notice the perspiration stains under my arms from my quick jog. I didn't invite her in, she just followed me through to the kitchen. She made herself comfortable sitting at the table and whizzed her eyes around.

"My, you have done wonders here. When I heard that Felix had employed a housekeeper I didn't believe it. I'm really pleased you are here. Rose? It is Rose?"

I nodded and asked whether she would like some tea. She let out a loud, "Super" and pointed at the fruit cake I had made and left on the side.

"That looks yummy – shouldn't really, but if you insist."

I made her some tea and put a slice of cake on a plate. I doubted she ever ate cake, she was too slim. She was one of those women who were anxious about their figures.

"So, how are you settling in?"

I had been at the Manor for months and I was bewildered by this person in front of me and why she had turned up now.

She must have realised from the look on my face and she dropped her voice to an ambient tone.

"Rose, I am Felix's sister-in-law. We have known each other for years, I knew his wife, we all grew up together. I'm married to Felix's twin."

"His twin!" I exclaimed. "His wife?" I uttered.

"Yes, Rose. Fergus, Felix's twin."

I went pale. I could barely take it all in.

"Look, are you OK?"

"Yes, of course, yes, sorry, it's just that I know nothing about Felix. He rarely speaks and there are so many questions I need to ask about his life and the Manor."

Bunnie's voice grew serious.

"Rose, Felix has had a great tragedy in his life and he's never got over it. His brother and I have done our best to keep our eye on him but he's impossible, I'm sure you realise that?"

I could not stop myself and I blurted out that I had been into the bedroom and that there was a bed full of blood. Bunnie looked concerned and took my hand in hers.

"Where is Felix now?" she asked.

"At the trees with the standing stones."

"Ah, I should have guessed. He's up at the Callow."

Bunnie leaned in towards me.

"Make some more tea Rose and let's talk."

As she weaved her tale I began to understand why Felix bore such sorrow.

Bunnie was the daughter of the Edwards and she lived in the house that I had seen across the moors that morning. Fergus and Felix were the only children of Vivian and Stephen Langley and were sent off to boarding school in Shrugsborough as soon as they were eight. Vivian and Stephen had more love for their dogs and blood sports than they ever had for their children and spent their days according to the season, fishing, hunting or shooting. *Vivian, the swan-woman in the photograph, I thought.*

In the summer months, when the boys came home, Bunnie and Hannah were their playmates.

"Hannah?" I asked. "Who is Hannah?"

"Was, Rose, who was Hannah," she corrected me and she continued.

"Hannah was the daughter of the Dakin family, farm labourers to the Manor who had worked and lived on the Callow lands since it was first built. Hannah was beautiful with marvellous sage coloured eyes and it was always she who led us into mischievous trouble, sometimes scrumping or playing rat-a-tat-tat down in Churchbury. The boys were enamoured by her and over the long summers we would trek across the moors taking picnics, riding our ponies and swimming in the lake. It was idyllic.

"We all grew and Fergus, Felix and myself were ushered off to university. We were all in our last year when news came that the twins' parents had been killed. Vivian and Stephen had decided to skate on the frozen lake. You know, the one down by the church. Vivian was warned not to skate in the middle but she was reckless and the ice cracked and she fell through it. Stephen frantically attempted to save her but they were both dragged under by the current and never seen again. Ironically, Vivian is a name that means, 'The Lady of the Lake'."

I saw the irony in that but it seemed like some twisted fate that Vivian was so swan-like. I asked whether they ever dredged the lake but Bunnie said that no-one knew how deep it was so their bones were left below to rest. She told me that the safest place to swim was from the shore by the church. As she spoke I think she realised that this information wasn't appropriate and she added in a small voice, *'should I ever wish to do so, that is...'*

I closed my eyes to visualise myself bobbing in the water and the glassy hand of Vivian reaching out to grab me as she swam up transformed into a swan.

"After that Fergus and Felix came home and as Felix was the eldest son he managed the farmland.

"Hannah went to the local school. She never went to university but secretly I think she waited for Felix to return home. One day she came up to the Manor. She had changed in those three years and had become a remarkably gorgeous young woman. Felix was smitten and soon they were married and Hannah moved into the Manor.

"Fortunately, I managed to keep Fergus's eyes on me and not long after Felix and Hannah were wed, we were married too. Those were lovely days. Fergus moved into my parents' home and helped to manage the estate. We would often join Felix and Hannah hacking out on our horses or chugging out on tractors to meet for dinner and drinks. Coincidentally, Hannah and I fell pregnant at the same time."

My brow narrowed as I thought of Felix's wife with child. It was unimaginable to think that he had experienced such happiness. I was curious to find out what happened to Hannah and her baby.

Bunnie saw my expression but made no comment.

"We both got near to the end of our pregnancies and we were due in January. We had a harsh snowfall that year, the roads were impassable and Felix had no telephone. The only way out of the Manor was by tractor.

"The rest of this story, Rose, is my own assumption because no-one really knows what happened that night."

What was she about to tell me, I thought. Bunnie took a deep breath.

"Hannah went into labour and Felix settled her into bed. Not the room he uses now but the bed that you found. I think his plan was to drive to the village in the tractor and to bring Dr Comickery back to the Manor but Hannah was frightened and didn't want him to leave her. The snow was deep and it would have been difficult getting down to the road even in the tractor. So, Felix lay with his wife as her pains came. He brought hot water and clean towels and I think he was convinced that he could bring that baby into this world based on no other reason than he had successfully delivered a lot of lambs by himself.

"Hannah pushed and nothing happened. By my reckoning she must have been in labour for at least twenty four hours and still no baby came. The snow fell harder swelling the earth into mounds of white. Felix, not knowing what to do, brought a knife from the kitchen and cut his wife's vagina. It worked because it opened her up and she gave birth to a son and then she gave birth to another son, smaller and more frail. Hannah fell into a deep sleep and Felix placed his sons into a drawer, firstly lining it with a pillow and covering them in a blanket. Why he didn't put them both in the cot, God only knows. Perhaps he just wanted to keep them warm. There was no heating in the bedroom as the boiler had frozen. He brought them down here, right there by the fireplace and put the drawer on the rug to warm them. Next he went back to his wife and flopped onto the bed beside her. Just for a moment. Unwittingly, Felix fell asleep and when he woke his wife had gone.

Panicking, he searched the gallery, the bathroom, the other bedrooms and then he came down here."

Bunnie pointed to the glass door leading out to the undulating garden.

"The twins were still in the drawer. It was a cold night. The moon was full and Felix traced the spots of blood where his wife had stumbled towards the Callow."

"Why? Why did she go there?" I asked.

Bunnie sighed.

"We can only guess that she was searching for her boys, perhaps she woke and saw that they had gone. Her brain was draining away all sensible thoughts as her life blood was leeching out. Felix eventually found her lying on the mystical stone in the Callow circle. She was dead, Rose."

I saw the mist in her eyes and I stifled the dewy droplets in my own.

"And the boys Bunnie, the boys?"

"Well, that's the saddest part Rose. In his hurry to find Hannah, Felix ran out and left the door open and the boys grew cold and death seeped into their tiny bodies and they passed away."

"Oh God!" I breathed. "Poor Felix." *I thought of my own son.*

"Felix carried her body all the way back. It must have been terrible being weighed down in the snow. He lay her in front of the fire hoping to warm her back to life, I suppose. God knows how he must have reacted when he realised his sons had died. Anyway, he placed each twin to cradle in her arms. Then he lay down next to them waiting to die. Two days later, when the snow had settled, Fergus, claiming to have a prophetic psychic connection to his twin, drove his tractor as far as he could up to the Manor and walked the rest of the way. He found the four of them lying there."

I looked over at the hearth imagining that awful sight.

"I don't think Fergus has ever got over the shock. It was dreadful, Rose, you really can't imagine. Somehow, Fergus has managed to move on. I'm his wife so I know it's always remembered, under the surface but he has tried desperately to lay those ghosts to rest for the sake of me and his own children. Having them, I think, Rose, has helped. I believe that Felix feels he has no-one to live for. He's stuck in that time and he can't or won't let go."

I made more tea whilst Bunnie composed herself. She had just told me the saddest story I had ever heard and I looked towards the fireplace where Felix sat each night, his mind wishing so hard that things were different.

"Anyway," she said brightly, "I only just found out you were here because I had to post some accounts in Churchbury and the postmistress told me all about you. It's lovely to meet you, Rose. After that story, I bet you can see why Fergus and I are really happy that you are here."

"Do you ever see him?" I asked. "Felix?"

"Now and again, mainly at the hunt but sometimes he comes over to shoot at our place. Actually Rose, that's one of the reasons why I am here."

She went on and suggested that I could go over for some extra work on shoot days if I wanted. She explained that she was always looking for help.

"You can meet Fergus too. Oh, and my twin boys and Emily."

I barely heard her. Sipping at my hot tea I was thinking hard about the tragic tale of Hannah and her sons.

"The blood in the bed, Bunnie, is that Hannah's?"

"Yes, Rose. It's her blood. Felix just can't bear to let her go, that's all that is left."

"It's macabre, Bunnie, it's just not right."

"Fergus and I have tried to persuade Felix to let us come and, well, you know, sort things out but he absolutely refuses.

95

He's a stupid, stubborn man. He gets it from his mother, the stubbornness. And like his own father, he was besotted with his wife."

I stared at the entrance to the cellar wondering if it was Hannah's ghost in the tower. Bunnie jolted me out of my thoughts.

"Rose, Rose, we have a shoot next Saturday. Would you like to come and help? We'll pay you, of course."

"For sure." I was thinking that it would be nice to earn some money of my own. I didn't even ask her how much.

"Your twins?" I asked.

"God yes, boisterous boys, although actually they are not too bad now. They're seventeen and Emily is twelve."

"What time?" I interrupted before she could tell me any more about her family. A jealousy was stirring in my heart yet I didn't know why.

"Early as you can. Seven o'clock would be fab."

I smiled in response and Bunnie got up to leave. Hesitating, she said,

"Rose, are you OK here? You know with Felix? If there is anything you need or want please do let me know. You are, well, I hope you don't mind me saying, you are awfully young. Probably not much older than my boys."

I smiled meekly and showed her out.

"Saturday then?"

"Saturday," I said.

When Bunnie had gone, I cleared up our cups and munched on the cake she hadn't eaten. I was tired and I made a cold dinner for Felix and left him a note saying I was unwell and that I'd left food in the fridge. I went back to the Lodge and crawled into bed. My eyes were hooded as I wept and I drifted to sleep and dreamt of Hannah and her twins and the bed of blood. I wanted to summon Eliza but she did not visit my dreams.

PART THREE

The cross of soot

CHAPTER 7

The next morning I went over to the Manor as usual. I was feeling stressed and burdened with the story that Bunnie had told me so to keep my mind off things I collected up all the cleaning products I could muster and threw them into a bucket. I stood in the grand hallway and tried to make a decision about which room to clean. I even found that choice hard but in the end I chose the library.

The task of bringing this room back to life was too much for me. My body was taut and I had no inclination to work, so instead I sat at one of the tables and left the bucket by the door. I studied an atlas where it had been left open. It was hand-coloured and showed a map of Great Britain and France.

The date was 1643 and the inscription was in inked calligraphy. Swathes of forest covered the country and there were name places that I did not recognise. I skimmed the page to find Shrugsboroughshire and there it was, a dashed line marking its border next to Montgomeryshire and the Callow Crest was sitting in the south west of the county to identify its location. The Manor must have been important as it seemed to be the only house marked out. Bunnie's house wasn't there. I noticed the church drawn by the lake and it also had the Callow Crest. I suppose it made sense that the Manor would have its own place of worship. Browsing for a while I tried to recognise places on the map. I searched for Birmingham but I could not find it. There were counties like Radnor, Brecknock and Merioneth. It said that these districts were held by the king and this included Shrugsboroughshire. Which king I wondered and I also wondered what connection this old house and its occupants had to do with royalty. I looked over at the bible, securely chained to the table and went to study that too. It was an expansive book with broad sheets. The first pages were crammed with the names of births and marriages all the way back to the first occupants of the house.

Sir Francis Langley commenced building the house in 1570. His son, also a Sir Francis, a noble duke as the second son of the peerage and aged twenty-six, inherited the land and continued to build and remodel the Manor. His painting of it was dated 1578. In 1594, he married Marguerite an illegitimate daughter of Louis Ferdinand, Duke of Nevers. The marriage took place at the church by the lake, St Laurence's. Ferdinand's jealous wife, Henriette of Cussac, sent Marguerite, who was a mere sixteen-year old, to marry a man thirty years her senior. Henriette most certainly had her revenge as I considered how Marguerite must have felt arriving here in the wilds of Shrugsborough with no friends or family. I felt for her, she was so young; like me.

Lord Francis had an interesting history returning home after the fifth religious war at Dormans. It was many years before the couple had produced any children but Francis seemed to have spent a lot of his time fighting Protestants abroad. Somehow he wriggled his way into the Court of Elizabeth I who bestowed him with the land of Callow. This vastly extended his original plot of land and all of this, despite his dominant Catholic heritage. They had two sons who were baptised Francis Robert and Christopher James in 1604 in St. Laurence's Church. Aged fifty-six, Francis died in the same year that his twin sons were born.

I looked around the room. It was just possible that the pictures and ornaments in here were ones that he had brought back with him. I hoped that they gave young Marguerite some solace. She must have felt very alone here and I was glad that her two sons had survived and I hoped they gave her the love she deserved.

Marguerite and Francis' eldest son Francis married a princess and she too came to live at the Manor. Marguerite survived to see her grandchildren born by Isabella, a Spanish princess. Marguerite died in 1635.

Isabella had eight surviving children, the youngest being her twin boys. Her other children were all girls and she had, it seemed, two early miscarriages. Isabella claimed to be the great granddaughter to the mad queen 'Joanna of Castile'. It was also listed as her father being Philip II of Spain marked as *illg.* I knew this meant that she was illegitimate. She was twenty-eight when she married the second Francis who was only 21. Interestingly, she had called her eldest daughter Joanna. I studied the pages hard trying to make sense of the writing. The 's' was written as 'f' so it took me some working out. It said that the twins were born, in the year of our Lord 1635. She called them Felipe and Charles. She had given birth nearly every year since her marriage. There was a note at the bottom of the page and it read:

"Felipe, the eldest son, is marked by a Cross of Soot and he will inherit the land and title of noble Duke, Lord of Callow.'

'A Cross of Soot?' What did that mean?

Felix's lineage was all laid out in this book. I found it fascinating. The only thing I knew about my family was that my mother was Welsh and my father was Scottish. I didn't even know where they had been born.

All Felix's dead relatives were either buried or remembered in St. Laurence's church and I resolved to visit in the near future.

Reading on, I travelled through time to the nineteenth century. I couldn't help notice that many sets of twin boys had been born and happily most had survived. Always at the bottom was a footnote, '*Marked by a Cross of Soot and he will inherit the land and title of Callow.*' I was getting tired, my eyes straining in the poor light. I reached the 1800s and I thought of the wine lingering in the cellar and then of the 1958 bottle sitting on the dresser waiting to be drunk.

My feelings about Felix had changed considerably. Just a day or so ago I thought he was a murderer. Now I was reading his ancestry and how he had become the Lord of this house and the land as far as I could see. I also understood why his mood was black and tortured.

Over supper I told him about Bunnie's visit and how she had asked me to help out at the shoot.

"Would you mind taking me please? I need to be there early, about 7 a.m."

Felix lifted his eyes from his plate and studied me. I tried not to give anything away, the fact that Bunnie had told me his sad tale, but I could tell by the way he looked at me that he'd guessed.

"Shall be going myself so no problem, I'll take you Rose."

I noticed Felix had bathed and dressed well on the day of the shoot. His nails were still grim as was his hair but he had made an effort. We held no conversation on the journey and it felt strange to me, to be sitting so close to the man who had caused me much confusion.

Bunnie's twins were handsome, young men. They wore rugby shirts and jeans and their faces were speckled with freckles. Emily was budding into a teenager. She wore a brace across her teeth and her brunette locks were tied into a single plait. She wore an apron tied at the front just like her mother over a pretty dress. In fact, she was the image of her mother. There was something about the boys' looks and mannerisms that reminded me of Felix.

Bunnie was already busy filling pans with vegetables and rolling out pastry. Her hands were dusty with flour so she greeted me with a generous grin and asked me to join the boys who were chopping parsnips. One of the boys fetched me a plastic apron and handed me a knife.

Trying to break the ice, I asked the twins their names.

"I'm Archie and this is Gregory. You can tell us apart because Gregory has the Cross of Soot."

His words made me stare at Gregory who had his head down, his light brown hair covering his face. Hearing Archie's words, he lifted his head and gave me a jolly and cheeky expression as he swept up his fringe. In the centre of his forehead was a birthmark in the shape of a cross. It was blueish black and clear in its form. Seeing me gasp, he laughed.

"Uncle Felix has got one too. It shows who was born first and it's definitely me."

As he spoke he turned to Archie who looked bored. He'd probably heard the retort many times. Gregory teased Archie saying that he was going to inherit Callow Crest Manor and that if Archie played his cards right he would 'do up' the milking parlour and he could live there with Gregory's favourite cows.

Bunnie bellowed over, "Boys, do get on, we've got twenty mouths to feed today."

Then she turned to me and said,

"Greg is an anomaly. Actually, he shouldn't have a Cross of Soot as Fergus, his father, is the second born. Somehow, he inherited the birthmark. There is actually only a few minutes between Felix and Fergus, perhaps the genes were so strong that in this case it passed to Gregory. We've just accepted it as a family thing."

What she may have said to me was that Felix's eldest dead twin had a birthmark too but this matter was brushed over and I suspected that this was the way in which Bunnie and her family dealt with the tragic events that had become Felix.

Her words gave me a keen desire to examine Felix's forehead but he had disappeared out of the kitchen as soon as we arrived.

The kitchen had high vaulted ceilings and a big range together with two electric cookers. In the middle of the room, where the twins and I were working, was a table about ten feet long supported by numerous legs, with a top ingrained with stains and cut marks. There was ample room for us to work and Emily joined us bringing flour and suet and herbs to make dumplings. Across one side of the room pheasants were hanging with legs of pork, salted and unappetising. There were wide uneven stone steps in one corner and I guessed they led to the ground floor of the house.

Bunnie came over and asked how we were getting along as she needed to roast the parsnips.

"Nearly done, mum," Archie said.

"Great, leeks next."

Bunnie went to a pantry and came back with an armful of leeks. Just as she did the back door opened and in came a chubby woman. She appeared slightly older than me and she wore thick-rimmed glasses and her hair was sleek and black. She had blue eyes and cream skin and her cheeks were pink. Despite being a little overweight she looked healthy, like someone who spent a lot of time outdoors. She gave me a friendly smile.

"Rose, this is Betty Dakin. She lives not far from you and she is an angel and one of my poppets."

Betty smiled again and I flashed her a smile back.

"Now, Rose, Betty. Who wants to be front of house waiting on and who wants to be in here dishing up?"

"I'd prefer to stay in here if you don't mind, Bunnie, Betty?"

"That's fine if you are OK with that Betty? Betty is used to it anyway, don't want to frighten you away just yet Rose."

I didn't want to attend to twenty men who would probably be drinking too much and leering at me.

That's what I imagined anyway, so I was happy to stay in the steaming kitchen with the twins. As the morning progressed and the kitchen began to fill with sizzling delicious aromas of tender meat and spices, Betty and I got chatting.

On the lane that led up to the battered track to the Manor and down in the hollow were semi-detached tithe cottages. Betty, her husband and two children lived in one and her mother and father-in-law lived in the other. I detected that her accent was different to the other people I had met in Churchbury and she told me that she was from Wales.

"Over the border, someone's got to keep the gene pool going as they are all related to each other around here," she laughed.

The way she spoke reminded me of my mother and I felt a pang wishing I could see her.

"Come and visit me, you can easily walk down from the Manor."

"I will, I will," I said, glad to have found a person of my own age to talk to and I instantly liked Betty.

All hell broke loose when the shooters arrived hungry and demanding. The twins and I worked tirelessly filling large bowls with endless quantities of vegetables, roasted, mashed and boiled potatoes and Bunnie sliced up meats of game and beef and pork and created glazed gravy from their juices. Betty and Bunnie brought the plates back clean and Emily showed me how to stack them in the dishwasher whilst we shared the rest of the washing up between us.

I hadn't realised that the shooters would be back for afternoon tea so no sooner had we cleared up after lunch than Bunnie set us all preparing cakes and scones and laying out trays with honey and jams and chutneys, crackers and cheese. The twins sliced the leftover meats and Bunnie brought out two dozen china teacups, saucers and plates ready to be filled with tea. Once we had finished and while we waited for the shooters' return, Bunnie poured us percolated coffee from a machine.

She produced a plate of sandwiches and we all sat at the table chatting and enjoying our break.

Fergus entered the room and I could not keep my eyes off him. His waistcoat was open and his shirt was unbuttoned at the collar so that dark wisps of hair were sticking through. His cords were brushed bottle green and he wore thick socks like Felix. He was identical to Felix only clean shaven and very handsome. Handsome in an outdoor rugged way, his skin was brown and his cheeks were veiny and rouged. I could see where his sons got their good looks from. Bunnie introduced us and he appeared to be very interested in me squeezing himself between me and Betty at the table. In his eyes I saw mischief and fun as he smiled teasingly.

"Well, you're a curiosity aren't you Miss Rose?" he said.

"Don't pick on her, Fergus," Bunnie said.

His dark eyes reminded me of Felix so much, that I found that I could not speak. He fondly put his arm around me.

"Welcome to the madhouse, Rose, lovely to meet you."

"You too," I managed to squeak not being able to lift my gaze from his face. So this is what Felix should look like, I thought.

He and Bunnie chatted about the shooting party, who was there and who was shooting well. Soon it was time to serve afternoon tea and our little gang of workers got back to our tasks and Fergus left to join his party. When Emily and I had the last load in the dishwasher and dried our hands after the unending cleaning of the fine china, (this was not allowed in the dishwasher) we all sat at the table.

Betty's husband arrived to take her home and did not stay because he had their children in the car. He was tall and freckled with bright ginger hair and a toothy friendly grin. She said 'goodbye' and invited me once more to visit. I promised I would. Bunnie said that Felix shouldn't be long and to join her in the sitting room for a drink. I followed her up the stone steps into a very spacious hallway decked with holly wreaths and a large glistening Christmas tree. We went through to an airy sitting room. Two sofas were covered in chintz and the curtains matched. A round low table sat centred in front of the marble fireplace and was covered in stacks of glossy magazines. Bunnie poured some red wine and I slumped into a chair feeling sleepy. Fergus came in and helped himself to a drink and sat next to his wife on the sofa. He folded his arms around her,

"That went terrifically well, darling. Compliments all around as usual. The food was scrumptious." He looked over at me.

"How did you find that, Rose?"

"Knackering," I laughed.

He raised his glass.

"Well, I know that Bunnie could not have done any of it without the backroom support so well done and thank you."

He got up and went to the bureau and handed me an envelope.

"Your wages for the day."

I took it and then Fergus asked if I would be able to come again next week on Boxing Day and I said I would.

We all heard Felix shouting in the hall.

"Rose, I'm leaving."

I got up and Fergus came up close.

"Felix is rough around the edges but he does have a heart of gold. It's been very difficult for Bunnie and me. Bunnie told me

107

that you found the bed. Look, once all the shoots are over, let me come to the Manor and sort things out. Don't forget, if there is anything Bunnie and I can do to help please just let us know."

"Thank you, I will." I said.

"Fergus, how old are you?"

He looked at me bluntly,

"Do you mean how old is my twin, Rose? We are forty five and Felix is three minutes older than me. Our birthday is 6th June. Anything else?"

I thought about asking him to have a chat with Felix about his hygiene but decided to leave that until next time.

We heard Felix call again and I hurried to join him in the truck to go back to the Manor. We spoke little on the way home. I was doing my level best not to keep staring at him. My mind was whirring thinking about his morbid tale and what had happened after Fergus had found him, laying next to his dead wife and his children wishing to die. Also, I could not help thinking how handsome a man he would be under his untidy beard and long hair.

"I met Betty today, she seems really nice."

He nodded and sarcastically said he thought that she probably was.

"She's invited me to visit and Bunnie and Fergus have asked me to help out again next weekend. Will you give me a lift please?"

"Becoming quite the socialite, Rose," he said again with a hint of sarcasm.

I ignored him and we arrived and I watched him as he trod across the cobbles back to the kitchen. Before I went into the Lodge, I gathered a bundle of logs from the stack in the corner. It was the angle where the Lodge garden wall married up to the east wing of the Manor. This wing was dilapidated and a tree was peeping out of the roof at the gable end. It was an area that I hadn't explored and it looked unsafe. The entrance of the wing was near to the tower and I thought of the woman in the window. I looked up in the fading light but I only saw gloomy panes of glass staring back at me.

Unmerciful rain woke me. It was heavy and lashing diagonally as I crossed in the morning to the Manor.

I had hoped to walk across the fields to visit Betty but the rain was unrelenting.

Opening the pantry door, I scrolled up and down the shelves wanting to find something simple for dinner. Because of the rain, I was changing my plans for the day. I was going to search for the key to the tower. I was convinced that the ghost of Hannah resided there and I wanted, inexplicably, to speak with her. I know this sounds peculiarly stupid now but my mind was fixed on it. I believed that making a connection with Hannah would cease the haunting of Felix.

Treading down the cellar steps I shone the torch with zeal into each black shadow searching for a hook or nail where the key might hang. As I shook the racks searching for the key the dust on the bottles made me sneeze. After about an hour I realised this was fruitless and thought that the key was more likely to be hanging somewhere more obvious. I went to the creaky door and shone the torch around the frame but nothing. As I walked up the steps to the gallery I lit up the walls as I trod but again nothing, no sign of a key. When I reached the gallery level I opened the door and slid around the tapestry. The tapestry obscured the windows behind it making the corridor dark and dour. I pulled at the edge, where I had come out, to reveal the door and drew the tapestry from that end as far as I could. I studied the door surround looking for a hook and key but I only saw peppered oak where death watch beetle had been boring. At the other end I pulled the tapestry hard. As I tugged it snagged and I bent down to see what it was catching on. Piled against the wall, beneath the leaded windows, were paintings of various sizes. I lifted the tapestry over and across so that it ran smoothly and I leaned in.

The first picture was of a landscape family scene. A diminutive woman in a dove grey dress of Elizabethan style was surrounded by her children. I counted them, eight, six girls and two boys. Standing rather proudly was a man whom I gathered to be her husband. He was dressed in black and his head was dwarfed by the white ruffle around his neck. He held a sword at his side. All the figures were bedecked in jewels. I shone the torch on the woman, she had a large sapphire ring on one finger and an abundant string of pearls linked with emeralds and rubies tucked into her cleavage. She wore gold and ruby earrings and in her raven hair a diamond tiara.

"Isabella," I whispered and stroked my fingers gently on her face.

I swept the canvas with the torchlight to her sons. Identical twins. I had to bring my eyes right up to study the boys' foreheads. Sure enough, the boy standing nearest to his mother had a birthmark, just like Gregory's, only deeper and black, in the shape of a cross. The twins looked about nine or ten but were already taller than Isabella. It was difficult to tell how tall their father was as he had been painted in the corner of the frame almost as if he was posing for a portrait of his own.

Behind this painting were more gilt and exquisitely carved frames mostly depicting women in costume from across the centuries. Some were of landscapes that I recognised as the Callow lands. I reasoned that someone had moved them here, from the east wing, to save them and stored them hanging the tapestry to protect them. That person was clever and thoughtful and I sat on the hard floor for hours marvelling at the skill of the artists.

One study showed a girl and in the bottom corner her named was inscribed, 'Marguerite *1594.*' She was youthful and yet her eyes looked sad. Was this Marguerite I wondered, the sixteen-year old bride of Francis? She wore a gown of velvet in moonlight blue and at the seams of a linen cap were revealed brown curls. Her cheeks were peachy and her skin translucent. The artist had highlighted her eyelashes so that they accentuated her eyes spotted with hazel.

I was so distracted by the pictures that I hadn't realised the time was sailing by. I looked down the gallery to the wide hall where the staircase ended and then I looked towards the bedroom door. The rain was dreary and even with the new light threading through, the view was depressingly lethargic. Momentarily, I was caught in a mood of sorrow. I felt sorrow for all those women who had lived here, their lives disregarded and their presence and impact on this gloomy house hidden behind a tapestry. My eyes welled and I grew morose and I began to cry. My shoulders heaved as I wept. I felt alone and discarded like the people and belongings in this house.

I had no-one. My father had punished me for something that was not my fault and I looked at Marguerite punished for being born out of wedlock. The rain was exuberant and fell sharp like splinters against the panes bringing a chill wind with it. I gave up looking for the key and returned to the kitchen. The weather matched my mood and lasted for the whole week.

I managed to cook the turkey and all the trimmings but the meaning of Christmas Day was lost on me. Felix opened some wine and offered me a glass but I sat motionless staring into the distance. He picked up on my emotion and he seemed to be making some effort to engage me. I hardly noticed for my mind was in turmoil about other things. Why, I was thinking, should I remain here? I could go back to Birmingham and find myself a job as a secretary and maybe a flat to live in. I could support myself and leave this place that had no welcome for me. I left Felix and the Manor and returned to the Lodge taking a turkey sandwich with me. He watched me leave and I could see a glimmer of disappointment cast over his face. In the evening, sitting by the fire I noticed his present under the tree.

I had forgotten it.

The next day Felix drove me over to 'Langley Hall'. Unlike last time I didn't join in the cheery banter. I was sulking and I was jealous of all the things that Bunnie and Fergus had: Their children, their house and modern accessories but mostly their obvious love for one another. I don't think that I had ever felt so depressed, not even after Patrick's death. For though his loss was real, I was feeling a loss for things beyond my reach.

At break, Betty came to sit next to me and said that I looked as if I needed cheering up.

"Oh, I'm just a bit fed up that's all. This rain is bloody persistent and I can't get out or do anything."

"I know, I was hoping you would call this week but I suppose the rain stopped you".

"Betty, I'm thinking of leaving, going back to Birmingham."

"Why, have you got family there, Rose?"

"Not as much," I replied telling a white lie. "But I'm not sure I can live in the Manor anymore.

"Felix is an abrasive character and he's not much company."

I wanted to tell Betty that Felix kept a bed of his dead wife's blood but it sounded weird.

"What you need Rose is a plan."

I gave Betty a half smile and carried on chewing at my lunch.

Through the season, at the end of each shooting day Fergus gave me an envelope. I piled them up having no idea how much was in them, but I hoped it would be enough for my fare back to the Midlands. Even perhaps to put down a deposit on a rental flat. Time rolled on until the grass was green and fresh and I could see daffodil heads ready and waiting for the joy of March.

Snow had come sprinkling the valleys like icing sugar in a snow globe but this year the weather was not too harsh and the snow had melted away as quickly as it had come.

Felix would be busy with lambing, meaning his return times would be erratic. I washed some tea towels and hung them in the kitchen garden. It was a long rectangle with a door to the ruined and burnt out milking parlour and another one leading off to the walled garden. Betty said that I needed a plan. Perhaps I could rejig this garden, or, at least bring it back to what it once was. The task was monumental and I couldn't do it by myself. Chickens could live in the milking parlour if it was made safe. The roof was missing. Shards of burnt wood tentatively hung under it. I looked around me and then flushed the thoughts away as I was more set on returning to an office job than staying in this desolate place.

Betty invited me to her cottage and as I strolled down the lane I looked around at the distensible landscape. Clouds rested merrily in a blue blanket and the sun courageously sneaked a tittering peek above them. There was no doubting that I was in a serene and beautiful location except I was still in no mood to appreciate the rarity of Shrugsboroughshire.

As I arrived Betty was waiting in the doorway.

"I could see you for miles in that red jumper, you look nice in it. Come in, come in."

The little cottage was homely and Betty pointed to photographs of her children arranged on the stair wall up to the landing, *"Rogues Gallery,"* she laughed as she led me through to her kitchen.

A table topped in red Formica with white painted legs was propped against a wall and dark wood fronted her modern cupboards. She boiled the kettle and made us tea inviting me to sit.

"Drink your tea while I put out the lunch."

"Oh, I'll help," I said politely.

"No, Rose, it's all right, honestly it won't take a minute."

Soon Betty had laid the little table with a home-made quiche, a salad bowl and potato salad.

"Help yourself to everything, Rose. We don't stand on any ceremony here."

I filled my plate chomping on the quiche, which was delicious and watched silently as Betty ate. She was not particularly overweight but she was chubby. Her fingers were delicate and she ate her food daintily not speaking until she had finished her plate.

"More tea and chocolate cake. I made it this morning so it will be good to grab a slice before Tom and the kids come home."

Her cake was rich and moist and I asked her for the recipe.

"I think the secret Rose, is to use the eggs as fresh as you can."

"Do you have chickens?" I asked.

"Yes and a cat and a dog and a rabbit. It's like a bloody menagerie here and guess who ends up looking after them all? You got it, me!"

I didn't think the time was right for me to question Betty too much about Felix and Hannah but to my surprise she voluntarily began to tell me.

"My husband 'Young Tom' is Hannah's cousin. We are Dakins."

As Betty spoke her gentle voice made me feel restful. Her accent sang and she reminded of my mother.

"Well, there's a big gap between my Tom and Hannah 'cos Tom's parents never thought they could have children and to their surprise up he pops when Gwyneth is forty. It was a heck of a shock. Tom is their only child. Hannah lived right here."

"Here?" I exclaimed as I looked around the kitchen trying to envisage Hannah's presence.

She continued.

"Hannah's dad is my Tom's uncle. Hannah grew up in this cottage and Tom in the cottage next door. There was some doubt whether Hannah and Felix would make a family but at last she fell pregnant but not before she was about thirty. Then you must know what happened to her and her babies, Rose?"

"I do, Bunnie told me. Betty, what happened to them all after Fergus found them?"

"Fergus got through the snow somehow and picked them all up and put them in the tractor trailer.

"Making his way through the heavy drifts he took them down to the undertakers at Churchbury. Mr Blakeway laid them out on cold, flat stones."

Just like Hannah had laid on that sacrificial stone on top of the Callow hill, I thought.

"Mr Blakeway telephoned Dr Comickery to come and write up the death certificates. Obviously Hannah and the twins were dead. But to his horror, he found that Felix was still alive. His bodily functions had slowed in the cold so that he seemed dead but he wasn't.

"Dr Comickery called for an ambulance and he was taken to Shrugsborough Hospital where they revived him. Like Lazarus, it was a miracle, Rose."

"What happened next?"

"Felix was kept in the hospital for a couple of months until he was deemed well enough to come home. I think, to be honest with you, it was more mental health issues. Not surprising really when you think what he went through. You know, Hannah and his little mites."

Betty let out a long tssssk.

"Did you meet Hannah?"

"No, she'd died a few years before I met my Tom at a Farmers' Ball. Her parents, Susan and Frank both died of broken hearts so they say. In a way it turned out well for me and my Tom as we have this house and his mum and dad are nice, they don't interfere too much and they're great with the kids. Fancy coffee this time? Sorry, it's not as posh as Bunnie's, ours is out of a jar."

We chatted on for a while. Soon Betty had to leave to collect the children from the school bus, the same one that I had journeyed on to come back to Callow Crest Manor.

Betty kissed me on the cheek.

"Don't be so down, Rose. Come back next week and we'll take a walk. Weather's picking up." She pointed at the sky.

"I'd like to visit the church, you know the one that you can see from the Manor, by the lake. Is it far to walk?"

"No, I know a short cut. Bring a picnic and we'll make a day of it. I'll meet you at the end of your track after the kids have caught the bus in the morning. Say, nine o'clock?"

"Lovely," I said and I kissed and hugged my new found friend.

Feeling uplifted, I wended my way back up the lane to the track leading to the Manor. I reflected on the conversation with Betty and what had happened to Felix and his family. My mind was swelling with the idea of leaving the Manor and that meant leaving Felix too.

When I reached the courtyard, I was startled to find my mother sitting on a plant pot in the sunlight.

CHAPTER 8

Mum stood up to greet me. She looked awkward but I ran to her and wrapped my arms about her.

"Mum, mum! What are you doing here?"

She seemed overwhelmed by my emotion and once she had managed to release me from my lock, she kissed me on the cheek. I knew from her expression and the way she looked down to the ground, that something was wrong.

"Mum, what is it? Is it dad?"

We sat at the scratched pine table in the Lodge and mum explained why she was here. I was astounded to see her and her face lifted my heart and her voice settled me, as Betty's had done earlier that day.

Dad had a heart attack. He was only fifty eight. I reached out for mum's hand.

"Oh mum, I'm so sorry."

She took a tissue from her bag and blew her nose. She was crying and the tears stained her make-up, her cheeks streaking white lines through her rouge powder.

"It's worse than anything in the world, Rose."

I patted her hand. "Tell me, mum."

"He was with Pat when it happened. He was having sex with her," she blurted.

Mum looked directly into my face waiting for my reaction. I began to giggle. It was wholly inappropriate but my giggles became guffaws and mum could not help but laugh inexplicably with me.

"Rose, what's so funny? I've just told you something that we should be ashamed of. Why are you laughing?"

"Mum, I'm sorry but I was just thinking about Pat with her shiny blue eye shadow and what she must have looked like when dad expired on top of her. Good Lord, what expression she must have had on her face!"

"Horrified, I would have thought," mum replied. "Her makeup would have ran!"

Moving the conversation back to a more serious note mum told me the funeral was next week.

She added,

"I managed to find you from the Post Office Box number. When I arrived in Churchbury the post mistress knew all about you and she ordered me a taxi. I was waiting for nearly three hours outside Rose and I had to drag my bag up that track, nearly killed me it did!"

"Sorry mum, I was visiting a friend."

"Well, I thought you could come back with me tomorrow, help me with the flowers and that."

I looked at my mother. She was clinging to her dignity and I knew her well enough to know that dad's funeral would be planned perfectly to give him a good 'send off'. Of course, Father O' Dowd would conduct the service.

"People only need to know he had a heart attack, Rose. No one needs to know where it happened."

Putting her hand on my arm, she said,

"You will come won't you, Rose? I'm sorry about that other stuff, you know, between your father and you. He was your father after all."

Her Welsh accent seemed more pronounced than usual and I gazed back at her. She was still a young woman but dad had made her grow old before her time. She was worn out from looking after his needs, both physically and mentally.

"Of course I will, mum. We'll leave tomorrow. You can have my bed and I'll sleep on the sofa."

I left a note for Felix saying that I would be back in a week, '*due to my father's funeral*' and came back to the Lodge to find mum in the kitchen making cocoa.

We lit the fire and sat together in the sitting room.

"It's nice here, Rose. You've landed on your feet. Tell me all about your work. Does your employer live in the big house then?"

Telling mum about Felix and what I had found out about his family fascinated her and she let me drone on unwinding my story. It was a good feeling to share my emotions and I felt my muscles relax. When I had ended my news she made no judgements. She changed the subject.

"I was born not far from here. That valley to the west towards Wales, there's a tiny hamlet, well not even that really, called Llwety Pool. My dad had the farm. My brother looks after it all now. I haven't been back since I married your dad. And, before you ask me, no, I'll not go back to Llwety Pool. The insurance will pay off the mortgage and I'll carry on working at the school so I can cope with the bills. I've still got some friends, well you know plenty that didn't sleep with your dad anyway."

We sniggered at that.

"Rose, if you want to come back and live at home any time you know you are welcome."

"I know mum, thanks."

Mum had arranged for the taxi to pick us up at 9 a.m. so that we could catch the 10 a.m. bus to Birmingham. Churchbury is a small town compared to Birmingham. It's like a village,

119

only bigger. People were dashing about, on their daily business and I knew it would take me some adjustment to mingle in the madding crowds of a big city. *God, what would I feel like in Birmingham?*

When the taxi parked outside mum's house I noticed that dad's car was still in the drive. We lived in a pleasant area and the road was uniformly lined with bay-windowed semi-detached houses. Neat gardens and concrete driveways fronted the row of precisely spaced-out lime trees. Net curtains filled the bay windows and ours was identical to everyone else's.

When we got inside mum told me to put my case in my room. Memories flooded back. There was a Marc Bolan poster pinned on the wall. I had made a red felt heart and written in black felt tip pen, *'I love you and I'm going to marry you when I grow up'* and I had covered his heart with mine.

My room was at the back of the house and I looked down into our garden. It was fenced with wooden panels and I recalled dad treating them with varnish each spring. He grew clematis and roses up them and his pride and joy were his colourful dahlias. Now the garden looked bare and plain. The stepping stones to his shed were covered in moss. The garden was overlooked on all sides and I felt hemmed in. I longed for another view. I heard mum calling me down for tea.

As funerals go, I think you could say that dad's went well. Under the circumstances, mum decided not to hold a Wake. Father O' Dowd shook my hand on the way out of the church.

"'Tis nice to see yer, Rose." His handshake was like touching a jelly fish and I tried to keep my face expressionless for I despised this man.

My only emotion was one of guilt as I felt no loss for my father.

I didn't tell mum but I saw Pat enter the church and sit at the back. She was dressed in black from top to toe. Her face was covered in a lace veil. I knew it was her. She gave the game away by her long pink painted nails and stained nicotine fingers.

I felt bitterness towards her because of how she had made my mum feel and I hoped that Trevor gave her a terrible time. She deserved it, I thought maliciously.

Linda came and it was nice to see her. She looked well and excitedly showed me a large diamond engagement ring. She couldn't stay long needing to get back to work and I watched her drive away astounded that my friend could drive, clutching her address and telephone number as I waved her goodbye.

Afterwards at home, mum and I sat in the kitchen. We had angel cake and mum poured out some sherry.

"So what are you going to do, Rose?"

"Tomorrow mum, you and I are going shopping in the Bull Ring to cheer you up and I am going to buy you an iced bun and a cup of tea!"

"That's lovely, darling."

It was clear to me, at the end of my day in Birmingham centre, that I yearned to be back in the countryside. I would go back to the Manor and review my situation from there.

Mum cuddled me goodbye in the way that only mums do and promised she would write. I was sad to leave her but I thought that dad's death would be the best thing for her.

Before I left she handed me a large brown envelope.

"It came here for you Rose, don't open it now. I have a suspicion that it's from Wayne."

I looked down at the envelope and there was the logo of a solicitor's firm across the back. I rammed it into my suitcase and kissed mum goodbye.

To my surprise, when I arrived back at Churchbury, Felix was waiting for me. At first I didn't realise that it was him. I thought it was Fergus by some coincidence standing at the terminus.

"Hello Rose," he said picking up my suitcase.

I was speechless. I kept staring at his forehead to make sure it was Felix looking for his Cross of Soot. He must have noticed as he lifted his cap and there it was marking him out from his younger brother. I was amazed that he seemed to know what I was looking for. I found myself quiet.

He cleared his throat.

"Fergus came over to the Manor and we had a long discussion. I've had a bath, Rose. What do you think? Smelling of roses now am I? A rose for a Rose, eh?"

Words escaped me. He turned to me as we drove up and over the hills waiting for me to say something.

"Nice, Felix. You look nice." These words were all I could think of to say but he seemed happy enough with them.

I went into the Lodge and sat for a while. There was a vacant space in my head and I knew it needed to be filled but I could not for the life of me work out with what. I felt confused.

Afterwards, whilst I was at the Manor, I prepared supper. Felix brought in two crystal goblets from the Georgian room and poured out some wine. It was the bottle I had picked from the cellar.

"A welcome home treat, Rose. Here you go."

As we ate together Felix topped up my glass.

"Good choice Rose, I'll have to send you off to the cellar again."

A shiver went down my back, thinking about the cellar and where it led to.

The wine made me brave.

"Felix, I've been thinking."

"Oh no, when a woman thinks it usually means she is going to speak and when she does it's because she wants something," he joked.

I grinned happy to hear Felix cracking a joke.

"I've been thinking that I need a project. Something to stimulate me. Cleaning this house is fine but I need more Felix.

122

How about the kitchen garden? I'd like to have some chickens. Betty's cakes are delicious because her eggs are really fresh when she bakes them. And I'd like to repair the greenhouse in the walled garden to grow vegetables and flowers. I can't do all that on my own, I need help."

He stopped eating for a moment letting my words sink in.

"Old Tom," he exclaimed. I'll ask Old Tom. I think he's pretty much retired now helping Young Tom out on the farm now and then. He could probably do with the extra money."

"Betty's father-in-law?"

"Yes, I'll call on him tomorrow."

I wondered if Betty knew why I hadn't met her for our picnic. I hoped Felix had got a message to her.

"By the way Rose, sorry to hear about your father." His voice was automatic, it was as if he didn't mean it and he was just saying it for the sake of it.

"It's OK, thanks Felix."

We drank the bottle of wine between us and then Felix insisted on opening the port. The wine tasted fine but the port tasted like vinegar so we abandoned it.

Felix told me he was going to look at some puppies in the morning and he asked me to go with him to help him choose a dog and a bitch for the farm. I agreed to go, wondering about his attentiveness towards me. Perhaps, after all, he had some sympathy and understanding for my loss.

Back at the Lodge, my mind was keenly drawing-in the vision of Felix. The new Felix. He was still wearing his filthy cap and his hair stunk flowing out beneath it. Somehow I was too emotional to think about such things and I fell into a deep sleep.

I awoke to the sound of Felix beeping the truck's horn. I had overslept. It must have been the wine. Hurriedly, I got dressed, ran some toothpaste around my teeth with my finger and pulled my hair into a pony tail.

As the truck bumped its way along the track Tarbo slouched in the trailer. On the way Felix enlightened me about why he was buying some new dogs. Basically, Tarbo would keep the young pups in order and they would learn a lot from her about bringing in the sheep. Old Tarbo, wise and fond of her keeper. I wondered how she would take to new company. I thought she still missed Buster. She seemed a lot quieter in his absence.

The pick-up puffed along and up over a hill to the east. We pulled up at a farm I didn't recognise to the sound of dogs barking in the yard. A bluish-veined and plum-faced farmer came out to open the gate for us and tipped his cap to Felix. He took us to a barn. The straw smelt damp. A sheepdog with one blue eye and one brown eye was being suckled by six puppies all wagging their tails and she looked grateful when the farmer prized them off to hand to me and Felix. There were two that had black patches over opposing eyes, a dog and a bitch and I fell in love with them. They were so cute. I was thinking that with the right upbringing they would be terrific dogs, not ferocious like Buster. Felix spotted me patting and cooing over them.

"Let's have a look at these two then, Rose."

We travelled back with them sitting on my knee.

The next week I arranged to meet Betty sending a message to her via Felix who had gone to speak to Old Tom about my project. I was pleased because Old Tom had agreed to come twice a week and Young Tom would come and help, once the lambing was over, with the heavier lifting and digging.

This time, when I ambled down the track, my head was full of my project and I felt excited.

I had completely rejected the thought of returning to Birmingham. Betty was waiting for me under the mythical watching dogs and she waved. I waved back with a new spring in my step.

Her rosy cheeks gleamed from the exertion of walking up the hill but she told me the exercise would do her good and she'd decided to meet me so that we could walk back to her house together.

Wandering along the lane we gossiped and Betty told me how she had more or less fallen in love with her Tom at first sight. She talked about her children, Jacob and Molly, who each had red hair like their father.

"You must meet them, come for tea next week."

I felt as if Betty was doing all the hard work to keep our friendship going so I asked her if she and her family would like to come to tea with me.

"At the Manor?" Betty's voice was filled with caution.

"No, at the Lodge, where I live."

She thanked me but seemed reluctant to visit me there and instead insisted that it would be much easier on her part, if I didn't mind, if I came to her. Jacob and Molly, she explained, are fussy eaters. She made the excuse so as not to put me to any trouble I thought.

I heard a hint in her voice that neither she nor her family wished to come to the Manor or indeed the Lodge as guests but I didn't feel it appropriate to push and ask her why.

"Come on Tuesday and we can have a good old natter. The kids are at school so we won't be disturbed."

Tuesday came and Betty talked about her wedding and the children's christening at the church by the lake where we were heading. The church heaved under local aching stone, its Norman tower turreted and ominous. We walked for a while where the graveyard edged the lake and we stood watching the swans and ducks bibble and bobble. The wind blew chilly and Betty took me to the other side of the church which was sheltered. A bench seat had been placed against the wall of the church and the sun drenched our bones as we sat; just looking at the stillness of our view.

We both heard the sound of a car on gravel and looked over at the latch gate. A tall man was entering, dressed in a dark suit and I noticed that he had a dog collar around his neck.

"I think it's the new vicar," whispered Betty.

As he came closer we gave each other a knowing look. He was the most handsome man I had ever seen. He was smiling as he grew near. He had a broad smile that emphasised his good looks. About six feet tall, he had lush brown hair flecked with blond and when he stood next to us we saw he had amber eyes that seemed to twinkle.

"Hello ladies, taking in the spring sun?"

Betty almost curtsied. In fact, if I hadn't been holding her arm I think she would have bent down all the way.

She was staring, her mouth open. I stood next to her also staring in wonder at this attractive man before us. After Barry had raped me and the experience I went through because of him, I never thought I would want to be with a man, yet I could not help the rumble in my heart and the popping of hormones coursing in my blood as I stared at him in a quiet shade of lust.

He looked back at us with all modesty. He behaved like a man who was well used to receiving admiring glances.

Pulling myself together I gave him a flirty smile.

"Yes, it's a lovely day for it," I said. "I'm Rose Howard and I live at the Manor, well not actually the Manor but in the Lodge, and this is Betty Dakin."

"Rose and Betty, how nice to meet you both." He held out his hand for us both to shake.

"I'm Gabriel." He looked at me specifically.

"It gets worse. It's not just that I am named after an archangel but that my last name is 'Goode'."

When Betty took his hand in hers she had some difficulty letting him go. He extracted himself and asked if we had been inside. Betty shook her head still staring up into his eyes.

126

"Pleased to meet you Gabriel," I responded. Like Betty I allowed his hand to stay in mine for a little longer than necessary.

"Well, let's go in."

I hesitated and in that brief moment he was able to see the doubt in my eyes.

"You don't have to, it's just that I'm new and I wondered whether you ladies could fill me in on some history?"

Betty talked keenly making her way around the path to the vestibule.

"Absolutely, come on then Rose," she said.

"I was raised a Catholic. I'm not sure I should go in. Is that allowed?"

Gabriel swooped his honey eyes around my form. He had a passive gentle voice.

"This ancient church was Catholic once you know, Rose. All are welcome in God's house."

I followed him as Betty opened the wooden door and he stood back to let us enter first.

Betty was doing her best to impress our new vicar with her knowledge and I found myself absorbed in the information she was giving as she bounced along pointing at this and that. On the walls were rusty nails where the Stations of the Cross must once have hung. I remembered the church of my childhood and the only station I could recall was Veronica as she wiped Jesus' tears.

The church was large and lofty and the ceiling was decorated with five-pointed stars on a cobalt-coloured background. Huge jardinières, on marble blocks, filled with bright and perfumed flowers, stood at the end of the altar table. The church seemed homely and lived in. A single painting of Jesus hung on one wall. His immortal eyes were spurred with pain and abandonment from his crown of thorns. Inscribed plaques recorded years of Felix's family whom were buried either in the church or in the graveyard.

Gabriel followed Betty around like an obedient dog and I broke off squinting my eyes in the kaleidoscopic light thrown in from the stained glass windows. In themselves, the windows were works of art. Angels, shepherds and Mary holding the baby Jesus and Jesus holding a lamb were stained in magenta, ochre yellow, brown and reds. Their saintly colours streamed in making pools of tempered green.

I came across a marble and elegant plaque in memory of Lord Callow and his sons. The black writing read:

Viscount Horace Beverley Langley

Captain, 68th Regiment.

Killed by a Russian sniper at the Battle of Sevastopol 1855.

Herbert Mortimer Langley

Lieutenant, 68th Regiment

Wounded in the Great Hurricane of Balaclava November 1854.

Died 15th October 1904 at Callow Crest Manor

His body lies near to this place. In his lifetime he bore a Cross of Soot.

At my eyeline there was a similar but less ostentatious memorial plaque:

Near to this place lies the mortal remains of

Colonel Robert Langley, Lord of Callow

Mercer's 'G' Troop

Wounded at the Battle of Waterloo 1815

Resigned his Commission 1819

Died at Callow Crest Manor 1864 aged 80 years, father to Horace and Herbert.

There was no mention of a Lady Callow. I thought this was perhaps because she had no army record. I was so transfixed reading the scrolls that I didn't hear Gabriel come up behind me and tap me on the shoulder.

"Everywhere you look in this church reflects the history and the lives of the people from Callow Crest Manor. Come over here Rose, Betty wants to show you something in the north transept"

I dutifully followed. On a marble tomb lay carved, presumably in near likeness to their living selves, two people on the top. The man was dressed with a ruffle around his neck. He was resting his feet on a dog and in his clasped hands he held a crucifix. There were remnants of olive paint in the folds of his wife's skirt. The marble pillars were candy floss pink and drizzled through with lilac swirls. Protecting the tomb was a blackened railing deterring parishioners from leaning over to touch their hallowed images. Above the canopy that covered them, as if they were sleeping in a four-poster bed, were some words in Latin. Gabriel obliged us by translating.

Here lies the mortal remains of his Grace, Duke Francis Langley, Lord of Callow. In the name of our most reverend God and on behalf of his most Glorious Majesty Charles I, supreme head of the Church of England, who here declares in his reign his utmost indebtedness for his strident candour and fortitude in preventing those who willingly usurp the blessing of his Majesty. Lord of the Callow and his wife, the Princess Isabella.

"That may be interpreted as a rough translation," Gabriel said looking at Betty and I who were both staring at him adoringly.

Here was Isabella's last resting place. At the end of the tomb it showed the dates they had died. Isabella outlived her husband by twenty years. Seeing her tomb, I turned to Betty.

"The Cross of Soot. Betty, I have seen a picture of Isabella and read the family bible and it mentions the Cross of Soot. Do you know about it?"

She motioned us to sit down on one of polished pews.

"Lord Francis Langley," she moved her head towards the grand edifice, "the second one of the Manor, well, let me tell you, he and Isabella had six daughters, and as legend goes, she at last gave birth to twin boys. They needed a male heir you see what with having all those girls. His Lordship, afraid that he would not be able to tell which son was which, ordered the nursemaid to bring a bucket of soot so that he could mark a cross on the eldest son's forehead. Of course, it was very important in those days to know which son should inherit and as the twins were identical he was worried he would not know which son was which.

"The nursemaid, oh what was her name, Maud, that's it, Maud Thompson, in her hurry, went to the kitchen fire and filled a bucket with soot and returned to his Lordship with a piece of kindling. Not realising that the soot was still boiling hot from the fire he dipped the twig in the soot and marked his first-born son with a cross.

The baby yelped as the soot scalded and scarred his delicate and new born skin. Realising the soot was still hot he turned and whipped the nursemaid and beat her until she was black and blue and threw her out of the Manor. Poor girl, I expect she was a bit dim. Her descendants still live on the Callow estate and I'm afraid they're still a bit, well you know, not quite all there some of them.

Outside, Maud spat on the ground and she cursed that the Cross of Soot would mark the eldest son of any twin in future generations. That's how come Felix has it and young Gregory. Oldest boys of twins you see."

I thought about Hannah and whether her oldest child bore the Cross of Soot.

Gabriel listened intently. He didn't seem convinced about Betty's story but I believed her. After all she and I had seen the Cross of Soot on Gregory. Felix had shown me his own to convince me that it was him on the day he met me in

Churchbury. I trusted that Gabriel had no belief in legends and rather he thought of the Cross of Soot as a natural birthmark. He was kind enough not to say anything to the detriment of Betty's tale. And yet, I detected he was stirred by the story and his pretence of scepticism was a façade. *There's more to him, I thought.*

"Thank you, Betty and Rose. How you have enlightened me today. I must dash as I have a meeting with the bishop about something rather special." He did not divulge what the 'something special' was about and got up to leave.

"I'd like to visit you both sometime if I may. I would really like to get to know my parishioners."

He looked at me with his succulent eyes sucking my soul into them as if I was drowning in a peach.

"Rose, you must feel welcome here, any time. If you ever want to convert will you let me know?

"I'd be happy to teach you the ways of the Church of England."

As I smiled at him my mind was savouring the idea that this would be a fantastic excuse to spend some personal time with the new vicar but it wasn't the right reason for conversion, so I politely thanked him and said that I may think about it. When we were sure he had gone Betty grabbed my arm.

"He's bloody gorgeous! Oh and those eyes, Rose. Did you see his eyes?"

I laughed and pulled Betty's arm into the crook of mine and we went outside to the spring glow and I agreed that he was the most pleasant thing I had set my eyes on for a long while.

We ate our packed lunch on the little bench seat and we jabbered on together throwing out ideas of what his special meeting could be about. We gossiped about his pure skin and what a well put together and handsome figure he was.

On the way home Betty almost forgot to tell me, having been distracted by the vicar, and being very animated, that Tom

131

had bought and fitted a new washing machine. A 'front loader'. She declared it was one of the happiest days of her life when Tom and Old Tom had plumbed it in.

"Rose, all you have to do is put the washing in, shut the door, put the powder in the dispenser and switch it on. Walk home with me and I'll show you, you'll love it. While we've been out today I left it to run all by its self. Can you believe it?"

I was very admiring of Betty's new appliance. It certainly was a timesaver. I had been hand washing my clothes and towels letting them dry on a rack above the range in the Manor kitchen. Felix hardly ever gave me any of his clothes to wash and I only washed my bedding if the weather was in the right mood to dry it. However, if I had a washing machine I could face up to the one thing I had been considering for some while. The bed of blood.

Old Tom came to the Manor and we set about the kitchen garden. It was hard going but very satisfying as the changes were fairly instant. I had discussed the purchase of a washing machine with Felix suggesting that Old Tom would plumb it in the boot room. I was currently in Felix's favour as Old Tom and I had made the garden safe for the puppies to play in. He was fearful that they would escape and worry the sheep so he had kept them locked up in the boot room and tied them in the back of his truck with Tarbo during the day. Now they had a chance to play and frolic and run freely.

Betty arranged to drive me to Shrugsborough to purchase the washing machine. I met her at the end of the drive as the track was too rutted for a normal car to drive down. On the way I asked her if she knew a shop where I could buy a new bed and sheets.

Shrugsborough is a delightful town. The River Severn runs through it and the border snakes through the town on three sides. There were lots of individual shops in a neat market square and cafés with seats outside where people were drinking coffee; people watching. Betty gave me a tour and we shopped, spraying on perfumes and trying on clothes. She took me to a larger store that sold 'white goods' and picked out the same model of washing machine as her own. I ordered it arranging the cost on Felix's account. Then we went to another floor, where beds were impeccably made up with luxurious throws and quilts and I ordered a double bed with a velour cream headboard. Betty helped me choose a duvet set, thinking it was for me she insisted on a flowery peach cover. I hadn't the nerve to explain that it was a replacement for the bed of blood.

In one of the cafés, I ordered my favourite tea and an iced bun and we sat outside. I thought of mum and suddenly remembered the brown envelope she had given me which I had not yet opened. I would try to remember to do it sometime soon.

I'd had fun and bought some new jeans. My old ones were threadbare and because they were my only ones they didn't get washed very often. I could not remember the last time that I had worn a skirt or a dress. Probably at the office, I thought, and quickly stopped thinking about those times as I did not want to feel sad.

Betty dropped me at the end of the lane and I carried my bags home swinging them at my sides. Betty would arrange with the two Toms to collect and plumb the washing machine in next week and she said that the men would collect the bed for me too.

CHAPTER 9

That evening a storm raged. It was violent and restless. The minimal electric in the house was knocked out and Felix and I scrabbled about for candles. I went to the library, as I had seen some fat round ones in an old iron stand and took two of them into the kitchen. We had a cold supper of ham, bread and cheese. I hadn't lit the range so Felix boiled water on the fire, fixing iron rods from the old bread oven into the bricks, so that we could have a hot drink.

I told him that the washing machine was coming next week and offered to start on his clothes. He did not answer that question but said,

"The puppies need names. Would you like to choose something for them?"

There was no internet in those days. When I had learnt to type it was on a clanging school typewriter and you had to press down extra hard on the ampersand key. At the office I had progressed to an electric model. Home computers were still a thing of the future. But, I had books, lots of them in the library and I told Felix that I would choose names from one of the books in there.

Crashing thunder and flashing lightning kept me awake. The Manor was in darkness. Felix had checked on the dogs. The puppies, who had been squealing afraid of the noise, snuggled up to Tarbo, as he patted them and reassured them. He went up to bed as I left.

From my bedroom I could see a light flicker in the tower window. I screwed up my eyes to peer across the courtyard and there she was. The woman in the white flimsy nightgown scratching at the glass, her gaunt body pressed hard against it. I could hear her above the whipping weather,

'Where are my boys? Where are my boys?'

I snapped the curtains shut and put my pillow over my head and tried to sleep. My dreams were muddled and festooned in confusion with images of the woman in the window and Eliza calling to me.

The earth was still bruised from the night's storm as I performed my usual morning routine and then went across to the Manor. I made myself a mug of tea and headed to the library. I felt tired, disturbed by dreams and the night's weather.

Sitting at one of the tables I began to open the dusty books. Some made no sense to me at all as they were filled with geographical statistics and maps of France. Belonging to Lord Francis, the husband of Marguerite, his spidery signature was scrawled in the front of each book. The pages were in velum and the covers in calf leather. Francis had been vain enough to commission a history of his battles and I was curious about how he had raised his fortune and fallen into favour with Queen Elizabeth I. He had been her enemy to start with and much against her as he stood firm in his Catholic beliefs. He had married Catholic Marguerite and his son to a Catholic Spanish princess and I wondered how and where they met or whether their marriage had been arranged. They were secrets from the past that I would never know.

I flitted through the pages bored with his achievements until at last I figured it all out. Lord Francis Robert Langley was a spy! Sadly, I realised reading on, that he had caused the death of many people, including women and children. I looked around the room. Was all this worth it? And, reading on I knew that his son was a devious man too. I now knew why the second Francis stood aloof in the painting of his wife Isabella and their children. He was displaying to the world that the jewels and lands he had acquired were from his own inherent and despicable scheming. I tried to imagine the wedding couple at the Church of St. Laurence, adorned with the Stations of the Cross and the smell of incense as he and Isabella attended Mass. Perhaps they sailed across the lake to get there. Did he pray for forgiveness, I thought? I wondered how he felt when his nursemaid had cursed his family with the Cross of Soot. So many questions left unanswered. I wished I could go back in time, I wished the walls of the Manor could speak.

Being so absorbed, I had to force myself to put the book to one side and began to search for puppy names. After a while I found a book of mythology and chancing my luck thumbed through. I found stories of Phoebe and Thor. I chose those names and I hoped Felix would like them.

There was much to do and Old Tom came up to the Manor each week. One day, as we worked, the rain fell and I invited him into the Manor for tea.

"I'll sit in the old parlour if you don't mind, Rose."

"No, don't be ridiculous, come to the Lodge, come on, I have Victoria sandwich cake and you'll catch your death out here."

He seemed not to mind me asking him to the Lodge, rather than the Manor and as I sliced cake and poured tea whilst the rain pattered the rooftop I quizzed Old Tom. He always wore the same clothes. Rough greeny-black trousers which he tucked into his wellingtons clamped in by woollen beige socks, an old sand coloured shirt and braces. I often saw him lift his cap to scratch his head and he was bald but somehow I remembered him as having lush salt and pepper hair.

"Tom, why don't you want to go into the Manor? Is it because of the ghost of your niece Hannah?"

Tom considered me and my question for a while sipping his tea, nibbling on his cake.

"That's not the ghost of Hannah Dakin." Frustratingly, that was all he said. The rain stopped and he got up to go outside. He had one arm leaning on the door as he pulled on his boots. Then he turned towards the window in the tower.

"Seen her me self, Rose. Fair put the wind in me sails she did. She was calling and calling for her boys. Wouldn't shut up. There is nothing more frightening than to hear the call of the dead. I shot off down the track and I ain't been inside that Manor since."

I didn't know what to say. I desperately wanted to ask Old Tom who she was but he went quiet. Apart from thanking me for the tea, we rarely spoke as we continued digging and weeding and mending in the garden.

When Felix came back I suggested the puppy names to him. He liked them and I felt pleased with my choices. I began to chat idly about the book I had found about the spy in his family.

"We have him to thank for this," he said as he pulled up his cap to show me his Cross of Soot.

"Actually, Gregory showed me his too. Bunnie said that his is an anomaly. It is a bit weird that Cross of Soot, don't you think Felix? The new vicar said he thought it was more likely a birthmark but I prefer the Lord Francis and nursemaid story."

"Have you met the new vicar, Rose? Where did you see him?"

"In the church. I walked with Betty the other day and he turned up while we were there. He is very nice, very nice indeed."

"I expect he'll be turning up here soon, they usually do."

137

"I'm sure he will. Your family is so closely associated with St. Laurence's; in lots of ways.

"It's a pretty church, Felix, and so old-fashioned. I love the way the grass runs down to the lake."

"Be careful near the lake, Rose, there's a bit of a current and you need to know where it is safe to swim."

On these subjects it was difficult to speak with Felix. Mentioning the church would evoke thoughts of Hannah and his sons. Mentioning the lake would make him think of his parents. It seemed that everything in this place was tinged with sadness.

"Take me there for a swim one day then," I said brightly.

Felix dropped his fork on his plate.

"And when do you think I have time to do things like that?"

He looked angry. I changed the subject quickly.

"I'm looking forward to the new washing machine."

"Whatever makes you happy," he replied.

Conversation dried up after that and I was glad to return to the Lodge. It was still cold enough to light the fire so I made myself cosy to read a romantic novel I had fetched from the library. On the inside dust cover it read, 'To Vivian, my darling wife, love Stephen.'

Sprinkling rain had refreshed the landscape and as Felix neared the end of the lambing season it was a joy to see their little bodies gambolling in the fields and suckling on long suffering ewes. Knowing that Felix would be out, tending to his flock, I had been up since sunrise. As I trod up the sweeping staircase I felt like I was heading into a fog of doom. Felix, I knew, would not appreciate my interference but I hoped that he would appreciate the good intentions behind my actions. My only thoughts were to release him from the bed of blood.

The two Toms were bringing the new bed and washing machine in a clunky horse box. Old Tom would not enter the Manor but he was happy to work in the boot room so I was hoping that Young Tom would entertain my resolutions and help me later. With a hard will I rallied forward to the bed of blood armed with a screwdriver and a hammer.

Smells drizzled at my senses. Rotted flesh invaded my nostrils and licked at my mouth and ears. Hurriedly I opened the window, its panes dashed with splattered mould and I looked at the view beyond. Stunning skies and luxuriant meadows greeted me. I wanted to let the scene, the smells, the comfort into this room as an exorcism.

Beginning to sort through the wardrobe I gave up after a while as so much of his clothing was not worth saving. Jeans splattered with cow dung were ripped. Knitted jumpers were snagged and moth-eaten. He'd probably not worn any of it since Hannah died, so I turned my attention to the bed.

Hurling back the cover and doing my best to ignore the cascade of burnt red dust that showered me, I packed it tightly into a bin bag. I stuffed the pillows into another bag and then looked down at the sheet that was left. My stomach lurched and I could see remains of blobs of human waste decayed and spreading out like a drug-induced abstract. Taking a deep breath I tugged at the ends and squashed it into a bag tying the top tightly not wanting anything to escape.

The decomposing mattress was heavy and I struggled to pull it off. I nudged it out of the room and down the gallery to the top of the stairs. Letting it slip it bumped on its back trip-trapping until it came to rest at the bottom. I pinned old sheets over it to hide the stains from Young Tom.

The iron-bed frame seemed to have all the nuts welded together. I grunted and sweated with steely determination to dismantle them. The bed struts were heavy too and I had to carry each part separately. Once I had created a pile of debris in the hall, ready to dispose of later, I began to attack the devastation in Felix's old bedroom.

Returning to his clothes I decided to put the majority into bin bags and the rest I threw in a pile to be washed in my new machine. Now the wardrobe was clear, I cleaned away the grime and dirt with copious amounts of bleach and disinfectant. Satisfied, I left it to dry and I vacuumed the carpet mopping it over with soapy water. I washed the skirting boards and windows and polished the door.

The bedside tables each had tall lamps on them. The shades were scorched and threw up an army of dust and I thought that I would buy new ones next time I went to Shrugsborough. I could tell which was Hannah's side of the bed as in the cabinet I found some sanitary towels, a pair of pretty silver and amethyst earrings and a book. She had inserted a bookmark to return to read at a later time. The poignancy of one of her last living actions overwhelmed me with sadness.

The space for the new bed was now ready and the room began to smell of fresh air and soap. On the dressing table was a wedding photograph of Felix and Hannah. I studied the woman of Felix's haunting. She was blonde and her skin was clear. Her green eyes shone with happiness and her face looked serene. In her flowing white wedding dress she looked like a being from another world, ethereal and fairy-like.

Felix looked handsome wearing a navy suit and a pink rose in his button hole. He was clean shaven and his hair was cut smartly with his fringe lopping over his forehead. Each of them looked out at the photographer full of hope and ambition for the future ahead of them.

In Hannah's drawers, clothes were folded neatly. Her petite underwear was soft and clean. I imagined Felix peeling her clothes from her shapely body on their wedding night. Her image came to life and I saw them lying on the bed pulling at each other's clothes. Her muse-like face smiling at Felix showing her white teeth and her pursed full lips kissing his lean body. Felix's muscles hard under her touch as he entered her, teasing her nipples as his tongue met hers...

I rapidly placed her lingerie back in the drawer.

Hannah must have sorted out Felix's clothes as one drawer was arranged with his socks and pants.

He had not touched them since as they lay unused like soldiers on parade.

I noticed that most of Hannah's clothes were in the drawers, no dresses or skirts, just jeans, tee-shirts and jumpers. That much we had in common.

I pulled hard to drag the dresser forward so that I could clean behind and something fell to the floor. Two large keys hung on a bull-sized ring. Picking them up I paused and saw a hook on the back of a stilt holding the folding dressing mirrors. It was antique and covered in cobwebs so had not been removed for some time. Uncertainty swayed in my head, back and forth, forth and back. I tried to put them in my pocket but they were too bulky so I went to the gallery and hid them behind the painting of Isabella and her family.

Morning was hurrying by and the Toms would be arriving soon. I pushed the dresser back. A bottle of perfume called, 'Dana' was half full. I opened it and wet my fingers dabbing the scent behind my ears. It smelt nice and I thought of Hannah sitting here rubbing it along her cleavage; she the object of Felix's adoration.

The two Toms arrived and I greeted them both with tea and biscuits. I was hoping to persuade Young Tom to help me carry the new bed upstairs and to help me dispose of the old one. He was reluctant but agreed. Old Tom set about preparing the plumbing for the washing machine whilst Young Tom and I carted the new bed to Felix's bedroom.

"This place has seen better days," he said looking around.

"I'm doing my best Tom, you should have seen it before. This bed will make all the difference for Felix."

"Does he know it's coming, Rose?"

"Kind of," I replied.

Young Tom wasn't stupid and he knew that this was being done without Felix's blessing but there was something about Old Tom and Young Tom which meant that they did not pry into other people's business and they expected people not to pry into their own. When we had put the new bed together I fetched the new bedding and Tom helped me fill the cover with the new quilt. Afterwards he lay on the bed declaring that even he could sleep on it. I took that as a compliment.

We cleared up the mountain I had formed in the hall and Young Tom took the rusty bedstead to the milking parlour and I took the bin bags to the metal drum where we burned the garden rubbish.

I stuffed the first bag in and poured a little petrol over the top and threw in a match. A fireball spluttered black smoke that choked at my throat but I stood silently as the flames killed the bed of blood. A shiver sprinted down my back as I thought of what Felix would say about his refreshed marital bedroom where his wife bled out. A bed that he could not bear to let go of even after all these years.

Old Tom was calling me.

"It's in Rose, have you got anything to wash to try it out?"

I knew that the boot room was the deepest part of the Manor where Old Tom would venture and I appreciated his morning's work. I handed Old Tom some tea-towels and we all stood mesmerised as the machine tumbled the cloths round and around. I wanted to put Felix in the washing machine too.

We sat drinking tea and eating fruit cake under the shade of a willow tree soaking in the moderate spring air letting the weak sun warm our bones. Young Tom got up to leave.

"Thanks for the tea, Rose. Oh, by the way, Betty said to come down next Thursday as she's going into Shrugsborough if you fancy a trip with her?"

"That'll be perfect, Tom. What time?"

"Meet her at the end of the track just after nine. And, I hear you two have met the new vicar. All she's done is go on about him."

"I can't think why," I replied mischievously.

"Thanks so much for coming and helping, Tom. I couldn't have done it without you." We waved goodbye and I watched the horse box ping along the track out of view.

Old Tom and I continued on with our work. The garden was looking tidy and a robin flew in now and again chirping and digging for worms. Chopping at the matted ivy Old Tom had cleared the doorway of weeds which led through into the walled garden. We concentrated on planting vegetables and bringing the lawn back to life. In a corner, Old Tom instructed me on how to prepare a bed to grow 'cut flowers' and I enjoyed scratching in the dirt to remove weeds and moss.

I had covered the mattress in sheets pinning them in before Young Tom helped me drag it out here and we made a bonfire specifically for it. Now the flames were dying I had a sense of rebirth.

Leaning on my spade I looked over at Old Tom, his back bent pulling up some defiant root and I smiled. I now felt that I had a purpose in my life and my emotions were balanced by the calmness of this place.

My comfort didn't last long.

PART FOUR

A heart burned in a strike of change

CHAPTER 10

At the end of the day, when Young Tom came back for Old Tom I went to the kitchen to make supper. My muscles ached and I let loose a loud yawn. On this evening all I wished for was a bubbly bath and to snuggle up in bed for an early night. Anticipation of how Felix would react to the new bedroom would have to wait until tomorrow. Leaving his supper in the oven I fed the chickens and plucked some tulips. I went up to the bedroom and closed the window and placed the vase on the bedside table. The room smelled fresh and I felt more than pleased with my travails.

There was some doubt in my mind however about what I had done and how Felix was going to react. Perhaps Felix would be upset but I was sure that he would realise my reasons for doing it. Fergus and Bunnie had been trying to achieve the same result for years. Fergus had even promised to come and sort it out but I knew he would never have the time.

Every part of my body ached and I relaxed in the bath until my fingers crinkled and the water grew tepid. Wet hair stuck to my back as I went downstairs to lazily fix myself a sandwich. I had left the brown envelope on the table and thought it was about time I opened it. None of its contents were unexpected. It was the divorce papers from Wayne's solicitor. I didn't even read the documents, I just signed the bottom and sealed them in the stamped addressed envelope before flopping into bed.

Something made me wake. Intuitively, I went to the window expecting to see the woman in the window but she wasn't there. I crept back into bed.

Suddenly, Felix burst into my bedroom his face red and his shoulders hunched. He was trembling. As he spoke his eyes were devoid of emotion. The derision in his voice was like a snake bite.

"You fuckin' cunt! You stupid fuckin' little bitch!"

I was frightened and I could sense that he was straining to stop himself grabbing at me. I sat in the bed with the covers under my chin and stared at him blankly.

Then he began to cry. Fat tears brimmed in his eyes and plopped down his cheeks.

"You've taken her from me. Hannah, my Hannah. There's nothing left."

Composing himself, he looked me hard in the eye.

"Out of here, Rose. By tomorrow. Do you hear?" His voice rose to a tumultuous crescendo.

I nodded and he left. I heard him slamming the door on his way out and then the slam of the door at the Manor which set the dogs barking.

Frozen for a moment, I sat transfixed staring at the space where he had stood. Tears came and I shook. He had scared me and I found myself dumbfounded not knowing what to do. After a while I got up and frantically packed my small belongings into my rucksack. Outside a storm was sneaking across the moors and I felt the ha, ha, ha of a cruel striking rain as I left the Lodge. I made for the track and scrambled towards the gated entrance to the lane. Dark sky whipped clouds above me where stars played peek-a-boo and the trees lining the route leaned threateningly and seemed to screech out at me to go away. There was a flurry of scrapings on a window and I saw the woman. She was visibly upset beckoning to me to come back. I watched her. She was distraught and trying to shout above the cracking thunder. Her voice echoed in the torrid air,

"Where are my boys, where are my boys?"

Then I heard her scream my name, 'Roooooose'.

Coldness carelessly tapped at my heart as my fright made me rigid. Again, 'Roooooose' and I shivered. Then I sprinted down the track afraid, afraid of the woman in the window. Afraid of what I was going to do next. Afraid that I would never see Felix again.

In a short burst the rain had soaked through my meagre clothes and I was shivering. My skin was white as I ran out of breath at the end of the track. I had to lean against one of the pillars where the beasts growled maliciously down at me. A splash of lightning exposed their grim posture and my imagination saw paws gesturing me onwards. No mortal, it seemed, wished me to go back.

Felix had shocked me from my slumber. I became wildly awake and fortuitously I'd grabbed my purse. I had enough money to catch the bus back to Birmingham but I didn't know what I was going to do until the morning. It was 3 a.m. The black ceiling fumbled my thoughts. Should I trouble Betty or Old Tom? Not possible I thought at this early hour. I stumbled on trembling through the lashing rain that punished me as I walked. My shoes filled with water and rubbed at my toes as I wended down the lane and the long walk to Churchbury. The cold harried my aching bones and I sat for a while letting the elements curse me with their rage.

A voice rang in my head as I buckled under the weight of my situation calling Rose, Roooooose. I blew into my hands to warm then and then...

A bolt of searing pain ran through me like a knife in soft butter. I passed out.

When I opened my eyes I thought I had died and gone to Heaven. I mean this not in the nice way. Not the same as when people exclaim the phrase receiving their heart's desire but in the way that I thought I had died. Figures in white were circling me and some of them were speaking but I could not understand what they were saying. I thought they were angels and when I opened my eyes fully I looked for Patrick.

A man held my hand, "Rose, Rose. It's OK, you are in hospital. You were struck by lightning."

"Lightning?"

"Yes, and you are a very lucky girl. Rose you have burns down your left-hand side but all things considered they are not too bad. You will heal Rose and lead a normal life."

"Lightning? Normal life?" I was confused. Where was I? There was a glare from the lights that hurt my eyes and the man's voice seemed amplified. He got up and brushed my hair from my forehead.

"It's a shock, Rose but you will be fine. Rest and treatment for your burns for a couple of weeks and then you can go home."

I was attached to a drip and a machine that seemed to be tracing my heart.

"This needle here Rose is morphine. You just press it down when you feel the need for some pain relief. All right? Do you understand?"

I looked to where he was pointing and nodded.

My left side? What did he mean?

When I was able to leave my bed and go to the toilet, I lifted the hospital gown to reveal patches of bandages covering my trunk. They continued down my leg. The damage to my skin was hidden by the shrouds that wound around me. I looked like an Egyptian Mummy.

What had happened to my body was not what was worrying me. I could not stop thinking about Felix and my home at the Manor and what it all meant to me. The magnitude of what I had done and the effect that it had on Felix dawned on me and I longed to see him to explain.

A nurse came to tell me that I had a visitor. I hoped Gabriel did not notice my disappointment when he came to my bed. He was grinning at me and leant over to kiss me on the cheek.

"Rose, how lovely to see you. You look well actually. The lightning missed your face. God was on your side that night, Rose."

I thought about what he was saying and I didn't think that God was on my side at all. How could he let this happen to me? Nevertheless, I smiled back at Gabriel, happy to see him. I did my best not to let it show that I had hoped he was Felix.

As we chatted he told me what had happened. After he'd calmed down, Felix had returned to the Lodge at about 4 a.m. Realising that I was missing he went out to look for me. He found me lying on the road. Thor and Phoebe had barked to alert him otherwise he would have run over me. He brought me straight here.

He came back for me, he came back for me.

Gabriel chatted on. It turned out that his visit to the bishop was to be granted a special licence so that he could be married to his fiancée, Fiona, by the bishop in St Laurence's Church. He suggested that Betty and I could do the flowers and extended an invitation to me and Felix to attend his wedding. I wondered how Betty would feel about us doing the flowers together. I knew she did the flowers a lot in the church and she was one of the church wardens but I had no experience. I decided it would be fun and I was sure that any excuse for her to gaze on Gabriel's earthly manifestation of joy would appease her.

"Is there anything I can get for you Rose? I could drop into the Manor and pick up a few things if you like?"

"Nothing, Gabriel."

He lowered his voice. "Is everything all right, Rose? What on earth were you doing out on such a night?"

Uncontrollable tears fell down my face as I explained to Gabriel the events, purposefully leaving out the episode of the woman in the window and how she had called to me, thinking that he would not believe me.

He took my hand, then he delicately held me to his chest and I loved the feel of his body next to mine. I needed his warmth.

He released me.

"Rose, you need to rest. Take advantage of being here and leave this to me."

Before I could respond he walked down the hospital ward and his shoes squeaked on the shiny floor.

I drifted between being awake and asleep. My mind was confused about reality as I constantly dreamed of Eliza. We would have meaningful conversations about me going back to the Manor as she sat on my bed caressing my forehead. Her words encouraged me to get well. She told me I was needed. When I awoke from those dreams, I found it hard to adjust to the bustle of the ward and the living people who worked there.

Betty visited bringing flowers and sweets and she sat by the bed chatting merrily. She was disappointed to learn that she had missed Gabriel but she cheered me up no end.

"When I heard what had happened Rose, I just couldn't believe that you had gone out on a night like that. Honestly, what were you thinking?"

Betty wasn't going to give up her prying very easily and I could tell that she expected an answer.

"I was sleepwalking, Betty, a horrible dream about a ghost in the Manor and I was running away."

She didn't believe me but she did not press me on the subject again.

Two days later a nurse came to tell me I had a visitor. I expected it to be Gabriel and when I saw it was Felix I employed my surprise by frantically pumping morphine from

152

the drip into my arm. Awkwardly, he sat on the chair next to the bed. He had brought me some lemon squash, grapes and chocolates. I was amazed when he took my hand.

"Rose, it's good to see you. When I saw you on the road I feared the worst."

I opened my mouth to speak but he interrupted me.

"Just listen Rose, please. Look, I have had time to think and Gabriel came by the other day and what he said made sense. I mean."

He seemed to flounder not being able to find the words he needed.

"Hannah," he started.

When he said her name I shuddered a wince from a green-eyed heart.

"Hannah, well she was the love of my life and I just couldn't let her go. I'm not sure you'll understand but she was everything to me. Now she and my boys are in their graves at St Laurence's and I have mourned them for over seventeen years. But you Rose. You have given me a new lease of life. I see things in a way that I haven't seen for years. You work so hard at the Manor and I have been ungrateful. I would like you to come back."

His eyes softened. I recalled him that night standing in the doorway restraining himself and the abusive words that he called me.

"I miss you being around, Rose."

My relief reverberated inside me. For all my time at the Manor, I had never thought of Felix in a truly romantic way, although I was growing very fond of him. I found it difficult to accept that I needed his care and attention. If I admitted it, I think I was falling in love with him but I was afraid of how vulnerable that made me. I feared the touch of any man and I had never had a proper relationship with one. I perceived my role with Felix as what? I didn't know what. His words were compassionate and for the first time as he looked at me I detected care for me in his eyes. I wanted him, I wanted to go back to the Manor but still I was unsure exactly why. I just knew that I wanted those things, the things that Bunnie had, the things that Betty had but seemed unattainable to me without sacrifice. I felt that I had already sacrificed many things including my dead son.

Something stirred within me and I stared back.

"I'm so glad you came, Felix. I need to explain, to tell you."

He squeezed my hand.

"Shh, it's OK Rose, I know what you were trying to do, there's no need to explain."

He continued to hold my hand until he left.

My dreams were enhanced by the morphine and I would wake sweating and calling out to Eliza.

Night staff would bring a cold flannel and place it behind my neck to cool me and adjust my pillows to make me comfortable. My eyes would close and soon I would be walking in meadows over the Callow lands. Scanning the horizon I would make out the figure of a giant bearing a relentless load on his back. I would gesture with my hand towards the slope of the hill indicating for him to rest a while. Here we would sit and drink tea made from wild herbs. When he rose to leave I suggested that he could lighten his load and continue his journey by emptying his bag of boulders. He smiled a toothy grin and lifted his bag. Renewed from the healing power of the magic tea, he shook out the contents so hard that rocks and stones and boulders fell to the ground like a showering rainstorm. I had to rush and run away for fear of being hit and then I would wake feeling out of breath and delirious.

When I was released from hospital Felix came to pick me up. He looked different somehow as if a great burden had been taken from his shoulders and he looked youthful. I discerned the good looks of his brother as he had trimmed his beard and he smelled of lavender soap.

He helped me settle in the Lodge and looking around told me what a lovely homely place I had made it. Then he supported me up the stairs to my bed. When he gently tucked me in I grabbed at his hand. He turned my hand over in his and kissed it.

Felix took me to my hospital appointments to have my burns cleaned and new bandages placed over them until I was ready to have them removed forever. The reflection staring back at me showed ugly red slivers that shattered and burst at my skin. When the heat struck me the scorch on the surface had created a line that stretched out from my torso to my toes. The doctor told me that because I had been sitting down the strike had missed my heart. Strangely the scar ended at my waist at the curve where my body was bent and began again at my thigh. Naturally I was repulsed but my mind was absent of self-pity as all I could think of were Felix's words. He wanted me back.

Bunnie came to visit bearing flowers and champagne which we drank in the afternoon which seemed wicked. She rattled on about Langley Hall and Fergus and her children and I waited for an opportune moment to ask her about the ghost in the tower.

"Ghost, Rose? Are you still on any medication? Gosh, that's a thought, should you be drinking this champagne?"

"I've seen a ghost in the window. The night, the night that it happened she called me by my name. It's as if she wants my help in some way. She calls for her boys too. I thought it was the ghost of Hannah but Old Tom said it wasn't her and actually Felix told me she is buried at the church with her twins so why would she want to haunt us here?"

Bunnie looked at me oddly as I continued.

"I dream of a woman called Eliza. It's as if this all happened for a reason. You know, me being here."

"Seriously Rose, are you still on medication? Sorry Rose, can't help you on that one. It was a filthy night, you probably witnessed a flash of lightning in the window. It was nothing more than that."

It was obvious Bunnie wished to avoid the subject so she changed it.

"Now, what do you think of our new vicar? He's a bit of a dish, don't you agree? We're all invited to the wedding and I met Fiona last week. Poor girl, he was trawling her around the parish like a trophy, but she seems rather pleasant. A bit jolly hockey sticks but I think she had good humour about the whole thing and Gabriel clearly adores her."

"Yes, Betty and I are doing the flowers. Christ! It's in four weeks. I'd better link up with Betty as we don't have much time."

When Bunnie left she affectionately kissed me on each cheek.

"Lovely to see you back and looking so well. Don't overdo it. Terribly busy so probably won't see you 'til the wedding. I'm sure you and Betty will do a great job of the flowers. No more dreams about ghosts, hey Rose?"

As she was going I called to her.

"Bunnie. Why are you called Bunnie?"

"Bethany, I'm Bethany but Felix and Fergus couldn't say it when they were little and called me Bunnie so it stuck."

"I like Bunnie," I said waving.

She waved goodbye and stepped up into her 4×4.

I went back into the Manor. Cautiously, I went to the staircase and held the rail as I listened to the oak creak and my bones creak as I made my way to Felix's old and refreshed bedroom.

I could tell, because of the indent, that he had sat on the bed. His clothes were still in the pile where I had left them and I picked them up to take to the washing machine. The tulips were folded over the vase, drained and limp, so I juggled to carry them in one hand and tucked the washing under my arm. On the way back down the gallery and passing the tapestry, I remembered the keys I had hidden there. I resolved to come back and collect them as soon as I felt better. For now, for once, I heard what other people were telling me and let myself back to my chores with an easier attitude. My scars grew tight as they healed and sometimes the pain kept me awake. On those nights the woman appeared at her window and I whispered over the courtyard that I would come and help her soon.

Dr Comickery came to see me and congratulated me on my recovery. I made him tea and he drank it gratefully.

"I came to visit Felix whilst you were in hospital. I'm not breaking any patient confidentiality Rose, just letting you know that I was doing my rounds."

"And how did you find him?" I asked. "By his smell?"

He laughed. "He needs you here, Rose. I hope you will remain here a while."

"I will doctor, for as long as he needs me."

Old Tom had continued to work in the garden and it was looking shipshape. He gave me messages from Betty and I was meeting her in a couple of days for a trip to Shrugsborough. The outside world seemed distant as I pootled about doing my best to keep on top of the housework. One evening, as I sat by my fire at the Lodge, Felix unexpectedly came in. I offered him tea and we sat together in my sitting room.

"I've been thinking. It seems to me that we could do with some more help. There's a lady on Home Farm who's looking for some part-time work and I've asked her to come and help you at the Manor."

As I watched him, sitting by the fire, I thought about his trips to the Callow Stones, Hannah's bed of blood and the graves at the church. Felix was a complex man and yet I realised he yearned for simple things.

"Thank you. What's her name?"

"Mrs Thompson. She's got a bigger beard than me," he joked, "but she is really nice. I stop by for tea now and then. She has known me since I was a nipper."

My jealous heart was relieved that she was not a 'young thing'.

"Thompson? Any relation to the infamous cursing nursemaid?" I asked.

"Actually, yes. How do you know about that?"

"In the library." I did not want to blame Betty for any indiscretion.

He looked at me suspiciously but passed over the matter.

"Mrs Thompson is unmarried but we all call her *Mrs* Thompson because she bullies her common-law husband so much that he is known as Mr Thompson although actually his name is Jones. She's quite a character but she's a hard worker."

Felix appeared to be embarrassed by our intimacy and got up to leave. He faltered at the door.

"Rose, I am sorry..."

"Don't, it's OK. It was my fault."

"See you tomorrow then. Goodnight, Rose."

Soon the Manor was full of light and was slowly being relieved of dirt as Mrs Thompson and I set about our work. She came three mornings a week. She was overweight and struggled to bend down or should I say she was fine about bending over but found it difficult to straighten up again. She wore an orange nylon overall tied around her middle with brown cord. She always brought with her some old-fashioned carpet slippers to wear as she cleaned and her stockings were wrinkled around her ankles. Mrs Thompson smoked, although never in the house but the smell lingered on her. She had a smoky, earthy scent. When she smiled I noticed that two teeth were missing at the sides of her mouth. She was a great gossip and filled me in on everything I desired to know about Felix.

"First born boy twin has the Cross of Soot. 'Twas Isabella by all accounts. Well, not her exactly but her husband, the man what made this place so lavish." She waved her chubby and wobbling arm above her head.

"He was so shocked to hear his wife had given birth to twins that he sent for the nursemaid to bring some soot from the fire. Stupid girl brought it hot and as Francis made the cross on his son it burnt into his flesh scarring him for life."

As she spoke I shivered stroking at my own scars. She seemed oblivious to my feelings.

I had heard this story before but Mrs Thompson's version sounded much more dramatic.

"He needed to know the eldest boy, see. Yer know, the one that was going to inherit all his land. All of this." She waved her arm again with the same dramatic effect as before.

"Reckon that nursemaid was secretly a witch as her curse was strong. All the eldest twin boys since has been born with the Cross of Soot."

I was truly fascinated by her tales and to encourage her I made striking responses. Lots of oohs and ahhs and 'no-nevers'. Mrs Thompson seemed very proud of her association with the cursing nursemaid. Since then, she told me, some of her female ancestors had been ducked in the village pond for gossiping and some had been accused of being witches. This wasn't hard to believe. Despite her penchant for sitting and drinking tea and eating biscuits, domestic drudgery never seemed to bother her.

I tentatively broached the subject of the ghost. Much to my annoyance the postman arrived just as I hoped she would enlighten me. There was a letter from my mother, I recognised the postmark.

Dear Rose,

I hope this letter finds you well as it finds me.

As you know the circumstances of your father's parting were troubling to me and of course to you. However, I don't think any of us took a thought about poor Trevor. As it happens he called to see me. He's left Pat and he's moving in with me. Things are happening fast Rose but I am putting the house up for sale and Trevor and me are buying a bungalow together in Solihull. I hope you don't mind, I think you always liked Trevor.

We are also going to Benidorm in a few weeks and after that we wondered if we could visit. I'd like to show Trevor the countryside by you.

I hope my news is not too much of a shock, darling. Please write and let me know when we can come. I need to talk to you about your belongings and what shall I do with them when I move and stuff like that.

Love mum xx

PS – Linda says will you write soon? She's getting married and wants you to come to her wedding.

"Not bad news Rose," Mrs Thompson enquired as she strained over me to read the letter.

"No, Mrs Thompson. Not bad news. Actually, the best news I've had for a long time."

We set back to work and I thought of mum with Trevor. I was pleased and amazed that she was going abroad. She had always said that she was frightened of flying. I remembered Trevor at my wedding. His cheap wife who called me quiet. I recalled he had looked embarrassed to be part of it so I gave him the benefit of the doubt, for now, about his intentions with my mother.

I wouldn't tell her about my accident. Accident? Was that what it was called when you have been struck by a bolt of electric force? I would wait until she came with Trevor and I wrote later that evening asking her to come in August before the shoot season started and after Gabriel's wedding. The year was rolling by.

Betty and I had our trip to Shrugsborough and we ordered plenty of flowers to decorate the church. We both agreed on meadow colours of cornflower blues, soft pinks, buttercup yellow and mauves. Three days before the wedding, Betty drove down to the church and on a glorious summer's day, we organised where we would place the pilasters. Betty had the idea of ordering some lilac ribbon. We wound it around the pillars and Betty skilfully tied large bows which we hung from the arches over the pew ends.

On the day before the wedding, we arranged magnificent floral structures to adorn the grey-stone church. As we brushed the floor wafts of incense were sent up forming perfumed clouds in the tapestry of leaded lights.

Once we had finished Betty suggested we sat by the lake for a rest. I lay idly on my back, my front still sore, picking at a daisy from the mowed grass that swept down to the water's edge. I watched water boatmen miraculously manoeuvre over the surface and willow herb softly wave their pink heads. In the sunlight the lake shimmered and at the landing dock a boat tapped at the posts.

"Whose boat is that Betty? And the boathouse?"

"The boat and house? Oh. It belongs to Felix."

I sat up and looked at Betty. She was sitting with her legs out in front of her.

"Where's Hannah's grave Betty? Do you know?"

She gave me a look as if to say that I should know better to ask. Reluctantly she got up.

"Come on then. I'll show you."

We walked to the other side of the church where the graves were more sheltered from the grazing lake wind. Yew trees grew outwards casting elongated shadows over the mottled

161

headstones. Family names repeated themselves joined by birth, marriage and death laying taut against each other.

"Here, Rose. She's here."

I don't know why I had expected something grander but her grave was as modest as those around her. Local stone was used and beige letters carved out her name. Lady Hannah Langley and her twin sons. The boys had given names and etched out I read, Stephen Francis Langley and Herbert Paul Langley. Such grown up names for two tiny angels, I thought.

Betty was quiet as I read the inscriptions out loud.

'Here lay the bodies of Hannah, beloved wife of Felix Langley and mother of Stephen Francis and Herbert Paul Langley of Callow Crest Manor. God smiled upon them and took the angels to heaven whilst they slept on 6th January 1962. Forever missed.'

"She was very beautiful, Rose. Like a fairy queen. Such a sad thing to happen."

"But I thought you had never met her, Betty?"

"No, but Old Tom and Gwyneth have photographs and my Tom remembers her, she was his cousin after all."

"Of course, Betty. I'm sorry."

Betty smiled and asked, "Come back and meet Gwyneth for a cuppa?"

We drove back in silence each of us thinking about Hannah and her boys laying in earth.

Gwyneth was the tiniest woman I had ever met. Despite her height she had the most enormous breasts and when I entered the kitchen she was taking the weight off them by leaning them on the table. Young Tom had her bone structure and blue eyes. She wore her hair in grips in a bun on top of her head and it was thin and slate. Not getting up she bade me to sit down and Old Tom filled a brown teapot with fresh tea leaves and hot water

162

and popped a knitted tea cosy over it. I was sure that Gwyneth had knitted it. The kitchen was warm and the layout was similar to Betty's. The décor was old-fashioned. The walls were covered in a paper pattern of teacups and jugs in a psychedelic way which reminded me of the flooring in the Lodge kitchen when I had first moved in.

Gwyneth was very pleasant and chattered excitedly about the forthcoming wedding. Gabriel and Fiona had been busy, it seemed, visiting as many parishioners as they could manage. Gwyneth was pleased about that and related how they had sat, just where I was sitting now, drinking tea and eating Bara Brith.

Old Tom, accustomed to her chatter, grinned at me now and then and asked how I was getting along with Mrs Thompson. I told him that we made a great team and made a mental note to myself to ask her about the woman in the tower. This would have to wait until after the wedding. Betty offered to drive me up to the end of the track and just before I left the car she said three things to me.

The first was that she would see me tomorrow. The second was that it was about time Felix fixed the track and the third was why hadn't I learned to drive?

Learning to drive was not one of those things I had ever thought about but I looked at Betty with new eyes and told her that I was going to learn soon. I recalled my envy watching Linda driving away.

"About time, too. You can't rely on me for a taxi forever."

CHAPTER 11

She was right, of course. Driving would be a new distraction and that night I spoke to Felix about it. He agreed to pay for me to have lessons and said he thought that it was a fabulous idea. His moods were much more convivial and he had brought a bottle of champagne up from the cellar.

"What's the occasion?" I asked as I watched the glasses fizz.

"The wedding tomorrow and to you Rose."

"To me?"

"Yes, for getting better. Do you think you could cut my hair?"

"For the wedding?"

"Yes, for the wedding. Better not let the side down."

"Only if you go and have a bath and take that cap off and shave off that beard while you're at it. I'll put the bottle in the fridge."

"Well, I wasn't expecting you to drink it all while I was gone, Rose. What sort of haircut would you give me after drinking all of that?"

"A better one than you have now," I said and we both laughed.

I heard the boiler splutter as he ran his bath. I cleared up the dishes and then I heard him call me from the bathroom.

"Rose, I need a towel Rose, Rose?"

I grabbed a couple of clean towels from the cabinet on the gallery floor and went to the bathroom. I knocked the door waiting for a reply. There was no answer so I opened the door and went in. He had his back to me. The bathwater was scummy and his hair looked black and clammy. I didn't know if he had heard me so I went to him and touched his back. He took my hand and gave me a sponge.

"Wash my back for me Rose?"

I hesitated. His shoulders were broad and lean and I smelled lavender rising up from his skin. I put the towels down and took the sponge and I began to soap his back. I saw his tenuous muscles move and his spine bones shift as I lightly caressed him. He never spoke. I continued moving my hand in circles and drenched his skin with the scummy water to remove the soap.

"The towels are here. Come down when you are ready and I'll attack that hair. I only drank half the bottle so you'll be all right. You can always put your cap back on if it's a disaster," I joked.

Instead of leaning over to grab the towels he stood up. He made a feigned laugh and I saw his lean bottom, his torso and as he bent down for the towels I saw his penis and balls hanging down. I looked away embarrassed.

When I got back to the kitchen I nervously poured myself some of the champagne and drank it down in one gulp. When he came in he was dressed in a clean shirt and cord trousers. His feet were bare and his face was clean shaven. His damp hair was clinging to his scalp.

"Felix," I uttered astounded by the change in him. Regaining composure I pointed at the chair I had put by the fireside ready to cut his hair. He was handsome and rugged and beautiful and I felt like a schoolgirl wearing my emotions all over my face. He looked to where I was pointing and sat down.

His hair was thick and knotted so I poured some cooking oil into my hands then sleeked my hands through his hair and began to comb out his locks.

He sat still and quiet. He had poured two glasses of the champagne and was sipping on his as I struggled with strands that probably had not seen a comb or brush for many years. I was as gentle as I could manage and intermittently I stopped to drink. Eventually his hair was knot-free and I began to clip. At first I made delicate snips and then I grew brave and chopped away styling as best I could. I had never cut anyone's hair before so I crossed my fingers and hoped that it would turn out well. He went to the hall to look in the mirror and when he came back he greeted me with a 'thumbs up'. I began to brush the hair from the floor and as I did so he came to me. He slipped his arm around my waist and whispered,

"Come, follow me Rose."

He held my hand as he led me up the stairs towards his bedroom. I hesitated. At the door he stopped to kiss me. Full and hard on my mouth, his hot breath sweet from the champagne. I responded as he fervently groped at my tee-shirt ripping it over my head. He undid my bra and moaned aloud as he moved to cup my breasts and kiss, caress and suck at my nipples. He took my hand again and we went to the bed. His bed. He took off his shirt and cords and he was naked before me. Aroused, his erection, with a life of its own, bobbed in desire as he pulled at my jeans and my pants. I was nervous and scared. We lay on the top of the cover and he kissed and caressed me all over. I was conscious of my scar. He dragged his finger along the line and then he licked me between my legs and kissed and touched me tenderly bringing me to an orgasm. I thought I was going to die in ecstasy. Murmurs whispered in the night air as I gripped a bed post as he entered me gently and groaned when he quickly came. As his body trembled I kissed his neck and ran my fingers through his hair. He lay on me for a while and then he took my hands to lift me and motioned for me to get beneath the covers. His arms about my body made me feel secure. I didn't want to be anywhere else in the world. We made love three times that night.

When I woke, he was gone. I checked my watch and it was 9.30 a.m. I had slept like a baby and I was behind schedule. I ran to the Lodge and bathed and dressed for the wedding. Betty was waiting for me at the end of the track and we drove off at speed.

"There's something different about you this morning. You look lovely Rose, very serene."

"Thank you Betty, so do you."

She was dressed in a duck-egg blue dress that billowed from under her bust and she wore white low-heel shoes and a white hat with a white rose in her cleavage.

"Enjoy the view while you can, Rose. This look won't last long once my two are around."

Betty was talking about her boisterous children.

My dress was plainer and Betty had helped me choose it. It was cut on the bias mint green and chiffon and hugged at my curves. I wore beige sling-backs and no hat but when we got to the church I pinched a rose of butter colour and stuck it in my hair.

Although I say it myself, and I know in great conceit, Betty and I had done a marvellous display and the church looked beautiful. The scent of the flowers masked the old aromas and it was a particularly hot day, even at that hour, and the windows burned bright for Gabriel and Fiona's wedding.

During the service I sat with Betty and her family. Trying not to be obvious I searched the pews for Felix. I couldn't see him and thought he was probably at the back or with Bunnie and Fergus. I was right because outside, when Gabriel and Fiona posed for photographs by the lake, I saw him talking to them. He saw me and I smiled making my way to speak with

167

the group. However, Bunnie had grabbed Betty and was coming towards me. She was overflowing with her compliments about the flowers and Betty and I were very humble about our efforts.

I travelled with Old Tom and Gwyneth to the reception in Churchbury. At the pub I was pleased to see Brian and he ensured that my glass was frequently topped up with champagne.

"Gosh Rose, you look lovely," he told me with surprise.

I was flattered and thanked Brian telling him he had made my day.

The seating arrangements meant that I sat with Betty and her family and I took some umbrage at not being sat with the Langleys. Then I figured that it would not be right for a servant girl like me to be sat with them. Based on Gabriel's deep faith, I had expected the wedding to be a sombre affair. The best man was his friend from Oxford University and he relayed stories of Gabriel being caught when trying to fly his underpants on the college flagpole and other such capers. The champagne made me quite drunk and I laughed loudly surprised at the best man's speech. Felix looked over but I ignored him supposing that I wasn't good enough for him and his kin.

Some sort of madness had got into me during the reception party, as I chose to avoid Felix and made a bee line to dance with James, the best man. As the evening wore on I kicked off my shoes so that my soles became black.

Betty came to dance with us and we spotted Bunnie beckoning us to join her at the bar. We left James to his dancing, his alcohol consumption making him look like Bambi on ice.

"Felix looks amazing, Rose. He looks like a different man."

In my drunkenness I was tempted to say to Bunnie that it was because we had made love all night but I managed to stop myself and said,

"I cut his hair with the sheep shears!" I winked at Betty.

Later, Betty came over to where I was dancing again with James and some of the drunken locals where we were attempting the hokey-cokey.

"Old Tom's leaving. Do you want a lift?" she shouted above the revellers singing 'we all do the hokey-cokey' as they bashed into us.

I made gestures with my hand and mouthed that I was going back with Felix. Betty gave me an odd look. She left gathering up Molly who was asleep on a chair in a corner and I watched her go with her family at her side.

Felix was at the bar chatting to some local farmers and I tipsily approached him. He seemed to be frowning at my behaviour. Loudly I demanded that he take me home. I was holding my shoes in one hand and my handbag was swinging precariously in the other. Felix took hold of me to steady me and we went to his truck.

"Rose, how much have you had to drink? You're drunk!"

"Not good enough for you, am I? Happy to bed me but not to be seen with me in public?"

"Rose, you are ridiculous. Let's get you home."

"Which home Felix?" I slurred. "Your bed or mine?"

I don't remember much more as I think I conked out. I was still in my dress when I woke and my shoes were in the open doorway. *'Oh God, what had I done last night?'* My mouth was dry and I brushed my teeth three times to get rid of the foul taste on my tongue. I had ruined everything.

To my surprise, when I went to the Manor, Felix was waiting in the kitchen. There was a fresh pot of tea and toast on the table. I thought he would be angry with me. I was foolish and stupid but most of all I was confused.

"Here have some tea, it will help with the hangover. And, eat some toast."

I feebly took the mug and munched at the buttery toast. As soon as it hit my stomach I felt sick and I rushed to the toilet.

Vomit was in my hair and bits of food stuck in my teeth. I looked dreadful.

Back in the kitchen Felix sat at the table.

"Rose, we can't go on like this."*Oh no,* I thought. *He wants me to leave.*

He edged closer towards me.

"I've disgraced myself and in front of everyone," I uttered the words with my head down not wanting to see the look on his face.

"Rose, will you marry me?"

I gasped hardly believing what I was hearing. It took some moments for the words to sink in.

"Felix! I, I... yes Felix, yes I will."

Taking me in his arms he kissed me and then I had to rush to the loo to be sick again. He was laughing at me and took a towel to wet and wash my face.

"Rose, my beautiful Rose. You are like a rose, sweet and fresh in the morning dew."

I glowed.

"Oh Felix, you have made me so happy. I have something to tell you. I've been married before."

"I know."

"You know? How do you know?"

"Because you left the divorce papers on your kitchen table and I could not help but read them.

"Has your decree absolute come through yet?"

"Yes," I replied. "I wondered how that happened? Did you post the letter whilst I was in hospital?"

"Yes, I have to say that I took the liberty of doing so. I hope you dunno mind, Rose?"

I smiled at him. "No, I *dunno* mind."

"Well then, you'll need to invite Gabriel up for tea after his honeymoon and we'll set a date for our wedding around Christmas."

That soon, he was keen and I'd agreed. My heart was saying yes, yes, yes but my mind was filled with doubt. I brushed the nagging thoughts away and did my best to focus on my marriage to Felix.

There was no need to invite Gabriel as he and Fiona turned up riding their horses to the Manor a day or so after their return from their honeymoon. They had brought snapshots of them basking in the Caribbean sun. Gabriel did not look like a vicar. His body was bronzed and his hair was dashed with streaks of blonde. *He looked more like a Greek deity*, I thought. Fiona looked like a model in her bikini and I felt jealous as I thought of the scars blemishing my body.

Her complexion was golden and freckled and she looked attractive in her riding gear as she sat at the kitchen table with her arm looped through Gabriel's as they pored over the photographs. Fiona worked as a solicitor in Shrugsborough and she was a keen horsewoman. I asked if she hunted and she mentioned that she wanted to join the local hunt. I suggested that I would mention this to Felix and perhaps Bunnie if I saw her first. She looked at me with feigned kindness but she said that she had already met the Master to organise signing up. I think Fiona was making a point that she was more than capable of doing things for herself. Her manner cut an edge that wore through our friendship for as long as we lived.

Gabriel commented about Felix's appearance at the wedding. He did not mention my drunken behaviour and I hoped that this was because he hadn't noticed.

I waited a while before telling them my own wedding news. Each exclaimed that they thought this was wonderful. Gabriel released himself from Fiona and gave me a hug. They declared that Felix and I would be good for one another and Gabriel said that he would be delighted to marry us. I blushed in my excitement.

Mrs Thompson or Mrs T. as I had grown to call her was mystified when I told her about me and Felix.

"Never thought he would recover from Hannah. They were true child sweethearts. Reckon the day she went up there," she pointed her flabby arm upwards in her usual fashion, "was the day that Felix died too. It's good news young Rose. Good news. Just what this house needs." She seemed uncertain but I could see the facts dawning on her as she spoke.

"I'd like to increase your days Mrs T. as I will need to spend a lot of my time planning the wedding. Do you think you could do some extra hours for me?"

"Rose, you need an army to sort this place out. I guess we shall 'ave to do the best we can. You just let me know what you need me for and I'll fit in."

To her surprise I hugged her.

"Nearly spilt me tea, silly girl." Mrs T's pretence of being flustered did not fool me. She was grateful for the work and happy about me and Felix too.

"Mrs T., there's something else. I need to ask you something."

"What's that then, Rose?"

"Have you ever seen a ghost in the Manor?"

She looked at me incredulously, not knowing what to say and turned a little off colour.

"You are a silly girl, Rose. What an imagination you have. No, I've never seen a ghost and neither have you. It's this old place makes you think you see things that aren't really there."

There was something about her tone which made me disbelieve her. She didn't give me the opportunity to carry on as she whisked up her duster and headed off to the hall mumbling under her breath.

My period came. Felix and I had used no contraception and I nearly cried when I saw the blood spot in my pants. I would have to visit Dr Comickery for contraceptive pills. I caught the bus into Churchbury and called in to see Mr and Mrs Davis. They were delighted to see me but like everyone else, it seemed, a little bewildered by my wedding news. After tea and cake, I booked mum and Trevor in for two nights. Not knowing their sleeping arrangements, I booked a twin-bedded room as a compromise. It would be easier for them to stay here.

Dr Comickery was pleased to see me and smiled widely when I told him about our impending marriage. He gave me my prescription and I headed to the chemist to exchange it for birth control pills. Control was my key. For once I was taking control of my own existence and as the sun beamed down on the snuggled town of Churchbury, I caught the bus back home with a confident countenance.

On a lingering early August afternoon Gabriel rode up to see me. I heard the clip-clop of his horse on the courtyard cobbles. He had his gown pulled up around his waist and as ever I felt unsettled about his dog collar. From the look on his face I realised that he had something serious to tell me. Sat in the kitchen he explained that he could arrange for us to be married at St Laurence's, despite Felix and I having been married before. The snag was that I should convert to the Church of England for this to happen. I drank in his spectral figure as he spoke. He had a voice that soothed and was nurturing and before I knew it I was writing dates in my diary to visit him for my conversion.

I would walk down to the rectory enjoying the meander down the lane towards the church. Fiona was never at home during my visits. She would be in Shrugsborough at her office.

At my first lesson, arguments raged in my head as I felt uncomfortable about rejecting the Pope's authority and referring to him as the 'Bishop of Rome'. These innermost thoughts had been ingrained inside me by my father and the plentiful Masses I had attended led by Father O' Dowd. I found it hard to dislodge them.

Gabriel enjoyed sharing his views with me and I came to realise just how much of a Christian man he was. His devotion to Jesus to God to his Church was evident to me. His eyes shone with enthusiasm as he spoke about 'Our Lord' and he was a man that I knew I could trust as his faith was deep and sound.

He was sympathetic to my view and we spoke of history and the Reformation and he told me of the similarities between the two churches. I was amazed to learn that I could still use my rosary for prayer. The beads of my faith had been tucked in a pocket of my rucksack. I felt that God had rejected me after my son was born and buried. Religion had left a bitter taste. Gabriel was persuasive and time had healed some of the pain. Before long Gabriel had arranged my confirmation. I was a good student and I enjoyed my visits and our long discussions in his study. During my visits I found Gabriel's weakness. He made insipid tea and served it with stale biscuits. In the end I would go to the kitchen and make the tea myself; a stronger brew. This was Fiona's kitchen. Her signature was all over it. Neat and tidy and well presented, a little astute, just like her.

I did not need to be baptised as already being baptised counted which was of some relief to me as I did not want the embarrassment of going through another ritual in front of the congregation.

On a morning, where the autumn threatened to leech out from the trees in golden hues, Felix and I drove to the church. I was being confirmed with some local children and Betty and Bunnie held candles for me as we prayed. Gabriel, smiling, marked with holy water the sign of the cross on my forehead. I repeated some of the words he said in unison with the children. Afterwards we all received Holy Communion. I felt awkward being watched by the brethren of the parish for being part of this special service particularly at my age as I sat next to children smartly dressed for the occasion. Behind me, I sensed Felix smirking and Gabriel proffered a wink which made me giggle as I opened my mouth for bread and wine to become part of the Church of England.

Gabriel gave me a gift, a copy of the 1662 version of a Book of Common Prayer. I wondered that an original probably lay in the library shelves but I beamed up at our gorgeous vicar and thanked him for his kind thought and I promised to read it. I felt some regret that my sessions with Gabriel would now end.

Felix and I went back to the Manor and I cooked a lunch and Felix fed and played with the dogs and went to the cellar to fetch wine. Tarbo creaked, her limbs stiff and tired. Whilst Felix and I were making love on that Sunday afternoon, Tarbo lay on her bed and fell asleep forever. Felix found her. He was distraught and he went to the walled garden and dug her a grave next to Buster.

The patch was overgrown and for the first time I noticed a row of mounds.

"Is this where all the past pets have been buried?" I asked.

Felix kicked at the earth.

"All along this wall, Rose. Dogs and cats rotting in the ground since God knows when. These last six bumps have been family dogs. My mother's Chihuahua, my father's black Labrador. Kane and Tallulah, my first sheepdogs and now Buster and Tarbo."

He hugged me. "Poor old Tarbo."

"Yes," I said in a sympathetic voice. "Poor old Tarbo."

He bent down to fill in the hole with dirt and hesitated. Picking up a clump of sod he pulled at the roots and tore something out. Holding it up in the light he cried,

"Rose, come here, look. It's a ring. A jewelled ring and it looks like gold."

He handed it to me. I recognised it at once, it was Isabella's, the princess from Spain. I rubbed off the mud and Felix followed me like an obedient dog back to the kitchen where I ran it under the tap. It was gold and the large stone was the colour of topaz skies. I asked Felix to bring some cotton buds and I washed the ring in mild soapy water. It revealed its beauty to us when Felix dried it with a tea towel. I wanted to say that I knew who the ring had belonged to but I was afraid to tell Felix that I had been nosing around his house. I thought he would be angry. But, perhaps, it was going to be my house now too.

He scratched his head.

"I've seen this ring somewhere before, Rose. In my mind I can see it on a woman's finger but I can't think where."

"Probably on one of those old paintings," I said.

"Yes, you are right, that'll be it. Here, Rose, try it on."

He slipped the ring on the third finger of my left hand. It fitted perfectly. My fingers were as small as the ring and I held up my hand for Felix to see.

"That's the engagement ring sorted out, Rose."

"What Felix? Really?"

The sapphire in the ring was enormous. A tingle ran up my arm and I felt awkward wearing Isabella's ring. I was terrified of losing it so when I was working, I kept it on the windowsill over the sink. Mrs T. admired it greatly.

"Fancy finding that in the ground. Might be more out there, Rose, think of that?"

What it did make me think was that I should buy Felix a wedding ring and when Old Tom gave me Betty's message about visiting Shrugsborough I thought it would be an ideal opportunity. Felix had removed Hannah's gifted and binding wedding ring from his finger. He had left it on the bedside table so I took that with me for the measurement. I held it in my hand and I thought of Hannah on her own wedding day. Whether it was the ring or my mood, sadness and grief came over me. I put it in my purse and snapped it shut.

It turned out to be fun hopping around the town and browsing around jewellers. Betty and I had lunch in our favourite café. She had been indifferent about my

176

announcement. I think she was uncertain because she understood Felix's history. But when I asked her to be my maid of honour she came around and we hunted for a dress for her to wear. We also visited lots of bridal shops to seek out my wedding gown.

I had asked Betty's daughter to be a flower girl and her son to be a page boy. Jacob seemed reluctant but Molly had jumped up and down in excitement. I chose a duck-egg blue for them both as Betty had looked so nice in that colour at Gabriel's wedding and a dark suit with a blue waistcoat and tie for Jacob.

I thought about my first wedding. My extended waistline. Gruff Wayne and my father. This wedding was going to be different.

Trying on heaps of dresses I eventually chose a plain ivory silk with a sweetheart neckline. I insisted going into the changing room on my own. I hated anyone seeing my scars. I chose a duck-egg blue ribbon to tie under my breast and to continue the wedding theme I booked a morning suit for Felix with the same coloured waistcoat as Jacob. Betty and I enjoyed our trip and on the way home we gabbled and chatted about our day.

"Have you thought any more about driving lessons, Rose?"

"Oh yes, I need to find someone to come to the Manor."

"'Bout time you had a telephone up there, Rose. You should talk to Felix, he of all people should know how important that is." She emphasised the *he*.

She was referring, of course, to the night that Hannah died. Ignoring this I told her that I would talk to Felix about it.

In the meantime, I'd arranged for my driving lessons and they were going well. With luck I would be in a position to take my test early in the New Year. Mum and Trevor said that they would buy me a second-hand car as a wedding present. This was generous. I was excited about having the freedom to drive myself.

177

Gabriel had suggested 22nd December as our wedding day, commenting that the church would be at its best decorated ready for the Christmas season. It was just about enough time for me to organise everything. I arranged the wedding reception at the Callow Arms. Brian was astounded by my news and gawped at me for a while until it had sunk in before he went to get the diary to write in the date.

Betty helped me organise the invitations and to allocate people at the wedding tables for the breakfast. On one of our excursions to town I collected Felix's new wedding ring. The shopkeeper asked what I wanted to do with the other band that I'd left with him. I hadn't thought about it. I would replace it in Felix's bedside cupboard and asked the jeweller to give me a box for it. Secretly, part of me wanted to throw it in the lake.

Mrs T. and I had stopped for a coffee break. For a reason only known to her, she chose to casually drop into the conversation it was she whom Felix went to when he needed to buy things from the lists I'd left. All those shopping baskets he had dropped off came from her. He never went into town, she told me. On those visits, Felix and her partner Ivor would chat about ley-farming on account of Ivor's experience of working on the Callow lands and he would hand me your lists.

"I must say young Rose, it came as a surprise to us, we were very puzzled by you. I'm sure Felix wouldn't mind me saying that we are like parents to him."

I had seen photographs of Felix's parents and I could not imagine anything more opposite. However, I had not met 'Mr Jones' so I chose to be silent. Did I detect a hint of jealousy? I wasn't sure but I could imagine very well Mrs T. mothering Felix. She told me that she had a son of her own, Richard, who was in his forties. Mrs T. spoke of him proudly and it was obvious that she missed him a lot. He was working in Sheffield for a steel company. He married a woman called Anita. That wasn't her real name she told me. She was an Asian girl with a

178

similar name but Mrs T. couldn't pronounce it so she called her Anita. I sensed that Anita was resented greatly by her mother-in-law.

"Only places I've seen Felix Langley is up on the Callow Stones and down at the grave at the church."

She mischievously added that it was known that Felix would sometimes sleep on the top of his wife's grave. The previous incumbent had to have words. Apparently, Felix had responded by telling him to go to hell.

Inwardly I was upset by what Mrs T. had told me so that when I next saw Gabriel, I asked if he ever saw Felix sleeping on Hannah's grave. Gabriel assured me that he had not seen any evidence of Felix doing that. I was relieved as I only wanted Felix to concentrate on me, not his dead wife. I felt cross with Mrs T. for mentioning it. She never spoke of it again but I remember how I felt. Everything always came back to Hannah. Dead, cold Hannah.

In the black of the night I awoke shivering. My dream was of Hannah rising up from her grave as Felix lay waiting to caress her. She was wearing her wedding dress and the pair lay entwined, the white of her dress smeared with mud as they kissed and made love. I drank some water and cried myself to sleep.

When mum and Trevor arrived mum looked terrific. She was blooming and still had a tan from her holiday in Benidorm. Trevor appeared awkward but I purposefully levelled my conversation to him so that he felt included. Mum announced that she and Trevor were to marry once Trevor's divorce came through, sometime next year they hoped. When I showed her my engagement ring she swelled with pride and babbled to Trevor in excitement. I prepared lunch and then we took the path to the Callow Stones. Trevor was in good shape and we walked together as mum dragged her feet stopping now and then with the excuse that she was taking in the view.

"I'm looking forward to meeting Felix," Trevor said. "Does he play golf?"

I laughed out loud at the thought of Felix playing golf.

"I take that as a 'no' then?"

"He's far too busy with the farm, Trevor. It's his life."

"Not too much of his life, Rose. He needs to leave some time for you."

I looked at Trevor. His thick hair was swept back with Brylcreem and he smelt of Brut aftershave. He was also tanned; a deeper brown than mum's. He looked healthy and trim in his golfing top and chinos. I looked over at mum. She looked well and younger dressed in jeans and a pink blouse. She'd taken to wearing sunglasses on her head, like Bunnie, I thought. Her new image suited her. Trevor would look after mum, I knew.

"You'll meet him when we get back, he's coming home early for tea. We thought we would drive into Churchbury for a drink at the Callow Arms if you fancy?"

"That would be nice, Rose, your mum will like that."

Trevor waited for mum and when she reached us he placed his arms around her shoulders as the pair faced out towards the rolling moorland. When we walked around the circle to the other side mum pointed down the valley.

"I was born down there, Trevor. About ten miles along the valley."

We stared to where she was pointing as she went to sit on a rock to enjoy the splendour and peace. Suddenly, I realised what mum was saying. It sunk in. I hadn't really registered it before but mum's family was from around here. I exclaimed loudly,

"Mum that must be what drew me here. What a coincidence that you lived so close and I came here. Oh, I know I told you about the two old ladies at the bus stop and how I had overheard their conversation, but honestly mum, I think even if they hadn't even been there I would have found my way to Shrugsboroughshire on my own. Mum, I keep dreaming about a woman named Eliza. They're really vivid and she calls to me. She called to me when I was in Birmingham before I knew this place existed. Do you know who she is?"

Mum looked hesitant. Trevor was observing me and then we both looked at mum.

"Well, I do recall there was an Eliza, I think, back in the family tree somewhere. But it was a common name. You're right though it is strange how you ended up in these parts but I don't think you should fill your head with such nonsense; it's a coincidence, that's all."

I began to protest but Trevor moved to where mum was sitting and put his arms about her.

"It's very quiet here, isn't it Rose," he said almost whispering.

By his tone, I realised he wanted me to shut up. Perhaps he could see what I couldn't in that this conversation was painful for my mum as it brought back to her upsetting memories.

On the way back I told mum to 'bin' all my things from home. I had lived without them for this long so obviously didn't need them. She asked me if I was sure. I told her that I was. My past was the past and that was that.

"I can't believe you are my same timid little girl Rose. You were always so quiet and now look at you. Making such big decisions at such a young age."

Poor mum! When I told her about the lightning strike she nearly fainted. It took me a long time to convince her that I was feeling fine and that scars were scars and I could live with them. She wanted to see them but I wouldn't let her.

She handed me an invitation to Linda's wedding. I rightly suspected she was trying to cheer me up. Linda was getting married in July of the following year at a posh hotel in Birmingham city centre. I planned to ring her, once the telephone had been installed, to tell her that I too was getting married in December and to ask her to come with her fiancé.

Over supper, I realised that I did not know Felix as well as I thought I did. Mostly, I think he was glad to find something in common to talk to Trevor about but as it turned out Felix did play golf and Trevor invited him to his golf club in the Birmingham suburbs for when we went over to his and mum's wedding. Mum and I talked about my wedding and then we left for the pub. As we chatted Felix turned to Trevor and said,

"Three weddings I've been told about in a week. Wedding this and wedding that."

"It's your fault," I exclaimed from the back, "you started it!"

Trevor looked at Felix, "I think you did Felix, I think you did."

Felix shrugged his shoulders and pulled into the car park at the Callow Arms.

I had not been there socially since Gabriel's wedding. I was worried that people would say something about my behaviour. However, it was the usual crowd at the bar and a few tourists tucking into high piled plates of food at the tables. Brian greeted us with a grin and Felix ordered us all a drink. While he was at the bar mum whispered to me,

"Rose, Felix seems really nice. From what I can gather he is transformed. When I nipped to the loo there was a lady in there talking to her friend who said that she barely recognised him. She thought he was his brother. You said he had a twin brother Rose, Fergus is it? Do you love Felix, Rose?" Mum was being very direct. I knew it was because she was worried about me. "I only ask because he has had a troubled past. This has all happened very suddenly." She was talking rapidly as if she wanted to get all her questions out before she forgot them.

I patted her arm. "Yes mum, I do love him. I've grown to love him."

"The age gap, Rose," mum began but I hushed her and told her that I knew what I was doing.

The weeks moved quickly like a high speed train hurtling towards its destination. The days were like its wheels moving clickety-click, clickety-click as I prepared for the wedding. I was also keeping up with my driving lessons. A telephone was, at last, installed. Mum and I could now chat on a regular basis and I enjoyed speaking with her about plans as the wedding drew near. I rang Linda and she and Charlie could make our wedding. I was really pleased. Linda was bursting with news as she had bought a horse and called it Patsy and she and Charlie had moved in together. They were living in a Warwickshire village and their cottage had a paddock. It was her dream come true. She was excited for me, too.

"It's funny how things turn out, isn't it Rose. You living out there and me with Charlie. We've gone up in the world, ain't we?"

I had never thought about my position as 'going up in the world' as Linda had put it. For me, it was about moving on, a natural occurring progression and perhaps if I was honest, about running away from my past. I was reinventing myself and in her own way, and probably without realising it, Linda was, too.

On the morning of our wedding, Felix drove us to the church in his pick-up truck. Traditionally, he was not supposed to see me before I arrived at the altar, but it was the only way that we could get down the track. There was no point in hiring wedding cars as they would be wrecked and I refused to walk down it in my wedding dress.

Felix held me tight and said that I looked beautiful.

"I love you, Felix."

He did not answer me but shuffled me into the front whilst the dogs, now big and strong, leapt into the trailer. He had cleaned the truck and placed a tartan blanket for me to sit on over the passenger seat. We arrived at the church and Fergus ushered Felix ahead of me. Betty fussed over my dress and then the organist played and I walked down the aisle on my mother's arm. Mum cried all the way along but I fixed my eyes on the altar ahead not wanting to cry and spoil my make-up. Rows of pews were filled with Felix's family and tenants and their families. Betty and her children sat with Young Tom, Old Tom and Gwyneth.

After Gabriel asked who was giving me away, mum said, 'I am' and then went to sit next to Trevor. She was the only person amongst the congregation that was truly related to me. All the while I held Felix's arm shaking with nerves and excitement. At the end of the ceremony Gabriel invited Felix, 'to kiss your bride'. Felix gave me a long and passionate kiss and the congregation whistled and cheered and clapped as we left grinning down the aisle together for photographs. Outside we were showered in confetti. It was a cold morning and the ground was covered in an icy frost. In my flimsy dress, I did not feel the cold as my love was burning with desire for Felix. Felix had placed a gold band on my finger and Isabella's ring greedily soaked in the dim rays of sunlight so that it sparkled brightly like my heart.

Tenant farmers had tied empty beer cans to the rear of the truck so when we left the church for the Callow Arms we bumped and clattered along. We laughed and giggled and he rubbed his hand on my thigh finding my garter.

"I could stop the truck right here and take you Rose."

"Not with the vicar and his wife following behind you don't," I screamed with laughter.

I fell in love with Felix. He was now my husband. Deep inside I knew that he would never love me in the way that I loved him. In my heart I knew that he was still in love with Hannah. Her memory and the memory of that tragic night haunted him every day.

The reception was a triumph. Felix's speech was short. He spoke of me. His beautiful wife. *'She can cook and clean and with Old Tom's help she's not done a bad job in the garden. Next job is to test her in the farming business. Can't wait to see her with her arm up a sheep's bottom. Let's see how she holds up to that one shall we?'*

Of course, he was joking and I thought he was a bit coarse but he made me realise that I was in some ways indispensable to him even if he was not entirely in love with me. His farming companions find his speech hilarious. I could see mum wince out of the corner of my eye.

Fergus, of course, was his best man. He could barely read his speech as his eyes went misty and his bottom lip wobbled so overcome was he for his brother's new found happiness. Our reception guests pulled out paper tissues to blot their runny noses. I looked across the room and saw and understood why all those people were upset. Hannah. It was my day, supposedly one of the best days in my life and I was sharing it with a person in a grave. A paradox on my wedding day. Everyone happy for Felix but sad for their remembering. What were they thinking? Why weren't they thinking of me. Why wasn't I in the spotlight? I was furious and jealous and I decided I would find a moment to throw Hannah's gold ring in the lake and make a curse like Maud Thompson had cursed those twins. My rage was powerful and I fought against my emotion of disillusion. What a foolish girl I had become. Felix would never love me. This room was full of his friends and family, his tenants. All who had known Hannah since birth. All who remembered her today of all days. Even Linda wiped tears from her face. At last Fergus regained control and raised a glass to the bride and groom. I swallowed hard and raised my glass to drink myself into solace.

I'd hired a Country and Western band and the caller shouted out the dance moves so that everyone could join in. Our guests jigged about on the dance floor and the young farmers grew drunk. Sausage rolls and beer got stamped into the carpet as the merriment grew stronger.

185

In a corner I saw Charlie and Felix chatting for ages. They had animals in common as he was a vet and Felix a farmer. I had never seen Felix so animated in conversation with anyone before and I watched him studying his mannerisms trying to learn more about the man I had just married.

Linda and I had a few moments to talk and when the time came for me to throw my bouquet, she caught it.

Felix avoided drinking too much and later that evening when our guests were still revelling, we sneaked away. Felix was a tender and considerate lover and that night we shared our love over and over until we both fell asleep in each other's arms. I put my thoughts of envy into a box but I kept the key ready to unlock them when the time was right.

There was no chance of us having a honeymoon because of the farm commitments so the next morning I got up and cooked a massive English breakfast. We were both ravenous from our lovemaking. It was my birthday, too.

We had not discussed having children and I was finding it hard to broach the subject with him but over breakfast, as he dipped toast into his eggs, I asked him, quite bluntly,

"Felix, shall we have children?"

"More than anything, Rose. More than anything. Actually, let's not waste any time." He inclined his head towards the door and up the stairs but I laughed and said,

"He and I had too much to do and anyway I would have to see the doctor about coming off the Pill."

"Didn't know that you were on the Pill, Rose?"

"Well, it was a precaution, Felix, I didn't want to waddle down the aisle."

The words reminded me of my first marriage. This conversation chilled me, its rawness. My husband who knew little about me and I who knew so little about him. I felt reckless and wondered whether I had married in haste. The cruel and bitter pill of resentment tasted fresh on my lips.

In this moment, I longed to tell him that I had lost a son too but no time ever seemed appropriate, certainly not now.

"I've got time to practise, Rose. Come on it's our first day of wedlock. And oh yes, your birthday.

"Did you think I'd forgotten?"

He stuffed the last piece of bacon into his mouth, scooped me up and carried me upstairs to pleasure me and him all over again. Our art of conversation may have been sparse but our art of lovemaking was profound. Afterwards he handed to me a set of keys.

"A 4×4 car for you Rose, so you'd better hurry up and pass your driving test!"

I hugged him.

Mum rang to wish me happy birthday and I told her not to worry about buying me a car. She was happy for me.

Dark months yawned into blackness as the sky grew cold and dappled clouds skipped overhead threatening snow.

Bunnie and Fergus invited us to have Christmas Day with them and I loved being in their warm house. The twins and Emily opened their presents under the tree, its branches bent under the baubles and tinsel. After a scrumptious lunch we all sat by the fire. I offered to help with the washing up but Bunnie would not hear of it. Fergus poured brandy and the children insisted that we played charades. Felix and Fergus grumpily declined. The two of them went to Fergus's office to no doubt discuss farming.

Hilarity filled the room as the rest of us tried to fathom the mimes that we wrote down secretly on pieces of paper. Ridiculous clues for television shows and films to act out. I was useless as I had not watched a television for years. At the end of the game I turned to Bunnie.

"I love your home, Bunnie. I want to make the Manor more homely but I don't want to make demands so early in our marriage. That's not the reason why I married Felix. I love him,

I really do and he's changed so much, I don't want to force him to make more changes so soon."

"He's certainly changed, Rose. You have brought us our old Felix back. Fergus is so happy with you Rose, you are a miracle worker. For more years than I can remember Felix has mourned Hannah and his babies. It's so lovely to see that Felix has a future. Take things one day at a time, that's my advice. Things are always difficult at first. When I married Fergus it was hard for him to adjust. This is my inheritance, not his. Although, we are, in fact, related far back."

Hannah, again, Hannah. In every conversation. Why couldn't people realise that she was dead. I was Felix's wife, surely people could see that?

Tipsy from wine and probably feeling more relaxed to talk about herself than usual, Bunnie talked about her family's history.

"A woman called 'Honora' married into the Langley family. It was in the Georgian era and she had come from fashionable Bath. Imagine coming from that environment to the isolation of the Manor? Apparently, she was great friends with Georgiana, the Duchess of Devonshire and they shared many secrets together. She must have missed her friend terribly and the elegance of that society.

"She hated the Manor so she built this house and moved in. Legend has it that she lived here whilst her husband remained at the Manor each of them refusing to budge. Somehow they had children together so it can't have been all bad. I am a descendant of hers. If you did the genealogy I think that Fergus and Felix are my cousins somewhere along the line."

I was fascinated as she spoke and I recalled an oil painting with a woman with flirting eyes and the ostrich feathers in her oversized wig. I felt sure that it was her whom Bunnie was talking about.

A chain of thoughts filled my brain and I thought of the woman in the tower. I had often thought of her. I wondered if there was a painting of her tucked behind the tapestry and then I remembered the keys I had hidden behind Isabella's painting. I resolved to use them and find the woman in the tower in the New Year when the season had settled.

PART FIVE

Footsteps that tremor on the tower stairs cause a shudder in your heart.

CHAPTER 12

We spent New Year's Eve wrapped up in warm jumpers hitched up by the kitchen fire. After supper Felix poured brandy into crystal glasses and the liquor burned at our inner tubes and filled our lungs with heat.

Life resumed to our normal routine. Felix stretched out his days on the farm, working all the hours that daylight would allow, and I meandered around the Manor completing chores with new vigour. Mrs Thompson was not due for a few days, as she had taken time off to be with her own family. Richard and Anita were visiting and I thought of Anita probably being totally ostracised by her mother-in-law. Being Indian, I made the assumption that she probably wasn't a Christian and didn't celebrate Christmas and part of me felt rather sorry for. I suspected Richard felt it was better for everyone for them to remain in the north.

Daydreaming in the snug, I envisioned making this room comfortable. A place where Felix and I could relax. Somewhere where we could sit and read and be close to the large hearth. It was uncomfortable sitting in the kitchen in the place where the twins had died and a painful reminder of Felix's other life. I would stare up at the painting of the Manor. Finally, I worked it out. The tower was absent. That's what was different. It did not form part of the original building, that's why it wasn't in the first Francis' painting. The snug could become our new together room, away from sad and lonely memories.

I broached the idea of opening up the snug and redecorating it with Felix. His response was hesitant but finally he agreed. He allowed me to engage some local workers and I set about removing the items of furniture, ornaments and pictures so that there was a clear space to begin. Firstly, I cleaned and scrubbed the fireplace until it gleamed.

Visiting Churchbury, I picked out some wallpaper in a cool, calm light green with exotic flowers painted in muted yellows that glared out with romantic promises. I felt it was in keeping with the room. The wood panels had been removed. This room would be cheery. I rolled up the tatty worn rugs and planned to store them in the long gallery when Mrs T. came back to help me. My senses and intuition told me that great changes were going to happen at the Manor and if I had my own way a lot would be because of my actions.

I chose a silver grey carpet and pastel green moire curtains. The two fireside chairs were old but comfy and their colours blended with the rest of the room. Once everything had been completed I began to wash the rare and delicate ornaments and placed them back arranging them to suit myself. Instead of replacing the oversized painting, of an ancient ancestor above the fireplace, I chose a gilded mirror from another room and persuaded the decorators to hang it for me. I placed two pink candle holders, with crystal droplets, on the mantel which lit up the room as their light reflected in the mirror and gave off a whole new ambience. I managed to persuade the decorators to take the rugs away and throw them into a skip.

When I showed him the completed room, Felix loved it. He kissed me determinedly wanting to make love to me on the new carpet. He had only just come in from his work and he smelled of sheep so I fought him off giggling and promised that we would christen the room with our lovemaking once he had bathed and changed. While he went off to do that I dished out supper. We ate and he just kept staring at me with a devilish grin knowing that his pleasure was soon to arrive.

As it turned out, it wasn't ideal making love on the carpet as I got 'carpet burn' on my front and it rubbed on my scar. We changed position and I sat on top. He came quickly, aroused by my breasts bobbing around and the feel of his penis penetrating deeply into me. I was beginning to realise that Felix's desires for sex were insatiable. I wondered if he had had sex with anyone else over his years of mourning but I guessed not as his link to Hannah was so strong. I enjoyed Felix's lovemaking. I found him erotic and neither of us minded being naked together. He adored my breasts and he would stroke them in bed at night, lulling himself to sleep as he lay arced next to me.

There was a stirring inside me which I recognised. I thought I was pregnant.

Mrs T. loved the new room and expressed that I had a flair for décor. She suggested that I should tackle some more rooms in the house. She made me think. Felix never questioned the money side of things but I had no clue about what we could afford. Was the neglect of this old house because of his grief or was it down to money? These were things that I didn't want to ask. Felix and his parents had allowed the east wing to dilapidate and I could only guess that this was because of finance.

I kept my notion of my pregnancy to myself. I would only be sure after a pregnancy test and so I booked in to see Dr Comickery the next week. Looking down at Isabella's ring I thought of the generations of women before me who had given birth to children fathered by the men of this place. Dare I believe that I was continuing in their footsteps?

Brighter days were beckoning, the grey turned into washed-out blue and crocuses forced skyward to greet the expansive light as I went over to the Lodge to give it an airing. Having been busy with the decorating and distracted by my impending pregnancy test, it had been some time since I had thought of the woman in the tower.

As I crossed to the Lodge I turned to look up at the window. To my surprise she was there. Standing perfectly still, her face a shadow. Her sadness overwhelmed me. Her misery clung to her; an aura of black.

I hurried along and when I returned to the Manor I went to find the keys that I had hidden. Tentatively, I went to the stairwell and tried each key in the lock until a surge of creaking wood splintered and cracked as I pushed the door inwards. My whole body was trembling, I felt scared, really, really scared. I took a deep breath.

There were a few winding steps which led me to a room that I was not expecting.

The room was square and surprisingly big and lavish. An ebony table with twisted legs sat at the end of a four-poster bed and an enamelled bowl of fresh mimosa sat on its top next to red calf skin books piled on their sides, their titles etched in gold. Deep crimson damask hung around the bed posts and I felt the deepness of the rug beneath my feet. I stood wide-eyed at the view before me.

In the window, where I'd seen the woman, was a tall silver candelabra with the candles burned out. There appeared to be another room leading off and I glimpsed through the open door a table set with a wash bowl and pitcher and I could just make out dresses hung and luxuriating in the dappled light. It was evident to me that someone was living here; and it appeared, in some luxury. The linen on the bed was brilliant white and the pillow slips were edged in lace. A throw of crimson damask fell neatly across the bed. At each side of the bed was a cabinet and on one I saw a bible. It was open with a black beaded rosary tagging the page. I took a deep breath as I took the courage to nervously call out, 'Hello, hello. Is anybody there?' No-one answered, so with my heart beating fast and the hairs on the back of my neck erect, I walked into the little room. It was obviously a dressing room and ladies' accoutrements filled the spaces. I noticed more beautiful dresses and a black velvet cloak hanging on the rail. There was no-one here so I returned to the bedroom. It was empty and I walked across to the window. As I leant against the window, to the view below, I pictured myself looking up to this spot where I had often seen the unhappy soul of the woman.

Suddenly, a freezing breath tickled my neck and a soft voice whispered, "Rose", as an icy finger dug into my back. I froze, too scared to turn. The voice grew louder as my name was called again. Quivering, I turned and I gasped at the vision before me. It was the woman, her dark Titian hair flowing about her shoulders, her face thin and bony and I stared into black eyes deep and mournful. A shiver crept over me and I opened my mouth to speak but nothing came.

"Help me Rose, help me find my boys," she almost screamed into my ear frightening my innards.

Her garment was so thin that I could see her nipples and the shape of her pubic region. She reached out to me with her delicate hands and cried in desperation her voice rising, "Rose, help me, Rose. Where are my boys?"

I was so afraid, I am ashamed to say, that I scampered out of that room as fast as I could. I chased down the stairs and slammed the door behind me not stopping to lock it and ran to my bed where I lay under the covers trembling and staring at the door afraid that the apparition was following and coming to get me.

Flickers of light touched the window and eventually I ventured out of bed and opened the door determined to make my way to the kitchen. I took the long way round, too afraid to enter through the gallery door and down through the cellar. With each step I expected the prod of a thin cold finger into my

197

sweaty back but I made it to the kitchen and quickly made a cup of tea. I sat down to draw my breath. I felt chilly so I lit the fire and sat next to it watching the flames lick the burning logs as I played out the scene in my mind trying to make sense of the woman in the room.

It wasn't Hannah, I was sure of that. I had seen her photograph and this woman bore no likeness to her. She seemed to be from another time and yet I could not work out how she came to be there. Who had brought the fresh flowers, particularly as they were not in season? The room was well looked after and there was fresh water in the washing bowl. I kept looking over my shoulder as I thought that she may come to join me at any moment. Thankfully she did not but it took me hours to have the strength and courage to leave my chair and prepare for Felix's return. I decided to keep this encounter to myself.

Anyway, I may have imagined it. I heard that pregnant women behaved in strange ways at times so I blamed it on my condition. I pushed silly thoughts to the back of my mind and tried to focus on my visit to Dr Comickery and I looked forward to breaking my good news to Felix. However, I was disturbed, knowing that I had come face to face with a ghost. When I thought of the woman in the tower my brain felt like a spider was crawling across it.

Felix commented that I was quiet that evening but I shrugged it off saying that I was tired. Mrs T. and I were working on the library I told him and there was much more to be done than we had at first imagined.

"I'm going to catalogue all the books and this means taking them all out, dusting and cleaning and recording each one. Some of them are so ancient, darling that the dust rises up like a gathering storm and gets into our nostrils and throats. I don't understand how the house has been allowed to fall into such a state of disrepair and quite frankly, a mess." And then I added, "The east wing is falling down and it's dangerous."

I said the words without thinking and immediately I regretted it. Each letter, each syllable sounded like a slur on Felix and his parents. But worse, I knew, on Hannah's attention to the house.

Felix stared at me long and hard. He took a deep breath. I could tell he was trying to brush over my comments.

"My parents did not care for this house, Rose. Actually, no one has cared about this house for a hundred years or more. But I find myself the heir whether I like it or not and you are now my wife. Rose, if you wish to care for it, that's up to you but don't expect me to ever love this vengeful, cursed place."

His voice was spiteful but I don't think he was aiming it at me. He was trying to encapsulate the history of the Manor and how it had spent, at times, its worth on its inhabitants.

I was feeling bold.

"Do we have any money to do it up?" I asked, emphasising the *we*.

"We can manage the centre and the west wing stables but the east wing is a loss to us, Rose."

There was some warmth in his voice and I took advantage.

"Will you give me the go ahead to start refurbishments, Felix? I know that I have no right to say this but some of your heirlooms, that you don't seem to care for, are probably valuable and perhaps we could sell some to help us fund the changes. What do you think?"

I held my breath.

"Would that make you happy, Rose?"

I nodded longing to tell him that I was keeping a secret that I knew would make him happy too.

At the surgery Dr Comickery asked me lots of questions and arranged for my records to be sent from my old doctor's practice. I realised that he would find out that I had been pregnant before so I was honest with him.

"You promise you won't tell anyone?"

"Rose, what is discussed in my office is highly confidential. I have taken the Hippocratic Oath you know. It's not for me to tell you what to do but it may be a good idea to tell Felix? It's just that it may make you feel better about the whole thing, I'm sure he'll understand."

"It's not about understanding. He will I know. It's just... it's just that I want to be positive about the future and not to dwell on the past. What with everything that Felix went through with Hannah."

He bent his head when I said that. That name, Hannah. Then he asked, "Did everything in your pregnancy go well, Rose? Sickness, bleeding anything else I should know about?"

"I had some morning sickness but all went fine until Patrick was stillborn."

Dr Comickery leaned towards me over his desk with a serious face.

"We have new technology, Rose to help prevent that and I am going to send you to the main hospital in Shrugsborough for a scan."

"A scan? What's that?"

"It's nothing to worry about and it won't hurt a bit."

I took the train to travel to hospital feeling apprehensive and staring out of the window. What was this scan and would it hurt my baby? I had put off telling Felix until after this visit unsure about what was going to happen. I checked in at the reception and sat in a waiting room filled with other expectant mothers at all stages and ages. A nurse called my name twice before I realised it was me. I was so used to being Rose Howard and when she called Mrs Langley I had ignored her thinking it was somebody else. She led me to a single room where she asked me to undress to my underwear and to put on a gown.

The smells of the hospital reminded me of my stay after the lightning had struck me and I looked down at my scars healed and pink.

In a short while she came back and explained that she was going to spread some gel on my tummy which would feel cold. She was right, the cold penetrated my stomach and made me twitch.

"Just relax."

Rolling her arm around she picked up pictures from inside my womb that showed on a screen. I was fascinated and amazed. She did not speak but observed the screen intently as I screwed my eyes trying to make out the pattern of life in black and grey.

"Nothing to worry about, dear but I am just going to bring the doctor in to have a look. Won't be a tic."

Dread overcame me. Something was wrong. I began to sweat and I could feel my heart beating irregularly in my chest.

A doctor, who seemed just a little older than me, came in with his white coat swinging out behind him. He held out his hand.

"Hello Mrs Langley. Nothing to worry about. Nurse has asked me to check your scan." He smiled as he shook my hand.

He made noises, hmm and ah and I watched the back of his neck pimpled like a youth as he moved his head.

"You are quite right nurse, well done."

The nurse beamed up at him.

"Mrs Langley, not sure whether this is going to be good news or bad but there are two in there. Twins, congratulations."

I gasped and then I cried and the nurse took my hand. She shared a glance with the doctor who then left.

"It's a bit of a shock, dear having twins?"

"No, you don't understand. I am so grateful that everything is all right."

"Of course it is. Two strong heartbeats. Look, do you want to see?"

I nodded and watched as she pointed out the little beans spinning and beating inside me.

When I left that room I could not stop smiling. I was elated and I wanted to dance and jig and I wanted most of all to tell Felix.

April sunshine lit my journey home from the train station as I caught the bus and it wound its way back to the countryside around Callow Crest Manor. Lambs gambolled and jumped in delight as they baaed and bleated seeking out their mothers. Fluffy clouds ambled in the sky and I wanted to skip about and leap on their cotton wool cushions.

Impatiently I waited for Felix to return home. I was bursting at the seams.

We sat through dinner and then I suggested that we moved to the snug. I had lit the fire and poured him a brandy ready in anticipation that he might be shocked by my news.

Once he was comfortable and before he got too suspicious of my actions, I curled up at his side and announced,

"Darling, I... we... well, I'm pregnant!"

It took a while for my words to penetrate his mind as he unscrambled them.

He stared at me and then,

"Rose, Rose, you clever girl. Oh my God! Oh my God!"

Then he began to fuss and pile cushions up behind me and it wasn't until he calmed down that I told him that I was having twins.

He frowned. His Cross of Soot furrowed deep in his brow. I sensed his worry and the memories of his little sons. I said nothing.

Then he held me in his arms and kissed my face.

"Twins Rose, twins. I'll bet they'll be boys, they always are."

CHAPTER 13

Felix had obviously called in on Mrs T. as the next time she came she had her friend Alwyn with her.

"Glad to hear your news, Rose. Alwyn's come to help. Felix wants to make sure that you get lots of rest."

I wasn't ill, I explained, I was three months pregnant but neither woman would hear of me doing chores. Alwyn seemed to be a shy person. She was exceptionally thin and she wore the same apron as Mrs T. which looked baggy on her and the cord around her middle was looped twice round her small waist. Like Mrs T. she smelled of cigarettes. She rarely spoke but repeated the end of Mrs T.'s sentences.

"Lots of rest", she smiled at me.

However, I would have been bored resting, so I set about in the library sorting through the books and making towers on subject matters, biology, ornithology, travel, history and so on. My predecessor had shelved the books by author. They probably had great insight to each writer but the books were so old that none of us recognised them; so I catalogued them by subject and then in alphabetical order by last name. This way you could put your hand on any book under each category. It was tiring work as there must have been near to a thousand books. Some were falling apart and I felt that this collection warranted an expert eye so I found Yellow Pages to seek out someone who could at least put some value on them as I had noticed that many were first editions.

There was no-one in the local area but I found someone in London who agreed to travel up to Shrugsboroughshire to have a look. I offered to pay his fee and expenses and put him up at the Callow Inn.

Meanwhile, I took my driving test and passed first time. Felix was so impressed that he gave me money to buy whatever I wanted for our twins.

"Plenty of shopping trips – make sure you include a cot and blankets, be sure to buy plenty of blankets," he said.

I spoke to mum who screamed down the line at me in her joy at being a grandmother. When she had calmed she told me that it was bad luck to buy things before the babies were born. I ignored her thinking that it would be very unfair if anything happened to my twins on the strength of me buying cots, nappies and babygrows.

"That's brilliant news about passing your test, Rose. I'm glad Felix has bought you a decent car. Only the best for my grandchildren. Trevor and I were looking at a Mini in Solihull, only one owner but a 4x4 is much better and now you can drive it. They'll be more room for the twins. It's been sitting on the cobbles for a while, I wondered when you'd get around to it."

I listened to my mother stating the obvious. What was important was that we had found each other again. I wanted mum to be part of my children's lives. Mum rattled on a bit sometimes but she had become a new person since meeting Trevor. I couldn't help feeling that dad died for a reason. To give mum a new life. A happier life.

Driving gave me some independence which meant that I could bring over my expert man each day for a week and return him at the end of the evening.

On my first solo drive to Shrugsborough I sweated all the way. I managed to find a flat car park by the river and parked a long way away from the other cars as I slowly and carefully reversed into a bay. I got better at driving, with practice, as the years went by.

When our expert arrived he was dressed in fawn cords, a checked shirt, a crimson tie, brown brogues and a jacket with arm patches. He smelled fresh like a sea breeze. I guessed he was about forty and probably homosexual not that this bothered me. He was what my dad would have called a 'poof'. I fell in love with him in a way. Guy Hudson-Jones. Not sexually, of course, but because he was so knowledgeable and intelligent, I fell in love with his mind. After a few days we both realised that a week was not long enough for the work so he agreed to stay for a month.

One morning, on entering the library, we saw the tall iron candle holder knocked over and candles had rolled over the rug and some had landed on the bible table. Guy helped me put it back upright and return the candles to the holders. Four were missing. I remembered that I had taken two so we began to hunt for the other two but they were nowhere to be seen.

"That's odd," Guy said.

"Very odd," I replied.

"Perhaps it was a ghost, Rose?"

I must have gone pale as he hurriedly apologised saying he didn't mean to frighten me. He insisted that I sit down. He had impeccable manners.

Naturally, the woman in the tower had been lingering in the back of my mind but this felt very strange and I had a strong inclination that this was her hand. Or the hand of someone else not of this world. I felt it unlikely that she would ever leave her tower as she constantly watched from the window to seek out her sons.

Guy looked at me feeling that he had hit a nerve. He said no more and got back to work exhaustively compiling records. He

205

kept his records in an A4 ruled hardback notebook. I rather marvelled at his beautiful cursive handwriting.

Guy was interested to see the rest of the house so I offered to show him around. When we got to the long gallery I pulled back the tapestry to show him the paintings. I pointed out Isabella and her ring and he was dumbstruck when I showed him the sapphire on my finger.

"Goodness Rose, it's amazing. Fancy you finding her ring, it's astounding. It looks stunning on you."

The door to the cellar was open and a draught seeped out towards us. I shuddered.

"Where does that lead to?" he asked pointing to the door leading to the east wing at the end of the gallery.

"The east wing runs at an angle at the end of this gallery but it's blocked off as it is mainly derelict and this door leads to the cellar. You know, a quick entry and exit for the servants to the bedrooms."

I did not mention the tower above.

"A fascinating house, Rose. What a shame it has been allowed to deteriorate so badly."

"That's going to change, Guy. Felix and I are very keen to restore it to its former glory. It is such a big project and well, I don't think I am going to have much time to oversee it soon."

I patted my stomach to indicate my pregnancy.

"Well, I would be delighted to help for a fee of course. I have some experience. I've nothing booked in for six months so I am happy to see the project through and extend my visit."

"Let me talk to Felix," I said thinking that this would probably be a good idea.

Guy moved into the Lodge at the end of May. He stayed for six months and then travelled back frequently as the renovations took over a year in the end to finish but a lifetime to complete the total restoration of objet d'art. He had good connections and brought a coterie of expert historic renovators and builders with him and they stayed at the Callow Inn. Brian was very accommodating and gave us a good deal for the whole of their stay.

The men quickly got to work and rooms were sealed. Mrs T. and Alwyn continually chastised the men for creating dust and they found themselves wafting their cloths around scaffolding and workmen. It transpired that the roof needed completely renewing and the costs to the refurbishments grew. Felix would groan but then he would come and pat my tummy and say that it was all worth it.

I found myself stretched in all directions advising Guy, instructing Mrs T. and Alwyn and working with Old Tom in the garden which was a great respite. My belly grew and my breasts became heavy. I had to stave off Felix's advances in the bedroom using an old wives' tale as an excuse: 'it might hurt the baby' but actually it was because I was exhausted. Dr Comickery arranged the appointments at the hospital and I had further scans on the little beings inside me. The midwives and the obstetrician were pleased with the way things were going. My stomach protruded out and my twins developed basking in my womb. Through the whole of that summer I oversaw the refurbishment. Bunnie visited often and would make me sit and drink tea bringing home-made scones and jam and cream churned fresh from her cows.

One day she quite openly said that she was glad that Felix would have an heir as Gregory, with Archie's help, had enough land to cope with at Langley Hall. I was glad about that. I was growing to like Bunnie very much and I did not want the question of inheritance to spoil any of our family's relationships.

For some reason, Betty never came to the Manor. I could only guess that it was to do with 'class'. She was happy to go to Langley Hall as an employee but I think she felt uncomfortable about having tea at the Manor with me. I thought this was a shame as I was just like her after all. The fact that I lived in this grand house changed nothing about the person I was or where I had come from.

Marrying Felix came with a title of, 'Lady'. For a girl like me with my roots in Birmingham, I found this uncomfortable and for all my life I avoided using it.

Mother visited with Trevor, she was looking forward to being a grandma. Trevor teased her saying that he would have to trade her in for a younger model, now that she was going to be a grannie, but it was plain for all to see that he adored her.

Escaping the bedlam of the house, mum and I took a walk to the church. It was a wonderful summer's day. We wended along chatting merrily, watching buzzards soar and smelling the heather and the effervescent prickly gorse burnt bronze.

As we drank in the day I turned to mum and said,

"Mum, why don't you want to visit your family in Wales?"

We had reached the bench by the lakeside and I was glad to sit as the weight of my twins bore down on me.

Taking my hands in hers she spoke in her gentle accented lilt of Welsh and Birmingham.

"Rose, I can't believe you haven't worked it out? Think about your birth date and the date me and your dad got married."

Lately, and I blamed this wholly on my pregnancy, my mind was befuddled. I knew that mum was about thirty when she gave birth to me and she was now just over fifty. I was concentrating on her age. My hormones were all over the place and sometimes I found myself doing odd things like putting my handbag in the fridge.

Realisation dawned on me and I lifted my gaze to my mother's face who looked frightened of what I was going to say.

"I'm glad he's dead, mum."

"Don't say that, darling."

"But mum, he was such a hypocrite. The way he treated me when I was raped and fell pregnant and all the time he knew that he had made you pregnant out of wedlock. He deserves to be dead for the way he treated us both."

Mum didn't comment on what I had said. She merely replied, "Now you know why I can't go back. I'm not ashamed Rose and neither should you be but I'll never forgive them for the way they treated me. My parents and my brother. They made me feel so ashamed so bad about myself that I couldn't bear it. That's why I left. I couldn't imagine bringing up a child in that environment. They never forced me to marry Alex and leave home. But, and this is a big but, I was getting older and I thought that I would never leave the farm. I was passed over by the local boys as a teenager and I thought I would die an old maid. I felt I had nothing to lose with your dad. It was pure coincidence how we met. I had a friend called Sharon who had just got divorced and she wanted to go to Birmingham for a night out. Well, I say she was my friend but really it was down to the fact that I was the only single female left around. She had booked a hotel for the night. Sharon had been to Birmingham many times. We went to bars and ended up at a night club. I loved it Rose. It was so lively and vibrant and so different to what I was used to. Anyway, as it turned out, Sharon had already got a man. She'd arranged to meet him and she went off with her bloke. I was quite drunk, I'd never drunk so much before and your dad offered to take me back to the hotel. One thing led to another. Luckily, he gave me his phone number and I contacted him as soon as I realised I was pregnant and then I walked out of that farm forever. We had sex in the hotel you see, it just happened. In a way I think I thought, 'why not?' I was a virgin and I didn't want to die as a virgin, Rose. As it turns out, I love where I am. I love being in Birmingham and my job at the school. I would never have found Trevor. Things turned out right for me without my family and it will turn out all right for you too, Rose."

She squeezed my hand.

"The difference is that you have me Rose and always will." Then she exclaimed, "Twins! I can't believe it!"

"That all might just have been too much information for me mum," I squirmed. "I didn't need to know about the sex bit!"

She nodded and said that it was the truth and that there was nothing wrong in telling the truth. I wanted to tell her about the way dad's behaviour had upset me but I kept quiet. I was thinking I would tell the truth about how dad had made me feel but there was no need. Mum knew how I felt and it hurt. I could see no point of prolonging the agony and discussing it.

I suddenly had an urge to show mum Hannah and the children's grave. She looked sad as we stood over Hannah's grave and the tiny mound next to it.

"I visit Patrick now and again, Rose. I know it's difficult for you out here but I take some comfort in it. I thought you wouldn't mind."

I thought of Patrick lying in his own earth and smiled gratefully at mum. Words were not necessary. There was an unspoken understanding between us. Mum put her arm around my shoulder and held me tight.

On the leisurely stroll home she told me the names of flowers and birds that she could remember from her days on the farm and I got to know a whole different side to her.

Trevor had snoozed in the snug on one of the comfy chairs and I made tea whilst mum went to wake him. This was about the only room in the house that hadn't been disturbed by the builders. Before mum went to shake Trevor, she told me that his divorce from Pat had come through. She looked pleased and radiant. I had a new mum and she had a new daughter.

They were pulling the kitchen apart but I had managed to heat a cottage pie from the freezer. Felix was sociable and had joined us for lunch but had gone back to farm. I spied him on occasions up at Callow Hill. The black smoke from his exhaust would give him away as his truck panted up the steep incline. I'd noticed with mum that there were fresh flowers on Hannah's grave too. A few days later, Old Tom was pulling on some defiant dandelions and I was sweeping up debris with a witch's broom. We often joked that this was my other form of transport and we would laugh despite making the same joke many times. Sweeping was about all I could manage as bending down was now becoming difficult.

We were both surprised to see Guy approaching us with a remarkably sensuous woman at his side.

She had blonde, shoulder-length hair and wore dark glasses. Her lips were full and round and filled with luscious pinkish, orange lipstick. Her slim yet curvaceous body was dressed in a navy skirt suit and she wore a striped purple blouse with the buttons open to the tip of her cleavage. She was tiptoeing across the path in high heels avoiding the garden rubbish that I had swept into piles. By no fault of her own she made me feel ugly and aware of my swollen ankles and swelling form which ran from one part of my body to another with no distinction.

Guy was smiling broadly and introduced his companion who, as she got closer, I noticed smelled of expensive perfume.

"Rose, please meet Dr Kay Osborne. She's come to look at your paintings."

Dr Osborne put out her hand for me to shake and she shook it firmly.

I leaned on the broom and placed one hand on the base of my spine. I wasn't huge yet my pair of babies seemed to fight for space inside me and pushed and heaved at my womb to make it grow so that I felt enormous.

"How lovely! Do you want to see them now?"

Guy was impatient and began to usher us all back to the Manor.

"Actually, Guy, I was just about to make a jug of juice. Shall we sit in the garden for a moment first? I promised to take some out for Old Tom and the builders."

Reluctantly, he sat with Dr Osborne beyond the wreck of the kitchen through the French doors to the rolling horizon. Mrs T. was around and took the tray from me to serve so that I could get back to my guests.

I must admit that part of me was slightly annoyed that Guy had brought this woman to the Manor without asking me. Who was she?

Guy began to introduce her but she butted in continuing the introduction for herself. She had great credentials with a degree and masters in art history and she had worked her way up at one of the leading London museums. She had a specialism in medieval art but her overall depth of art history was phenomenal. She said that we could call her Kay. She looked at me with a sneer. It was a look of contempt. I knew this career woman thought I was throwing my youth away to domesticity.

Once refreshed, I took her and Guy to the long gallery conscious of my fuller figure as I walked beside them. I held back the tapestry to reveal the paintings roughly leaning against one another. I perceived that she was not happy in the way they had been left and she tasked Guy to help her take them out to the main landing so she could examine them better under the light of the windows. A cool breeze rose up from the door to the cellar so I shivered and told them that it would be better if I left them to it.

"I understand from Felix that there is a lot more in the attic?" She spoke to me as if I were a servant.

"You spoke to Felix?"

"Oh yes, we passed him on the road before the turning up the track."

Inside my head, 'And I bet he thought you quite the delight,' my mind offered up the envious words without me thinking.

"If you go along to the central gallery there is a staircase behind the door leading upwards. Be careful in those shoes, Kay." That was the most malicious thing I could think of to say. In a clumsy way I was letting her know that she should have been more prepared in the way she had dressed.

She nodded. They were so engrossed in the paintings that they did not notice me leave. I went back outside to find Old Tom chatting to Mrs T. and Alwyn. They looked embarrassed as if I'd been the subject of their conversation. I smiled pleasantly still basking in my retort.

July came and Felix and I went to Linda's wedding. It was a grand affair. Felix wanted to leave early. I made an excuse, blaming my pregnancy, saying I was tired. Felix hated being away from his farm and fretted the whole time we were away. He drove and swore at drivers until he made me laugh. I put my hands over my tummy and said that I was shielding my babies from his bad language and he laughed too.

Leaving the reception, Linda confided in me that she longed to have children of her own. I invited her and her new husband to the twin's christening and kissed her goodbye wishing that I could have stayed a little longer.

Summer turned to autumn and the Manor took on a different shape as the roof was dismantled and then slowly put back together.

Lately, I had dreamt about Eliza. She was constantly calling to me. My dreams were vivid.

"The roof!" I said it aloud. Felix startled, sat up in bed.

"Are you having a dream, Rose? What about the roof?"

"Yes, it's a dream. Sorry darling, go back to sleep."

I had been dreaming about the tower and what impact it would have on the room when the roofers came upon it. I needed to visit again and I would have to summon up the courage tomorrow.

Noise was filtering through from a radio and I could hear the banter of the workmen in the distance as I made my way up to the long gallery. I pulled back the tapestry and saw the paintings all bubble wrapped. Kay and Guy had been busy and the protective covering sealed the images away from the world. I felt sad for Isabella and her family and Honora and all the people in the paintings hidden away for who knew how long. I promised myself that I would hang them back in the east wing one day. I checked the attic doorway, which had been left open and I could hear Guy and Kay murmuring above.

The door to the tower was unlocked. My heart beat fast and I tried to steady it by breathing deeply. My bulging width scraped against the lean walls of the steps as I trod up to the lavish room. I was afraid, very afraid. The first thing I noticed were the two new candles in the window. *"That's where they got to,"* I thought.

The room was deathly still. The mimosa in the bowl looked fresh and there was the smell of lemon-scented perfume. I called out,

"Hello, it's Rose, I'm here. I'm here to help you find your boys. Are you here?"

She appeared slowly at first transforming from a shimmer out of the bed. I saw the indents of her body in the damask before she became the spirit of the person that she had become.

I felt sickly and went to sit on the bed trying to control my breathing. In through my nose, out through my mouth. She shocked me out of my concentration by moving in close beside me. I felt the weight of her body next to me yet she looked as light as a feather.

Taking my hands she looked me in the eye, her own black eyes imploring.

"My boys, Rose, where are my boys?"

214

"I don't know," I said. "Who are your boys?"

She whispered their names into my ear her breath smelling like sweet cherries. Then she took a strand of my hair and curled it behind my ear.

"All will be well for you Rose but be careful with your heart." I wondered what she meant.

"Promise you will find my boys so that I can rest?"

I promised. I recognised their names.

When I stood up to leave I turned to her but she had gone. Hoping she could hear me I said,

"There will be noise on the roof but don't worry it is workmen making repairs." I hesitated but no response came. "What is your name? Please tell me in some way, I need to know."

Her voice was hoarse as she whimpered her name into the still air. 'Jane Dakin'.

A noise in the window made me turn and I saw a girl straightening the candles. From her clothes I guessed she was a maid of sorts and she saw me look and nodded her head as if it was commonplace to see me.

I rushed down the steps to the gallery, my heart pounding, my brow perspiring.

"Ah, there you are Rose." It was Guy.

"We've come across some lead piping in the attics which need replacing. Actually, I'm guessing that the whole house has lead piping that will need to be stripped out. I'm afraid it's going to cost rather a lot of money, Rose."

My mind was so far away that I simply replied that he could get on with it. I went out to the garden to find Old Tom but he wasn't there so I sat on the wall soaking up the last rays of the autumn sun beneath the shade of a willow tree and thought about how I was going to reunite Jane Dakin with her sons.

CHAPTER 14

At last most of the work was coming to a close. Parts of the house were transformed. I now considered that the most exciting part was to come, which was to choose the décor and curtains for each room. At her cottage, Betty and I trawled over wallpaper books for hours on end. Bunnie helped too and gave her suggestions when she visited for an update. She loved all that side of things having chosen all the décor and furnishing for her own home. Guy was finalising the major details of the project and he also guided me to be sympathetic with the building and to be aware that much of the old furnishings, ornaments and paintings would be going back and I needed to consider where. I busied myself with this for a while each day feeling the kicks and yawns inside me as the twins grabbed for space to grow.

The twins were due in mid-October. Mum and Trevor put off their wedding until the following year; mum wanting to be around for their birth. Guy and I planned to be in a position for the work on the Manor to be almost complete for Christmas. The new kitchen had been installed and we had the luxury of central heating. I figured that there was still a lot of finishing off to do around the house but Guy had been a nit-picking and strident project manager and everywhere was at least looking freshly plastered. In some rooms electric wires were still draped across walls and ceilings waiting for light fittings to be installed.

As the master workmen finished each room and the decorators moved in, Mrs T. and Alwyn came into their own as they tidied and cleaned around them. There was still much to do but Felix and I were happy because the Manor was at least prepared enough for me to bring our babies home.

As the workforce reduced the house became quieter. Mrs T., Alwyn, Bunnie and I had lengthy discussions about where to hang paintings and place the ornaments but I mainly followed Bunnie's lead. She introduced me to the style of William Morris and I thought his designs went well in many of the rooms. I picked out wallpapers, my favourite being the, 'Strawberry Thief'. I had curtains made for the library in his rich patterned fabric of reds and gold birds. The drapes added some warmth to the space and I felt some self-gratification when Bunnie said that she thought they were the best possible choice to show off the ancient books.

I was glad we had reached this stage as I grew weary. Felix kept saying that I was doing too much but he understood my need to do something. Sitting around feeling heavily pregnant was not my idea of fun. I needed things to distract my mind. Jane Dakin lay heavily upon it.

Guy had left leaving a huge interim bill. To his credit the work was terrific and he had catalogued not just the library but filled a book itemising all the works of art in the house. He was as excited as I was when I extended my invitation for him to come back and restore paintings and objet d'art carefully in the spruce almost refurbished Manor. He and Kay had found a great many more items of worth in the attic rooms including paintings. Next time he came he was going to arrange for everything to be brought down for inspection. I detected a hint of excitement in his voice and wondered whether any of the paintings were rare or valuable.

217

Behind a wardrobe in our bedroom, I found an avant-garde period painting. Before Felix moved out of the bedroom he'd shared with Hannah, this room had belonged to Felix's parents. It was a painting of his mother. I pulled it out and examined the fine figure of a woman. She was Vivian wearing a sleeveless long silk pastel blue dress. She was so elegant and slim. A string of pearls were tied in a knot beneath her small breasts. Vivian wore a wry, sardonic smile. I was gazing at her when Felix came into the room and stopped abruptly when he saw his mother's portrait.

"Oh, you've found the Dalí of mother. You can ask Guy to sell it, I've never liked that picture. Mother hated it too, that's why it was shoved behind the wardrobe."

He said nothing else and left. I was left staring at Dalí's portrait of my mother-in-law. I could understand why Felix didn't like it. Dalí had encompassed her cool demeanour somehow and a lack of lovingness in her eyes. He had painted her face in blues and white making her whole being seem cold and blank.

I tasked Guy with doing something with it. Guy was not very good at hiding his feelings. He was excited by the painting and astounded at my casual manner towards the artist's creation.

"The thing is Rose, everything in this house has such provenance."

However, unbeknown to Felix I told Guy never to sell it.

The kitchen was refitted with pine wood cabinets and a newly tiled floor which was easy to clean.

In keeping, the shabby windows in the Manor had been replaced with specially made leaded double-glazed ones and a new French window at the end of the kitchen had been fitted the width of the wall so as to take advantage of the wondrous and spectacular view. It let in daylight and the kitchen took on a new sheen. We had left the original fireplace but I had bought a new rug and new chairs cleansing in some way the horror of Felix's most dreadful night.

Thinking long and hard I finally decided how to help the woman in the tower. I would talk to Gabriel. Neither Guy nor the workmen had stepped a foot in her tower and for that I was glad as I did not want Jane to be disturbed.

One morning in the library, I was drawn to look at the tall candlesticks. How did the candles end up in the tower, I wondered? Someone must have come down for them. Someone that I must have released at my last visit stupidly leaving the door unlocked. Jane had burned out the old ones as she searched for her boys each night through the window. I was quite afraid and hoped and prayed that whoever it was would not venture out again. I suspected it was her maid but I was still not convinced that what I had seen was real. I was then drawn to the bible. Guy had left it open and I bent to read it. He had moved it to a lower, wider table so that it could be opened without any further damage to the spine on a book rest. It was more than a bible as it contained sheets of paper or vellum that had been meticulously sewn in. I looked admiringly at my curtains; they looked perfect.

I flipped the page, bored and restless. Inserted was a document folded flat and tied in a faded red ribbon with a seal across it. I took it to a winged-back leather chair and sat with my feet rested on the opposite one.

It read...

I, Colonel Langley, in the year of 1833, do declare that Jane Dakin do be my wife by lawful means having been wed on August 3rd in this same year of our Lord. The said, Jane Dakin, is also the mother of Horace Melverley Langley and Herbert Mortimer Langley twins born of her on August 3rd in the year of our Lord 1833. Due to the sorrowful mind of the aforementioned Jane, it is with great sadness that her two sons do be taken from this place three months hence to the house of Eliza Thompson, good woman of this parish, and to be her ward until such time that each son reaches 21 years.

Jane Dakin shall have no awareness of the placement of the boys and will remain at Callow Crest Manor until she be parted from this life in the care of my sister Annabel Langley.

Signed: **_Robert Langley_** *Witness: Rev'd William Arbuthnot* **_William Arbuthnot, Rev'd._**

I reread it. Eliza? Eliza? I dreamed of Eliza and I was certain that she was the same person.

'Of sorrowful mind?' What on earth did that mean? I imagined Eliza was kind but how wrong could I be? She was taking Jane's boys. I made a small scream, angry with myself for being seduced by Eliza's angelic presence in my dreams.

Eliza had brought me here, she wanted things to be well. What things? Was this connected to Jane's boys? The words of the letter troubled me.

One of Jane's sons died in Sevastopol, I remembered the plaque in the church. Would his spirit return to the lands of the Callow? I read on worried for Jane and whether she would ever see her sons again. He must have been her youngest child, I recalled from the bible, as he had died with no heirs.

Jane's surviving son came home, decommissioned from the army due to his wounds. He was twenty one when he and his brother had gone to fight for Queen and Country. Their father was at least fifty nine when Jane gave birth to her sons. I wondered how old Jane was. She seemed very young to me. I hated Lord bloody Langley even more for that.

Perhaps the colonel was cared for by his son, a returning hero? And then, when I looked up some other records in the Manor's inventory of that time, I saw that the household was being run by Eliza Thompson. She must have moved in to take care of them both, I thought. I searched but there were no records of Jane, other than the piece of paper to say that she was in '*sorrowful mind.*'

I rang Gabriel. He was pleased to hear from me and announced that Fiona was 'expecting'.

I congratulated him and passed on my regards to Fiona.

"Such wonderful news, Gabriel."

For a moment I envisioned Gabriel making love to Fiona. I could not summon the image, Gabriel seeming too saintly for earthly pleasures and Fiona too prudish. Despite my inability to conjure up their lovemaking, they were having a child together.

"It's early days, Rose so keep it to yourself for now. Wednesday? Let me check the diary. Yes, that's fine, I'll come to you. Keen to see the restoration."

Felix supposed I was tired when I gave excuses to go to bed early and I did not correct him. It was because I wanted to lay in the quiet to think about Jane Dakin and what had happened to her. I decided that the only way to find out was to ask her.

Autumn was threatening winter days so I was too afraid to leave my visit to the tower to an evening when the dark veiled the Manor. It was easier for me to visit on a day when Mrs T. and Alwyn were out and naturally Felix would be on the farm.

I crept along the gallery to the stairwell and again braced myself to trace my steps to the tower. When I entered it was just as before. Out of the corner of my eye I thought I saw someone attending to the mimosa. It was the maid, a small girl with a chubby face. She caught my eyes with her friendly ones and scurried off to the ante-room.

I sat on the bed and soon I felt Jane's body close to mine. Her cold breath softly blew on my cheek.

"Please tell me your story, Jane."

Her eyes opened wider.

"How kind of you to ask, Miss."

I won't deny that people will find this an incredible happening. But as I sat next to a woman, dead for over a hundred years, she clasped my hands in hers as she unfurled her story to me. My twins lay sleeping lulled by her velvet voice and I felt the base of my spine crunch against my muscles as I fidgeted to sit comfortably on the bed.

Without exaggeration and in some distress, Jane related her tale. Aged only fourteen, she had been a milkmaid at the Manor. She was a good child of a local family. A virgin. As one of six daughters and four brothers her job was important for she was contributing to the upkeep of her large family.

Jane had worked in the milking parlour since she was twelve but she proudly told me that she could write her own name. "*I did so on the marriage certificate,*" she told me.

The Lord of the Manor was often out of the Callow lands and no doubt had business elsewhere in London and Paris. Suppressing all signs of emotion she carried on.

"*'Twas at the end of the day Miss Rose when I was working in the dusk light I heard a noise. At first I thought it was bats come down to feed on the cows. I knew it was unusual for a visitor as likely there would be only me and Bertha, Daisy and Lottie the cows. I looked up to see the Lord Callow his eyes burning upon me. I sat on my stool, keeping on with my work but he did not leave. He came upon me Rose.*"

Now she was struggling as I knew she was reaching the climax of her tale.

"He came upon me Rose and disabled me in my movements. He thrust me to the ground, the milk spilling on the floor and he took me like a man does his wife."

She began to cry. I put my arm around her shoulder and I felt her bones and cold flesh.

Instantaneously, she told me, she knew she was pregnant. For months she hid it from her family swathing her belly in strips of cloth.

"I was so ashamed," she cried, "for the raising of a child out of wedlock was the deepest sin."

I wanted to shout out that it wasn't her fault. Her story resonated so much with my own. With some concern I asked her what happened next.

As terrible fate would have it, his Lordship was back from his administrative work for the new queen in London. He was prowling with the urge to seduce his servant and found her in agony. She went into labour in the parlour whilst milking the cows. He had been away from the Callow for months and Jane was surprised to see his shadow lurking in the darkness. Surmising quickly that the baby was his he took her to the Manor to the room in the tower. He summoned the vicar and his trusted evil-hearted sister Annabel.

The Lord of the Callow insisted that they be married at once and sent his groom for the vicar.

"Make these bastards my heirs," he bellowed at the vicar.

Despite his reservations, the vicar nervously married them, his hands shaking as he held the bible. All the while Jane was in a deep and painful labour. Annabel was a witness with young servant Biffy Hankins who had been quickly summoned. Annabel and Biffy were very much afraid of Lord Callow.

When Jane delivered a son the vicar quickly christened him. He bore the 'Cross of Soot' so there was now no doubt that Colonel Langley was the father. They named him Herbert. Jane held her son and then wailed as the pains returned. Another son was born, smaller and frailer but alive and crying. They named him Horace. The vicar repeated the christening ceremony. Jane's twins were baptised and she was married in a shake of a lamb's tail.

Cradling her new born sons, Jane held them to her breasts relieved that the pain had subsided feeling the burst of jelly and blood between her legs as the afterbirth spilled out. She looked up at Lord Callow and his sister. A fearful and great intuition took hold of her. They were whispering together and Annabel was nodding in agreement. Annabel's piercing blue eyes were cruel and she had sharp, thin features. Jane began to shake. Kind Biffy Hankins saw Jane's fear and she wiped her face with a cool linen cloth and sat on the bed stroking the babies. Lord Callow did not even go close to look at his sons, he simply left with his sister in tow.

Locked in the tower, Jane nursed her babies. Her sons suckled well and grew strong. Then about three months later wicked Annabel arrived in the tower carrying two wicker baskets. She was accompanied by Biffy who was holding her head down not wanting to meet Jane's anxious face. Instantly Jane realised that her sons would be lost to her forever.

Many times she tried to escape from the tower but the walls were thick, she was high up and the door was constantly locked. The only person she saw was Biffy. Biffy was an ignorant girl and Jane thought her not to be quite right in the head. She was kind and Jane's only companion. Biffy would, in her own excitable way, tell Jane about what was going on outside. The Lord had burned down the parlour and Biffy told Jane that her parents thought her dead, caught in a terrible fire, there was no body to bury. Poor Jane wept, thinking of her parents and siblings, all who thought her deceased. With Biffy she had discussed getting a message to her family. Biffy had cried and said that the Lord would whip her to death if she did such a thing. After that, Jane took pity on Biffy and didn't ask her to help her again. Lord Callow had imprisoned Jane. His cunning plan demonstrated his malice and hard heart. Jane's poor family swept my mind as they grieved for their daughter believing her burned to ashes. No daughter to bid farewell. She had gone out to work never to return.

Jane's favourite place was by the window that looked out over the courtyard. She never lost hope of seeing her boys and she would sit for hours watching and wondering if Lord Callow would ever return them to Callow Crest Manor.

Five years went by and Biffy took care of Jane bringing fresh flowers and keeping her company as she was kept locked in the tower. Annabel was in charge of all Jane's needs. Her brother gave her an annual allowance so that Jane could be fed and clothed. Annabel bought Jane clothes to wear. Beautiful dresses and a black velvet cloak. But Jane never even tried them on because she knew there would be no need. She knew that she would never leave the tower. Despite Biffy's pleas, Jane remained in her milking clothes never wanting to accept anything from her prison warder. Annabel would grow cross,

"Don't think that you'll ever see your sons again. My brother has made sure of that. I wish you had burned Jane Dakin and that your ashes had gone to hell. Because of you I am stuck in this house day after day. You stupid and ignorant girl."

After her tirades, Biffy would wait for Annabel to leave the room and then rush to put her arms around Jane to comfort her.

One day, Biffy awoke feeling unwell. Her throat hurt and she could feel the glands in her neck were swollen. Her head was bursting and she had a fever. She needed to get to the Manor as Jane would be waiting for her breakfast. Biffy made the porridge and poured milk into a glass and set them on a tray.

225

She went to the tower and together with her deadly germs gave Jane the tray of breakfast.

"I needs to tell ye summit, Miss," Biffy said. "Your boys are with Eliza Thompson all well an' all that. Seed them wiv me own eyes this morning riding on ponies across Callow hill they was."

Lord Callow had devised a plan to remove his sons and to place them with Eliza Thompson. Eliza was his mistress and he already had three children with her; twin girls aged ten and a son aged twelve. Here he hoped the scandal of Jane Dakin would not be discovered. However, he would acknowledge Jane's boys as his own once they reached the age of majority. He would pay for their keep and schooling. He had mapped out their lives and he would pay for their commissions into the army once they reached twenty one.

Eliza was amenable to the situation as he provided her with a good allowance so that she knew that none of them would starve. 'Home Farm' was generous with a good orchard and vegetable garden. He would worry about his sons' introduction into society circles when that time came. His eldest son Herbert would inherit his title, the Manor and all the land for he bore the Cross of Soot. I looked at the table at the end of the bed. The tray was still there, the porridge left uneaten.

The next day Biffy struggled to come to the tower and lay on the bed next to Jane, hot and unwell. Jane thought of her sons with Eliza and a jealous rage struck out at her. She cursed Eliza and tossed and turned as she slept in fever.

The two young women died together that night, their hands conjoined on the bed. Annabel caught the fever too so everyone connected to Jane, apart from Lord Callow, took their secret to their graves.

Jane did not forget her sons. Even in death, she yearned and prayed for her sons to return as she sat by the window each day and night looking out with hope and cursing Eliza Thompson.

Silently weeping, I took her little face into my hands and kissed her delicate cheek. Her skin was translucent and she was as cold as marble.

"I know where your boys rest Jane and I will take you there. But first you must be patient as I need some help, which will come, I promise this following Wednesday." I did not have the courage to tell her that one son had died abroad. Of course, I knew nothing of what happened to our souls after death, I only hoped that I could reunite Jane with her sons.

Jane gently nodded. Then she suddenly grabbed at my arm.

"I cannot leave this place, I must wait here for my boys."

She was pleading but I knew that somehow she would have to leave the tower but as yet I didn't know how.

I left. Jane's story filled my head and I vowed to return her to her sons, somehow, I didn't know how but I would.

Felix looked astonished as he watched me speed down the stairs. Hours had passed without me realising and he was home.

"Everything all right? You're not in labour are you dashing about like that?"

I got to the bottom of the stairs and took my husband's face in my hands and kissed him in the way that I had kissed Jane a few moments ago but with passion.

"Everything is fine, darling," I reassured him trying to stop my hands from trembling.

As the week went dully by I waited for Gabriel. When he arrived we spent at least two hours going around the Manor as he marvelled at what had been achieved.

"Transformation," he kept saying. "It feels so warm."

In my new kitchen we sat at the table together drinking coffee.

"It has made such a difference now that you have repaired the track up to the Manor Rose."

"Oh yes, it seemed silly not to get that done while we were sorting out everything else."

"Rose, I am guessing you have asked me here for a reason. If it is about the twins' christening you know, of course, I will be delighted to do it. Have you chosen any names? Christian names, I hope?"

I laughed. Felix and I had not discussed names but I had an insight into Felix's strong sense of old-fashioned names, so I guessed that he would have some lined up.

"No Gabriel, no names yet and yes, you are right, there is a reason why I asked you here."

I'm not entirely sure what Gabriel was thinking as I unravelled my story. His face barely changed and I dared not look too hard for fear that he would conclude that I was completely mad. My heart stood still and when I finished I felt the twins kick me back to life.

At first I thought he would take his leave as he went to stand.

"Take me to the tower, Rose."

That was all he said and not answering I led the way.

We sat on Jane's bed. His fresh face showed no willing enchantment in respect of the room nor did he utter any words as I called Jane to join us.

His first inclination of someone else in the room was when he shifted his bottom as Jane sat next to him, bringing the ice of death with her and blowing it over towards where we sat. We saw a girl light the candles in the window.

I looked at Gabriel. "That's not her, that's her maid Biffy."

On hearing her name Biffy looked over at us and smiled and as she blew out her match she dissolved into the air.

I spoke to Jane looking at where she sat beside us watching Gabriel's face who seemed nonplussed at witnessing the form of a girl wither away before his spiritual eyes.

"Jane, this is Gabriel and he and I are going to find a way to reunite you with your sons."

Gabriel shot me a disdainful look as he spoke,

228

"Jane, I know you are here but you must listen to me. I cannot do this now, I will have to come back. We need to say the right prayers, complete the correct rituals and remove you from this place. I cannot promise, I'm sorry."

Again he looked at me.

"This is not an exorcism, Rose. We cannot make promises that we cannot keep."

The door to the dressing room slammed shut which made us both jump and I felt my twins wriggle in surprise.

She appeared before us with angry eyes. Gabriel remained amazingly calm.

"Jane, you must leave this place if you want to see your boys. They are never coming back Jane, not even in death. Do you understand? They are at peace."

She stared at Gabriel. I was afraid that something violent was going to happen and I got up to move towards the door. Jane did not notice me, she had fixed her eyes firmly on Gabriel.

Suddenly and without anyone touching it, the breakfast tray fell to the floor, the beautiful china smashing in its wake. I jumped but Gabriel did not flinch.

He spoke again, "Jane, if you want to be with your sons you must obey and listen to what I am saying. You *must* leave this place."

Once more the dressing room door was opened and slammed. We heard her voice but there was no vision of Jane, just an outpouring scream that made me grip Gabriel's arm hard.

"I vow to you that I will not leave this place until Eliza returns my sons. Where are my boys? I am their mother not she."

Then all became quiet. Gabriel and I sat on the bed for at least half an hour waiting and recovering from our ordeal until

Gabriel took my hand and led me back to the cosiness of the kitchen.

"Gabriel, what are we to do? She doesn't want to leave."

I had poured him a whisky.

"Yes, Rose. I know."

"What did you mean when you said this is not an exorcism? Jane is not an evil spirit, Gabriel. She just wants to be back with her sons."

"I'm just saying it's not that easy, Rose. We have to remove her from this house to a sacrosanct place to St. Laurence's Church. Her sons are at peace Rose we cannot remove them to the Manor where their souls will remain for eternity in purgatory. I need to do some research to find out how. It may take some time. Does Felix know about this?"

I shook my head.

"Who is Eliza?"

"Eliza is a woman in my dreams. She called me to this place to help her. She said that if I came, all would be well. But she lied to me Gabriel. Eliza and Lord Callow took Jane's children away and she kept them as her own. She was his mistress and even had the gall to come and live at the Manor knowing all the time what had happened to Jane. Even, her faked death."

Gabriel listened to me patiently. He said little and arranged to call the following Wednesday.

My impatience for the week to pass quickly rubbed off on Felix. He put all my recent moods down to my confinement. I noticed, as my time drew near, he became surly and once or twice I had to remind him to wash and clean his teeth. I suppose he was worried about the impending birth and I knew that quite frankly the memory of what had happened to his dead wife and sons would never leave him, even though we were starting a new family together.

One evening in the snug, as we lay with my legs outstretched over him, I did my best to reassure him that everything was going to be all right. He did not look convinced and his temperament was like the old Felix, sullen and withdrawn. I was too tired to make the effort to console him and hoped that he would change once the twins were born. I bore no charitable emotions for Felix. I just felt that until then he was going to have to get through on his own.

CHAPTER 15

Gabriel arrived equipped with his bible and incense.

"I shouldn't really be doing this, Rose. It's just one of those things I am in conflict with having experienced something similar in my parent's home as a child. We have to keep this between us. Your word is vital. And, I must go to Jane alone."

I understood and swore on his bible that I would not tell a soul about our indiscretions. I was right about Gabriel, I thought, he was deeper and more spiritual about such things than he let on. I was desperate to ask him what happened to him as a child.

"Your childhood, Gabriel?"

"Rose, we can talk about this another time. Something happened in India where I was brought up. My father was a missionary there. Look, honestly, there is no time for this, just trust me, eh? I'd like to go to Jane now."

"There's something I'd like you to give her please, Gabriel?"

I handed him a cloak. It was made of black velvet and I had taken it from the ante-room in the tower. On the bed, I had laid out a dress and socks and boots that I had found ready for Jane to leave in.

"She'll need to be warm where she is going. Please make sure that she wears it."

He nodded and took it from me. His eyes were filled with dread and fear and he had gone a deathly shade of white. I hugged him and kissed his cheek.

"Thank you. It means a lot, Gabriel."

He bent and kissed me on my forehead and left.

Gabriel was gone for hours. I sweated over the sink peeling vegetables and preparing stew for dinner. I wondered what was happening in the tower. The time dragged and I could not bear it. I desperately wanted to know what Gabriel was doing. Doubt rose in my mind as I fretted and worried about what was going on and whether Gabriel would be able to truly release Jane. She evidently was serious about not leaving the Manor. That poor, wretched girl! When I thought of what she had gone through my doubt changed to anger and I wanted to slap Lord Callow, Colonel bloody Robert Langley, sharply in his face. And Eliza with him. I thought she was a bitch. My heart palpitated as I paced. I chopped the vegetables with vigour and slashed the knife through in a subdued rage.

I felt very scared. The lights flickered and then went off completely. The late fading light was grey and overcast and I lit a candle. I began to walk up the stairs to the gallery but my body was chilled by the sound of a woman's screams: Jane's screams. I could hear the smash of things being thrown around and the thud of heavy furniture being scraped across the floor. Above all, I could hear Gabriel's voice shouting above Jane's.

"Be gone from this place, be gone Jane Dakin," I heard him bellow.

Jane let out a long heart-stopping wail and I turned on my heels and scampered back down the stairs as fast as my pregnancy would allow me.

I poured a brandy, a small one to calm my nerves. In one sip the twins spiralled inside me as the heat chased through my veins. The radio came on by itself even though there was no electricity and then it went off again. Then all the lights came

233

back on and I heard the whirr of the new boiler in the boot room kick in. I was shaking and I could not imagine what Gabriel was feeling. For a moment I doubted whether he would be able to release Jane as she was so unwilling to leave her prison tower.

At last, Gabriel appeared in the kitchen and slumped into a chair. His face was red and sprinkled with perspiration. My lungs stopped for a while as I took in his body. He was spent. Whatever engagement he and Jane had encountered had exhausted him.

I made him strong coffee and gave him some brandy. He did not speak for about fifteen minutes and then he just said,

"She's gone Rose, but not without a fight."

How had I doubted him? This man before me whose faith was so strong.

As he stood up I hugged him. I wanted to ask him what had happened but just at that moment Felix unexpectedly appeared from the boot room.

"Oh yes," he said rather too flippantly. "What's going on here?"

"Gabriel came to talk about the twins' christening. He's agreed to bless them for us, isn't that lovely?" I spoke hurriedly trying to cover up the real reason for him being there.

Felix, acting like his old self, grunted.

"Well, so he bloody well should, 'tis my church anyhow."

I felt embarrassed at his rudeness to Gabriel who was the kindest and most genuine man I had ever known.

Gabriel said he would see me soon and left.

It was torturous. I wanted Gabriel to stay and drink more brandy to calm his nerves and to tell me what had really happened in the tower, but I heard his horse's hooves clip-clop in the courtyard. I imagined him trotting home with thoughts swirling in his head. It was hard to embrace the meaning of what he had done. There would only ever be me for him to discuss it with. When he got home, perhaps Fiona would think

234

that there had been a death on the estate; it was impossible to think that she would see deep into his true emotions and what he had gone through. She would have no idea. Poor Gabriel! At that moment I longed to be with him and to comfort him like a mother.

Felix understood that he had come in at the *wrong time* I could see it in his face as he glared at me and stalked out of the door calling Phoebe and Thor. His manner reminded me of the times when he summoned Tarbo and Buster and he looked dishevelled. Ignoring Felix, I went to bed for a lie down. My stomach was like someone had put a beach ball under my top. Tears fell and I cried myself to sleep.

It was dark when I woke and Felix was not next to me. A drawn-out ache stretched across my back and I went to the loo to pee. Water gushed out and I knew my time was near. I called out to Felix but he did not come so I pulled my weight off the loo and made my way to the kitchen.

Felix was sat watching the last embers flicker by the kitchen's fire. He turned to look at me. I think my expression said it all and he ran to the telephone and called for an ambulance.

At the hospital, sitting next to my bed, Felix held my hand and whispered words of encouragement. There was a new drug for pain relief which was injected into my back. This was frightening but being scared was outweighed by the relief of the pain that had overcome me. My main feeling was of surprise, I had envisaged my labour being far worse. The new drug worked and I was even able to sit and chat with Felix as we both watched the rise and fall of my contractions on the monitor.

Rupert Felix and Percy Henry were born with three minutes between them. They were identical and good healthy weights. Rupert had a birthmark on his forehead. My eldest son, he had the 'Cross of Soot'. When I noticed it I laughed and kissed him gently. I was the happiest woman in the world and Felix's face

235

was beaming. In that moment I had not only gained two sons but also a portion of the love of my husband.

PART SIX

Raising the babies with the dead

CHAPTER 16

When we came back from the hospital, Callow Crest Manor had a different aura. I stopped to look up at the window in the tower as Felix carried the baby chairs in from the car. Jane was not there. I knew she had gone. I hoped to see her again one day.

Bunnie had brought over a casserole and on the kitchen table was a huge bouquet of mixed blue flowers. There were also cards from the Edwards' family, Guy, Old Tom and Gwyneth, Betty and family and people from the estate. There was one from Gabriel and Fiona and a gift of a silver cross for each son.

Never having had living babies before, I was absolutely clueless as to what to do with them. I had never guessed that the luxury of them sleeping would not last. I was terrified as when one son would cry then so would the other. Somehow, I managed to work out how to sit with each on a breast to feed them but they were hard work and I was constantly changing nappies and I never seemed to sleep. Felix continued to be out on the farm and when he returned he would kiss me and then kiss his sons. He always wore an expression of being in a dream when he gazed down at them.

This sad, old house was now filled with the sound of crying babies and the background noises of whirring utilities. I cherished and loved my new dishwasher and my washing

239

machine and when I used them I thought of the women before me who had lived in this house without modern comforts; Isabella and her snooty, corrupt husband, the gorgeous Honora who deigned not to live here, building her own dwelling over the vale and I thought of the child bride, Marguerite and of course, of Jane.

I had not had chance to see Gabriel and I telephoned to arrange the christenings. He answered the phone in a rushed voice.

"Sorry Rose, I've got to rush off, one of my flock is dying and I need to perform the Last rites. Let's speak soon."

We quickly arranged for a christening for the boys and we put in a date for March when they would be five months old.

For the first month, Mum came with Trevor to help settle me and my new boys into my new life of motherhood. When they left I wept and felt worried that I would not cope on my own. Mum squeezed my arm whispering in my ear to tell me that I was a strong, young woman and that she was proud of me.

"You'll be fine," she said.

Mum and Trevor were away for Christmas and the New Year, somewhere hot but I'd forgotten where, as they were always dashing off on trips lately. I felt alone and vulnerable as I nursed my babies. I missed my mum.

I longed to speak with Gabriel. This became more pressing as one night when I got up to feed and settle the boys I heard a noise in the gallery. The door creaked as I opened it and I tiptoed out trying not to wake Felix. I saw the figure of Biffy treading along the gallery towards the staircase. She was looking about her as if searching for something or someone. Neither Gabriel nor I had considered Biffy and now she was alone seeking Jane. A shiver ran down my back.

We celebrated our first Christmas together as a family. Feminists may well criticise me but I loved my new kitchen and being in it. On Christmas morning, Felix declared out of the blue that he would be at home for the whole day which delighted me. I set about preparing Christmas lunch with all the trimmings. The twins were thriving and my figure was decreasing and I began to feel well. In the hall Felix had cut a pine tree from the estate and climbed up a ladder to place a fairy at the top. The sparkling fairy lights lit up the space and the Manor rejoiced in its warmth. Now they had been cleaned, the old men in the paintings seemed to have shifted their gaze towards the tree in the middle and were smiling in seasonal merriment.

Of course, the twins were oblivious to their first Christmas but Felix and I bonded as he helped me around the kitchen, periodically checking on his sons asleep in their cots. He went to the cellar and brought up some wine. I had a few sips over dinner and Felix drank the rest. We went to bed to seal our love bringing the twins upstairs to put in their cots at the sides of our bed. It was the first time for a long while that we had sex and we both fell back on our pillows giggling and kissing and stroking each other until the boys squealed for attention. Felix commented on my breasts admiring their increase in size as I took each son to feed whilst he stared at me and them in disbelief.

The New Year flew by and spring blew in like a lion through March as the date for the christening drew near.

I telephoned Gabriel.

"Fee's in labour, Rose. We are just leaving for the hospital. Oh dear Lord! It's all happening too fast, Rose, she's not due yet. Pray for our child and my wife, Rose."

His voice was laden with concern and then he added, "Ring in a few days, Rose and we'll finalise everything."

He sounded worried and I could hear Fiona yelling at him to hurry up and get in the car. Gabriel rang next morning to say that Fiona had given birth to a little girl. She was quite the premature little thing but beautiful. She was to be called, Judith. I passed on my congratulations.

I'd already written christening invitations to Bunnie, Old Tom's family, Guy and his partner and Linda and Charlie. I discussed with Felix who would be godparents. Naturally, for our eldest son, he chose Fergus and Bunnie. This was a *fait accompli*. As each child needed a godfather and a godmother I chose Betty and Young Tom to be Percy's. I thought of Linda and hoped that she would not be offended at me for not asking her to be this role model. The trouble was she lived so far away and we only saw each other, perhaps twice a year. Linda and Charlie were already godparents to Linda's brood of siblings' children so I felt she would understand and my pangs of guilt were eased. Betty, after all, was my nearest and had become my closest friend and I hoped she would agree. I remembered Betty's reticence about being my bridesmaid. I understood it was a class issue, something that related to the status of her family and the Manor's inhabitants through history. I may be the, 'Lady of the Manor' but I was working class too and I wished she could see that point of view. Felix agreed to my wishes but he declared that he had not realised that I was so close to Betty.

It just showed how little he knew of my days at the Manor. In a way I was grateful. I thought about Jane and the fact that I had managed to keep the secret of her and the tower hidden from Guy and his entourage of builders.

Mum and Trevor arrived displaying raw skin and healthy faces. Mum was overjoyed at seeing the twins and showered them with clothes and teddies.

On the eve of their christening, a blustery wind had blown overnight so I wrapped the boys in thick blue blankets as the air was brisk. Felix swiftly fixed them into the car seats fearing they would get cold. He must have been thinking about his sons

242

lying in the drawer by the fire and I rushed to kiss him. He looked at me strangely as we got into the car.

Fiona was there and we cooed over each other's babies. Her little girl was wrapped in a pink shawl and bonnet. Judith's face was rosy and chubby and she was thriving. She looked exactly like Fiona until she opened her eyes which were like Gabriel's. I looked down at my boys. Each had the same shaped head, brows, nose and lips. I could only see reflections of my husband. If their looks were judged on my own it would be hard to believe that it was me who had given birth to them.

The service was short and Gabriel christened the twins in the ancient font which stood at the front of the nave. It was of grey stone and looked cold but Gabriel assured the congregation that the water was warm. He marked Rupert with the sign of the cross over his own natural one and he squawked.

Percy never made a sound and from that day forward I knew that he would be the quieter one of my sons.

Felix headed off with the car seats, the twins tucked into them and asleep. Everyone was leaving for home back along the country lanes. I looked around the church. There was a warm glow from the many candles and as the March wind blew, leaves made a soft patter against the stained glass windows. Gabriel pulled at my arm.

I had been to some of his services but I had been so busy with the twins that this was the first time we had been on our own.

"Wait, Rose," he said.

I stopped and looked up at his serene face. If God sent angels to earth then Gabriel was certainly one of them.

"Rose, wait awhile."

We stood at the end of the aisle together looking up to the altar and the magnificent arched window. The white of the sunlight lit the ivory and pink colours of the figures emphasising their religious imagery.

Gabriel had put his arm around my waist but I hadn't noticed. Looking back, I think it was because he wanted to hold me still.

"Eliza. I need to talk to you about Eliza."

"And I need to talk to you about Biffy," I said.

Gabriel was about to say more but mum came in calling me to hurry as she wanted to get back to the Manor to fill the vol-au-vents. I smiled and pressed my hand into Gabriel's.

"Let's sort out a visit. We'd better go as mum will be expecting us and you'd better make a big hoopla of eating her buffet or they'll be no peace for either of us!"

Grinning, he said he would see me there.

Mum fussed over the twins and I was delighted to see Betty and her husband and children in the kitchen tucking in. I guessed that Gabriel must have persuaded her to come.

"I am so glad you came, Betty."

"I can't believe I haven't been up here before. It doesn't feel haunted at all."

Young Tom shot her a glance.

"Oh, I know what you mean," said mum overhearing.

"It's just as well, what with those two little mites and their mother dying here, the place has got a whole new atmosphere, don't you think?" Mum was oblivious to her indiscretion.

Betty said she could not compare, not having been inside the house before. Then Young Tom spoke saying he had noticed the difference since he had come to help me remove the old bed.

It was Betty's turn to flash him a look.

Gabriel, Fiona and Judith arrived and Gabriel came over balancing a plate filled high with food and a glass of champagne. Overhearing us he said,

"It's since Rose came here. It is like it was meant to be."

"What was meant to be, Gabriel?" asked Felix coming over.

"Rose coming here, Felix. She's changed everything. We've all noticed it."

Felix did not reply. He shuffled away to fill his plate.

"More champagne anyone?" said mum. "Come on Rose, this cake that Gwyneth has made looks delicious. Time to slice it I think?"

Later, I managed to find some time to speak with Gabriel and arranged a meeting. Fiona was taking Judith into Shrugsborough to visit her parents the following week so Gabriel asked me to visit him at the rectory on that day.

I was up early and fed the boys. I had been expressing my milk for a couple of months and this made feeding times much easier as someone else could help me. Mrs T. and Alwyn were more than happy to sit and chat and suckle the boys on their bottles. I was always grateful for the rest.

Felix was out on the farm tending his lambs and I knew he would not be back until late evening. The wind had blown itself out and there was blue sky with a warm tinge of spring sun as I strapped the boys into their car seats.

By the time I arrived at the rectory, the motion of the car had rocked them to sleep. The rectory was late Georgian with big windows and a smart door with a heavy brass knocker fashioned into the shape of Jesus on the cross. It made up part of a small hamlet called, Laurence Well. There was the rectory which was about half a mile's walk from the church, a tenant farm and a pair of cottages and that was it. All were owned and rented out by my husband. I rang the bell and Gabriel answered taking one of the car seats from me as I went in. Once we had settled the twins, he led me into his study and kissed me on both cheeks.

"I'm so glad you came, Rose, you look well."

"So do you. How's Judith getting along, is she sleeping? Fiona looked well at the christening."

"Judith is a good sleeper. Fiona keeps waking her up worried that something is wrong but she is just content. I hope it lasts."

We continued to chat for a while making polite conversation. I was sitting at the end of his desk and Gabriel was sat in an antique captain's chair. There was a familiarity of the room from my conversion days and I recognised an old book smell. The walls were lined with them. Not all theological, I noticed. I spied some of the titles, books on Buddha, Hinduism, the Muslim faith together with Scott's exploration stories, Dickens, Darwin and Austen. There was an old map of his parish hanging on the wall, burning in sepia tones as daylight lavished beams on it through the long sash window.

He took my hands in his and looking at me with his incredible eyes he spoke. His voice was like a lullaby and I felt myself being hypnotised by his pitch.

"Rose, it's good to see you. I've been wanting to catch up with you for quite a while. I have seen Jane."

I gasped.

"Where Gabriel, where?"

"In the church. She's with her sons, at last. You have reunited them after all these years."

"Not me Gabriel. It was you."

"Well, I may have a hand in the process but it was you who went to the tower in the first place and it was you who came here purely on your intuition, Rose. Tell me truthfully, was there any other reason why you came to the Manor?"

I thought. I thought about the two ladies on the bench at the coach station and my trek across the hills.

"I confess Gabriel, I can't think of any other reason."

"Are you sure? What about your dreams?"

I looked around his study. There was a whole section of books on one shelf about interpretation of dreams.

"Eliza," I said.

Gabriel nodded. "Eliza. I think she brought you here and what's more, I don't think she is the evil person that you think

246

she is. I think she wants to make amends with Jane, that's why she called for you in your dreams, Rose."

My heart began to flutter. What Gabriel was saying made sense but why me?

"Why me?" I asked loudly.

"Well, that I don't know but I think it is something you need to find out."

"How can I do that especially as I don't know what it is I'm looking for?"

"Only time will tell, Rose. I don't have all the answers, I wished I did. Try and see the good in everyone, Rose. Let's walk to the church. Do you think it's warm enough to take the twins out? Looks like a glorious day," he said looking through the window.

We each carried a twin, leaving them in their seats, down the track to the church. The lake was gleaming and shimmering in the light and the swans looked regal and graceful as they swam across the water.

There was no breeze, just the gentle hush of the lapping water on the shore. Daffodils were dotted around the graves and some held fresh flowers in stone vases.

Inside the church we placed the twins' seats on a pew at the back and Gabriel took my hand as we walked down the eastward aisle towards the Langley plaque. We stood quietly. Gabriel raised his arm and I looked to where he was pointing.

In the faint light I could just make out the form of a woman. She wore a black velvet cloak and moved in an ethereal glide. She went towards the plaque and pursed her lips to kiss it. Then she knelt and putting her hands together in prayer, her mellow voice echoed into the buttresses. I watched in silence. Gabriel's body was so close to mine that I could feel his chest ebb and flow with each breath.

247

When the apparition had finished her prayer she rose and stood facing me. She smiled and lowered her head a little placing one arm over her chest. Then she was gone.

"Oh Gabriel, it was Jane. It was Jane, back with her sons."

I squeezed Gabriel, tears falling down my cheeks.

"Thank you," I spoke into his ear on my tiptoes. He smiled back at me, his own gorgeous eyes misty and we both left for the rectory.

Mum and Trevor married in the summer at Solihull Registry Office with a small meal afterwards at their local public house. Their wedding was a quiet affair and only a handful of people attended. Mum was happy and looked lovelier and younger than her years.

She and Trevor adored the twins and made super grandparents. If I ever needed help they would arrive at the drop of a hat. I offered to drive this time, recalling our last journey to Birmingham and Felix was happy to let me but he still shouted abuse at other drivers as I tackled the busy Birmingham traffic.

After mum's wedding I had pangs of guilt realising that I had never visited her in her new home. I promised myself that I would take the boys as often as I could. As much as I wished to avoid the milling crowds I decided that it would be good for the children to come to a big city. As soon as they were old enough I made up my mind to take them to the Hippodrome to see a pantomime and to stay over with mum and Trevor.

The boys grew healthy and strong. Twice a week, there was a playgroup at Churchbury village hall and I would drop them off to play whilst I went shopping or now and again I would treat myself to having my hair done. I would bump into Gabriel parking to drop off Judith and he would dash off here and there to see one of his parishioners. I always found it strange to see Gabriel behind the wheel of a car. It suited him much better on top of a horse.

Gabriel and I never discussed our secret but I desperately wanted to talk to him about Biffy. I had frequently noticed her around the Manor. My presumption was that she was looking for Jane and I worried that in reuniting Jane with her sons we had caused a great sense of loss for Biffy and forced her to be lonely in the tower. Ridiculously, I never found the time. My sons took all of it up and when they weren't I was asleep.

One night when the twins were about three-years old I heard the pad of feet outside the bedroom. I thought it might be one of the twins so through blurry tired eyes I went out to the gallery. Biffy was walking steadily down the corridor towards the tip of the sweeping staircase and the boys' bedroom. Suddenly, I noticed Percy. He was rigid staring at the apparition stepping towards him. Biffy stopped and caressed his hair. Percy smiled up at her but then she quickly moved on through a sea of lath and plaster in the direction of the west wing stable block.

I looked down at my son. He didn't see me. He stretched and yawned and went back to his room. I followed and tucked him in. As I bent to kiss him on his forehead he smiled up at me,

"Don't worry mummy, it's only Biffy, she won't do any harm." Stunned, I crept away back to my room and got into bed. Felix was lightly snoring and I lay awake until the morning light, staring at the ceiling and wondering how to broach the topic of Biffy with my son.

At breakfast, after Felix had left, I started the conversation by asking the boys if they had slept well. They looked at me oddly as this was a new question to them as they'd always slept well since they were old enough to walk and run about.

"Good," said Rupert. Percy copied his brother, "Good."

"Did either of you have any dreams? You know, about pirates or sailing ships or, people of any description?" I added.

"Yeah, I dreamt about a pirate who took me to an island and I had to escape by swimming through sharks," said Rupert.

"No, you didn't," said Percy.

"Yes, I did," said Rupert.

This started a feud between them so I left the subject and poured out some milk.

Not long afterwards I began to feel sick in the morning. I was pregnant again. When I announced this to Felix he whooped for joy. Then his face changed,

"My God! What if it's twin boys again, Rose?"

I would have managed but Felix was quite a lot older than me and I sensed that he was worried about being around for his sons when they were teenagers and young men.

"Best get yourself off for one of those scans again, Rose. Mrs T. can look after the boys."

It would never cross Felix's mind to take care of the twins by himself. That side of parenthood never occurred to him.

I went to see Dr Comickery for a pregnancy test and the usual check-ups. He arranged for my scan. This time I cried with relief because it wasn't twins. A single egg lodged in my womb was waiting with bated breath to form into a human. I wished for a girl.

Guy was still working his way through the collection in the house and we had become accustomed to his visits with his partner, Ray. I put them up at the Lodge so they could at least sleep together. I didn't want them to feel any embarrassment by staying in Churchbury where as a homosexual couple they might not be welcome.

Guy and Kay had brought down a number of paintings from the attic. In the bedroom, that Felix and Hannah had shared, we moved the new bed to another room. We ripped up the carpet and as part of the original refurbishment the window was repaired. In here we stored the pictures from the gallery. Guy and Ray were itemising them and covering them to protect them for their journey to London and Paris. Guy reeled off names of famous artists from across the centuries. He arranged for Kay to visit to oversee the final arrangements.

Over a cup of tea, she told me that she was sure the painting of Honora was by Gainsborough and was worth a lot of money.

"It should be in a gallery. Are you willing to sell it?"

I knew that Felix would never agree to the sale of the pictures as they were his ancestors and a record of all the people who had lived here. I explained this to Kay.

"But it's such a shame that no one can see her. It's the most sublime painting."

Her eyes began to shine just like I had seen them when she and Guy had first discovered the artwork.

"Perhaps you would agree to exhibit some of the paintings of your husband's family on loan?" she insisted.

Guy looked at me with pleading eyes. For him I would persuade Felix to agree.

"I'm sure that will be fine, as long as you arrange the insurance, I'm afraid my husband is far too busy."

Guy smiled with some relief. Kay continued without taking a breath,

"There's a much older one, not a relative I think, which I think is a self-portrait of Raphael? Do you know if he had any association with the Manor?"

Guy was nodding in excited approval.

I said I didn't know. There were so many paintings but if they wanted to check in the library they may find some answers.

Kay nodded and Guy said,

"Kay would like to take it to London, along with the others, to have the picture verified. If it is a Raphael it could be worth a lot of money. Do you think you could speak to Felix about it?"

I agreed. Guy said that we needed humidifiers in the store room so I would need to speak to Felix about that, too. He

251

suggested the sale of the Raphael may help to buy them with lots of loose change, of course, he added jokingly.

Felix was amenable about the verification of the paintings and to lend them to galleries. Art and culture were not his interests and when I jotted down on a piece of paper how much Kay thought the Raphael was going to be worth, if it was genuine, he gave a wide grin and said that I could do what I wished with it. Even though he bore no interest in the masterpieces, he would not agree to sell any of the ones linked directly to his family name. Felix was much the same about many items and I began to change my opinion of him. Possession meant more to him than caring, I thought.

Once the pictures had been stored safely and Kay and Guy had chosen the ones that they were taking away, the tapestry was removed to the central gallery. The difference in the light that came in was sublime. The tapestry looked better in its new place and the colours looked more reverberant. During that time, I would stand and stare at the door that branched through to the entrance of the tower and I'd think of Jane and wonder about Biffy.

Over that summer, Felix decided it was time that the twins learned to fish and swim. We all trundled off to the lake and I set up a picnic on the grass by the church. Whilst I was setting up, Rupert let slip that daddy had taken him and Percy to see their dead little brothers and daddy's other wife in the churchyard. This worried me but neither Rupert nor Percy seemed disturbed by it so I decided to let it go even though I wanted to scream.

Felix would take our little boys out in his truck and Rupert, in particular, enjoyed being out of doors. On this day he was keen to get into the boat. I watched as they jumped into the vessel making it rock. Felix barked out orders for them to be steady. He let them take an oar each and I watched laughing out loud as they rowed themselves round in circles. My little boys, only three-and-a-half years old but behaving like little men. They were wearing their armbands and the fluorescent orange glowed brightly in the reflection of the water. Felix handed them both a fishing rod and under his instruction, Rupert stood up to cast out into the water. He was strong and efficient, relishing this moment of testosterone-filled bond-ship with his father and brother. Percy followed suit but as he cast out with his body's weight behind him, he fell overboard.

I jumped up watching the scene as if in slow motion. Felix dived in and I could see Percy bobbing about, the orange of his arms splashing in the water. Then he was gone.

When they came ashore and I'd wrapped my two sons in towels and rubbed them dry, I swore at Felix. Rupert and Percy looked shocked.

"Don't be angry, mummy," Rupert said. "It was fun."

I banned Felix from ever taking the boys on the lake again.

"Come on Rose, he's all right. He's got to learn to swim."

He went to hug me but I was having none of it and once the boys were dry we drove back to the Manor in silence. When I calmed I informed Felix that I would take the boys to the sports centre for proper swimming lessons.

That night I woke with familiar stabbing pains in my lower back. I prodded Felix out of his slumber and ordered him to telephone Mrs T. to come over and look after the boys as I needed to go to the hospital.

After a short labour, our daughter was born at 6 a.m. The little girl that I had longed for. As ever, Felix was wide-eyed and bewildered. He had tears in his eyes as he cuddled her.

"Vivian. Can we call her Vivian?"

"That's a nice name, Felix."

"Let's call her Vivian Rose," he said.

CHAPTER 17

Linda and Charlie had started up a branch of their practice at the edge of Coventry. Sadly, Linda could not have any children of her own.

"Me fallopian tubes are gunked up," she told me. We were sitting drinking tea in the kitchen as she held sleeping Vivian in her arms.

"Well, you are more than welcome to share my crew," I said trying to sound buoyant.

I felt so sorry for Linda. She was surrounded by children on all sides, it seemed cruel that she could have none of her own. I decided to ask her to be Vivian's godmother there and then and she agreed.

Over the years, Linda threw herself into her animals, compensating, I thought, for the lack of a child. When I went to Birmingham I would visit Linda and Charlie on a long way around home. Rupert enjoyed these visits as Linda was knowledgeable about horses and he liked to follow her around her stable watching how she handled her horse. Linda loved my children and she would buy them expensive presents. Charlie and Linda would visit us but I could not budge Felix away from the farm so mum's wedding was the last time that we travelled anywhere together.

Before long, the twins demanded a pony each of their own and Felix gladly gave in. He would take the boys out on long hacks and soon they were as proficient at riding as their father. It was evident to me, and probably to everyone else, that Felix was grooming Rupert to take over his role on the farm. The birthrights of my sons were pre-determined. Fortunately, Rupert was the one who enjoyed venturing out with Felix over the Callow lands and never doubted his birthright and what the future held for him. He was very like his father and had a temperament, which at times, was dark like Felix.

Percy grew quiet and studious. He would mooch around the library reading the old books. He did a history project for school and he would spend hours researching his ancestors. The internet had come along which made things much easier. He was fascinated by the paintings and the stories I told him about them. He was outraged when he learned that we had sold the Raphael.

I argued with Felix about which school the twins should attend. They were eight-years old and had settled well at infants school in Churchbury. I was worried about moving them. Felix wanted the boys to board at his old school in Shrugsborough. In the end we compromised and agreed that they could be weekly boarders coming home at the weekends.

Percy liked to trek outdoors on his own and would wander off for miles across the Callow estate and come back with fossils. He ingratiated himself with the tenant farmers and their families and he would come back and tell me tales of how he had been given tea and cake. When he grew older it would be beer and crisps.

Once Vivian was old enough to have a pony of her own Felix bought her one. Judith was also mad keen on horses, like her mother, I thought, and she kept her own grey Welsh pony with Vivian's in the stables in the west wing.

Felix had built a ménage where the children could practise jumping and dressage skills but riding horses was something that had never attracted me. One afternoon, during the long school summer holiday, Felix was with the children and their ponies in the ménage and I could hear lots of squeals and shouts as each child took their turn going over the jumps. He saw me approaching; I liked to watch as all of them took pleasure in their horses. Judith was there, as she nearly always was. We all called her Judy, her brilliant amber eyes gleaming haughtily. Felix shouted over to me,

"Come on Rose! Come and have a go on Tripper."

Tripper was Rupert's horse, bigger than the others but suitable for a ten-year old. The children, encouraged by Felix, began to shout to me to come over and sit on Tripper. Really I should have made the assumption that I was going to fall off by paying attention to the name of my son's horse. Feeling under pressure, I reluctantly agreed to sit on Tripper. Rupert swung off with childish athleticism and Felix helped me up into the saddle.

"All right luv, just hold on to the saddle at the front here and I'll walk you around."

It actually felt quite pleasant and I grinned as Tripper walked around the edge of the arena.

"Good Rose, that's good, let's try a trot."

With all the children watching he made a clicking sound between his teeth and Tripper began to trot. My feeling of security disappeared as I felt the change in the movement of the horse jiggle beneath me and my bottom slapped ungainly on the saddle.

"Well done mum, you've got it," shouted Percy.

I looked over to him where he sat calmly on his bay and in that action, I promptly fell off. I didn't hurt myself but the embarrassment was too much. It was further prolonged by the arrival of Fiona who simply let out an, 'Oh dear!' with the exact haughty glint of her daughter.

Brushing the sand off my jeans and faking some dignity, I walked back across the ménage to the gate. As I passed Fiona I said, "Good morning." As I left, I heard them all laugh at my expense and I stormed back to the Manor feeling bruised and humiliated. After that, I swore I'd never ride a horse again.

Vivian had thick brown hair with wild and uncontrollable wispy fronds at the front. Her teeth were straight and even like mine. Having older brothers seemed to make her resilient and she and Judy, who were inseparable, would get away with teasing Rupert and Percy about all manner of things. They all grew up together, attending the same school and spending holidays riding their ponies across the moors and over the hills, swimming and fishing in the lake, which I was supposed not to know about, but of course, I did.

Time has an efficient way of passing you by without you ever noticing. This can be cruel as it forgets to remind you to stop awhile and watch the hands of the clock tick and tick until childhood and its magic has disappeared into a land far away and forgotten.

Archie and Gregory had been to university and Emily was due to follow soon. Bunnie's sons chose to remain and live and work in the county of Shrugsborough. They were natural rural men living and working on the farmlands of Langley Hall.

Because of the wider age-gap, the cousins did not see a lot of each other but Rupert would drive a tractor and trailer with Felix over to Langley Hall and bring back a ram or sheep. He liked to shoot, so he and Felix would go together when it was the season. From an early age, all the children hunted. Fiona would ride up to the Manor and collect Judy's pony which the girls preferred to keep aside Vivian's. They would all trot along the drive to the main lane to meet up with the hunt. The traditional colours and noise of the hunt were etched in the landscape.

On those occasions, I would worry about one of them falling off. All the children had experienced trips and falls from the backs of their ponies. Mostly this happened when I wasn't there. The soonest that I would hear about it was to be told exaggerated tales of bravado and proudly shown bumps and bruises when the children arrived home. Often I would wince at the sight of them but somehow it never stopped them from riding again. Sure enough, when Rupert was aged only fifteen, he took a tumble over a jump. Thankfully, he was wearing a hat but he banged his head hard and broke his collar bone. He was upset as he had been chosen for the school rugby 'A' team and now he couldn't take part. I loudly noted the fact that not being able to write was more important, but he just shrugged his shoulders. In their teenage years, Rupert and Percy lacked the art of communication and words were replaced with grunts.

"How was school?" I would ask.

Grunting noises closed the conversation rapidly.

The larder was constantly raided as my young sons grew and became strong. Mrs T. adored the children and she had a big hand in helping me bring them up. She would arrive with tray-bakes and Rupert and Percy would gorge on them as she sat and watched with a satisfied grin.

After his fall, Rupert suffered persistent headaches. Dr Comickery sent him for tests and eventually it was found that he needed glasses. Wearing them singled him out from his twin which made it easier for the teaching staff at school. I realised that the boys weren't saints and that they sometimes pretended to be each other. Rupert had a long fringe which covered his birthmark so it wasn't very easy to tell them apart. When Felix and I attended the boys' parents' evenings it was regularly hinted to us about how naughty they were.

"High spirited boys, full of enthusiasm..." they would say.

I knew it would be Rupert who would instigate any mischief.

Around this time, I received a call from Betty who told me that Gwyneth had passed away. She sounded very upset and she told me that Old Tom was beside himself with grief. They had been together for over sixty years. I rarely saw Old Tom these days. On a slow basis he had retired from his gardening job. I missed Old Tom helping me weed and dig and our days of working alongside one another turning clumps of soil into beautiful flower beds. Before he finished he began to bring Jacob with him who had inherited his grandfather's passion for gardening. Jacob was tall and slender and had red hair like his father, Young Tom. He had Betty's easy way about him and seemed mature beyond his years. He never lacked confidence in showing me how to manage things in the garden.

When Felix and I went to Gwyneth's funeral we learned from Betty that Old Tom had been concealing the fact that he had lung cancer. Betty blamed it on his pipe smoking. A few months later he passed away. When I heard the news I sat on the bottom stair and cried. Felix was visibly upset and we both drove down to see Betty and Young Tom to offer our condolences.

"I know it's not the right time, but Jacob or Molly are welcome to have the tenancy in the cottage next door. I'll keep it vacant for them."

"Thanks, Mr Langley," Young Tom replied.

I found it odd that he referred to Felix as Mr Langley. I always felt on the most friendly terms with Betty and Young Tom and their children but I suppose they felt some deference to their landlord.

After Old Tom's funeral we planted a tree next to his favourite seat in the orchard in the walled garden, which was now bountiful. I missed his company. Never being a man of a lot of words, when he did speak it was always worth the wait. I had learned so much from him.

Beavering away in the garden I looked over at Jacob, taller than his grandfather, a handsome young man. I realised that this house made its history by repeating things. I ordered an inscribed wall plate which Jacob and I hung on the door to the walled garden: Old Tom's Garden.

Rupert scraped through his school exams. I would try and speak to Felix about him but he was nonchalant about Rupert's education.

"There's no point in him being a great scholar, Rose. He will have his work cut out here. What do you think I've been doing with him all these years?"

He was right, I knew, but I insisted that he went to a local agricultural college to learn land management.

Percy, on the other hand, worked hard at school. I was so proud when he announced that he had gained a place at Cambridge to read art history and classics. He never brought a girlfriend home. At times, I wondered if my son was 'gay'. That was the label for homosexual men then. It sounded so much nicer than, 'poofs' as my dad would call them. I would not have minded at all if Percy had brought a man home. I think he understood that about me. Although Guy and Ray had been visiting for years I think it would have been difficult for Percy to face up to his father and brother about his sexuality.

As far as they were concerned, sheep mated with rams, cows with bulls and pigs with sows and that was that. When Guy and Ray would visit, Felix would sometimes take off his cap and scratch his head and say

"It's not normal that, Rose," as he looked over at the Lodge.

I would look at him and think, *look who's talking, a man, who for years, kept a bed of his dead wife's blood...* But I would say nothing to keep the peace.

CHAPTER 18

One afternoon, I found Vivian sitting on the piano stool. She was only nine but she was so much more mature than her brothers. That was the nature of girls. She was tinkling on the keys, picking out some simple tunes. When she saw me she looked up and asked,

"Mum, do you think it would be OK for me to have some lessons? Mrs Bainbridge teaches piano after school on a Monday and as I don't have any clubs would it be all right if I went?"

"Of course, darling," I responded. "I'll telephone school to arrange it."

Vivian smiled at me.

I went to the old gramophone player and picked out a Charleston record and started to dance around the piano. I grabbed at her hands and pulled her off the stool and we danced together around the piano still topped with silver frames and filled with my daughter's ancestors. I didn't notice Felix standing at the door coming to see who was making the noise. When the music finished Vivian left for the stables. He winked at her on the way out and said,

"Your namesake played the piano you know, Vivian."

I put on a Cole Porter 78 rpm record, *Night and Day*. Then he came and put his arms around me and we swayed until the music stopped. I felt elated as this was a rare moment of shared affection outside of our bedroom.

When I took the three of my children to pantomimes, plays and concerts, Vivian took to our visits to Birmingham with the most glee. When the boys became disinterested Vivian and I would go together and stay with mum and Trevor. Vivian wasn't fazed by the vast crowds or the bustle of the big shops and theatres. She delighted in them. When she was thirteen, the school had taken her class to London and she vowed to me then that she was going to live there.

Percy and Rupert had learned to play guitars and on rare nights we would gather in the drawing room and our children would entertain us with their musical talents.

My lovely dogs, Phoebe and Thor, passed away and were replaced by working dogs from a vinaceous-faced farmer. We named them Brandy and Snap. Vivian had rescued a cat which promptly gave birth to six kittens. I had forbidden her to keep them but I would find them in odd places, warmly curled up and purring and I weakened and helped Vivian to choose names for them all.

Felix realised, that as the children got older, I needed some company around the house, so he brought me two Jack Russell puppies. I trained them so that they shadowed me everywhere and we let them sleep in their baskets in front of the kitchen fireplace. I called them Pixie and Trixie and they soon became part of our family in such a different way from the working dogs that Felix and Rupert kept.

Rupert and Felix spent a lot of time together. They were so similar it was quite remarkable. It was easy to tell if they were in a bad mood as their birthmarks would deepen and become blacker as they furrowed their brows. I wondered whether they had long conversations. Certainly, Felix would spend time teaching Rupert to drive a tractor, a combine harvester and how to plough and sow in straight lines. Sometimes, I thought it would be nice to be a fly on a wall to overhear them. There was a closer relationship between those two than with Percy.

Felix lacked the finesse that Percy craved. He sought Gabriel out for this and he would walk to the rectory and spend hours with Gabriel discussing Darwin, God and the classics. Gabriel enriched Percy with enthusiasm and the pair enjoyed their long discussions.

Percy shunned crowds and when he was too old for me to persuade him to come to the theatre he would wander off to the museum or the art gallery. He would meet Vivian and I, Judy too if she had been with us, at the train station with a grateful look to be going home.

Rupert had ceased coming to Birmingham from an early age.

"Dad needs me on the farm, mum," he would say. "That's far more important than watching some poof ponce around in tights."

God he was like his father, I would think. Or was there a patch of my father in him. I hadn't heard the word poof for years and I wondered where Rupert had heard it.

"Don't be rude, Rupert. Male ballet dancers are probably more physically fit than you are. I bet they would beat you in a hay bale-throwing competition any day."

"Yeah, well, sorry mum but it's just not my cup of tea. Honestly, dad needs me here."

"Of course he does, darling," I would say, knowing that he was right.

Most nights I slept well. Felix was virtually asleep as soon as his head hit the pillow but occasionally I would need to get up to go to the bathroom. Often I would see Biffy trawling along the corridor, running her hand along the wall. Percy was home, a break from university and as I crept to the bathroom, having become quite accustomed to seeing Biffy walk about our house, Percy came out of his room. Biffy was just gliding past

263

when he caught sight of her disappear into the walls of the east wing. I didn't know what to do or say so I just stood there limply.

"Mum, don't worry, it's OK. I came out here on purpose to see if Biffy was still around."

"How do you know she is called Biffy?" I asked.

"Because she told me."

I went into the bathroom and Percy went back to bed.

Felix and I had the strangest of relationships. He made love to me often and as the children got older he was cajoled into remembering my birthday. But we never spoke about his life with Hannah or when things cropped up to remind us of our past. They were ignored; left unspoken. When I came to the Manor I found Felix's lost soul and my burning desire was to redeem him. Personal issues were never on his agenda. I found in Percy that same quietness. There were things better left unsaid and I never raised the subject of Biffy. Somehow, he knew her name and like me, he wasn't frightened by her ghost.

Betty had come up to the Manor to see me. Jacob was to be married to a girl from Churchbury. Her father was our vet and I recognised her name when Betty told me. As we were both church wardens she asked if I would open up the church on the morning of the wedding. I agreed, of course, and accepted her invitation to my family to attend. Tentatively, she asked if I would help her with the flowers. She also asked me if Jacob and Helena could have Old Tom's and Gwyneth's cottage. I agreed and promised that I would make arrangements to bring the house up-to-date with fittings and decorations. Betty beamed at me.

Gabriel telephoned to say that Mrs T. had taken a 'turn' and that it was probably a good idea to visit. I had never been to Home Farm which she had inherited down the line from Eliza Thompson. I was surprised that it was fairly grand. It was the only house on the estate not owned by my husband. It had a large door and leaded windows. Black beams looked freshly painted and wisteria clung to the white plaster. The garden was full of flowers and there was a greenhouse on the side lawn abundant with tomatoes.

It was her son Richard who answered the door.

"Lady Langley, how nice of you to come. I'm afraid that mum is not well, not well at all."

I flinched at his reference to me as 'Lady' as I stepped inside the house where Eliza Thompson had resided all those years ago. It was a gift to a mistress by a rapacious old man.

A bed had been brought down to the sitting room where Mrs T. was propped up by an inordinate amount of pillows. There was an air cylinder by the bed and from it two tubes went in to her nose. I could hear her breath rattle. Her huge form filled the bed.

An Asian woman with kindly eyes came in to offer me tea. Anita, I thought.

Gabriel was sat by her side with her son. Mr Jones, her partner, had passed away some years before and I felt slightly ashamed that I had never met him. Anita came in with tea for us all and laid the tray on a table just as Mrs T.'s throat gurgled and she took her last breath. Anita looked at me with startled doe eyes and I led her out to the kitchen taking the tray back out with me. I poured out the tea and we sat for a while whilst Gabriel completed Mrs T.'s last rights and Richard said goodbye to his mother.

On the day before the funeral, I walked down to the church to organise the flowers. On the way I heard Gabriel calling from behind me. He had been down to Betty's cottage to finalise the wedding plans for Jacob and Helena.

It was a long time, a very long time since I had the opportunity to speak with Gabriel alone.

"No horse today, Gabriel?"

"No, Winston's lame and I thought the walk would do me good. It's a beautiful day, don't you think?"

We walked to the brow of the hill and stopped to look over a gate to the countryside spread out before us like a magic carpet.

"You're right, Gabriel, it is a beautiful day."

We drank in the scene and then after a while as we meandered along I plucked up the courage and asked him what had happened to him in India.

He looked down at me with his penetrating eyes that seemed to be able to read your mind.

"You remember me telling you that?"

"Of course, Gabriel. You promised to tell me one day and I guess, well, here is the day."

"I told you my father was a missionary? Well, he and my mother were extremely busy so they appointed an Ayah to look after me. An Ayah is a person like a nanny. I loved my Ayah she was like a mother to me. She had the patience of a saint and she would sit with me for hours telling me stories of the great Buddha and of how he came to be. I was fascinated by the tales which were so contradictory to the ones that my father told me from the Bible.

"In the middle of the night, when I was aged about nine or ten, my Ayah suddenly appeared at my bedside. She was rocking me frantically urging me to get under the bed. In my grogginess I obeyed and crawled under. Within a few seconds the room began to shake. I heard the crumbling of concrete and plaster fall all around me."

"What was it? An earthquake?"

"Yes, an earthquake that lasted only a few minutes but seemed like a lifetime. It was devastating.

"But I was safe because my Ayah warned me to get under the bed. Our bungalow had imploded all around me and both my parents were dead."

"Oh God, I'm so sorry Gabriel. And your Ayah?"

"Dead too, Rose."

He looked crestfallen.

"Thing is Rose, my Ayah was at her own home five miles away at the time. She was nowhere near our home yet she came to me, to save me. I can't explain it. I think it was God's doing. He wanted me to be saved so that I could be his representative on Earth."

We walked in silence the rest of the way. I didn't know what to say.

At the church I busied myself with tidying the hymn books and dusting the shelves. After a while, Gabriel called me to sit with him on a pew.

"Eliza!" He said nothing more as he took my hand.

"What about her?" I replied.

"Yes, indeed, what about her, Rose?"

I bit on my lip.

"Rose, I've not mentioned this to you before but don't you think it is a little strange that your middle name is Eliza? There is a connection between you, I feel it. I feel it as strongly as I did that night when I hid under the bed. We need to find out why." He went on, "Isn't your mum's middle name Eliza too? And wasn't she born around here somewhere? That's a bit of a coincidence in anyone's books."

I shrugged my shoulders.

"One day we probably will know the connection Gabriel but not now."

I looked around the church.

"So many marriages, christenings and deaths. It's history constantly repeating itself. My life is too full at the moment Gabriel to think about Eliza. It's not the right time."

He patted my hand.

"I know Rose, I know," he said reassuringly. "But the time will come, Rose."

He took a breath wondering whether to raise the subject but said, "Is Biffy still wandering the corridors at the Manor?"

"Yes, we still have Biffy," I answered matter-of-factly. "She's like part of the furniture. By the way, did you know that Percy has seen her? Once as a child but more recently."

"Yes, he told me on one of his many visits, Rose. Don't worry, I didn't divulge anything about Jane. I merely said that Biffy was looking for someone. Biffy's hauntings will stop Rose when you resolve your issues with Eliza."

I wanted to feel the urge to release Biffy but now didn't feel like the right time. There was something on my mind that I had not yet shared with anyone. I was worried about Felix. Just lately his memory seemed to fail him. He seemed to have no sense of recall and at times he seemed to forget my name and the name of his children.

I felt at odds at Mrs T.'s funeral. I mourned her loss, of course, I did, she had been a big part of our family; yet my thoughts were blurred as I felt anxious about my husband. I sat with Richard and Anita and put my arms about them and handed over a regular amount of tissues as we all wept. When she was lowered into her grave a ray of sunshine lit the sunny spot that was sheltered by an ancient yew. It had taken ten pall bearers to carry her coffin which was large. She was a big woman in size and character. I felt sad. The children were sad too.

"I'll miss her flapjacks the most," said Rupert.

I went to the church very early on the morning of Jacob's wedding. I was looking forward to the occasion and Jacob's bride was going to be driven to the church in a horse and cart decorated with flowers by her father-in-law to be, Young Tom. We still called him Young Tom even though his father had been dead for a number of years.

Alone, I busied myself with sweeping the aisles and straightening a floppy flower stem here and there. The light beaming in was crystal clear and waves of colour like spotlights lit up the interior producing a mellifluous, calm and peaceful atmosphere.

A sunbeam faltered as a figure walked through it. Jane! I watched as she seemed to glide over the medieval tiles, her cloak swirling behind her as she drifted towards the plaque on the wall. I stood breathless. I thought I could see the forms of two men dressed in red tunics standing proudly beside her. Each had a wide and trimmed moustache and on one I saw the vivid slashes of a Cross of Soot on his forehead. Jane knelt and closed her hands in prayer, crossing herself and shutting her eyes. After a few minutes she got up and stood silently touching the plaque with an outstretched delicate hand. I thought she hadn't seen me but then she turned and whispered into the air.

"Rose." Then the apparitions were gone.

Vivian and Judy were horse mad. There were many tears shed over the years as Mr Williams, our vet, visited to put down an old or lame pony and I would ensure that we did something away from the Manor as I could not bear for the girls to hear the gunshot. We would visit my mother or sometimes we would meet up with Linda in the centre of Birmingham for lunch. Then, I chose to travel on the train, it was much easier than the challenge of driving there.

I allowed the girls to spend an hour on their own to shop and Linda would remark about the times she stole tights from Marks and Spencer and we would giggle at her audacity. I watched as the girls toddled off explaining to Linda about my hard work to get them out of their jodhpurs even for a day. I doubted very much that they were like us at the same age.

On one occasion, as Linda and I exchanged woes about our lives and moaned about our husband's deficiencies over a coffee, two uniformed policemen came walking through the arcade where we sat outside the little coffee shop. I froze. Linda saw my face and then the two policemen came towards us. Quickly, she stood up,

"Let's go inside and pay the bill. Shall we?"

I couldn't move so she grabbed my arm and pulled me off my chair to go inside the little café. Linda took out her purse and paid the bill. I watched transfixed as the uniformed men walked by. One was very young, the other had grey hair peeping out from under his hat and his belt was tied tightly around his middle-age spread. It was Wayne.

Linda took hold of me waiting for them to pass by the window.

"You OK? That was him, wasn't it?"

"It was Linda, it was."

It felt strange to me that the perpetrator of all my grief was allowed to walk freely about the centre of Birmingham: To roam the streets in an authoritative uniform. I wanted to run after him, point him out and scream at the top of my voice, "*Do you know what he did to me? That man is a rapist.*"

"He's got no conscience, Rose," Linda said seeming to read my mind. "You've gone really pale, I think you need something stronger than coffee. Come on, let's walk over to the Mail Box and find a bar, there's a nice Italian one I know, me and Charlie go there after the theatre."

We sat sipping wine which calmed me. All I wanted to do was to find the girls, scoop them up and take them home.

Vivian had a rare talent for music and she could play any instrument. I suspected that she inherited this talent from her grandmother Vivian, as none of my family, as far as I knew, was musical. She always said to me that she would not choose music as her profession. She did not want to mix her hobby with a career. Vivian was a gifted musician and passed her grades with distinction. It was a natural progress when she finished school that she would go to university. Once she had a degree, she argued, she could get any job she wanted. She was a determined young lady and followed Percy to Cambridge coming out with a first class degree.

Judy went to university in Birmingham to study business management. Her choice of career seemed to suit her growing relentless trait of organising everything and everyone.

One day, Bunnie arrived looking thinner and pale.

"Whatever's the matter?" I asked.

"It's Emily."

"Emily?" I thought her to be ill.

"She's going to live in Australia. Oh I can't bear it. The other side of the world. Jon, her husband, has got a job with an Australian airline and they are going to settle there."

I knew, of course, that Emily had married a pilot. Something seemed to course through the veins of the Langley girls. It was a need to travel; a gypsy longing. I comforted her and made her coffee and did my utmost to cheer her up suggesting holidays abroad with Fergus now that the boys were running the farm. She dried her eyes and shot me a false smile. When she had calmed a little I uttered the words that I had been dreading for a while.

"How's Fergus' memory? I only ask because obviously he is the same age as Felix and his mind seems to be deteriorating just lately."

"Oh! No, well, no actually Fergus is fine. Are you worried, Rose? Perhaps he should see a doctor?"

"Oh, it's probably just that he has a lot on his mind. He's doing too much, as ever."

Dr Comickery had retired and there was a new young doctor at the surgery. Perhaps I would make an appointment. Sometimes I saw Dr Comickery and his wife walking the hills or the moors on the footpaths that ran through the Callow lands. I would wave and they would wave back. I had never once been for a walk with Felix on my own. When the children were younger we would walk out with the ponies but as I reflected, I realised that we had no romantic times together.

I doubted that I would get Felix near a doctor so I inwardly hoped that it was his age that was making him forgetful.

Alwyn retired and in the absence of Mrs T., I found two young Polish women to come and clean the Manor for two days a week. Ewa and Halina were startling in their efficiency and would arrive in their car piled high with their own buckets and mops and cleaning products. One would tackle upstairs and the other downstairs although the kitchen remained my domain. Soon after, I engaged their husbands and a team of their friends, also trustworthy and reliable, to help with odd jobs and to support Jacob in the gardens. Jacob was working full-time as he expanded and maintained the gardens and he appreciated the extra help. He grew an abundance of produce and my freezer was always overflowing with seasonal vegetables and fruit. Helena was already expecting their first child. I suspected that she may have been pregnant at the wedding but I was in no position to be morally affronted by that. Betty was over the moon. On a visit to her cottage one fine summer's day she told me that her daughter Molly had got a great job in Shrugsborough as a legal administrator.

"It's where Fiona works, isn't that great? She's also moving in with Billy, her boyfriend. You met him at Jacob's wedding. He's a plumber starting up his own business. They're buying a terraced house together in the centre of town. I'm so happy for her."

"It's excellent news, Betty. Gosh, you're going to be a grandma too. How do you feel about that?"

"I can't tell you how excited I am, Rose. It's made me so happy."

I was glad for my friend. We often visited each other and we always made some space in our conversations for Gabriel. Betty was, as ever, still enamoured by our dashing vicar and we would chuckle together about his handsome looks that never seem to leave him.

One day, in the stable yard, I noticed one of the Polish men taking a keen interest in the horses. I approached him as Vivian's horse nestled against his face, seemingly kissing him. He doffed his cap at me. In his Polish accent he spoke.

"You have very fine horses, Lady Langley."

"Thank you," I said. "You seem to know your way around them?"

"Ah yes, I do. I used to ride them in a circus in Latvia."

"Latvia, you are not Polish?"

"No madam, I am not. I am Latvian."

I felt embarrassed at my presumption.

"Well, it would be great if you would take over the responsibility of looking after the horses while Vivian, Judy and Percy are away. I think Rupert finds it a bit of a bind. I'll pay you, of course."

"I would like that, madam. Do you ride, madam?"

"No, I'm rather afraid I never have."

"Then I will teach you," he said.

I smiled at him graciously.

"Maybe, one day."

"No, soon, whilst the weather is good. You look like a natural to me, Lady Langley."

"Of that, I certainly am not. I tried once and I fell off."

"Only the best riders fall off, madam. I have fallen many times."

He looked rugged and his face was dark and swarthy with many pit marks and lines.

"Meet me here tomorrow, say at ten? I will teach you," he said.

"Perhaps," I exclaimed. "I'll check my diary. What's your name?"

"Žanis."

"Thank you, Žanis."

I was flirting with him and as I walked back to the house I felt really stupid. Žanis looked quite a few years younger than me. Lately I had been having hot flushes so I put it all down to the time of my life. Later that evening, after a long soak in the bath, I stared at my reflection in the mirror. My body had changed considerably in the last twenty-five years. My hips were broader, my breasts hung low, my stomach seemed to have developed in to a ball of lumpy flab and my scars looked crinkled. I didn't like what I saw. Where had Rose gone to, I wondered?

The age gap between Felix and I grew wider. Felix was in his early seventies. I could not remember the last time that we had made love. It seemed that his brain, or rather his anatomy, had forgotten how. In a way I was glad, as looking at myself in the mirror, I had no desire for any man to see me. I realised that I had been flattered by Žanis and decided to pull myself together. In the morning I would go to the stables and tell him that I had changed my mind about having a lesson.

When I arrived Žanis was holding Vivian's horse by the reins. She wore no saddle. Even in my own limited experience I knew that Ginger should be wearing a saddle. Žanis threw me a wide smile.

"The best horse for you to learn on in the stable, I think, madam."

"But where's her saddle?" I asked.

"Today you learn without a saddle. This is so that you can get the feel of the horse between your legs. You will like the sensation I think?"

I could not make out whether he was being suggestive but at that moment my resolve melted and I found Žanis helping me up on to Ginger's back.

"I'm surprised that you chose Ginger," I said as he led me to the ménage. "I mean, Vivian really only keeps her for hunting when she is at home now. Isn't she a bit headstrong?"

"Ginger, *he pronounced her name as Geengar,* is the best horse for you, madam. She is well schooled and she is a polite lady."

"Very well, but please do stop calling me madam. My name is Rose and calling me Rose is fine by me."

"Like a flower. You and your name are beautiful like a flower."

Žanis was rather irresistible but I maintained some decorum as he led me in a walk around the ménage.

"That's good Rose, very good. Put your weight into your bottom and relax. Ginger is a good girl she won't do anything unless you ask her to."

He walked me around for about half an hour then led us back to the stables. He took my arm as I slid off Ginger.

"You did well, Rose. Did you enjoy that? Come again tomorrow. I will teach you how to ride the Latvian way. You have plenty of time, Rose? You're not planning to go anywhere? I can teach you for one hour per day."

I looked at him. I could not tell if it was just his manner but somehow I thought he was flirting with me.

"No, I'm not going anywhere. I'll see you tomorrow. Thank you."

My muscles felt sore but I had enjoyed the experience. All my family rode and there were plenty of horses in the stables. I missed the company of my children and I needed something new in my life and riding a horse seemed logical. The thought of riding out over the moors did appeal to me. Anyway, that's how I justified it to myself for my time with Žanis each day.

Rupert had a Chinese girlfriend and that evening she was sleeping over for the first time. I was concerned about the pair sleeping in the same bed. Percy was at Cambridge completing his Masters and Vivian was away too. I wanted to chat to Felix about this but I realised that it would be pointless. Our conversations, of late, weren't sinking in it seemed.

I cooked supper. Rupert could not keep his eyes off An. She was a pretty young girl. Her black hair fell straight across her shoulders and her almond eyes expressed sincerity. Her conversation over supper was clever and bright. Rupert had met her in a bar in Shrugsborough and they had been together for about six months. Both her parents were doctors and had moved up to Shrugsborough from London. The way Rupert looked at her reminded me of the way Felix had looked at me when he wished for us to go to bed. Although Rupert made a good job of stretching out the evening, I knew that he could not wait to take An upstairs. Unexpectedly, Felix engaged An in conversation.

"That's a biblical name isn't it? Anne?"

An looked uncomfortable for a moment, then she smiled and replied,

"Actually, it's a Chinese name, it is spelt A-N just the A and the N. In Chinese it means peace."

"Peace? You'll get no peace with my son whatever your name is. My mother had a name that meant something. She was called Vivian and that means a woman of the water, or some such thing and she died in a lake so I hope for your sake that you die in peace as your name permits."

It was awkward. Felix seemed very lucid, yet his comments came across as being rude.

"Oh, peace," I said. "That's a lovely name."

Rupert and I exchanged a look across the table.

A scream awoke me in the middle of the night. I dashed out of the bedroom only to find An trembling at the top of the stairs. Her little body was soaked in perspiration. Rupert rushed out of the bedroom naked with a blanket and folded it around her. Looking at me he yelled,

"Bloody Biffy, mum. Half frightened An to death. It's about time you did something about her," he said gruffly.

He took An back to the room that he normally shared with Percy. I was dumbfounded for a moment.

"So Rupert knows about Biffy too? Why had he never said?"

An never came to our house again and Rupert never mentioned the incident to me. I think he felt bad for shouting at me. But he had a point. Something should be done about poor Biffy.

PART SEVEN

Sometimes we are inseparable
in life and even in death

CHAPTER 19

I believe that having children had made me less selfish. I no longer dwelt on things from the past. Felix's window of opportunity for future parenting was passing. As he grew old he forgot the things that brought us together, our children, this fragile house, my love for him.

Our expanded family grew and it had become a well-founded tradition that everyone came to the Manor on Boxing Day for a buffet after the hunt. I was looking forward to Christmas this year as all my children were home.

Gabriel had found Percy a placement at a school in India as a volunteer and he was coming back. Vivian was bringing her new boyfriend and naturally Rupert and Felix would give up the day to spend with us.

Vivian and her boyfriend arrived a few days before. My daughter looked different. She had been living in London for over a year and worked at the British Broadcasting Company [BBC] as a researcher. Her choice of job had not surprised me at all for she always had a curious mind. Vivian and Percy were alike in that way; although they took contrasting paths.

She was thinner which made her neck look longer, like her namesake. Her hair had been fashionably cut and it was obvious to me that she was very much in love with Bertie.

Bertie was quiet but polite. He was the type of person who would take some time to get to know. He was very attentive towards Vivian and seemed not to believe his luck in having such a pretty and intelligent girlfriend. I thought he underestimated himself. Bertie was tall and dark. He wasn't what you would call good-looking but he had a wonderful smile and kind eyes.

There was the question of sleeping arrangements and I broached the subject with Vivian.

"Oh mum! You are funny. You know we sleep together at home, in London, right? Dad probably won't even notice so as long as you are all right about it we'll sleep in my room. In the twin beds."

Vivian was pragmatic. I remembered when she had started her period aged thirteen. She came up to me saying that I needed to add some sanitary towels to my shopping list.

"Don't worry, mum, Mrs Needham gave us all a lesson on the birds and bees. Also, I sleep in a dorm with eleven other girls so I know all about this stuff. Do me a favour though, don't tell dad or my brothers, will you?" The situation was dealt with like the matter of fact that it was.

Vivian went to the snug to ring Judy and I could hear their excited banter from the kitchen.

Bertie didn't hunt so he was going to spend the day at home with me. I was grateful as I needed his help in the kitchen and he willingly offered his assistance.

Percy arrived greeted with a flurry of snow. He looked tired from his journey. I hugged and kissed him until he told me to stop fussing and went to his room for a lie down. My returning son taught little children in a land far away. He made me realise that I had never been anywhere. Mum and Trevor had visited half the world in their lifetime. They were arriving tomorrow, Christmas Eve and I hoped the weather would not be too bad. I worried about Trevor driving, he was in his eighties and it was a long journey for him. Thinking back, I thought of my mother at my age. She had looked so young, revitalised by her love for Trevor and his for her.

With all the children sat around the kitchen table, conversation flowed.

"No, seriously, say that again. Your dad is Frankie Tattoo?"

Bertie nodded. "Yes, he is. I am the product of his second marriage and I have another brother. Our mother is Lillian Birchwood, she used to sing in the pop duo Oca and Fifi. Do you remember them? My mum is Oca."

"Remember them! I've still got their poster on my bedroom wall!" exclaimed Rupert excitedly.

Bertie looked rather embarrassed by Rupert's questions but we were all impressed by his parents. I had heard their music booming out of the children's bedrooms for many years.

"Do you play anything?" asked Percy.

"Acoustic guitar but not as well as my father."

Bertie looked at Vivian for help. He felt out of his depth and it was clear that he did not wish to be the focus of attention. I wondered whether he shunned publicity. He must have grown up all around it.

"Hey boys, I spoke to Jude's today. She's coming up for the hunt. I think she's going to ride Winston as Truffles is lame.

"Ginger is in terrific condition. That new groom that mum's employed is marvellous with the horses. I took Bertie out earlier to meet the horses and he was there. What's his name, Žanis I think?"

"Or Žanis the Penis, as I like to call him," said Rupert.

Vivian playfully struck her brother.

"You are so coarse Rupert. The trouble with you is that you spend your day watching various beasts copulate. That's all you have on your mind, you're disgusting!"

I broke the bickering by announcing,

"He's been teaching me to ride, on Ginger actually Vivian."

There was an uplift of noise from the table expressing disbelief.

"Well, you all ride so I thought it was about time I did, too. I'll have you know that I can now canter quite confidently around the ménage and even go over a couple of the small jumps."

Percy piped up. "Well done mum, that's brilliant."

"Thank you."

I mockingly proposed that I would join them on the hunt but that I was needed to stay at home to make my renowned turkey, Brie and cranberry sandwiches, with Bertie's help, of course."

We all laughed.

"Well mum, your turkey, Brie and cranberry sandwiches are worth staying at home for, if nothing else." She added sadly, "We miss those years of Mrs T. being around to help."

"I do, too. The new girls bring their drinks in flasks and stand by the window at the end of the central gallery talking in Polish so that I have no idea what they are saying. Not a bit like Mrs T. who would spend half her working time sat at the table chatting."

We were quiet for a while until Rupert said,

"I miss her tray bakes."

In unison, we all said, 'We know, Rupert!"

I looked over at Felix who was half asleep in a chair by the fire. The boys went to tune their guitars. Vivian looked over at her father.

"Mum, is everything OK? With dad, I mean. Are you coping? I feel a bit rotten leaving you here while I'm in London."

I took my daughter's hand in mine and caressed her face.

"We are fine darling, honestly, don't worry." I squeezed her hard. "I am so proud of you, Vivian. Bertie seems really nice."

"He's asked me to marry him, won't that be wonderful?"

"Very wonderful," I said with excitement.

She looked over at Felix.

"Mum, you know that I would like a smart London wedding."

I sighed.

"No mum, it's all right. I know dad wouldn't travel. I'd like to have it here. A marquee on the lawn. Bertie's going to ask for dad's permission when he can find the right moment. Do you know that Bertie's mother lives in Shrugsborough? In the north and that she actually rides with the North Shrugsborough Hunt, so you see, it's convenient to everyone to have the wedding here. Promise, not a word to the boys, mum until we've told dad."

I woke Felix and we gathered in the drawing room. Rupert had lit a fire and it roared in the hearth as Vivian took her seat at the piano and guitars were played and songs were sung and Felix slept.

On Christmas morning, after breakfast, we all sat in the snug to open our presents. For a joke, Rupert gave Percy a plastic naked doll which he obligingly blew up. Felix bellowed with laughter and we guffawed raucously as she rose up and got caught in the chandelier and dangled above us. She remained there for months until Rupert remembered to take her down.

Trevor and mum had arrived safely and watched in amusement as we exchanged presents. Vivian disappeared to her car and came back with an odd-shaped gift. She was excited to give it and she wore a big smile.

"Here, this is for you two. A sharing present, Rupert, Percy, no disagreements, it's for both of you, from me and Bertie."

They unwrapped their gift and exclaimed delighted, thankful surprise.

"What is it?" asked my mum. "It's not another sex toy is it?"

We all yelped with laughter.

"No, Grannie, it's a metal detector for finding things buried in the ground."

Felix was particularly lucid.

"I found your mum's ring in the ground, you know. Show them Rose, the ring on your finger."

I held up my hand.

"Where did you find it?" Percy asked.

"I'll show you tomorrow," Felix said.

I pulled Vivian to one side to advise her that Felix was in good form today so it was probably a good idea for Bertie to ask the question. Then we began to shoo everyone out of the room, back to the kitchen for a cup of tea under some protest. I managed to grab Percy's arm and hinted that Bertie needed to be alone with his dad and he got the idea and supported my mother back to the kitchen.

We sat mum and Trevor by the fire and the boys sat at the table as Vivian and I made tea. We waited with bated breath and at last Bertie came in with Felix at his side.

"Rupert, I want you to go down to the cellar and bring back a couple of bottles of champagne. We all have something to celebrate, Vivian is marrying Bertie."

"Poor bloke," shouted Rupert mischievously as he gave Bertie a hug.

"Another wedding?" said Trevor rousing from his slumber.

"Another wedding. It will be the best one yet!" I told him.

We had lunch in the dining room using all the crystal and lovely china. I wallowed in the glow at having my family all around me and I felt joyous. That night, in bed and to my surprise, Felix tenderly kissed my lips.

"Thank you for everything Hannah. I love you."

Tears fell down my cheeks. I held my husband in the dark until he fell asleep.

"I love you too," I said.

CHAPTER 20

A hustle of family arrived after the hunt: Bunnie, Fergus, Archie and Gregory with their wives Christina and Verity and the five children they'd had between them. Also, Emily and Jon and her twin daughters, Elizabeth and Rebecca. Bunnie's eyes shone brightly, happy to have Emily back in the UK for a while.

Gabriel, Fiona and Judy came up later arriving with Betty and her family. Vivian and I went around with trays filled with sandwiches and sausage rolls, nibbles, cakes and mince pies. We drank champagne when Vivian announced her news. Gabriel agreed to take the service at St Laurence's and a date was set for the wedding at the end of August.

Small presents were exchanged and we all had a jolly time. The hunt had apparently been a marvellous event and a good ride out. I noticed Rupert talking fervently with Judy in a corner. She was wearing a red dress and high heels. Her strawberry blonde hair was cascading over her shoulders in large curls and her face was made up. Her lips were pouting with red lipstick and I saw a look in Rupert's eye that I recognised. Judy's body language showed that she was evidently enjoying her time with Rupert.

Betty came over.

"Thanks, Rose, it was a lovely 'do' as ever. We're off now."

Jacob held his son as he placed his arm in the crook of the back of his pregnant wife and we all kissed each other goodbye. They left through the main entrance and I opened the door for them to leave. There was a hush in the air as snow fell softly into the courtyard. The tree in the east wing was bare and caught the flakes on its branches making it look luminous and ghostly.

I went back to the kitchen to load the dishwasher. Fiona came in.

"Can I help?"

"Oh no, it's all right Fiona, I'm just going to load these few things and put them on before the next round comes in, thanks."

I expected her to leave but she dallied and sat at the table.

"Congratulations on Vivian's news. Bertie seems very pleasant. Judy is thrilled as Vivian's just asked her to be chief bridesmaid."

"Yes, he does seem nice, doesn't he?" I was taken aback, not used to Fiona's informality. I suspected she wanted to tell me something and she seemed to be summoning up the courage.

"It's our thirtieth wedding anniversary in the summer and we are having a bit of a party to celebrate. Nothing too big, a small marquee on the lawn at the rectory. It's your anniversary next year too, of course. I do hope you can make it. It will be before Vivian's wedding, in the beginning of July. Have you and Felix planned anything?"

I looked over at Fiona, at her long toned legs, her perfect face and hair and her crisp manner.

"No, I doubt Felix will remember so for us there is no point. At the moment we are just happy to get through each day. Yes, we will come, of course."

She stood up and took a deep breath.

"Rose, I wanted to talk to you about Rupert and Judy."

At that moment Vivian came in carrying a tray of glasses.

"What about Rupert and Judy?" she said.

288

"Oh nothing, it was something about the hunt. Sorry, I've forgotten," Fiona said and she left.

"Mum, those two, honestly, Rupert and Judy, you should have seen them this morning, they were racing each other like crazy, I swear, I don't know how they got away with it. Master Williams, you know that he's Helena's dad don't you? Well, he was absolutely furious with them."

I looked out of the window. The snow was casting a premonition on me. Vivian came beside me,

"They'll be no metal detecting for a while. That looks like it's going to settle."

"Mum, is it OK for Judy to stop tonight? We're going to have a few drinks and play some music.

"I think Fiona and Gabriel are leaving now."

Percy fetched their coats and I watched Gabriel wrap his scarf around his neck. The brilliance was fading in his eyes but there was enough penetration left in them to suck a person in. I felt uncomfortable with the secret feelings I had about his daughter and my son and I wondered what he would think if I told him.

Fiona kissed me coldly on my cheek and looked disgruntled. She had wanted to tell me something. I had guessed what it was and now we had missed the chance to speak.

Gabriel gave me a hug.

"Say goodbye to Felix and your mum and Trevor for us, won't you?"

He hugged his daughter and kissed her goodbye. "Hopefully, see you tomorrow, darling. We'll keep our eye on the weather. Rupert can always bring you down in the tractor if you get stuck. When are you back at work, Tuesday?"

"Come on Gabriel, you will miss your evening service if you don't hurry up," Fiona uttered as she stepped out into a blanket of white.

We watched as Gabriel started his 4×4 and skilfully drove it over the snow and down the drive. Rupert rubbed his hands together.

"Right, who's up for some wine?" The young ones disappeared into the drawing room. I heard Vivian play the piano and laughter and merriment coming through the door.

Bunnie's family were in the snug. They were saying goodbye to Felix. He looked drowsy.

"Bunnie, Bunnie? Are we having rabbit for lunch?"

"No, not rabbit for lunch, it's your sister-in-law."

Bunnie looked embarrassed but she shook his hand and kissed him on the cheek. Fergus shook hands with his brother and a faint sense of recognition came over his face as Felix stared up to his identical likeness. He began to hold Fergus very close to him and he turned to everyone and said,

"This is my twin brother. Have you met him? He's called Fergus."

There wasn't a dry eye in the room.

I ushered the family out and we said our goodbyes. As she was leaving Bunnie turned and said, "Is there any chance you can get Felix to a doctor? He seems to be getting worse, Rose."

"It's just the excitement and all these people in the house. He'll be fine tomorrow, I'm sure."

"OK, Rose, but if you need any help you know where we are."

As Bunnie left with her family the house became still again. The sound from the drawing room was stifled as the flutter of flakes seemed to have a quietening effect on the Manor, as it always did.

It was ten days before I felt it safe enough for mum and Trevor to drive back home. The snow still lay deep and thick and lined all the lanes. Gritters had been out in force and once they got to the motorway it would be clear all the way back to Solihull. I was relieved to wave goodbye. I had found it hard work taking care of everyone. Vivian and Bertie had managed to catch their train to London but there had been a number of delays.

Rupert attended to farm matters and once the drifts had cleared he took Felix out with him in the cab of the tractor. I had bundled them both up in scarves and gloves as the air was icy and I worried that Felix would catch a chill. The evenings drew in around 3 p.m. and January was a dull and listless month. By the end of it the weather was congenial for a trip outside with the metal detector.

I suggested they tried the orchard in the walled garden where Felix had found my ring. On their way out through the boot room, I found Felix with Rupert and Percy wearing his Wellington boots and shooting jacket.

"He's not going out with you, is he?" I demanded in a ruthless tone.

Percy took my arm quite roughly.

"Mum, let dad come out with us. He'll enjoy it."

I had never seen Percy being so forceful. I withdrew my arm and glared at him.

"I wasn't going to stop him, he just needs to be warm, that's all."

"Come on Perse," called Rupert. "Hurry up, let's go and find treasure!"

The ground was hard and cold. Rupert swung the detector over the frosty grass. Under a gnarled walnut tree they heard a beep.

"Do that again!" said Percy.

Rupert went over the spot again and Percy went off to find a spade. He began to dig. His brow sweated and Rupert yanked the spade from him and shovelled hard at the solid earth. Percy continued to wave the detector over the spot and it pinged positively until at last Rupert hit something that clanked. By now he had dug a square of about 2ft x 2ft. Percy knelt down and cleared the dirt away from the object.

"It seems to be a box of some sort, dig a bit more around the edges, Rupes and let's see if we can pull it out."

In the kitchen I was tidying away the breakfast dishes muddling over the way Percy had spoken to me. It was unusual in his behaviour. I realised that I had been over-anxious about Felix. The boys were right to carry on as usual with him.

The three of them sprang into the kitchen. Rupert and Felix were carrying a large chest by two metal hoops at its side and humped it down on the table.

"Mum, we found treasure. Look mum, let's open it!"

I could hardly believe it. They had only been outside for a short while and soon I was as exhilarated as them.

The chest was locked so Rupert suggested that he got a wrench.

"Wait," I said. "I think I have the key."

The boys looked astounded as I quickly set off to the bedroom. I took the iron keys from my bedside drawer where they had remained hidden since the day that Gabriel had set Jane free. There was a dramatic pause when I came back. The boys were dumbfounded wanting to know how I knew the key would fit and where I had got it from. They were brimming with excitement to see what was in the chest so Rupert tried the lock. We heard it crunch and release.

As he lifted the lid, the front piece unexpectedly fell down like a drawbridge and made me and Felix jump. The chest was built into compartments and there was a flat drawer on the top with further drawers beneath. Lying on the top was a long string of pearls interspersed with stones that seemed to be emeralds and rubies.

Some of the pieces I recognised from paintings from around the Manor. Felix was animated and focused on picking out pieces in silver and gold that were so encrusted with jewels that we were silent and bedazzled. A fine pair of silver candlesticks were so heavy that I could not pick them up and at the bottom of the chest were small moulded gold ingots.

There was only one person that I trusted to examine the contents of the hoard and that was Guy. I telephoned him to arrange a visit, not giving away the reason for his visit, but told him that we had discovered some more items of value for him to see. He had officially retired and I was lucky to catch him at home as he and Ray were often holidaying in Italy or France or to a Covent Garden opera. I extended my invitation to Ray but he was busy doing some work of his own.

When Guy arrived, Rupert took the chest to the snug and lit the fire so it was warm and cosy. When Guy saw the contents of the chest he gawped and gasped, speechless at their glory. A few days later Guy left for London with our treasure in the boot of his car. In his usual impeccable manner he had categorised each item and left me with a signed receipt of the contents.

He had advised me that he would have to declare the chest as 'treasure trove' but he doubted that our ownership would be contested as we had such great provenance for each item and it was after all, on our own land that we had found it. Guy was correct and we were entitled to the contents which were valued at millions of pounds, so rare and exotic were they. I suggested to the family that we all select a small piece to keep and that the rest was sold. My plan was to refurbish the east wing and everyone agreed. We also agreed to give a portion of the money to Fergus and his family. This was his inheritance, too.

Vivian made a special journey home to select some jewellery and she chose a pair of pearl drop earrings with ruby points set in gold. She claimed all the recognition of the find, reminding everyone that it was she who had given the present of the metal detector in the first place. Like the rest of us, she was amazed at the discovery.

293

Percy picked out a gold bracelet which he wore for the rest of his life. To all our surprise, Rupert took a gold ring set with brilliant diamonds and surmounted by sapphires with rubies on the shoulders.

"Who's that for?" asked Percy.

"Mind your own business," said Rupert.

I took the candlesticks, as I already had my ring and placed them on the mantelpiece over the hearth in the kitchen.

Percy began to investigate how to manage the project of restoring the east wing. He did piles of research in the library and spent hours poring over old photographs of how it once looked and how the rooms had been set out. My sons came up with the idea of dividing the east wing into apartments and running the whole as a business. It was a great idea and would help to secure the future of the Manor.

Richard telephoned to say, he and Anita had decided not to return to the house and were offering it to us as a first port of call for a sale. I spoke to Percy. He agreed that it was a good idea to buy it back. I tentatively touched the subject of Felix's bank accounts. I had no idea how much money was in them and his state of mind was not well enough to continue with the responsibility of managing them.

I contacted Fiona and asked if there was anyone in her law firm who could help and she arranged for Rupert, Percy and I to visit one of her partners. Shortly afterwards I became Felix's power of attorney and took control of our money. There was an awful lot of money: The sale of the Raphael, the hoard and estate money that had collected over the years. Fiona was charged with the purchase of the house and Percy and Rupert commenced the east wing project.

Over the months, Felix's mental health deteriorated. I was concerned that he would not see the east wing transformed to its former magnificence. I was more concerned about whether he would be able to walk Vivian down the aisle. He had always been a good sleeper but he had begun to walk about the gallery at night and I would find him having a conversation with Biffy. At times he didn't know who I was. I blamed this on his years of neglect after Hannah died, his working too hard, his lack of food and warmth and the grief that overcame him. I felt angry and resentful for those years as I wanted my husband back. Felix was diminishing. His body and mind were broken.

It was a cold winter and dragged out into the ends of February. I hadn't had a riding lesson for a while and I ventured out to check on the horses. Žanis was breaking ice on a water trough, his hands red from the cold.

"Good morning, Rose. How are you today?"

"I am well, thank you. And you?"

We chatted for a while about the weather. He assured me that the horses were well despite the cold conditions. He promised to carry on with my lessons in a few weeks.

Later that day, outside the large French windows in the kitchen, I heard Žanis calling me loudly.

"Miss Rose, Miss Rose, come quickly."

Percy heard the shouts too and hurried with me to look out of the window. Žanis was standing with his arms in the air as Felix stood astride before him pointing his shotgun straight at him.

"Get off my land you bloody peasant," he was shouting.

"Oh, my God! Dad, stop, what the heck are you doing?"

Percy rushed outside to where his father stood. Felix moved his arms so that the gun was now pointing at Percy. I watched silently from the window afraid to step outside.

"Get off my land, you buggers."

He pulled the trigger. Percy snatched the gun from his arms and threw it towards me. I ran out to take it shaking with fright. Žanis looked shocked.

"It's all right, mum, the gun wasn't loaded."

"Oh, thank God," I exclaimed.

"I'll take dad inside and make some tea."

"Žanis, are you OK? I'm so sorry, come in and have some tea, or something stronger?"

"It's OK, Miss Rose, I think your husband is a bit crazy but don't let him have a gun, he is dangerous." He rolled his finger at his temple.

"I won't. Are you sure you are OK?"

"Fine, Miss. I'm fine."

After that, Percy and I called the doctor who made a house visit. He examined Felix and suggested some tests. He would not confirm dementia until the tests had come through and told me that I needed to take Felix to the hospital to be seen by a specialist. He would arrange the paperwork.

"How long has he been like this?"

"A couple of years, maybe more, well, when the first symptoms set in."

"And you have been coping on your own?"

"Indeed doctor, I have. I have to tell you that whatever the outcome of the tests, Felix is going nowhere. This is his home and he will stay here until the day he dies."

"Well, if that is the case I can arrange for some home help. He's going to get a lot worse, I'm sorry to tell you. You may find you need it."

He looked younger than Rupert and Percy. He was wearing black trousers and a shirt but no tie. He introduced himself by his first name, Kevin. He preferred Kevin than to being called Dr Ward. He informed me that it was customary for doctors to be called by their first name. I felt uneasy with the familiarity and hoped that I was never going to be ill enough to call on Kevin.

"Thank you doctor for your time. I'll think about it."

My sons and I sat around the table. Felix was resting in bed. I warned them about what the doctor had told me and I asked for their opinion about employing a live-in nurse to come and look after him. We could afford to find one privately and I thought that consistent care would be better overall. It was hard to comprehend and I knew it was difficult for them as they were losing the character of the father whom they loved and adored. I told them that it was imperative not to let Vivian know as I did not want her to be upset. Somehow we would have Felix walk her down the aisle.

Percy sat in on the interviews with the nurse candidates and we found a nice Afro-Caribbean lady. Angelica had an un-fussy manner and an easy style of doing things. She organised a wheelchair and I arranged for a suitable car to be delivered so that Felix could have days out. It was odd to wave off my husband on those occasions as we had never shared excursions. The thought made me want to weep. He was barely the man I had married.

I organised National Trust membership for them both and Angelica would take Felix out for hours touring the properties owned by the trust in the area. She would come back saying how much Felix had enjoyed his outing which never ceased to amaze me. I found it hard to imagine my husband being pushed around a stately home admiring other people's work of art. I put Angelica up in one of the guest rooms, which had an en-suite and she joined me and the boys at meal times. She was not intrusive and we all grew to like her immensely. Her laugh was infectious and she had so many funny stories to tell about her previous patients from around the world that we found her jolly and beguiling.

Turquoise began to grace the sky as I strolled to the church for my warden duties. I glanced over at the lake only to imagine Vivian and Stephen being swallowed in the inky rippling depths. The water was dotted by small islands and a pair of swans had nested. Their necks formed a heart shape as they tapped their beaks as if kissing. Perhaps they were the reincarnation of Felix's parents?

The boat slapped against the dock, tied up in the position where the children had last left it. It needed a coat of varnish and I made a note to myself to mention this to Rupert. I carried a plant pot and I walked around to the graves where Hannah and her sons were buried and took her ring from my pocket. I dug into her grave with my hands and placed her band of gold in a tissue before placing it in the earth and covering it with soil. Then I put the pot filled with lily bulbs over the spot.

Later that afternoon, Žanis took me out for my first hack. May blossom sprinkled the hedges and their perfume pricked at my nostrils. Ginger shook her head up and down pleased to be out of the stables. I felt tense. Žanis was riding beside me on Judy's horse Truffles, so called because of his colouring.

"If you feel afraid sing a song in your head. It will help to calm you. The horses will be a bit fevered today because they have not been out together for a while. We will have a gentle walk."

High on Ginger's back I could see for miles. Soon I felt calm enough to try a trot and then a canter up Callow Hill. It was invigorating and I felt safe as Žanis kept his horse beside me all the way. When we got to the top we stopped on the Welsh side and I looked down the valley to where my mother had been born. I felt refreshed and on the way home I chatted casually with Žanis about his life in Latvia and his reason for coming to the UK. He told me that he missed his family very much but he was making a better life for himself. He had been to many places but he liked it in Shrugsborough as it reminded him best of the place where he had been born. His manner was calm and his voice cottony and as gentle as the delicate breeze that blew through my hair.

At home, the telephone rang. It was mum. Trevor had died.

Percy was in Shrugsborough at the architects and Rupert was on the farm somewhere. Angelica and Felix were out on one of their 'jolly days'. I resorted to leaving a note to explain what had happened and that I was going to Solihull to see mum. I decided to drive as I would probably need the car to drive mum around to funeral directors, florists and the church.

Arriving at mum's bungalow, there were no lights on and the front curtains were drawn. I rang the bell that chirped a tune from Tchaikovsky's *Nutcracker*. I heard mum shuffle to the door. When she opened it she seemed to have shrunk. I bent to hug her and we went to the sitting room.

"Oh mum, I'm so sorry."

"He died in the chair you're sitting in. I found him there this morning."

I made some tea and put out some clothes for mum to wear. She was still in her dressing gown. For supper I drove to the local public house and we sat eating fish and chips and I bought her a brandy. The drink enlivened her.

"At least he died in a chair and not in another woman's arms," she said.

"Well, there is that mum. Trevor loved you very much you know mum. What are you going to do without him?"

"Well, one thing is for sure, I am not going into one of those homes. I've seen them on television. People sitting in a circle asleep and drugged. I don't want that. I can look after myself and I will carry on at home. If you are thinking that I need your help Rose, please put that out of your mind. I'll be fine."

I stayed with mum until after Trevor's funeral.

CHAPTER 21

When I arrived home, Percy had the plans for the east wing and he'd laid them out on the kitchen table ready for me to see. It was designed so that the ground floor was split into six deluxe apartments each with an en-suite, kitchen and two bedrooms. The first floor was split into two larger apartments to accommodate bigger groups. At one end, at the right-angle where the gallery by the tower met the east wing, Percy had allocated a picture gallery. I was thrilled. At last we had a place to hang our family portraits. Percy engaged the workmen and the project commenced.

Vivian and Bertie were home for the Goodes' wedding anniversary. Felix's rapid decline was a shock to them both but I gave assurances that Felix would take Vivian down the aisle even if it was in his wheelchair. Her eyes grew misty and I gave her a cuddle.

Fiona threw a lovely anniversary party for around thirty people in a small marquee on their clipped lawn. A catering company cooked and served delicious food. Angelica brought Felix in his wheelchair and we sat together privileged to be seated on the top table with our hosts. Once we had eaten, the tables were cleared and the space was made ready for dancing. The weather was kind and the sides of the marquee were tied up to let in brief gusts of a light wind. Dulcet tones from a jazz band struck up as I kissed Felix goodbye. He was heading home with Angelica. He looked up at me and smiled. I revelled in these moments of slight intimacy between us. I desperately missed the arms of my husband around me.

Rupert had taken advantage of the free flowing wine and was loudly talking in a corner with a group of other farmers. Judy went to join them and he put his arm around her. He stroked her bottom and she didn't move. My suspicions were confirmed. There was something very familiar in the way that the two of them were so relaxed with one another.

I hadn't realised that Vivian was watching me and she gazed over to where I was staring. Suddenly, she blustered over to Rupert and swung his hand from around Judy. The scene unravelled in slow motion from there on in.

"I knew it. I knew it Rupert Langley. How long has this been going on Judith?" She used Judy's full name to enforce her question.

"Hey Viv, don't make a fuss. Look we were going to tell you. It's been a while. Calm down for goodness sake, you are making a scene." Rupert slurred his words as he was a little drunk.

"Grrr," Vivian exclaimed. "Why do you have to spoil everything? She's my best friend, you stupid fucking idiot."

Rupert put his hands out as if he was surrendering. Bertie was petrified seeing a side to his fiancée that he was unaccustomed to. I walked over and pulled her away. I drove us home leaving Rupert and Judy to apologise to Gabriel and Fiona. I poured some brandy and made coffee. Sitting in the snug I spoke to Vivian about her brother and her best friend.

"I've suspected for a while. I think Fiona was trying to tell me on Boxing Day but she never got the chance."

"I remember. I walked in on you, mum. I thought it was strange for you and Fiona to be having a tête-à-tête."

"Why are you so upset, Vivian? I think they love each other, there's nothing wrong with that. You should be grateful to Rupert for keeping your best friend in the family."

Vivian flushed.

"Why should I be grateful? Rupert has had a string of women. He'll end up hurting her and who's going to be torn between her sibling and her best friend when they pick up the pieces? Me, mum, me. Oh, I'm so fed up with the two of them."

"When the treasure was found and you all picked a piece from the collection, Rupert took a ring. I think it's for Judy. He's obviously very serious. Vivian, we've both seen him with other women but with Judy he is very different. I expect they are deferring an announcement so that they don't steal any of your wedding thunder. Try and understand, Vivian. Be kind. Don't do anything you will regret."

As I spoke Bertie continually nodded his head and wisely said nothing.

"I think we both know," I added, "that Judy is more than capable of handling Rupert on her own."

Vivian had a streak of jealousy in her voice. I recognised it in her, knowing that same streak ran through my own veins. Eventually, Bertie and I talked her round and she agreed to apologise to Rupert and Judy. Bertie was a likeable young man. I felt he was the right sort to be with my daughter.

Percy was proceeding well with the refurbishments in the east wing. Our timing wasn't best for the up and coming wedding as there was a lot of noise and dust. The tree had been removed allowing sunlight to blaze over the courtyard. It was strange not to see it there. In conversation with Percy I asked for his reassurance that the paintings would be hung in the gallery he had designated for them. I was nervous of my son's ambitions to make the east wing a profit returning extension.

"Mum! I can't believe that you are even asking me that. Of course, we won't be able to hang them all at the same time, there are too many, but we can alternate them. Look, tell you what, why don't you choose the first exhibition?"

I agreed and felt an inner pride at having that responsibility.

I was extremely busy with Vivian's wedding plans. Constantly on the telephone booking tables, chairs, chair covers and consulting my daughter over every detail. Betty had offered to help with the flowers and as ever she got stuck in relieving me of some of the tasks.

The lead project manager for the east wing build was a young sporty looking chap whose name was Shaun. His healthy face shone under his protective headgear. He approached me one day as I was crossing the courtyard to air the Lodge.

"Excuse me, Lady Langley, I'm glad to have caught you. I've been looking at the plans and I think there is a problem here." He held a clipboard and was pointing at a small scale drawing of where the east wing abutted the central part of the Manor. It was just at the place where Jane's tower had been built.

"Problem?"

"Yes, there seems to be an extra room. If you stand further back here you can see the window. It looks like a tower of some sort. Do you know if it encroaches in to the east wing?"

I looked up.

"Let me tell you that there is a tower but that it does not encroach on the east wing. It is a sacred place, a place of worship and must not be disturbed under any circumstances. Do you understand?"

I think my forcefulness shocked him.

"Yes, that's fine Lady Langley. I hope you understand that I just needed to check, that's all."

I softened my voice. "Of course, I understand. I would ask you not to mention your discovery to either of my sons. They do not know of the tower's existence which is of some miracle after all these years but I prefer it that way if you don't mind?"

303

He nodded and went back in to the east wing through a large roughly hewn arch that the masons had cut in the wall.

"Thank you," I cried out. He didn't hear me as he had pulled his defenders over his ears.

I continued to the Lodge. I wanted to air it as I had a secret plan in my mind about what I wanted to do with it.

Perhaps it was my conversation with Shaun but that night I had a fitful sleep. I woke and went out to the gallery only to discover Biffy sifting through the linen cupboard. She looked at me with disdain. Lately, I had found drawers left open and things thrown out. Biffy was searching for something and was not afraid to leave a trail of destruction behind her. She disappeared off down the stairs and I waited for her to return. When she did, she was clutching two church candles. So that was what she was looking for! I arranged for the delivery of one hundred church candles to be kept in the box in front of the door that separated the end of the gallery to the east wing. This door was bolted and had been for years as it was too dangerous to open. After that Biffy ceased from fiddling in cupboards and drawers. In death she was still lighting candles for Jane and her boys. I had seen them flicker in the tower window. She seemed totally unaware of where Jane had gone; back with her sons.

As I returned to the bedroom, I saw Felix standing at the side of our bed. He looked perplexed and angry.

I approached him and began to take his arms to ease him gently back beneath the covers.

Felix grabbed at my arms and then he took hold of my finger and started to shout,

"Give me back that ring, it belongs to my wife."

"I am your wife," I screamed as he tugged harder. "Felix, stop, it's me Rose."

"I don't know you. You are wearing my wife's ring. Thief, help, there's a thief!"

I tried to push him off but he gripped me harder. We got into a tussle and then, just as my sons and Angelica burst into the room, he punched me hard in the face and I fell to the ground.

"Thief, quick, get her, she's got my wife's ring. THIEF!"

Angelica dashed to her room and came back with a syringe and jabbed it into Felix's thigh. Rupert and Percy helped me up and I staggered, dazed and shocked.

"Mum, mum, are you OK? Can you walk? Rupert, see if mum can manage to get downstairs, I'll help Angelica with dad."

Dizzily, I leant against Rupert as we went downstairs to the kitchen and he sat me at the table and filled the kettle for tea. He waited for Angelica to come down with Percy and asked her to look at my eye. It was beginning to swell and I could feel it close. She wet a tea towel and then filled it with ice placing it over my eye and telling me to hold it there.

"You're going to have a lovely black eye in the morning. I'm sorry."

Percy made tea and we sat quietly for a while, my head throbbing.

"I think it would be wise to move Felix to another room Mrs Langley. I've noticed that there is a linking door from my suite to another bedroom. Perhaps you and the boys can make it habitable as soon as possible."

No-one replied to Angelica but we all knew that it was for the best. In that moment I had lost my husband forever.

Angelica had a way with Felix that was inexplicable. She was patient and kind and to the amazement of all of us he seemed to know who she was. We often heard her chatter to him explaining their goings-on in minutiae. Whatever her method, it worked and Felix remained happy in her care for many years.

The morning of Vivian's wedding arrived. Pure chaos reigned from every corner of the Manor. The marquee was put

305

up and tables and chairs were set out. Caterers arrived and delicious aromas seeped out from under its canvas. Betty came with Helena early in the morning to help with all the flower arrangements. Judy slept overnight, Vivian and she having reconciled their differences and Judy had received her blessing in the relationship with her brother. They were as they had always been, inseparable.

Vivian was having her hair done in her bedroom, her bridal dress hanging on her long standing mirror. Her bedroom was unchanged. Banners of gymkhana rosettes hung from the beam over her bed and over the spare bed, where Judy slept, were rosettes of her own pinned to the wall. It was a child's room and now this room was going to say a long farewell to the little girl who had occupied it, with her best friend, for twenty six years.

Vivian ran to me.

"Mum, can you believe this day has come? My wedding day!"

I looked at my daughter, the joy was shining in her eyes and she looked more beautiful than I had ever seen her. She threw her arms about me and kissed me on my cheeks.

"Mum, if I don't have the chance later, I just wanted to thank you for everything. Just because I'm getting married doesn't mean that I'm not still your little girl you know."

I hugged her. Judy, who had been sitting on her bed painting her long nails, jumped up and threw her arms around us both.

Vivian's wedding was one of the happiest days in my life. Linda and Charlie brought mother from Solihull and it was lovely to see my friend again. Angelica wheeled Felix down the aisle and Vivian held his hand. He seemed totally unaware of what was happening but with Angelica's prompts he gave his daughter away to an adoring Bertie. Gabriel carried out the service and beamed brightly at his own daughter, in her lilac chief bridesmaid dress, who looked stunning next to her best friend. Afterwards, at the reception and after the wedding breakfast when everyone who could was gathered on the dance floor, Judy caught the bridal bouquet. Angelica took Felix and tucked him into bed, in his new room in the Manor at 9 pm. and I missed him. The rest of us danced past midnight.

For a few days after the wedding festivities, the house was busy as people came to take down the marquee and remove the tables and chairs. Vivian and Bertie had left for their honeymoon. Percy was absorbed in the refurbishment once again and Rupert took leave for the farm. The house felt empty. Noises from the east wing were reducing.

Feeling lonely, I telephoned Guy with the excuse that I needed his advice to hang the paintings in the new gallery and he agreed to come and stay for a few days bringing Ray with him.

Žanis and I met at the stables each day. Guiltily, I fervently looked forward to seeing him. I would watch his strong tattooed arms saddle the horses and carry hay bales, as if they were cotton balls, across the yard. Sometimes, we refrained from talking but this day he had a suggestion for me.

"Rose, perhaps you would be better with your own horse. Ginger is a little big for you. You have small hips. I don't think you are used to spreading your legs so widely."

He was being suggestive again. I took some sensual pleasure in his remarks but always did my best not to show it.

"A horse of my own? But I've only just got used to riding Ginger?"

"I have been studying you. Your balance needs adjusting. At first I thought it was because you were inexperienced but now I think it is because you need a smaller horse, a pony."

"And do you have a pony in mind?" I asked.

"As it happens, I do. I will bring him tomorrow."

I couldn't wait for the next day. The night seemed long as I tried to sleep wondering what type of pony Žanis was going to bring me. I was disappointed. Out of the stable he walked an ugly bay gelding with a thick black mane and tail standing about 14 hands. Žanis noticed my disappointment. To cap it all he also handed me the bill for my new steed and his tack.

"Come, try him Rose, he is perfect for you, wait and see."

We rode up to the Callow hill and as much as I hated to admit it, my new pony was indeed perfect for me. I felt more connected to him as my legs reached comfortably down to tap him into canter. My back and muscles stopped aching as each day I rode over the hills and moors with my new companion and my new horse, whom I named Axis, because I felt in unison with his rhythm.

Žanis had become indispensable. Jacob appreciated his work in the gardens and it was Žanis I called upon for any odd jobs around the Manor. I had hatched my plan in my head but as yet I had dared not reveal it until one day when Žanis was sweeping the leaves and washing their dew from the yard.

"Where do you live Žanis?" I asked.

"I rent a room in Churchbury, Rose. It is OK. I have a bath and cooker of my own."

"Žanis, you are much needed at the Manor and I would like to offer you the Lodge to occupy. Your wage will remain as it is now, I don't expect any rent, you will be doing me and my family a favour as it is getting neglected. I will ask Percy to update it, it does need some updating, nothing has changed in there for over thirty years."

I expected him to jump at my offer but instead he looked at me with glassy eyes and said that he would let me know tomorrow.

The next day, Guy and Ray arrived. I was delighted to see them and I settled them into a guest room. I no longer cared what Felix or Rupert thought of my gay friends. Felix would not remember them and I was sure that Rupert had other things on his mind, that being Judy. Over dinner we discussed the paintings and how best to rotate and hang them in the new east wing gallery. In the morning, Guy and I bumped into each other at the end of the central hall and we looked down through the beautiful arched window, that covered two thirds of the wall, at Žanis and Jacob working in the garden.

"Very pretty those flowers down there Rose, very pretty." It was an evident double-entendre as he gazed at the bulking men.

"Just because you join the library doesn't mean that you can't buy a book," he said laughingly. I chuckled and replied,

"They're not for plucking Guy, not those flowers, not for plucking."

This made him giggle and he put his arm around my waist.

He became serious.

"You're not feeling lonely, are you Rose? You always seem to be on your own somehow."

I squeezed his arm.

"Sometimes alone Guy, but never lonely."

I watched Žanis dig and pull at the weeds. He sensed he was being watched and looked up to where we were standing. He grinned and waved and instinctively Guy and I waved back to him.

CHAPTER 22

The east wing was taking shape. Where the arch had been cut out, neat bricks curved in the entrance door and windows filled the space. Lines had been drawn for parking bays in the courtyard. Across the two floors glass gleamed and the roof seamlessly weaved its way into the old Manor.

Interiors were still being worked on. Percy had zoomed in on Guy and Ray during their visit and they had indulged him with ideas of colours and fabrics and layouts of the new apartments. As impeccably as ever, Guy had left me a plan of how he thought the paintings should hang. I gave it to Percy asking him to follow it through when the time came.

Vivian telephoned. She and Bertie had a wonderful honeymoon and she had just been given a plum job on a new television programme where she researched people's ancestry. She sounded very animated about it.

It was almost Christmas. Another mark in the calendar of Felix's ageing. I rode less with Žanis as the days grew colder. He eventually told me that he would move into the Lodge and I instructed Percy to get on with changing the central heating, adding a new bathroom suite and kitchen and changing the décor. He was most unhappy about the proposition, as he still had much to do in the east wing, but reluctantly he agreed.

Rupert, when he was not out and about on the farm, was spending his free time with Judith. Finally, he proposed and came to tell me on a bleak and windy night whilst I was sitting alone in the kitchen.

"Another wedding, mum! Can you believe it? I think Fiona will probably do most of the planning, it should be easier for you this time," he said with some relief.

My son. My reckless son was going to marry his childhood sweetheart. He had always loved Judy. They were alike. Paradoxically, the two were adventurous, yet home birds, loving their homeland and being adventurous within it. I thought that he had other girlfriends in an attempt to convince himself that he wasn't really in love with Judy. With the benefit of hindsight it was now obvious to me. He gave her the ring from the treasure chest.

Specks of snowfall sprinkled the giant's stones as I drove to the rectory to speak with Fiona and Gabriel. I was invited into the sitting room where Judy and Rupert were perched closely on a cream sofa. The fire was lit and baubles glistened on the Christmas tree beneath a nailed-in cross of Jesus.

Fiona brought in a tray of tea and Gabriel poured some out for me and handed me a plate of mince pies. For a moment there was an embarrassing silence. Gabriel and Fiona went to speak at the same time but Gabriel won over.

"I'm sorry that Felix couldn't join us."

"Me, too."

Rupert piped up.

"Mum, Gabriel would prefer not to marry his own daughter to me. Although, I mean I'm sure Gabriel would like to marry us but it's better protocol for someone else to do it. He's asked the Bishop of Shrugsborough to take the service and he has agreed, at St Laurence's, of course."

"Of course," I said biting into a mince pie.

"Judy, that ring looks gorgeous on you. How lovely it fits. It belonged to Marguerite, one of Rupert's ancestors. Her picture will be hung in the new gallery. I'd love to show you when it's ready."

"We'd all love to see that," said Gabriel. "Wouldn't we Fiona?"

"Oh yes, absolutely."

Fiona changed the subject.

"Molly's doing well at work. I hear that you have been very kind to Jacob and Helena letting them have the new house you bought from Richard Jones. They'll be much more room for them there."

"Yes, I'm not sure that Betty has forgiven me yet. I think she was rather enjoying having her new grandchild next door. It's nice to have some space from your mother-in-law."

"On that note mum, it is perfectly fine for me and Judes to live at the Manor, isn't it?"

"Well, not in your room, Rupert."

My mind withdrew for a moment as I thought of my sons' bedroom: Their twin beds with identical covers; the electric car track laid out on the floor, which I knew they still played with as sometimes I would hear the buzz of the motors, and the Airfix models pinned with wire dripping from the ceiling. Grown men, inseparable twins.

"I think you can have my bedroom. I'll move into one of the guest rooms. Percy won't thank us for it but I'll speak with him so that you can redecorate. Judy, please choose whatever you like, I really don't mind."

"Well, that all seems settled then," said Gabriel. "I've checked with the bishop and he is available on 24th July next year. How does that sound to everyone?"

I hoped that Felix would still be alive to see his son, who bore the same Cross of Soot as he, when he was wed.

Žanis and I rode down into the valley. Icing sugar cold flurried over the trees. Christmas had been and gone and my children were occupied once more by the jobs that filled their days. Felix was at home playing a memory game with a pack of cards in the snug with Angelica. I had watched them do this before. Over and over again Felix would select a downturn card and try to remember if he had previously turned over a matching one and try to remember where it lay on the table. On some days, he was lucid and clever and would snigger when he got it right. On other days he would repeatedly ask Angelica what he was meant to be doing and she would show him again. I never joined in. He would get upset. He didn't know who I was and he would turn to Angelica with pleading eyes for me to go away.

We were chatting idly. Žanis pointed to a copse of trees planted in diagonal rows. He jumped off his horse, he had his own now, I bought it for him, a bay mare the colour of Axis and she was bigger. He called her Dekla. Dekla, he explained, was a Latvian Goddess of Destiny and Fortune. He loved her. His way with horses was intriguing and mystifying. He would make a clacking sound through his teeth and all the horses in the yard or out in the paddocks would lift their heads and prick their ears. When he opened the stable doors the horses would go to him quietly, even Jack, Rupert's stallion, and follow him to the gate to the paddocks through an invisible boundary. Once inside, the horses would gallop, roll and frisk about. Dekla would nuzzle into his neck as if whispering her secrets in his ear.

I looked over to the end of his finger. Then he dismounted and signalled for me to do the same. I followed him as we led the horses towards the trees.

"Hold Dekla a moment!"

I took the rein and watched as Žanis began to scratch in the ground.

"What on earth are you doing?" I exclaimed.

He came towards me holding a piece of terracotta. I could make out that it had once formed part of a bowl or cup. The wind was feeble, protected by the slope of the valley, so I took off my glove to hold it.

"Wow! What is this you've found?"

"I think it is Roman. And, judging by the line of the tree planting, I believe Rose that this is the place where a vineyard was grown, back in time, in Roman times."

An aura of mystery shrouded him. How did he know all of this?

"Look, see how the trees are planted in rows. This is where the vineyards once stood. These old trees have been planted in their line. You have a vineyard here, Rose. You know, for wine! And the soil, see it is very chalky for these parts, ideal for grapes."

He took some soil and let it run through his hands. Even on this cold winter's day the soil was light and not like the thick clumps in the ploughed fields.

I let go of the reins and stepped towards him. He took me in his arms and kissed me passionately, his mouth open.

Over supper, I was explaining to Rupert, Percy and Angelica that Žanis had discovered a Roman vineyard in the valley. I suggested that Percy took the metal detector to scan for artefacts. I was lively and enlivened. I had a vision of planting a new vineyard in its place. It would be a new project for me. Clearly, Percy and Rupert were somewhat overcome with my manner but in the main thought it was a good idea. My instincts told me that I was being humoured. I promised Percy that I would take complete control of the project myself and that I would research the complexities of growing a vineyard.

Rupert frowned.

"So, you were out with Žanis when you discovered this?"

I didn't like his tone. It was accusing. My guilt of what had happened today blushed in my cheeks.

"You are spending a lot of time with him, mum. Do you think that's appropriate?"

Percy flinched.

"Oh, he's company for me." I looked at Angelica for support. She was unresponsive.

"Well, your father doesn't even know who I am, he spends all the day long with Angelica, you're on the farm and Percy is bound up with the final stages of the refurbishments. I need a project, Rupert. If your father was aware of this, I know he would sanction it."

From their facial expressions, I realised that the time I was spending with Žanis had been discussed. I suddenly felt ashamed and decided that the next time I saw him I would act as if nothing had happened between us. I made a conscious effort to keep out of his way for a while.

Nothing more was said.

I persuaded Percy to show me how to use the computer, to surf the internet and I obsessively gathered as much information as I could about vineyards in the UK. Percy moaned because the ink in the printer kept running out as I printed everything I found. It troubled me that my sons were not taking me seriously. They had forgotten about my inner determination for getting things done and I approached my new project like a dog with a very juicy bone.

There were undoubtedly hollow spaces in my mind and in my heart. Felix was the person that I loved, my children were the people that I loved but they were growing away from me in different ways. I was a middle-aged woman but I still felt young and enthusiastic. What I needed was a project, just like when I had turned my hand to gardening when those voids had needed to be filled before.

Through the internet, I managed to track down a pioneering wine grower from Kent who agreed to visit. When he arrived he bore the look of an outdoor man. His cheeks were ruddy and his hands were tanned and rough. Fred Albright had been a banker in London and one day he just decided to give it all up and turn his life around. His happiness showed in his eyes.

We took the pick-up truck along the tracks until we came to the spot where Žanis had found the Roman pottery. As Žanis had done, the first thing he did was to pick up a clump of soil and rub it between his fingers. He was smiling so I knew that this was a good sign.

To impress my sons, Fred Albright and I prepared a business plan for the commencement of turning the wood into a viable vineyard. Everything was in it, from the cost of felling the trees, clearing, digging, planting and the building of the wineries. In the first instance we would grow red grapes as Fred advised that they would grow better in the conditions available. Then we changed our minds deciding to plant both red and white grapes should one crop fail. In the space of two years we would be producing our first bottles of wine. It was, of course, an expensive production but we included in our plan the profit and losses and in five years the wineries would be in the black. We would also make some money from the sale of the timber. After long discussions, I received the green light from my sons to go ahead. Not that I needed this, as I was aware that I could have spent three times the money without it depleting the family wealth but I wanted their blessing. After all, the actions that I took now would affect their future and their children's future long after I was gone. The vineyard was my legacy to them.

PART EIGHT

Death is a lifelong friend who reaches out to greet us

CHAPTER 23

I always found it remarkable how quickly events could change our lives. Eventually the east wing was complete and Rupert and Percy, with Judy's help, had transformed the building. A small reception room had been built at the bottom of an oak staircase that Percy had found at a reclamation yard. When the telephone rang it bellowed out across the Manor from chimes fitted on the exteriors. No one wanted to miss any future bookings for our luxurious new apartments.

On the ground floor, the rooms were rectangular and each was identical in their layout. Sitting rooms faced out over the moors partitioned with granite top islands in modern kitchens and bedrooms with en-suite bathrooms that looked out over the courtyard. As well as the stairs, a lift had been fitted for people to carry luggage to the first floor. Two penthouse-style suites had been arranged leading from the staircase and along a corridor to the right. The whole of the interior design was lavish. To the left was the entrance to the picture gallery.

The Lodge had been brought up to date with modern conveniences and Žanis had settled in well. Feeling sure that Žanis was working in the gardens, I went into the Lodge to have a look around. The kitchen had been refitted and the floor had been replaced with clean wooden flooring which carried through the hall and into the sitting room. On the stairs was a deep beige carpet with thin red stripes at its border and this continued along the landing. The bathroom had been renewed with crisp white fittings and a new shower. In my old bedroom a modern cream wrought iron bed was neatly made. I looked through the window towards the tower. It was a long time since I had taken this view. I didn't hear Žanis come in. When I turned and saw him standing there I jumped.

"Do you find everything to your satisfaction?" he asked me sarcastically.

I searched my brain trying to find a reply. All I said was,

"Yes, I do thank you."

As I walked to the door he bowed and gestured with his arm. Then he grabbed my arm and began to kiss me. Frantically, he picked me up and took me to his bed. My senses were aroused as he unbuttoned my blouse and cupped my breasts as he kissed and sucked at my nipples which became erect. I held onto him as if I was going to die. He undid my trousers and pulled them with my pants down hard to my ankles and began to kiss me between my legs. In a flurry I became moist and I felt his tongue lick and scour for my clitoris as he made me come. I clung to him, desperate for him to enter me. He stopped for a moment to look in my eyes. Distracted, I felt his penis pulsate in my flesh as he penetrated deeper. His lovemaking was slow and he caressed every part of my body as his mouth tenderly brushed my neck.

I lay gasping with his head on my chest. An overwhelming guilt overtook me and I rushed to put my clothes on. All at once I felt foolish as he stared at me lazily.

"Don't worry, this is our little secret," he said as he reached over to find a cigarette.

I watched him light it. "It won't happen again," I replied with determination but inwardly, I was already wishing it would. Outwardly, I felt ashamed – a betrayer.

The next day I decided to ride out on my own. Axis whinnied as I left the yard, to Dekla's surprise, to be leaving without her. From that day on I avoided any opportunity to be alone with Žanis.

My vineyard project was in full flow. Fred Albright had seemed envious of the quick progress and my idea for building a wine-tasting room, a comfortable room for the staff, a café and a shop. He lacked the money to do this in Kent. I decided to make him an offer and we agreed that I would become a forty per cent shareholder with a princely investment to support him to copy my plans. It was a generous offer by me, which I based on his willingness to travel and help me when I had needed him to. The shaded, sloping valley was beginning to take shape.

Rupert and Judy were married in the July of that summer. We awoke to a shimmering hot day and the moors and hills looked beautiful as I dressed for my son's wedding. Sadly, Felix was too ill to join us, so I drove alone to the church leaving him and Angelica at home with the card game.

Younger ones enjoyed the day. It was filled with love and joy and humour. My own humour was melancholy as much as I tried to join in with the merriment. I so longed for Felix to be with me. Judy made a gorgeous bride and Marguerite's ring rested at home on her long finger. Rupert look self-satisfied, he bore very much the expression as Felix had on our wedding day, a little like he could not really believe what was happening to him. I studied my new daughter-in-law. She was tall and slim. The spotlights in the ballroom caught glints of red and gold in her hair which shone like copper and she had Gabriel's eyes. I looked to where Gabriel sat with Fiona. He too was watching the spectacle and he saw me. He threw me a wink and raised his glass. I grinned back at him, our two families united. I recalled his manner the day that he had cast Jane from the tower. Now, he looked like a different man. Grey whiskers flicked out from his temples and lines creased his eyes where a light was dimming but still had the strength to devour a person.

Vivian looked bright, Judy's matron of honour and as best man Percy delivered a kind and thoughtful speech about his brother and his life-long friend. Judy had chosen pistachio green as her colour theme and my sons wore cravats in that colour and were dressed in tail coats. They looked handsome. Percy would never marry, I knew that. I had two children married and a husband who didn't know what our names were and the thought made me want to weep as I observed a room of happiness.

The east wing was going to be full of guests ready for the shooting season. Gregory, Archie and their wives were running things at Langley Hall and visitors could book in to shoot and eat there as part of their package.

Fergus and Bunnie were visiting Emily in Australia. This had become a regular occurrence for them travelling twice a year. I thought of them, eating, sleeping, snoring in a plane together. Natural and normal things that Felix's mind had stolen from me. The rage in my heart would not lie still as it beat jealously.

In the kitchen I was clearing up and Angelica and Felix were sat at the table. Felix was watching me intently as I busied about. He began to stand up his weak knees creaking. Angelica went to stop him but he pushed her arm away. His eyes were burning and I watched as my husband raised himself in a challenging stance to confront me.

"Where is my bed? You damn bitch. I know it was you. YOU! You took her from me."

I had been dreading this moment. Hannah was bubbling near to the surface of his mind and she was rising to haunt me.

Angelica was shocked and began to fuss over him forcing him to sit down in his wheelchair and covering him with a rug. I didn't speak as she wheeled him away to the garden.

Before the guests arrived in the new wing, Percy and Rupert arranged for me and Felix to see the picture gallery. Angelica took Felix up in the lift. I chose to take the old route through the kitchen, down through the cellar and out to the gallery. With the tapestry removed, the area was light and airy. The panels smelled of beeswax. I wanted to walk in the footsteps of the ghosts of this house through the door for the first time in over a hundred years to the east wing. As I entered, Angelica was pushing Felix through from the opposite end with Percy and Rupert. Judy was absent, working at her office seeing out her notice. I wanted her to support me with the vineyard business and she had readily agreed.

Isabella's painting took pride of place above the marble fireplace on the uninterrupted long left wall. Percy and Guy had ensured the correct softness of lighting. In its mist Isabella's jewels glowed. The picture looked deeper, its colours richer. Her raven hair and strong dark features were lit up by her sparkling diamond tiara (now in the safekeeping of a London museum). I stepped towards her and looked at her delicate finger to see my ring. My finger was swollen and her ring pinched me. I wondered whether I would ever be able to take it off. Her frame was tiny. Her twin sons stood tall beside her. In that moment I yearned to kiss her, to thank her for her legacy and her inspiration to me to forge my own.

Rupert pointed out the Cross of Soot on Isabella's son and flipped his fringe to compare.

"That boys is really black," said Percy.

"Well, he was the first in the line to have it," I replied.

Angelica listened to our conversation and she walked to the painting to see what we were talking about. Then she looked at Rupert's forehead, then she went to Felix and tenderly brushed her hand across his brow. She understood without having to say anything.

The Dalí was hung next to the door I had come through which was marked, 'Private'. Out of the corner of my eye I saw Felix try to stand up and walk towards it. Angelica looked at me fearing an outburst. She coaxed him to sit down and wheeled him in front of the painting. In his eyes I saw an onslaught of confusion. Poor Felix!

"Is that mama? Is she dead? Someone told me she drowned. Mama, mama?"

"Angelica, I think that's enough for dad for today. Can you take him back to the Manor please?"

Percy took my arm as he spoke.

"Come on mum, look let's walk round together."

I took my time. Rupert was obviously bored and left with an excuse about the sheep. Percy stayed with me as I muttered and revelled in the sheer delight of seeing the pictures restored: Marguerite's young face, the first Francis and Honora.

"This one is by Gainsborough you know, Percy. I always thought she had a rather special look about her, don't you think?"

"Under all that dirt they found his signature, Guy told me mum. It's marvellous. She has always reminded me of Bunnie."

I looked at Honora and I could see what he meant.

"Percy, I don't think she belongs here. Can you arrange for her to be hung at Langley Hall?"

Percy went to open his mouth to say something but stopped himself. Then he nodded.

"Actually mum, I understand that Honora belongs with Bunnie, not with us, I'll arrange it."

We ambled and Percy stopped to show me a landscape. It was the one from the kitchen. Next to it was another. Percy told me that the two pictures had intrigued him and it wasn't until the other day that he had worked out what was different. The later one, dated about 1640 had a tower, whereas the first picture did not. As I listened I tried to keep my face blank.

"You can see the tower from the courtyard, I can't believe I have never noticed it before. But mum, if you didn't know it was there, then you wouldn't."

Percy had found the door to the entrance but he couldn't get in. It was locked.

I breathed a sigh of relief. A sudden realisation dawned on me. It was time for me to share the secrets of the tower.

The telephone screeched out from the office below and Percy left to answer it. I was fixated on the landscapes when he returned.

"Mum, it was Angelica, dad's taken a turn."

After a few days it was clear to all of us that Felix was not going to get better. He had had a stroke. He was dying.

I telephoned Vivian to come home and she arrived with Bertie looking distressed and tired. It was as if Felix had been waiting for her. We all gathered at his bedside watching the shallow rise and fall of his chest. His chest that had once held me, that I had kissed and stroked and lain upon.

In his last gasps he cried out, "Hannah, Hannah."

My children looked at me. Vivian began to cry. Rupert took his father's hand and shook it,

"Goodbye old buddy," he said.

Percy saw the look in my eyes. He saw the green-eyed monster lurking. I looked away.

CHAPTER 24

When Gabriel committed Felix's body into his grave at St Laurence's my children wept. Angelica wept but I did not weep for I dreamed of him in the arms of Hannah.

After his funeral we had a Wake at home. Fergus and Bunnie were away and Archie told me that they were withholding the news until they came home. Many tenants came. Betty came with Young Tom, Molly, Jacob and Helena. Helena had two young sons and she was pregnant with her third child. They were very grateful for the larger home and clearly needed it. Eliza's home...

Percy came by my side placing his mobile phone back in his pocket and he looked at me knowing I was going to ask.

"Who was on the phone, darling?"

"It was Fergus ringing from Australia. He'd had a premonition about dad and wanted to see if dad was OK."

"Did you tell him?"

"Mum, he already knew but yes, I'm afraid I confirmed the news."

I wondered if my twin sons would ever experience such telepathy. There had been no evidence to date. Probably, I thought, because Rupert only ever really thought of himself.

I was delighted when Linda and Charlie arrived. My friend threw her arms about me.

"Come for a ride out with me tomorrow?" I asked.

Linda looked at me surprised.

"Are you riding out on your own Rose?"

"Yes, Žanis taught me. Can you stay overnight?"

Linda eyed Žanis. She looked at me. In other circumstances I know she would have said something about him to me but she refrained.

"Sorry that we couldn't bring your mum but Charlie wants to drive on up to Stafford to look at some equipment for the practice which means that I can't stop. To be honest Rose, I don't think your mum's up to the journey."

"No, you're probably right," I said guiltily.

"Fancy you riding? I never thought I'd see the day. Another time?"

Linda and I never did get to ride together. Her expression told me everything.

"Linda, are you OK? You've gone very pale, it's not your monthlies is it?"

She laughed a little, "I know this is not the right time to tell you Rose but I've got some bad news I'm afraid. Well, you know I always had trouble with me tubes being gunked up and all that? I kept getting a dragging pain in my womb and Charlie persuaded me to go to the doctor. They gave me loads of tests. I've got ovarian cancer but worse, its spread. Two years at the most." She said the words sharply like she had been rehearsing them over and over again.

I looked at my friend and tears filled my eyes.

"Hey, come on, I need you to be strong. Keep in touch with Charlie, afterwards, you know, when the time comes, you will won't you, Rose?"

I hugged my friend. "Of course I will. Oh Linda, what am I going to do without you?"

"Live your life Rose, you're still young. If you do anything after I've gone promise that you will have an adventure. Why not go to France to look at some vineyards? Why not shag your handsome groom? Or have you already? I wouldn't blame you Rose. I know you well enough to want to wish you a drop of happiness. Felix's mind has been gone for years, I don't know how you managed?"

Thankfully, Rupert called me over to ask if there were any more sandwiches.

Žanis, came to the Wake, probably out of respect for his employer and he stayed for a short time. He chatted to Rupert as he sipped a glass of red wine. A pleasant thought tingled inside me. I thought of our lovemaking but surprisingly, I thought more of the fact that one day soon people would drink wine from the valley of Callow and thinking about what Linda had said, I would definitely visit France. I had already checked the box about my groom.

Vivian's eyes were red and heavy as she approached me.

"Mum, dad's mind was gone. I'm sure he meant to call out to you, not to Hannah. You know what he was like towards the end. He could remember the name of his first dog but not those of his children. I'm really sure that he didn't mean it."

My friend had just given me the most devastating news that I could imagine and poor Vivian chose to raise the subject right now. My mind was in turmoil, grief, guilt and despair. "Hannah," I cried. "She is the woman who haunted your father all of his life. Now she and your father have gone, as God is my witness, trust me, there will be no more hauntings in this house."

Gabriel heard my outburst and came over to me, reassuring people to carry on.

"I was naturally upset," he was saying in a loud voice as our guests gaped at me in astonishment.

Fiona watched as his put his arms around me and led me into the snug sitting me by the fireside. He poured me a brandy and one for himself.

328

"You OK? That wasn't like you, Rose."

"Did you know that he called for Hannah? His last words on earth and he called for her, not me."

"No Rose, I didn't know. I'm so sorry. It was his mind, he was living in the past. She was in his mind for years before you came along, you know that."

I nodded and gulped down the brandy.

"Linda's dying. Cancer. Will you speak to her, Gabriel?"

"Yes, I will. Oh God, I'm sorry, Rose."

"So am I."

The winter drew in. A dark veil descended over the Manor. News came of my mother's death. She had always sworn that she would never come back to these parts and she passed away from this life in the same chair as Trevor with an untouched glass of sherry and a piece of angel cake on the side table. My sorrow was deep. Percy arranged her funeral. He drove me to Birmingham and my mother was buried with her second husband in a plot that he had reserved for them at our old church. It was cold and blustery and leaves swirled over her grave as the priest sprinkled incense over her coffin. Percy sorted out clearing her bungalow and Fiona handled the sale. My mother and Trevor had left everything to me.

Angelica was leaving. She was saying goodbye. I had written out a generous cheque which I handed to her with the words,

"I hope this is enough for you to retire? Thank you for taking care of my husband so well. You need to remove the last three letters of your name for you are an Angel. We'll miss you, Angelica."

Angelica smiled and took the envelope. Somehow I knew that she would not retire. She would seek out another family and arrive like Mary Poppins on the tail of a wind.

Death lay dominant in my thoughts. Linda lasted a few months, not a couple of years as she had hoped. She and my mother were the link with my past. The first third of my life. Apart from what had happened with Wayne, they were not all bad times. Linda and I had fun at school. She stuck by me, as my mother did. Life felt unfair. Linda did not deserve to die so young.

My misery grew like a cancer and I had no interest in anyone or anything. I moped about feeling like a maggot was nibbling at the vivacity of my soul.

Percy had moved Honora's portrait and as fate would have it a replacement arrived unexpectedly. Jacob parked his truck in the courtyard which was unusual as he mostly parked in the yard by the stables. I saw him through an upstairs window and went down to let him in taking him to the kitchen. He was carrying an item wrapped in brown paper. I made tea and we sat at the table.

"Helena and I were putting stuff in the attic and I went up and found some paintings."

He had a strange and puzzled look on his face.

"Well, most of them are of landscapes but then I came across this one. Let me open it and show it to you, you'll see what I mean."

He began to unravel the parcel which measured about 2×4 feet.

"There's no doubt Lady Langley, this picture belongs to you."

I stared at a woman who looked uncannily like me. Her hair was the colour of mine, her skin was the same tone as mine but most of all, her eyes shone out to me just like mine.

Jacob seemed bewitched.

"Me and Helena, well, it's a mystery but she looks a lot like you. Any idea who this is?" he asked.

"Eliza, it's Eliza," I said. "Thank you for finding it, for bringing it Jacob. You and Helena are right to return it, thank you."

330

Later, I showed it to Percy. He was lost for words when he saw it.

My vineyard was reaching a climax. I rode out on Axis to the stoop of the valley and looked down across it. The main building was roofed in grass, an eco suggestion by Sporty Sam. I called him that because he would use his leisure time to jog over the landscape of the Callow lands. He was the project manager and with the architecture of the building he had received a prize for its design. A tarmac car park laid to one side entered from the B road that wound through the valley below. The other side of the road was skirted by the estate of Langley Hall. We had received no objections about the planning as naturally we had discussed everything with Fergus and Bunnie first. The question was, 'Would anyone come out here to see my vineyard?' Christina and Verity had begun an ice-cream making business and they opened a small shop near to the B road opposite the vineyard centre to help capture visitors. We planned to stock their ice-cream in the shop, together with meat and dairy produce from Langley farm.

To Judy's credit she had whisked up an army for the grape picking. The vines drooped heavy with their fruit. Even though there would be no wine this year, I decided to hold a party to celebrate the picking of our first harvest when it was completed at the end of October in the new building.

I took a ride out on my own. It was pleasant to have some time for my feelings and thoughts. I felt horribly ashamed of my encounter with Žanis and I could not erase those jealous thoughts from my head about Felix and Hannah. Suddenly, horse's hooves chomped at the ground behind me. Žanis stopped his horse pulling up at my side.

"How are you Rose? You look sad."

"Yes, I feel sad. Too much death in the air for me to bear."

I was in no mood to talk to him about my feelings so changed the subject.

331

"Look how things have developed in the valley. You inspired all of this Žanis. Did you realise that day when you scooped up the soil in your hands that it would be the cause of all of this?"

"No Rose, but I see that it makes you happy. I am glad for that."

Riding home, the only noise I heard was the last leaves of autumn rustling gently as they clung to branches not wanting to fall.

Vivian managed to take some leave and came back for my grand celebration of the grape harvest. The girls were thrilled at the condition of the horses. Žanis rode each horse each day to keep them exercised, apart from Jack, Rupert's horse, as Rupert often rode out himself to visit tenants. Žanis had cut sugar from their diet and changed their feed. The stables smelled of a fly potion he made out of garlic, lavender and lemon juice and a secret ingredient that he would not divulge to us.

Despite the grey weather, Judy was vivacious. Perhaps she had always secretly coveted becoming the next Lady Langley as she adapted to the role with gusto. It was a rare opportunity for the four of them to ride out together. Žanis groomed and tacked the horses and Rupert, Judy, Percy and Vivian went out for an early morning ride the morning of my celebratory harvest picking party. They rose early and I didn't hear them leave. Mid-morning the telephone rang. It was Percy.

"Mum, come quickly, bring the 4×4 we're at Lime Brook. Fetch Žanis for the horses. Quick mum, there's been an accident."

He didn't say to who or what had happened. I grabbed the keys and ran into the courtyard screaming at the top of my voice for Žanis. Thankfully, he was in the Lodge and came rushing out.

I ran, calling for him to join me, I could barely speak. I shouted 'accident'! Some people were just arriving to book into the east wing and I yelled at them to go in as the door was open.

I drove to Lime Brook to find Percy holding his own horse Streaker, and Jack. He was frantically waving his arms towards the other side of the hedge. I stopped the car and Žanis jumped out to take the horses' reins. Percy ran to the gate and leaped over it and I followed. There was an old man-made ditch to collect the water from the moorland and divert it down the valley. As part of the vineyard project a brown pipe had been placed in the ditch for the water to run through and link to the new toilet block. As yet, it had not been covered and lay exposed. Vivian and Judy, in their usual excitable fashion, had jumped the hedge not realising the changes on the other side. Percy and Rupert had called to them to stop but they could not hear as the wind whistled past their ears. Apparently, Judy's horse had clipped the pipe and tumbled, clipping Ginger's back leg which toppled them all.

Vivian was struggling to get up and Percy dashed to her side to help her. She was holding her wrist and looked in pain. Judy had been thrown and was lying still on the ground. Rupert had her head in his lap and looked up at me fearfully.

"Has anyone rung for an ambulance?" I yelled my voice carrying over the howling wind.

We looked up, there was an air ambulance approaching. Ginger and Truffles were laying on the ground. Ginger raised her head and I went to stroke her. Truffles' leg was clearly broken.

"Vivian, are you OK? Have you hurt your wrist? Is it broken?"

"I think so, mum. Oh God Judy, wake up!" she said.

The doctor leapt out of the helicopter and rushed straight to Judy. He questioned Rupert about what had happened as he took her pulse. Next he inserted a tube in her arm for a drip. Then he

333

and the paramedics placed a head restraint around her and then the paramedics carried her on a stretcher to the helicopter. He made a quick examination of Vivian's arm and instructed someone to take her to hospital in a car. There was no room in the helicopter as Rupert insisted that he travelled with his wife.

Percy helped Vivian into the front seat and I sat in the back as he took the wheel and drove us to hospital. I yelled over to Žanis to take care of the horses. He nodded and as Percy turned the car across the field I saw him tie the horses to the gate. I hoped that at least Ginger would survive.

At the hospital Vivian was taken away for an x-ray of her wrist. Unbeknown to me, she didn't have an x-ray for a reason I was soon to find out. The doctor assessed her and diagnosed that she had broken it and needed a plaster cast. Percy telephoned Gabriel and Fiona. When they arrived they looked washed out. The strain was evident as we waited for news. Eventually, Rupert came to find us. To our relief Judy was fine. She had regained consciousness and luckily she had broken nothing. Before we were allowed to wallow in the good news, Rupert sat next to Fiona.

"There's something I need to tell you all. Judy was, well is pregnant. Well, it's difficult, I'm not sure whether she still is, well whether, er, if she has lost both of the babies."

"I don't understand, what do you mean?" Fiona said, her face puzzled.

"We were going to announce it tonight at the party, Judy's pregnant with twins. Trouble is, she's bleeding heavily and the doctors don't know if she's lost them. They need to do tests."

"All we can do is pray," Gabriel said.

I went to find Vivian to break the news to her.

"Mum, I feel so silly but I've got some news for you too. I'm pregnant too. Oh God! I hope my baby's OK. Can you find a doctor for me? I'd like to be examined."

I stared at my daughter. My urge was to shout at her. *'What the hell did you and Judy think you were doing, stupid reckless girls!'* I saw the fright in her eyes and took her hand.

"Are you bleeding? Any tummy pains?"

"No, but mum can you get a doctor, please?"

A lady doctor came and examined Vivian. Then she arranged for a scan and to my delight I saw the form of a baby with a beating heart. It was such a wonderful moment after all my grief that I cried. We both cried and the nurse left us on our own for a while. The doctor came back and advised Vivian to rest.

"Probably not a good idea to ride any horses for a while," she added scornfully.

I looked at Vivian. "The doctor's right, darling."

"Don't mention my pregnancy mum, not until we know about Judy."

We went to find the others. A doctor had informed them that they were going to keep Judy overnight for tests and rest. He advised us to all go home as there was nothing we could do but wait.

I wasn't sure what to do about the party but decided to go ahead as it was too late in the day to cancel. Vivian took plenty of painkillers and she and Percy put on brave faces as we greeted guests and served canapés wishing for the evening to end. Rupert understandably stayed at home. The party was a success although my heart wasn't in it.

The next day Rupert rang me from the hospital. Judy had lost one of her babies. I didn't know whether to feel happy or sad but I was relieved.

I visited the picture gallery. One wall was bare, the wall where you entered from the apartments and there was also an empty space in one corner. I wondered why and thought I would ask Percy. Honora had been replaced by Eliza. I studied her face. She was plain looking but she had a kind face. Eliza

335

intrigued me. Her hair was neat in two plaits circled on her head. In my dreams her hair was always loose. She was a blithe spirit but now she looked elegant and precise. Her lips moved to speak but I walked away and glanced at each painting absorbing the untold stories within them. Voices. A cacophony of voices screeched as I nervously made my way to leave. I passed Marguerite and it felt like she was grabbing at my arm,

"Rose, Rose, will you be my mother, I am alone Rose, please do not leave me."

Isabella is jabbering in Spanish, I do not understand what she is saying. The first Francis is leering at me, the second Francis is sneering at me. I run away and my head throbs.

I sought out Percy and Vivian. They were with Žanis in the yard and I saw the back of a horse box driving away. Žanis was using a hose pipe to wash blood into the drain. Truffles had to be shot. Ginger was peering over the door as Vivian stroked her with her good hand.

"Is Ginger all right? How's her leg?" I asked Žanis.

"It is bruised but it will heal. She needs to rest it."

"No riding for a long time," I said with a mother's tone looking at Vivian.

"Percy, Vivian, I need you to come with me, please."

My children looked at me anxiously. They followed me into the Manor to my old bedroom as I took the ring of keys from the drawer.

"Mum, I always meant to ask you. How did you know that the key would fit the chest?" Percy said.

"I don't know how I knew, I just did. I think someone left them in a secret place for me to find one day. Come on! There's something I need to show you."

Percy and Vivian exchanged perplexed looks and stepped behind me wondering what mystery was about to unfold. At the door, which led to the tower, I took a deep breath as I turned the key in its lock. The room was nothing like how I remembered it.

A thick layer of detritus covered everything. The once vivid crimson damask had mellowed, the mimosa in the vase was dust. Candle wax dripped from the holders and had formed a pool beneath the window. I walked across to look at the courtyard below. There were some matches so I lit a candle. The air stirred. Biffy appeared.

"At last you came, Miss. At last, I have waited so long."

Vivian and Percy were watching me in silence as my body moved in response.

I took her cold hand in mine.

"Keep lighting the candles, Biffy. They've been moved to the linen cupboard so we can use the door through to the east wing. Have you been there?"

Biffy nodded. "But when can I go, Miss? Jane, she's gone, I can't find her. I search every night but I can't find her." She looked crestfallen.

"We'll find her soon, don't worry Biffy, I promise."

Vivian was dumbstruck hardly believing what she was experiencing. All she saw was me speaking into an empty space.

Percy took my arm.

"Is this a special place for you mum?" he asked.

"Yes Percy, in more ways than you'll ever know."

We left the room without speaking until we got back to the kitchen. Percy made tea and Vivian finally spoke.

"How on earth are we going to tell Rupert about this? He's got enough on his plate."

"It's all right. He knows about Biffy, he's seen her too. Vivian, have you never crossed paths with Biffy? I know Percy has."

"I think so but I always thought that I was dreaming. Crikey mum, what are you going to do? It's all a bit unbelievable. Did dad know about the tower and Biffy? And who is Jane?"

Vivian was pragmatic. Did she understand that she had seen a ghost?

Percy put steaming mugs of tea on the table and sat beside me.

"Your father seemed to be in denial about the goings-on in this house. For years I thought there was a ghost of Hannah in the tower. But it wasn't her, it was a lady called Jane."

I related the story to my children about my dreams of Eliza and how I came to be at the Manor. I spoke of Jane and her sons and why Biffy still glided through the galleries seeking her out. The air had grown chilly and Percy went to turn up the heating thermostat just as Rupert arrived. He looked drawn but pleased that Judy would be released from hospital tomorrow. I never got chance until the next day to ask Percy about the spaces in the picture gallery.

Vivian left for London with strict instructions from me to take it easy as she was carrying my grandchild. She had told Rupert her news over breakfast and he had reacted with a smile and a hug pleased that his surviving twin was going to have a cousin. Rupert left to fetch Judy and Percy was attending to guests in the east wing. I fancied a ride to clear my head but a gale was blowing in from the east threatening rain. Instead I chose to wander into the gardens. Jacob and Žanis and the team of gardeners we employed had transformed the walled garden. The Victorian greenhouses had new glass and were filled with large quantities of produce. A lot was going to be sold in the vineyard shop. Against one wall the row of humps had increased where working and family dogs and cats had been buried. Since Tarbo and Buster, three pairs of dogs had worked the sheep. Rupert was looking for a new pair as the current incumbents grew into retirement. I expected that Judy would pick their names. At each grave were little wooden crosses and I read the names, Buster, Tarbo, Phoebe, Thor, Brandy and Snap. I walked to the gnarled walnut tree and sat on the bench where

Old Tom and I would rest. Žanis appeared and sat next to me. He was carrying a rucksack.

"Are you going somewhere?" I asked as I pretended not to be surprised.

"Time for me to move on. I have stayed here longer than anywhere before."

"Moving on to break women's hearts," I replied rather cautiously.

"I think it is my heart that was broken this time, Rose." His voice was husky and tired. I found it sexy.

"What will we do without you? Jacob, does he know?"

"He knows. My cousin is sending his son from Latvia to come and work next week. He will be a good worker. He is like me in many ways, he loves horses and speaks their language."

"Of course, that's fine, we will welcome him. What's his name?"

"Žanis. What can I say, it is a popular name in Latvia!"

I laughed. "Thank you for everything, Žanis. The horses will miss you greatly."

He got up to go.

"More than you I think, Rose," he said looking down at me through his mysterious dark eyes.

"I'll let Percy and Rupert know." I refrained from acknowledgement of what he had just said.

"Tell them that Žanis the Penis says farewell."

Again I laughed and I wondered how he knew about their nickname for him. He bent and kissed me on my mouth. My stomach churned and I responded guiltily. I understood this would be my last kiss of passion and so I let him linger for a while. He stopped and tenderly kissed my neck. Then he cupped my face in his hands and spoke to me softly.

"Goodbye, Rose. Perhaps one day you will send me a bottle of your wine?"

"Where will I know where to send it?" I called as he began to walk away. His shoulders were hunched and already he had one hand in his pocket.

"My cousin's son Rose, goodbye." He half-turned his head and then gave me a wave as he sauntered cockily on the cobbled path down to the old wooden door.

"A case, I'll send you a case..." He was gone.

When Rupert and Judy arrived home Gabriel and Fiona came to visit and I made us all supper. As Judy's parents fussed over her I pulled Percy to one side and told him that I needed to speak with him before bedtime.

We sat in the snug. I told him that Žanis had left.

"He knew your nickname for him. He said to tell you that Žanis the Penis said goodbye."

Percy laughed, "Oh come on mum, you know that was Rupert not me."

"There's something else on my mind. Can you speak with Rupert and Judy as soon as she is better? I want to move back into the Lodge. I think the time has come for me to leave them to have the run of this house. Judy needs the space away from her mother-in-law and to make this her own home, Rupert and their baby. I expect you will stay too, Percy? Perhaps you can move into one of the guest rooms and your old bedroom can be for the baby and who knows, any future babies? Actually, Percy I have resolved to move to the Lodge tomorrow. Will you help me with my things?"

"Of course mum, are you sure?"

"Absolutely. And now, can you tell me why there are blank spaces in the picture gallery?"

CHAPTER 25

My first night back in the Lodge. Candles flickered in the tower window. I could see Biffy pacing the floor. When I slept I dreamed of Eliza. A long tireless dream as she called to me, her lips moving in her portrait. In the back of my mind I recalled Jane's words about being careful with my love. I had long forgotten and I still wondered what she meant.

In the morning, I summoned my sons in my best mother's authoritative tone. Judy was resting in bed. We went to the tower.

"Rupert, this would make a great home office don't you think? Percy, perhaps you can relocate some of the furniture around the house. I would like the bedside cupboards and the table with the twisted legs in the Lodge."

Rupert was mumbling. "What the heck is going on? Why didn't I know about this place?"

Percy hushed him explaining that he would tell all later. "Just do what mum says."

Percy lifted the rug to examine it. It was slightly moth-eaten but was of good quality.

"Hang on a mo, there seems to be a trapdoor under here. Rupert, give me a hand to move the bed."

We discovered a chamber. It contained an altar table, two silver candlesticks and a Bible. There was a silver bowl where holy water must have once filled it and a cross of Jesus hanging on a rusty nail.

"It all makes sense now. I reckon this tower was built to hide a place of Catholic worship. For sure, I bet it was Isabella, our Spanish princess. There was so much religious war and division of land depended very much upon which faith you followed during her time."

I went to the ante-room. Jane's beautiful dresses had decayed and the smell of lemon-scent had diminished. Over the coming days the boys set about emptying the tower room. Everything apart from the candles and the holder in the window. I think Rupert was glad of the distraction not knowing how to interact with his wife.

The winter faded and swallows arrived carrying the hope of summer with them. Their favourite nesting places were in the stables where I had come across Žanis' relative. He was charismatic but he did not flirt with me, he was young enough to be my son. I spoke with Jacob who was pleased with his progress. Our new Žanis had the same gypsy instinct with the horses and as soon as Judy was well enough Rupert bought her a lovely chestnut. We banned her from riding until her baby was born.

The space in the corner of the gallery was for a commission. It was a space for me! I was to be painted for posterity. As soon as Percy told me I drove to the drapers in Churchbury and ordered a made-to-measure cloak of black velvet.

To fill the larger wall, Vivian had been working on our family tree and this was going to be enlarged and fixed here. This was a gift to me from my children and a lovely surprise. I looked forward to seeing it with excited anticipation.

Eliza came to me in my dreams. Each night her tender words resonated in my ear. *'All would be well. Come to me Rose, come."*

On a pleasant May evening, Percy, Judy, Rupert and I were sat in the garden through the French windows on the seats that I had turned the right way up so long ago. Mimosa, agapanthus, spray carnations, eucharis, fritillaria, delphinium and forget-me-nots filled the beds throwing up their scents in the calm evening air.

The telephone rang.

"Hi mum! Just to let you know that the ancestry board should arrive in the next few days. I've told Percy but make sure someone is around to take delivery. And by the way, I'm in labour. I'll get Bertie to ring."

I went back to the table. Percy and Rupert were drinking beer and Judy was sipping a glass of cordial from a tall glass with a sprig of mint and ice.

"Everything all right, mum?"

"Vivian's in labour! Bertie will ring. She was more concerned about the family tree arriving..."

I had not quite finished my sentence, pondering on its gravity for a moment, when suddenly Judy let go a yelp and I heard a gush of water as she jumped up out of her chair.

"Oh my God, my waters have gone. Rupert, ring mum, quick and take me to the hospital."

Rupert telephoned me. "Mum, our eldest twin survived, you should see his Cross of Soot, it's really deep and black. He looks like me but I think he'll have Judy's eyes."

By the next afternoon I was a grandmother of two. Vivian had a baby daughter and Judy a son.

Gathering mimosa, I arranged them in the beautiful bowl from the tower on the table next to me where I stood very still in my long black velvet cloak. Underneath, I wore a pale blue evening gown, made of silk, which had belonged to Felix's mother. The dress was too tight for me but I had left it undone at the back. No one could see as the black cloak draped over me. I took the pearls from the chest that were interspersed with emeralds and rubies and fastened the diamond lock. As I did I felt Maud Thompson's oath weigh heavy upon me. I thought of the legacy of the Cross of Soot and my new grandson who bore the symbol of a curse. Charmingly, I smiled at Henry Fitzgerald who was adding the final touches to my portrait. He was sweeping his brush with a flourish filling in yellow-headed flowers with a dab and a swoop. 'Voilà!' he exclaimed. His eyes were bright with excitement and I stepped over to see my painting; I saw Eliza staring back at me.

At last the first bottles of wine were ready. We branded the wine, 'Callow Wine'. The vineyard, 'Callow Valley Vineyard' and the Callow crest was embossed on the labels. We stored twelve bottles of the red and the white in the cellar and I sent a case of each to Žanis via his namesake. In the end I hired a manager to oversee the process. I tried to be enthusiastic but my heart was just not in it. I was still grieving.

Judy had given up on running the business as she wanted to concentrate on her son and make the changes to the Manor that she desired.

Rupert had the view that this was Judy's home and as long as it did not interfere with his farming and his drinking nights in the Callow Arms with his farming friends, his view was that she could do what she wanted.

In my heart I always knew that this is what she wanted. She was casting me out and once more I felt unloved and the curse of jealousy in my blood.

The east wing was full of guests. It was always full of guests as word of mouth circulated amongst those who desired the uniqueness of the rooms and the open countryside with all that it had to offer.

The delivery men followed Percy to the gallery and after much huffing and puffing they carried the threads of the Langley ancestors up the stairs. Jacob and the new Žanis gave a hand to fix it to the wall. Once in place, Percy pulled off the protective cellophane. I looked around the room at the faces in the pictures who seemed to be crowding in.

"It's amazing! I wish Vivian was here to see it."

Percy hugged me. Jacob and young Žanis stepped back to admire it.

"I think there are some relatives of mine on there somewhere," Jacob said peering hard to figure out the map of descendants which confused him.

"Come back another time perhaps, Jacob? I think mum wants to study it on her own for a while."

"Sure, sure, we've gotta get back anyway as there is a load of turf coming for the new lawn outside of here for the visitors' garden." He nodded turning his cap in his hands.

I stood back. Vivian had cleverly printed the descending lines in different colours. She had done a huge amount of work and I felt sure she had used her connections and experience in her job to help put the tree together.

I traced the blue line from the top from the first Francis. Marguerite, her children, her eldest son's children. Passing Isabella I ran my finger along the lines until I reached Horace and Herbert. I stepped closer and I was drawn to a name that stood out: Eliza Thompson. Vivian had searched deeply. Trembling a little, I drew even closer and read that Eliza's eldest daughter had married Herbert. She was called Harriet and they had three children together.

From there a yellow line spread out.

My eyes must surely be deceiving me? I was perplexed. Percy was standing silently next to me.

"Percy, this yellow line, does this mean that Eliza Thompson was my great, great grandmother?"

"It seems so, mum. Gosh, look, you are related to dad. Vivian mentioned as much. I think she was a bit worried about

345

how you would feel about that. She said something about us children getting away without having two heads."

I could not find anything inside me to laugh at his joke. I needed to sit down. When your mother dies you wish you had asked more questions. Dig deeper about family history but I had left it too late. Perhaps my mother never knew the connection. It turned out that Felix Langley was my relation. It turned out that I had always belonged here.

What was Eliza trying to tell me? For many years, even before I set out on my journey to the Callow lands, Eliza called to me to come home. But why?

A murky cloud moved over the sun and shrouded the light through the window making it hazy. Feeling cold, a shiver ran down my spine.

I went to telephone Vivian.

"Thank you, darling. Yes, it arrived safely and fits perfectly on the wall. It is amazing. I wish your father could have seen it. How did you find out all the details of our ancestors?"

I listened to my daughter explain how she and Percy had scoured the records in the library and the help her colleagues had given in her research and the records in the church that Gabriel had helped source.

"Mum, we did some research on Jane Dakin and filled in the gaps."

"You've done a lot of work, thank you," I said gratefully.

I put the phone down, forgetting to ask my daughter how she and my grandchild were getting along.

Summer rolled into autumn. I felt restless but I didn't know why. Occasionally I rode out on Axis to breathe in the fresh air to help clear my head. I was happy for the staff to manage the vineyard. I had no interest in it or the harvest or the wine for my mind was in turmoil.

Vivian suggested that I went to London to spend time with my new granddaughter. Their three-storey home was in

Hampstead, that fashionable part of the city. As I now held the power of attorney, I bought the house for them and invested a large sum for Daisy, my grandchild and any other future grandchildren that Bertie and Vivian may produce. The boys had the farms, the land and the Manor. I had made a will and decided to leave the vineyard between the three children to do with as they wished.

Percy drove me to the train station in Shrugsborough.

"You going to be all right, mum? Can you remember where you need to change stations? Be careful on the tube, watch out for pickpockets."

"Percy," I said kissing him and patting his cheeks, "Stop worrying, I'm a grown woman, I'll be fine. Vivian's meeting me at Hampstead. I'll ring when I get there."

Vivian looked radiant. Motherhood suited her. Daisy was strapped in a harness tied around Vivian's waist and she was asleep. Tiny wisps of blonde curls crowned her head. When we arrived at the house she woke and stared at me with deep cobalt eyes.

"She's adorable Vivian. No, she's more than that, she is the most gorgeous child I have ever seen."

"Mum, you would say that, you are biased!"

I could see so much of Bertie in Daisy. Lillian, his mother, had been a pin-up and she still was very attractive. It was good to have some new genes in the family, I thought.

Bertie was a very hands-on father. Daisy's eyes would light up when he came into the room. At five months old she seemed alert and communicative. Vivian often sat her on her knee so together they could look at a book as Vivian read aloud the story. Daisy pointed at the animals, 'moo', she mimicked when she saw pictures of cows. I frankly thought my grandchild was a genius. Matthew, my grandson, received a lot of attention from Judy and Fiona but he never seemed as bright.

Their house was minimalist. Vivian and Bertie had no desire for clutter. I asked Vivian if she would like anything from the Manor and she merely replied that she would have liked Ginger and perhaps Žanis to look after her. Hearing his name made me blush. My guilty pleasure flipped through my mind. Like my mother, Vivian was happier with the full context of human society about her.

"On Friday, I've got tickets for a theatre trip, mum. *The Mousetrap*."

"Who's going to look after Daisy?" I retorted.

"Bertie, of course. Mum, you are so old-fashioned. I'll bet Rupert's never even changed one of Matthew's nappies, has he? Bertie's not like that. We share the chores and the care of our daughter.

"We are getting a nanny once I am back at work, but I don't want to leave it too long before I have another child. Mum, it's not like I'm running that old Manor and the estate."

She was right. I had never thought of things that way. My life had always been so strongly linked to the past and I wished to escape from the haunting ghosts. Dare I hope for a change in my future? Visiting Vivian was the tonic I needed. Her matter-of-fact attitude inspired me to get on with things and to stop dwelling on stuff that might never happen or otherwise, if it had, to let it go.

We went to the theatre. The smells and the atmosphere reminded me of when my children were young. A small awakening was ruffling at my feathers and as it wasn't too late when we returned, I telephoned Fred Albright.

I went into the kitchen where Bertie and Vivian were sipping red wine. I announced to them that I was going to France to visit some wineries with Fred Albright and his wife.

"I'm taking back the reins, I am not prepared to spend the rest of my days roaming around the Lodge with nothing to do." It was a statement and I meant it.

Vivian wrapped her arms around me.

"That's good news mum, good news."

There was a travel agents in Churchbury and so I drove in and sat with the petite young blonde girl, who smelled of jasmine, and worked out the travel details for our tour of French wineries. I had decided that I would pay for the expenses. I had never met Fred's wife but I hoped that she wouldn't mind meeting me. I would be the gooseberry in our threesome but I wanted to have their company. I was too afraid to go on my own. The trip was planned so that I would drive to Kent and stay over at their home. To break the ice, Mrs Albright would give me a tour of their vineyard. Then we would catch the train to Waterloo and the train to Paris. Fred was going to hire a car in Paris. He was well accustomed to driving on the wrong side of the road, something which terrified me and thus we would begin our tour. As I had never been to Paris, I suggested that we extended our stay so that we could have a couple of days in the city on the way back and Fred and his wife agreed. Because of my investment, it meant the Albrights could afford to hire a manager and she would take control of their business in their absence.

Percy was worried about me. He made me feel like a child but I could see his point having never travelled anywhere further than Warwickshire but I was so looking forward to it and he was reassured that I had the company of Fred and his wife Kathleen.

He looked tired. Percy was managing the east wing and was currently overseeing the management of the winery. I knew I was burdening him with a lot of work so I promised myself to give him a break when I got home. He was also putting on weight and I could see a ring of scalp appearing on the top of his head where he was losing his hair. Reality dawned on me that my sons were no longer boys but grown men. Rupert was a father and Judy was expecting her second child. Judy had keenly abandoned all responsibilities to do with the east wing, the vineyard or anything else to do with the estate. She was happy to fill her days by choosing décor and a new kitchen for the Manor. She also spent a lot of her time in Churchbury at the hairdressers and beauty salon so that I found myself looking after Matthew. He was a cute baby, although I felt, not as clever as his cousin Daisy, nevertheless he was developing well. He was the image of Rupert at the same age all except his eyes which were amber, like his mother and grandfather. I would look into them and see Gabriel.

Fiona had taken early retirement and spent her days riding and gardening. Her influence on the changes in the house came through her daughter. In an underhand way it felt to me as if she were saying that it was the right of her daughter to do whatever she liked in my old home. They both made me feel discarded so I was happy to be leaving the place that had held me in its grip for so many years.

Diligent Percy had written out directions for me to the Albrights. The journey took me five hours and for most of it I was petrified. I drove on the M6, past Birmingham and I thought of my mother, Linda and Patrick. An urge came over me as I wanted to visit their graves. It remained for a while but soon I was past the exit and I needed to concentrate on my driving and thought that I would stop on my return.

Kathleen was very nice. She was pretty for her age, probably my age I guessed. Her hair was cropped short. Women have a deep reckoning of other women and my intuition told me straight away that she was happy my intent was not to steal her husband. She must have thought it odd that I had arranged this trip but we bonded immediately.

"Please call me Kathy, everyone does."

Kathy had a great sense of humour, mostly directed at her husband. Over supper Fred opened some of their own white wine which tasted delicious. Then another and when we all woke in the morning, we had to be ready for 6am to catch our train, we looked worse for wear. We barely spoke as Kathy filled our mugs with fresh coffee and filled our plates with croissants.

Once we got to Waterloo Station we had all perked up and I was very keen to get going. I was going to France. Me, plain Rose, who had never stepped a foot out of her country before.

The train hauled its way along tracks and eventually through the great tunnel under the sea that joined our two countries. We drank more coffee and read magazines and then, after what seemed like a short time, we reached Paris.

The Gare du Nord was humming with throngs of people. There was a scent in the air that reminded me of almonds. Whilst Fred went to organise the car hire, he left me and Kathy sitting on a wooden bench with our luggage. I listened intently to the French accents and found them fascinating.

Somehow, things always brought me back to the Manor and I thought of Marguerite, the child bride, and how the familiar sounds of her own people would be a comfort to her.

A grinning Fred returned holding a car key and we followed him to an estate model which had plenty of room in its boot to hold our luggage. The roads in Paris are frightening but Fred steered his way through with great aplomb and soon the scenes of the city were left behind like driftwood floating in cobbled rouge lights and we hit the countryside.

Kathy and I both slept, me in the back and she in the passenger seat. When we woke we were entering the town of Bordeaux. Finding our sweet Bohemian hotel, we checked in and ordered dinner. After tender lamb, mashed potatoes, green beans and a rich glass of red wine we took a gentle tour of the old town.

We visited St André's Cathedral and it evoked hidden memories from the mists of time in my great line of ancestry. I had been here before, in another life perhaps? As I ran my hand

351

across the stone wall I could feel the clock of déjà vu ticking. I scribbled a note in my journal to ask Vivian to discover where Marguerite had been baptised.

In the morning, after consuming a continental breakfast and cups of refreshing freshly made coffee, we headed off to the Grand Cru Classé Château Pape Clement in Pessac-Léognan. We were supposed to be tasting the wine and discovering more about grape growth but we found ourselves wandering through the stunning gardens. I brought my journal with me and chatted to the gardener, whose English was very good, to ask the names of the flowers that I didn't recognise as I wanted to grow them at home.

"Why not? It is possible if you find a sheltered space you can grow all of these plants," he told me as I basked in his pronunciation of English in French tones.

Over five days we visited the Châteaux in Saint Emilion, Saint Julien and others. We learnt of the unique soil, the aspect and the micro-climate and I began to yearn for my little patch of France in the warm valley of Callow lands in Shrugsboroughshire.

"As it turns out, Rose, I think you will find that your land is more suitable for growing wine than ours in Kent. You lucky girl!" Fred retorted as we were packing the car ready to return to the capital.

Fred was tired from our drive back to Paris, so Kathy and I went sightseeing on our own. Fred had been to Paris before so he didn't mind remaining at the hotel to catch up on his sleep. We caught the open-topped bus. Kathy, and I had a good guide book and we decided to venture on the bus to Rodin's house. Nowhere in my life before had I been where the calmness and the grace of womanhood was steeped in the very air that we breathed. Rodin's view of women was marvellous and admirable. Kathy took my photograph by *The Kiss* and I made up my mind to purchase a sculpture to set in the centre of the gallery in the east wing. I hoped it would remind me of Rodin's house. Fred's words echoed in my head... 'You lucky girl!' I felt enthused about going home and continuing my vineyard project. For once, I felt happy to be a woman and for once, just in that moment, I wasn't jealous of anyone.

We visited Notre Dame and the Sacré Coeur Church at Montmartre and the market nearby. Even in the sombre falling light of the year, everywhere was busy with tourists. And even though I sensed the great dignity and beauty of the magnificent cathedrals in Paris, it was the one at Bordeaux that had bored its way into my soul and I felt great attachment to it but I did not know why.

Leaving Kent, I kissed Fred and Kathy goodbye, promising to meet up again soon and set off for home.

I was tired yet invigorated after my trip. Cautiously, I considered whether to stop and visit graves on the way home. It would be a sad end to my travels but I wasn't sure when I would pass this way again so I took the turning to Warwick and wound my way through pretty country lanes until I stopped at the church where Linda was buried. Her grave was fresh with flowers and I suddenly had a pang of guilt. I had promised Linda to keep in touch with Charlie but realised I had not spoken with him since Linda's funeral.

"I went to France, Linda, you'll be impressed with me," I whispered over her grave.

I inwardly recited a prayer and let a tear drop down my cheek as I thought of Linda laughing with me over some pointless joke and I missed her.

Then to my mother and my son. I drove to Birmingham to the church where I had first married in what seemed like another life. A great knot of tension wound in my stomach. Firstly, I visited mum's grave. In life, Trevor had spared no expense. Their shared headstone was elaborate and memorial words were etched in gold with ornate flower decorations carved at the bottom.

"I expect you and Trevor are on a beach in Spain somewhere aren't you?" I said aloud.

I went to find Patrick's tiny grave nearby. I became overwrought. I should have tended the grave at mother's funeral but Percy was with me and I couldn't let him see. Mum was the last person to visit my poor son's grave and there was still a vase of rotted flowers on the overgrown patch where she'd left them. I bent down and began to tear at the grass and weeds. A man was at another grave and watched me suspiciously as I tore at the soil.

"You all right, luv?"

I looked up at him. There was some faint recognition. My God! It was Ian, the spotty boy from school.

"Ay, is that you Rose Howard? I don't believe it?"

He looked at me and then at the grave of my baby and seemed to be putting two and two together.

"I heard what happened to you. I'm sorry I didn't stop to help that night. I was only young and I hadn't a clue as to what had happened to you. I'm glad to see you look well. Is this your baby's grave?"

I nodded.

"Come on, let me help you."

He went to his car and fetched a spade and a bag of spring bulbs.

"They're my parents over there," he pointed. "I usually plant some bulbs and tidy the grave at this time of year but you can have them, I can always get some more."

I smiled at him. I smiled at him for the kindness of strangers.

When we had finished he said, "Do you fancy a coffee?"

He took me to a café on the main street and we drank frothy coffee from large mugs. He told me his story.

Ian had gone to university to train as an engineer and got a job at one of the large car factories. He'd been married and divorced, no children. After his divorce he went back to live with his parents and cared for them until they died. His story was short, simple, uncomplicated. He liked classic cars and kept a MGB Mark 1 1967 Roadster in his garage.

"And what about you Rose? Where have you been all these years?"

"Where do I begin?" I asked.

"Well, you don't need to fill me in on what happened that night in the toilet but you can tell me where you live now and what you are doing?"

I told him how I had left Birmingham and heard the women talk about Churchbury at the bus station. How I had walked and got lost and found the Manor and how I met Felix. I spoke of my children and the vineyard and my trip to France. I didn't mention Hannah.

He was interested in the vineyard and gave me his phone number. I surmised that he was lonely.

"If you ever need an engineer, you know, or someone to help with the vineyard, let me know, Rose. I'm not too old for a new challenge and by the way, neither are you. Sounds like you had a calling to be there, Rose."

I took his number, thanked him for the coffee and left.

Driving back, my mind whirred as I was trying to figure out how Ian would fit into my new plans for the vineyard. How could I make him swear never to divulge my secret? I think part of me wanted to give him the chance to make things up to me but I also liked him. He was kind.

Percy was relieved to see me and came out to help me unload the luggage. He had aired the Lodge but a chill evening was stealing the warmth of the day as October skies charred the blue with dashes of purple and orange over the stretching moors. I hurriedly lit the fire and made some hot chocolate and

355

Percy sat with me by the hearth to listen to the tale of my travels in France.

"Mum, you don't need to bother Vivian about Bordeaux Cathedral and your feelings of déjà vu. I can do that. I'll check the records, no problem. You look tired from your trip."

"Yes, I am rather tired. I stopped to visit some graves on the way home. An extraordinary thing happened. I met a man who I knew years ago. I think I may ask him to come and help with the vineyard."

My son looked at me curiously. He knew me well enough not to question me too deeply but I saw worry etched on his brow.

"Don't worry, darling. He's a perfectly nice man and he has all the right credentials to help. Now, I must get some sleep as I have a busy day tomorrow because I need to check at the centre about the grape picking. I learned a lot in France and we need to get on. By the way, how is Rupert, Judy, Matthew?"

"Oh, they're all fine, mum. Judy's decided on a new kitchen; Granite tops and lots of stainless steel. I tried to protest that the style doesn't really fit with the Manor but you know what she's like. Her mind is made up."

"Yes darling, I know what she's like. Goodnight."

PART NINE

Now we are in the future as we must be, for this is where my story ends

CHAPTER 26

Ian was engaged as an employee of Callow Valley Vineyard and he took the cottage next to Betty and Young Tom. There was a garage for his classic car so he was pleased. He kept his house in Birmingham and rented it out so that he had enough money to buy another car and at weekends he would motor around the country meeting up with other classic motor enthusiasts. We never spoke of our past lives together and he made a promise to me that what happened in the past in Birmingham, remained in Birmingham and I trusted him implicitly. When he went back to check on his house he visited Patrick's grave and tidied it and left flowers. He kept my secret until the day he died twenty years later.

Percy discovered that the Roman site extended further than we had originally thought right across the B road to the fields of Langley Hall. The local authority were keen to excavate and the site became populated with students digging trenches. Ian's job was to oversee the archaeology and where possible he kept some of the finds in glass cases in the conference room at the vineyard centre. He was a quiet man. Occasionally we would share a glass of wine and chat about the vineyard.

"This land is wild and holds many secrets. It is ancient and below the Roman villa they have found archaeology relating to the people who lived there before them. One of the students found the remains of a chariot, probably dating back to Boadicean times, which has caused some excitement as you can imagine!"

I could tell that Ian was just as excited about the chariot but he never displayed emotion unless it was about his cars. His accent reminded me of Linda. Strangely, I liked this about him as it emphasised his steadiness and he was a true confidant.

Once, when I was riding Axis over the hill, I thought I saw some people chatting amongst the rows of vines dressed in Roman costume. I assumed they were staff instructed to dress up for tourists. It was a glorious sunny afternoon and they chatted as they worked trimming dead wood. A little girl ran to her mother, who was dressed like a Grecian goddess and she bent to kiss her. Her skin was olive and her hair was tied in a scarlet band. When I next saw Ian, I enquired who the people were. He told me that no-one was in costume on that particular day. More ghosts, I pondered, as I looked far away across the Callow lands. I think Ian detected the emotions in my eyes at times but never uttered a word on those occasions. Rather, he would engage me on another matter and pretend not to notice.

Our wine grew in reputation and over the years we received many awards. I would go so far as to say that our wine, in some cases, outranked the French.

I noticed that there was a regular visitor to the holiday apartments. He was a single male of perhaps forty years. Percy would take him on long walks and I would hear the zoom of his car as they drove off to Churchbury or Shrugsborough for dinner. They were obviously in a relationship. To reward Percy for his efforts, I bought two tickets for a trip to Italy. This included tours of Venice, Rome and Florence ending on the Amalfi Coast for a week. I booked luxurious five-star hotels for the whole holiday. When Percy opened the envelope he looked at me.

"Thank you, mum. This booking is for two people. Who shall I take?"

"Percy, you know who you should take." And that was all I said.

When he returned looking tanned and happy he went to the library to find out more about Marguerite. Lo and behold! I was right. She had been baptised in Saint Andrè's Cathedral and she had spent some of her childhood in the town. Percy was amazed at my intuition. I told him that when I followed it, it never let me down. After all, it was the reason I had come to the Manor.

Guy was visiting with Ray. They came as friends and I asked them to find me a piece of sculpture to put in the centre of the gallery. For two years Guy searched for the right piece. He was so meticulous. When my sculpture arrived I was enamoured by what she portrayed to me: A large piece of marble, creamy and tactile. A woman was carved naked curled on a rock. Her long hair was flowing over her shoulders so that her face was hidden. Why had Guy chosen this piece? Did he know me so well? In her repose she represented how I felt, coiled and hollow; remote from the world because my love was lost. My youth was lost; this house had stripped that from me. I named her, 'Chagrin Fantastique'. I never looked at her and thought of Rodin, I only thought of sorrow.

I telephoned Charlie, more out of guilt than anything else. I was fond of him in a way because he was Linda's husband. To my surprise a woman answered the phone who turned out to be Charlie's new partner. Charlie was at his clinic. We spoke for a while and I said that I would phone back but I never did. A year later I received a card with their new address. Charlie had moved and remarried. We exchanged Christmas cards but I never saw him again.

Years moved rapidly by. Vivian had three more daughters and she named them, Rose, Poppy and Lily.

361

"We're making a summer meadow," Bertie joked with me once.

Judy had two more sons. I thought she regretted not having a girl but she did not want to try for another child. I think this was more to do with not wanting to spoil her figure. Her sons all looked like Rupert but they had amber eyes that softened their swarthy looks. William, the middle son, was the one who spent most of his time with me. We would ride out together, bake together and he would love to hear my stories of the mischief his father and uncle got up to when they were young.

My granddaughters loved to visit the Manor. Rupert bought a brood of Welsh ponies and the girls would trot out with their cousins. Even Lily, whom we all babied as she was the youngest, would bubble with joy as she sat proudly, her back erect, her head high, as Judy held her pony on a lead rein.

I don't know why I felt jealous, why envy fortified my thoughts. It seemed that everyone had a purpose. No, it wasn't that. I had a purpose in my life, I had my children, my grandchildren and the vineyard. It was because I had no-one to share it with. I missed Felix and I yearned for his company. Felix was the person who I wanted to discuss my day's news with in the evenings. Most of all, I wished that he was alive to taste the wine and to see how the vineyard had developed: To witness first-hand how his family had grown; to see the east wing in all its magnificence; to listen to the paintings. Paintings that cried out to me to come to them and be still.

Rupert was often tied up with the estate but on Sundays he had decided to spend time with his sons. After church we would have lunch and I would play cards with my grandsons in the snug.

"Grannie's cheating at cards again!" they would scream.

Matthew was like his father in that he loved the work on the estate. Chugging off in the tractor cab with Rupert so reminded me of Rupert as a boy with Felix. History was repeating itself again.

Edward was the clever one. He read at an early age and often had his head in a book. He was just as boisterous as his elder brothers but there was a lot about him that reminded me of Percy. Percy was a fabulous uncle and our family would gather on long summer days on the lawn outside Judy's gleaming kitchen and watch the children play cricket. As blissful children's voices are carried by the wind across the lands of Callow, I can hear the tick, tick of the clock of time.

The fire was warming the sitting room as the air was frosty outside. I was reading a book in my favourite chair. Winter pansies bobbed their flower faces in the hanging baskets that swayed in the spring's unfolding breeze and I can hear the clang of the chains swinging. In the husk of a bleary mirage through my window, I can see that a car has pulled up. It is Betty. Hooray! Perhaps we are going shopping together, or down to the church to decorate with flowers, or perhaps to sit together to gossip and drink tea.

Then, I watch as she goes to the passenger side to aid an old lady out of the car. I realise that the woman I think is Betty is actually Molly, her daughter. My bridesmaid. Her red hair has gone and turned to white. Molly has brought Betty to see me.

We sit in the kitchen, the chairs are better here. Betty finds the low seats in the sitting room difficult to get in and out. Molly begins to make tea but I tell her, 'no'. Molly doesn't realise our routine as it is usually Jacob who regularly brings Betty for a visit. Betty and I always drink sherry and eat angel cake. Percy buys it from the new supermarket in Churchbury. Five hundred new homes have been built there, he tells me, so the big store is needed. I don't recognise the little town, it has changed so much, so many people. I don't shop there any longer. My sons bring all I need.

363

"Lady Langley, would it be all right if mum and I took a look at your family tree? I have started to put one together for our family, you know, the Dakin side." She is helping to steady her mother's trembling hand as she sips her sherry. I don't recall when she began to call me Lady.

I nod. I don't really want to go to the gallery but I agree. With one hand on my stick, I heave myself out of my chair. Betty is supported by Molly. She has arthritic knees and Parkinson's disease.

We shuffle to the east wing reception area, take the lift, then enter the room.

In a line we stand back to look at the family tree of the Langleys. I feel tired so I sit on a ladder-back chair in the corner. It is made of oak. Someone has moved it from the great hall. It is the chair that I sat on when I first came here. Looking down at my feet, I can't remember which one I had hurt. I prod each ankle with my stick. They feel swollen and squidgy. My hands are swollen too, dotted with brown spots and hard blue veins. Isabella's ring, next to my wedding band, feels tight and itchy.

Molly moves to study the sculpture and walks around it, leaving Betty who vibrates like a jelly fish.

"What do you think her story is?" I ask.

"Her story?" Molly runs her hand over her sinuous spine. "It's surprising how cold she feels," she says. She continues to follow contours and strokes the ebbing hair that falls over her hidden, dainty face.

"Like a woman who survives a great storm at sea. A tempest that wrecks her ship. She swims to this rock and waits."

"Waits for what?"

"To be rescued, of course."

"To be saved?" I reply. I say, "Some people think that she represents me. I hope she is not an omen? I call her 'Chagrin Fantastique', or, 'Sorrow Fantastic'."

Molly studies her form. "I know the French, I can see why you call her that."

She moves back to her mother still staring at the wall. I dare not look up at the faces in the paintings as I know that they are waiting for me.

"There are a lot of gaps. I'm expecting Vivian to fill in the spaces, you know, on the tree lines. None of my grandchildren are on yet. Actually, did you know that I am waiting for news from Matthew? The birth of my first great-grandchildren? Twin boys. Matthew's wife is being induced today. You never had children, did you Molly?" I am curt to her. "Like my friend Linda, surrounded by other people's but never having any of your own. Linda died a long time ago."

A tear creeps into my eye.

"How many does Jacob have now? Six or seven?"

Molly has her arm around Betty.

"Seven. Four boys and three girls. They're all grown up. Mum already has three great-grandchildren," she says rather triumphantly.

Betty was still staring at the wall.

"Everyone is dead," she says. "Fergus and Bunnie, we worked for them you know. Me and Rose. There's where we met. I think it is sixty years gone."

Her plump figure has shrunk. Her body is thin and her face is scrawny. The lilt and softness in her voice carried me to years far away. The last time I had seen my friend was at Fiona's funeral some months before. Gabriel had cried silently as his wife's body was committed to the ground. The grandsons we shared, tall, handsome and strapping, stood close to support the only grandfather they had ever known. Edward held Judy tight.

Vivian has erected a plaque in brass. Etched in red Gothic writing she hung it in the church next to the memorial of Jane's two sons and it reads, *'In memory of Jane Dakin, wife of Robert*

Langley, Lord of Callow and mother of Herbert and Horace Langley. May she rest in peace.'

"You realise the link Molly? Dakin?"

Molly said brightly, "Yes, I do, of course. Well, unfortunately, people die. But just look at this history on this wall. See how it is weaved into ours, mum? And, it must be a joy to add new names to keep the ancestry going. How wonderful to be able to add your first great-grandchildren."

She paused for a moment then she said, "We'd better get going. I don't want to leave dad on his own for too long."

"Before you go, can you help me soap my hand to remove my rings please, Molly?"

Back at the Lodge and after much tugging and some pain, the rings slipped from my finger.

"This ring is so beautiful. Such a large stone and your wedding band too. Do you have somewhere safe to keep them?" Molly stood wide-mouthed gazing at my bewitching jewels.

"Oh, I'll put them in my bedside cabinet." I made a wish inside that Vivian would find them.

"Thank you for bringing Betty."

Betty twitched as she made contact on my cheek to kiss me. I watched as Molly manoeuvred her into the car and I waved goodbye. "Goodbye, Betty."

Rupert and Percy had decorated the tower some years ago and converted it into an office. The change had clearly upset Biffy and sometimes I could see her crying as she lit the candles in the window for Jane. This made me feel dismal and I knew it was time for me to call to Eliza. I had put this moment off for too long. When I saw the faces speaking in the gallery I had been frightened. As I grew older my courage was diminishing for I knew I was drawing closer to seeing her in another life.

Frost lustily sprinkled the flowers in the tubs and made the courtyard cobbles shine as I walked to the Manor. I made my way to the kitchen, tiptoeing, not wanting to wake anyone. I crept down the cellar steps and up the stairs towards the gallery. Then, I opened the door through to the picture gallery and it creaked.

I had on my cloak and I lifted the hood over my head. Standing in front of her portrait I called to Eliza.

"Eliza, Eliza, it is me, Rose. Eliza?"

A whisper touched my ear and a wispy form unfolded beside me.

"Eliza," I breathed.

Eliza took my hand, her fingers were long.

"Eliza, why did you call me to come home?"

"You know why Rose, to save Jane's soul and to reunite her with her sons."

"And what of you Eliza? Am I summoned to save your soul too?"

My mind was thinking."What about my soul? What about the loneliness that rips at my heart?"

Eliza looked nervously around. Her face was drawn across her features. She had kind, hazel eyes and her long brown hair was braided in neat plaits across her head. A recognition of myself was in her mouth as she tried to smile her tension away.

"Don't worry, no-one will come," I said.

She gripped my hand tighter.

"I swear to you Rose, I thought Jane had perished in the fire. On her death bed Biffy's mother confessed that her daughter had been Jane's keeper. It was too late. Lord Callow had died. He married me a year before. Herbert, his son, married Harriet, our daughter. It was incestuous but I could not object for fear of my secret being found out. My secret that Lord Callow was the father of my children. I had sworn on the Bible never to tell."

"Your other daughter, what happened to her?"

"My other daughter lived here as their servant. She had been born with a simple mind. My son married a farmer's daughter. For generations I have called, but you, my child, were the first to let me awaken your dreams."

There was an unearthly silence. The room was dark as I had not turned on any light. A bright moon released its silvery beams that touched the floor in circles.

"I would like to rest in peace, Rose. I seek forgiveness for the wrongdoing of Jane."

Gabriel's words rang in my ears. He knew that this time would come. I thought of his peachy eyes.

His strength and faith overcame his fear when he banished Jane from the tower and I felt almost that he was standing strong next to me.

"I forgive you Eliza. The house of Langley forgives you. Rest in peace."

Eliza turned her head quickly as the door marked 'private' opened. Coming through it was Biffy holding out her hands to embrace Eliza. Eliza folded her arms around her. Biffy looked at me.

"Can I go now, Miss?"

"Yes, Biffy, you may go. I'll miss you."

"But wait, what of me?"

Eliza's breath was sharp on my cheek.

"The curse, Rose. 'Tis your turn to take the curse."

"The Cross of Soot?" I cry. My voice is hoarse and I fear most darkly Eliza's words to come.

"Nay, the Cross of Soot will always be and 'twill mark the sons of the Callow. Your curse sweet Rose, is to know thy name and thy duty. You are bound to watch from the window until you 'ere long may call to a dainty child unto yourself to come and be still and take your place for your peace."

I was left standing alone. A dwindling hush of her breath felt cold against my cheek. My back bent, my limbs weakened, my heart slowed. The realisation of my calling caused a great despondency to overcome me. I looked at the faces in the paintings. All were alive scorning and grabbing at my soul wishing me to die to protect their greedy spirits. For I am cursed. I gave my love and I am cursed. Beware of your heart. Jane, dear Jane she forewarned me of this curse and I let her go. For Eliza's sake I let her go. I want to shriek and fight and spit out an omen that will cure my heart of the green monster that lurks inside and now rises to its zenith. But I cannot make an outpouring of my envy for I am lifeless and old. As honey in a trap my revenge will reign upon this house but not now. I calm to face my destiny. I heard a rustle and saw Percy standing in the doorway. He looked pale observing the scene before him.

Eliza releases my hand. A shimmering mist of golden light fills the gallery. The faces in the pictures crowd in; watching.

"Rose. Be still, all is well." They smirk and grimace.

Percy is dazzled by the voices, by the light. My stupid son cries out,

"Goodbye Eliza, take care of Biffy."

"I will." Eliza calls.

The light dissolved and she and Biffy were gone.

"Mum, is that you?" Percy looked frightened. He hadn't recognised me. "Mum, I think I just saw a ghost. It was Eliza, I spoke to her. She took Biffy. Biffy is gone. Mum, after all these years, thank the Lord!"

"Yes, it is me Percy. Don't be afraid. Biffy is gone, Eliza is gone. I shall be gone soon my son."

I took his shaking hand and held it firmly in my own.

"Remember, I say fiercely, "It is me, Rose Eliza Langley. Lady of Callow Crest Manor and rightful heir."

ooOOoo

Half asleep I feel the strength of my sons lift my weary body. They sit me into Felix's old wheelchair and they are pushing me to the Manor. They put me in the guest room where Felix died. I am unwell. I feel debilitated. My body has given up listening to my brain.

My sons bring joyous news. My twin great-grandsons are born big and healthy. Upon their brow, each one has the mark of the Cross of Soot.

I have grown old and my time has come. I am lying in the bed where my husband called to Hannah as he parted from this life. My children are sitting around me. I can hear their muffled voices but I am not responding, I am staring into the distance where I can see visions. I concentrate harder to make out what they are.

There is Felix and Hannah is standing next to him. They are in a gathering and people are smiling and waving. Felix is holding two babies and Hannah has her arm touching his shoulder.

There is my mother. She is holding Patrick folded in a blue blanket. His eyes are wide open and he is blinking in the glittering light. I smile when I see him. She hands him to me and I smell the scent that I have missed for too many years.

Isabella greets me. Her frame is like a midget and she is wearing my ring. I rub my finger where it had worn a crease but it is gone. Bedecked with pearls she is standing with her children all around her. I see her twin boys. One has a deep scar of black on his forehead in the shape of a cross. I think of Rupert and Percy. I must go back.

Where is Gabriel? I miss him. Has he gone to be with his God with his haughty wife beside him? I loved him, dear Gabriel.

Then I see Jane. Her sons are tall and proud at her sides. She is cloaked in black velvet and wearing the clothes that I left for her so long ago. Her handsome sons beckon for me to come. But I want to go back, back to my bed in the Manor. My own bed where Felix and I made love.

Eliza smiles, her hazel eyes are keen and kind. "Come Rose, be still."

I inhale ready to take a step nearer. I hear my children, Vivian weeps. As I drift away, I reach out to the light.

EPILOGUE

My family have buried me at St Laurence's Church next to Felix in a grave by the lake.

I cannot rest. A curse lays upon me.

Felix ascends when the air is damp and the sky is heavy in slate-grey. Hannah, and their sons, linger in the shadows. Vivian and Stephen swim to the surface of the jet-jewelled lake and put their arms about their family. Felix's first family. Sometimes, when the moon casts a spell, I can see their skin glisten as they huddle in avaricious love. Admiration seeps smugly through their satin whispering mouths.

My wrath is severe. I am jealous and my envy takes me each dark night to the path beside the water. Wearing my black velvet cloak tightly around me, I tread the route back to the Manor. I enter through the large door and make my way to the cellar. Sweeping down the staircase I head for the steps to the tower. In this room I sit by the window and light a candle.

Here I wait where Jane and Biffy waited before me. The candle wax droops from its holder and I look out across the courtyard longing for someone to release me from my solace. Won't someone pity me and arise for my company? Please come and join me, someone. Perhaps it is you?

Eliza lured me here but she forgot about my own soul. She forgot my gift for calling the dead. I can hear the soil in the vineyard move as Roman spirits pluck the grapes. I can hear the weeping tears of my ancestors. But no-one ever hears me.

So many years pass. I don't recognise the faces that move around the Manor. Everyone I knew has gone. Jane warned me about the love that I gave freely from my heart. I repent at my peril.

My heart is broken even in my death. I am 'Chagrin Fantastique'. I wait... I watch... I am alone.

Tonight in your dreams you will hear me call, 'Come to this place.' My breath will shimmer like the whisper of an owl on the troubled wind. Do not wake. Hear me as the waxen light flickers and I wail across the starry night:

"For as long as I bear this covetous body, then never will I be at peace, and you, my friend, who has shared my story, will feel the brush of my cloak against your scared frozen arm and the weight of my curse will laden your heart."